Praise for the DI Marjory Fleming series

'A fascinating cast of possible villains is explored in this
skilfully plotted and well-paced novel, each vividly described,
entirely believable and never sliding into the usual parodies
of country folk. But its real strength is DI Marjory Fleming,
both tough and vulnerable as she struggles to track down the
killer . . . This book is delight, from its leisurely start to the
moving and unexpected finish. Even better, it's the second in
a series, so there's more pleasure to come.' *Guardian*

'Aline Templeton] has demonstrated that, just when we
Thought Scotland was saturated with detectives, a strong
Woman can elbow her way in and find a unique niche.'
Scotsman

'Loved it. She has become the crime czar of the Scottish
small town!' Val McDermid

'In fictional terms the combination of domesticity and
detection is very appealing, especially when it comes with a
detailed, vivid portrayal of a complete society . . . an interesting,
atmospheric and – I predict – televisual series.' *Literary Review*

'An unalloyed pleasure – an intelligent, character-driven crime
Novel.' Andrew Taylor, author of *The American Boy*

The DI Marjory Fleming series

Cold in the Earth
The Darkness and the Deep
Lying Dead
Lamb to the Slaughter
Dead in the Water
Cradle to Grave

About the Author

Aline Templeton lives in Edinburgh with her husband, in a house with a balcony built by an astronomer to observe the stars over the beautiful city skyline. She has worked in education and broadcasting and has written numerous articles and stories for newspapers and magazines. Her books have been published in translation in several European countries as well as in the United States.

ALINE TEMPLETON

Lying Dead

HODDER

First published in Great Britain in 2007 by Hodder & Stoughton
An Hachette UK company

This paperback edition published in 2018

1

A CIP catalogue record for this title is available from the British Library

Paperback ISBN 978 0 340 92227 9
eBook ISBN 978 1 848 94834 1

Typeset in Plantin Light by Hewer Text UK Ltd, Edinburgh

Printed and bound in Great Britain by Clays Ltd, Elcograf S.p.A.

Hodder & Stoughton policy is to use papers that are natural, renewable
and recyclable products and made from wood grown in sustainable forests.
The logging and manufacturing processes are expected to conform to the
environmental regulations of the country of origin.

Hodder & Stoughton Ltd
Carmelite House
50 Victoria Embankment
London EC4Y 0DZ

www.hodder.co.uk

For Ian again, with all my love and thanks for support, encouragement, and the title.

I

The wind had dropped with the sunrise. It was a beautiful May morning, with the soft, pearly light so typical of the south-west corner of Scotland, but it was cool still; vapour clung to the tops of the trees and there was a sweet, damp, earthy smell after a heavy dew. He got up to have a chilly shower – he must see if something couldn't be done about the hot-water supply – then dressed in his working jeans and checked shirt and went down the rickety staircase and across the living room to open the door.

The wooden shack, his home since he was freed on licence six months ago, had walls weathered by time and the elements to a soft silvery grey. It stood in a clearing surrounded by rough grass studded with the stumps of felled trees, crumbling and mossy now. Beyond that, a tangle of undergrowth formed a natural enclosure: at this time of year the grass had feathery seed heads and the creamy flowers of hawthorn and cow parsley gleamed against the lush dark green of nettles and docks. From a snarl of brambles, a robin was shouting a melodious challenge to all comers. Sitting down on the dilapidated bench outside the back door, he drank in the peace and freedom which remained a novelty still.

He enjoyed his work as a forester; his hands were hardened now and his muscles had strengthened so that he didn't suffer as at first he had from the physical demands it made. He had nearly finished repairing a path for ramblers; after that, he would be putting up owl nesting boxes as part of the Forestry

Commission's wildlife protection programme. When he heard the eerie cries on a moonlit night, he would enjoy thinking that the bird sweeping through the clearing on great, silent wings might have been a scrawny chick in one of his boxes.

Yes, he was a contented man in this simple, solitary existence, with only his books for company, though he would once have pitied someone who earned a meagre living by the work of his hands and didn't own a house or a car or even a shower with reliably hot water. But after eighteen months when there had been little else for him to do for hours at a time but think, he had come to the conclusion that serenity came from lack of expectation. Not happiness, no, but that was a luxury he had been forced to realize he couldn't expect. The nearest approach to it was this pleasure in the warmth of a spring morning and the tranquillity of his solitary world. It was tempting him to linger now, when he should really be getting ready for the day's work. Just five more minutes . . .

When the mechanical, insistent call of a mobile phone – a silly, chirpy little tune – broke the spell, his first reaction was one of alarming rage. He had believed himself alone and he was being spied on; it seemed a violation as gross as if he had been sitting on the bench naked. He had been under surveillance for too long to be rational about it.

Jumping to his feet, he headed towards the sound which seemed to be coming from the edge of the clearing where it joined a forestry road, his hands unconsciously balled into fists, angry enough to take on any intruder.

But there was no one to be seen. In front of him the track was empty and a moment later the ringing stopped. He looked about him uncertainly.

Could it be some rambler who had dropped the mobile nearby without noticing? It was a popular walk, winding up through the forest to a panoramic viewpoint. Perhaps, if it went on ringing, he could trace it and restore it to its owner. It wasn't likely to be far off the track.

Provokingly, the sound stopped again just as he emerged from the clearing, but it didn't take long for him to establish its source. There was a woman lying on her front, her head turned to one side, just beyond a screening hawthorn bush at the very edge of the track. She was wearing jeans, a white shirt and a light blue tailored jacket. She was dead.

It wasn't hard to tell. The long dark hair veiling her face was sticky with blood and on one side of her head a wound gaped, showing a glint of bone and a mess of tissue.

He staggered as if someone had struck him. With the random irrelevance of shock, he found himself thinking, *That's why you say, I'm staggered.* He shut his eyes as if it might be a bad dream, as if when he opened them a blink would have wiped away the monstrous sight.

Of course it didn't. She was still there, still as shocking in ugly death. He had never seen a dead body before. He steeled himself to look directly, to walk towards her. He saw that she was wearing trainers and her clothes were glistening with dew, then his eye travelled reluctantly to focus on the mutilated head. He was beside her now; he bent down and gingerly put out his hand to push aside the curtain of hair.

The shock this time dropped him to his knees. He knew who she was, though her hair, when last he saw her, had been close-cropped like a boy's and hennaed red. How could he forget that seductive mouth, the tiny diamond glinting in the side of her nose? – they had tortured him in dreams. But the mouth was sagging open now, the olive skin waxy and discoloured. The huge dark eyes, which had looked at him with what he had believed was love, were closed, one of them puffy and sticky with congealed blood.

The last time he had seen her was in court, when she had looked at the jury with those same limpid eyes and delivered the evidence which had put him behind bars. And if he called the police now, what would they assume? She was lying outside his house; there were his footprints in the dew-wet grass beside her body.

His world splintered about him. The sun was still shining, the birds were still singing, but it was as if a stone had been thrown at a looking-glass, showing up his tranquil, contented existence for the illusion it was.

At any minute there might be ramblers. Soon there would be other foresters on their way to a project up by the viewpoint. There could be no concealment then.

He wasn't going back to prison. That was his only coherent thought, and moving like a zombie he went back into the house to fetch a tarpaulin he used sometimes when the roof leaked.

As he walked back out again carrying it, his face was set in hard, emotionless lines. Turning his head aside, he wrapped it round her slight frame, then levered the package, rigid and bearably anonymous now, on to his shoulder in a fireman's lift. The inanimate body was surprisingly heavy, though, and he faltered a little as he took the weight. Then, regaining his balance, he set off through the belt of undergrowth, ignoring the thorns which snatched at his legs as he carried her in her tarpaulin shroud, the fading sound of the robin's song from the bramble bush an impromptu requiem.

It was eerily dark and quiet as he stepped into the green shade of the forest. On all sides, the trunks of the larches rose high above him, bare apart from the jagged spikes of old broken branches, with low cloud still lurking in their canopy of foliage. As he climbed the sloping ground, there was thick soft grass to deaden his footsteps and even when he stumbled on a concealed stone or snapped a twig the sound was muffled. With no scrub for nesting there was no birdsong; the silence, too, added to his sense of unreality.

This section of the forest was unfamiliar territory. He'd

never worked here, or felt tempted to explore; he had no idea how far it might extend before he would come to a track or one of the swathes of ground where timber had already been harvested. His every instinct was to take – it – as far as possible from his own back yard, but fit as he was, his burden seemed to be growing heavier and heavier. He blanked out the thought of how small, how slight she had been; all he was carrying was a dead weight which very soon he would be forced to set down, at least for a rest.

He could hear a sound now: the soft babble of water over stones which indicated one of the countless little burns running down the steep sides of the valley. He headed towards it, his breathing laboured, and saw that on the other side the trees were thinner, sparser and of more recent planting. He paused.

On the near side of the burn lay three great fallen trees, their branches dry as tinder and their exposed root systems linked, elaborate as a vipers' knot, to form a bank. They must have stood at the outer edge of the old plantation, unprotected against the winter storms which topple the giants of the forest as a man might blow down a house of cards.

Grimacing, he set down his load and sat down himself, leaning his head back against the gnarled root mass and closing his eyes. Despite the cool damp air, he was sweating and his heart was racing with fear as well as physical effort. Time was passing. He checked his watch: in half an hour a truck would come to take him to the project he was working on and by then he must not only be ready, but calm and normal.

There beyond the burn, the forest was beginning to thin out. This was a fine and private place to spend eternity, with the murmur of water and the guardian presence of the trees. A hollow had formed at the base of the bank of roots and with deliberate lack of reflection he picked up the formless bundle and laid it there. It looked neat, impersonal, a package not a person in its tarpaulin cover.

The tarpaulin . . . He dared not leave it. There was no reason why they should find – it – for years, until this plantation's turn for felling came, but he couldn't take the risk. It must have his prints all over it and there would be traces of his sweat, minute skin cells shed by his hands. In twenty years' time, thirty, they would still have his prints and his DNA on record. He had to take it with him.

When he removed it, though, she would become a person again. A person whose face he had seen on the pillow next to him, a person who had transformed his agreeable, respectable – oh yes, and dull, dull, dull – life first into a fantasy of enchantment, then into a horror of betrayal and despair. Circe. Delilah . . .

She was dead, he told himself. An inanimate body. A corpse. Her soul – if a soul could be discerned – was elsewhere.

With the resolve of desperation he stood up and with his head averted jerked the edge of the tarpaulin. He pulled it towards him, gathered it up and walked away without looking back to see how snugly she lay on her back, as if the cavity beneath the vipers' knot of roots had been hollowed out especially to receive her.

PC Sandy Langlands, his boyish face weary-looking after his night shift, emerged blinking blearily from the Galloway Constabulary Headquarters in Kirkluce just as DS Tam MacNee arrived for duty and got out of his car. It was warm already, early as it was, and there was a sticky, sultry feel to the air.

MacNee was wearing his customary summer garb of jeans, white T-shirt, black leather jacket and trainers, though the difference between this and his winter gear might not be immediately apparent to the casual observer, since it consisted only of dispensing with the semmit his wife Bunty insisted he don under the T-shirt when the weather was less clement.

At the sight of his colleague's haggard appearance, Mac-Nee's face brightened, his smile exposing the gap between his two front teeth. 'Man, Sandy, you look like the wrath of God! Heavy night?'

Langlands groaned. 'You could say. Lost five quid to Wilson, playing poker. We were on back-up and it was dead quiet. Not one call in from the patrol cars the whole time – the night seemed to go on for ever.'

MacNee's grin faded. 'I blame the weather,' he said bitterly. 'A week of this, and everyone's in a good mood. You know what the high point was yesterday? Two drunk and incapable – you couldn't even call them disorderly when they were just passed out in the park, not bothering anybody. Four of the lads went to that one and they'd to fight for the privilege.' He gave a resigned shrug. 'Oh well, I suppose it's desk work again today. I tell you, I'd have gone into the bank instead of the polis if that was what floated my boat.'

The constable greeted this assertion with a certain scepticism. Tam as a bank clerk didn't really square with his appearance, which was still that of the wee Glasgow hard man he'd been before Bunty, a sonsy lass from Dumfries who punched well above her not inconsiderable weight and had some very old-fashioned ideas about respectability, had taken him in hand. Tam on the other side of the counter with a stocking over his head was an altogether more plausible image, but Langlands refrained from pointing this out. He was too young to die.

'Right enough,' he said diplomatically. 'Well, I'm away to my bed anyhow.'

'You do that, laddie. I'll see what we can drum up to keep you busy tonight.'

MacNee went on into the building. The reception area was quiet, with only a couple of people in the waiting area who looked as if they might have come to inquire about lost property, and Naismith, the desk sergeant, was showing an elderly lady a leaflet about home security. It looked like being another quiet day and MacNee, with a sigh, went along to the CID room.

He was surprised to hear, as he reached the open door, the voice of DI Marjory Fleming in full flow. It wasn't often that 'Big Marge', as she was known to her subordinates in recognition of her commanding height and the personality that went with it, came down from the fourth floor to give someone a rollicking in public. Rollickings were usually private and painful.

'And if not, I'll have your guts for garters,' she was saying in a favourite phrase. 'Frilly ones, with wee blue rosettes at the side.' It was only this unexpected elaboration, and the gust of laughter that greeted it, which made MacNee realize what he was hearing. No one laughed when Big Marge was giving them laldie.

The voice was that of DC Jonathan Kingsley, a relative newcomer to the Galloway Force with a gift for mimicry which had proved operationally useful in working undercover to break up a drugs ring. MacNee had heard, with appreciation, his take-off of Superintendent Donald Bailey and suspected that there was a Tam MacNee too, which he hadn't heard, but he hadn't known about the Big Marge act. It was pretty good, especially considering Jon's normal voice had an English accent. Grinning, MacNee went in.

Kingsley stopped instantly. 'Uh-oh! Sorry about that. Back to your desks, guys!'

There were five other officers in the room. Four of them, exchanging sidelong glances, went back to their tasks. Only DC Tansy Kerr, her neat, gamine face flushing, said sharply, 'There's no need for that, Jon. Tam likes a joke as much as anyone.'

'Of course he does!' Kingsley's voice was offensively soothing. 'Morning, Tam.' He too turned away, but MacNee could see his smirk reflected in the expressions of the men facing him.

It was true, of course, that Tam and Marjory worked closely together. They went back a long way, having been partners from the time Marjory joined as a rookie, and her promotion hadn't damaged their relationship. Tam had no ambitions to rise to any sort of administrative post: he loved his job with its endless variety, and working with paper in an office on your own held no appeal when instead you could be out on the streets dealing with the public or here in the CID room enjoying the jokes and the cut and thrust that went with being on the team.

Kingsley was becoming a dangerously divisive figure. He was clever and an effective officer, but he was also arrogant and nakedly ambitious. He didn't like Tam, which was fair enough in its way since Tam didn't like him either, and in any group, the clash of personalities is a fact of life.

But it seemed now as if Kingsley's objective was to create his own gang, excluding MacNee from the common currency of jokes and complaints inevitably made by lower ranks about their superiors, subtly implying that he'd run to Fleming and clype – he, Tam, who had been raised in one of the rougher parts of Glasgow with an attitude to tale-bearing which made *omertà* look like a set of recommended guidelines!

He went to fetch the file he'd been working on the day before, and Kerr came across with a report she'd promised to look out for him. She must have dyed her hair again yesterday – it was kind of a hobby with Tansy – and it was bright yellow with a streak of dark green at the front.

MacNee leaned towards her confidentially. 'Maybe no one's liked to tell you, Tansy, but your hair's gone mouldy.'

Kerr didn't rise to the bait. 'Your problem is you've no fashion sense, MacNee. Look at Jon over there –' she raised

her voice to attract attention, 'see how he's colour-co-ordi-
nated? That funky beige shirt just matches the colour of his
teeth.'

There was a general guffaw at this and Kingsley shot her a
look of intense dislike. MacNee joined in, adding with malicious satisfaction, 'There you are, Jon. As Rabbie Burns says,
"*It's innocence and modesty/That polishes the dart.*"'

Kerr groaned and Kingsley scoffed. 'Innocent and modest?
You should have been at the pub after work last Friday.'

Cheered by this exchange, MacNee settled down to another
day of pushing paper. Maybe, if he tried hard enough, he
could find something in the files that would give him an excuse
to go out and interview someone. And if he did, he'd take
Tansy with him as a reward.

Detective Inspector Marjory Fleming set the paperweight to
the right of the computer screen on her desk, considered it,
then moved it back to the other side. She could, unusually,
actually see the surface of her desk, which the office cleaners
were forbidden to touch; pulling a face, she took a tissue and
removed the accumulated dust. Taking another one, she
licked it to scrub away the ring left by a coffee mug. It wasn't
a method you'd see used on *How Clean Is Your House?* but it
worked, sort of.

She picked up the pen pot which seemed to be acting as a
dating agency for ballpoints, producing hybrids which she was
ready to swear she'd never put there. Some had obviously
dried out; she threw those away, then tipped out the pot,
marvelling at the detritus of paper clips, rubber bands and
stray coins collected in the sludge of sticky ink blobs at the
bottom.

For once in her life, Fleming was on top of the job. There
was no outstanding Government form, demanding information on the number of breaths each officer took in making an

arrest. There was no major investigation at the moment, just the ongoing problems with alcohol and drugs, petty theft and vandalism which were all being satisfactorily dealt with at a lower level. She'd a couple of appraisals to do later and she was jotting down budget proposals to discuss with her superintendent, Donald Bailey, at their regular meeting tomorrow, but she'd had no difficulty in working office hours for the last week or two. She wasn't under pressure, and she wasn't enjoying it one little bit.

Perhaps she'd become addicted to the adrenaline rush that came from being permanently stressed and these were just withdrawal symptoms. But if she was honest with herself . . . She usually was, blaming Calvin, as Scots do when they don a moral hair shirt, but it was a habit she couldn't break, so she had to admit that one of the things she liked about her job was the white noise of permanent over-commitment which blotted out the voice of domestic conscience.

This last spell, she hadn't been able to plead overwork as an excuse for ignoring the dusting, snatching a ready-meal from the freezer and even, when it got right down to the wire, taking a mountain of dirty clothes for a service wash at the launderette – and how boring it was! Bill, her farmer husband, was more ready to help his wife than most of her male colleagues were theirs, as far as she could tell, but he had his own heavy load to carry.

And in fact, it was just as well she wasn't at full stretch at the moment. Over the years, it had been largely thanks to her mother, Janet Laird, that the household chores didn't get totally out of hand and that the Fleming children, Catriona and Cameron, actually knew what it was like to have good home-cooking as well as someone with all the time in the world to listen to them.

Janet had always behaved as if Marjory was still a lassie who had somehow acquired a husband and children to be gathered under her own motherly wing. And even Angus Laird – 'Sarge' to the officers of the Galloway Police Headquarters for more years than anyone had wanted to see him serve, and a father who had never forgiven his only child for being a daughter not a son – had served his time on the touchline when rugby-mad Cammie was playing.

Until recently. The last few months had seen Angus retreat into a strange and troubled world where his only emotion was rage at the terrifying confusion surrounding him. Marjory had watched impotently as her mother aged ten years and her plump and comfortable frame wasted away to alarming frailty. With her days and nights dedicated to preserving from actual harm the physical husk of the man she had shared her life with for forty-five years, corrosive anxiety had destroyed her cheerful serenity.

'Janet, you can't go on like this,' Bill had said to her gently, taking her thin hand in his. 'He's still strong. He could hurt you in one of his rages.'

Janet's brown eyes looked faded, as if the tears she had shed had washed some of the colour out of them, but she drew away her hand and responded fiercely, 'He still knows me, Bill, still calls out for me sometimes. And as long as he does, how could I leave him? What would he feel if he wanted me and I wasn't there?'

And Bill, recognizing defeat, had raised his eyebrows to his wife and she had shrugged helplessly.

That was the worst of it: Marjory was bad at helpless, and she wasn't very good at Bill's kind of philosophical acceptance either. While she went round regularly, Janet had an army of friends who were supporting her on the practical side so there was nothing for Marjory to do except fret over her mother's increasing distraction. Janet seldom managed to finish a coherent sentence while Angus was awake; it was almost as if, using the instruments of torture – sleep deprivation, uncertainty, fear – he was trying to draw Janet after him into his own disordered world.

Marjory couldn't bear it. 'A home – somewhere he'd be well cared for – you'll make yourself ill . . .' Whatever vow of silence on the subject Marjory made before she went to see them, she couldn't stop herself returning to it, and Janet would look hunted, as if her daughter's urging was one more burden she had to cope with.

Yesterday, with Angus for once asleep, Janet had said in a tone that was, for her, almost sharp, 'You're rich, Marjory. You have Bill and the children – you don't need me. But poor Angus – I'm all he has.'

Marjory had felt ashamed, justly rebuked for her selfishness, and that was on her conscience too today. Her relationship with her father had always been difficult. No son could have tried harder than Marjory to make Angus proud, but her success in his own profession had only made him bitter. In being promoted beyond the rank he had achieved, she had somehow diminished his life's work in his own eyes.

Intellectually, she'd recognized long ago that she would never win his approval, but emotionally a tiny hope had always remained of a more mellow old age. It hadn't happened, of course; in old age, in senility, you don't become different, you become more intensely whatever you were. She could never hope now for understanding, reconciliation . . .

But she couldn't, surely, be jealous that her sick, needy father was absorbing all her mother's time and attention? It was a most uncomfortable thought.

Restlessly she got up and walked to the window, a tall, fit-looking woman in her early forties with clear hazel eyes and neatly cut bright brown hair, showing only a few threads of grey at the temples. She opened it wide; it was very stuffy in the office today and she had an unpleasantly muzzy head. A fly flew in, then buzzed stupidly against the panes as she unconsciously drummed her long, slim fingers on the window-sill, looking out on the street scene below.

Fleming liked this vantage point with its view over Kirkluce High Street. Through the new green leaves of the plane trees below she could look down on the traffic, motorized and human, as it went about its business in the thriving market town.

It was particularly busy today, with the recently established Friday Farmers' Market. Popular with producers and consumers alike, the market gave the farmers a fair price instead of the pittance paid by the supermarkets, and the customers a chance to know where their food came from and what had been done to it on its way to their plates.

Bill would be down there somewhere. Raising only sheep now on a small hill farm, he didn't have a stall, but farming was a solitary life and he enjoyed the social side, catching up on the gossip and having a pie and a pint at lunchtime with some old mates. He'd have brought in eggs from Marjory's hens to the stand which their neighbours, the Raeburns, always took to sell cream and cheese from Hamish's dairy herd as well as Kirsty's dried flowers and home-baking.

Marjory consulted her watch. She could take an early lunch hour, pop out and have a chat with Kirsty . . . But it felt all wrong.

She sighed. This benign spell of weather had meant that even their regular clients were more inclined to strip off their hoodies and sit around, roasting their pale grey goose-pimples to an equally unbecoming shade of puce, than to get out there and do a dishonest day's work. It was just too quiet; that made her uneasy too.

Again, she looked at her watch: eleven forty-five. She'd done enough overtime, heaven knew, to tack on an extra fifteen minutes. There wasn't so much as a breath of air coming in through the window and the oppressive atmosphere was making her headache worse. She might feel better outside and then come back with more enthusiasm for checking through the files, neatly laid in her in-tray, for the first appraisal. Well, she might. It was always possible.

Feeling like a schoolgirl bunking off, Marjory hurried out, masking her guilt with an ostentatiously purposeful air.

2

Drumbreck, a scattered hamlet strung out around a sheltered inlet near the estuary of the River Cree, just north of Wigtown, was looking as slickly perfect as a picture postcard this morning. The tide was in; a pair of swans, exuding majestic indifference, sailed round the pontoons of the marina between the expensive yachts and dinky little boats which jostled and clinked as they rode their moorings, glossy paintwork shimmering in sun-sparkles from the waves, while a school of Mirror dinghies was circling round an instructor in an inflatable with an outboard motor. It looked stage-managed, an advertisement shoot, perhaps, for *Your Holiday Paradise*.

The houses too, tucked round the margin of the bay or on the rising ground which sheltered it, were all trim and freshly painted, even if a number of them showed the signs of being currently unoccupied: no car outside, half-lowered blinds, shutters closed on downstairs windows. By this evening, though, with a half-term holiday week ahead, it was a safe bet that the 4 × 4s would soon be arriving and this select little enclave would again leap into active social life which would become more and more frenetically social as the summer approached.

Within easy striking distance of Glasgow, Drumbreck was much favoured by businessmen keen to adopt the sport once described as standing under a cold shower tearing up fivers. Not all of them, perhaps, were as keen on the activities which took place on the heaving deck as they were on those which went on after the sun had sunk below the yardarm, but if seasickness, along with a degree of terror, was the price of acceptance in Drumbreck society, then it must be paid.

The Yacht Club by the marina, once a mere wooden shack for occasional sailors, had been transformed by a major fund-raising drive four years ago into a smart social centre with a swimming-pool, gym and squash courts.

It all drove up the property prices, so that by now almost none of the houses, whether substantial villas, with a bit of ground, or two-bedroom cottages, were owned by families native to the area. And it wasn't surprising, when Drumbreck was looking as it was this morning, with glinting water covering what lay beneath: at low tide, the boats now floating so jauntily would be stranded on the mudflats below.

A Land Rover Discovery appeared, turning cautiously into the narrow road round the bay then pulling up in a parking area outside a pretty cottage set above the road, painted the colour of clotted cream with bright green paintwork, and with a steep flight of steps leading up to it through a terraced garden. A buxom blonde, in jeans and a green camisole top revealing 'invisible' plastic bra straps, jumped out and went round to open up the back. It was packed with cases, boxes and Marks and Spencer carrier bags, and she stood back, hands on curvaceous hips, looking from it to the flight of steps with some distaste. A small child, strapped into his safety-seat, began a monotonous chant, 'Want out! Mummee, Mummee, want out!'

Her only response was an impatient sigh. Groping in her Prada bag for house keys, she prepared to embark on her unappealing task of haulage – no fun at all in this sultry heat. She was sweating already, just looking at what she had to do. First, though, she turned to look along the shore road towards the marina, shading her eyes against the glare from the water.

The nearest house was a charmless Victorian monstrosity,

large, sprawling and run-down, an eyesore in smart Drumbreck. The litter of diseased timbers, discarded plasterboard and chipped sanitary-ware in the yard to one side suggested a renovation project, but the way the grass had grown up round about hinted at slow progress. It had a large paddock to one side where a tall man in a blue-checked shirt and moleskin trousers seemed to be working a curiously small flock of sheep with a black-and-white collie.

The woman's face brightened. Taking a few steps along the road, she called, 'Niall! Niall!'

Niall Murdoch looked round. 'Oh, Kim,' he said, without marked enthusiasm. 'You're back.' He had very dark hair, falling forward at the moment in a comma on his brow, and with his strong features and deep brown eyes, he was a good-looking man; though there were lines about his mouth that suggested temper, they gave him a sort of edgy charm. He was looking sullen at the moment but his brooding expression could, with a certain generosity of spirit, be considered Byronic.

Kim's nature, when it came to men, was generous to a fault. She wasn't easily discouraged, either. Ignoring the complaints from inside the car, becoming more insistent, she swayed along the road to lean over the dry-stone dyke separating the paddock from the road.

'Yes, that's me just back to open up the house.' Her Glasgow accent suggested that it had been only recently refined. 'Here, it's great to see you! Like last summer, all over again.' Her smile was an invitation.

'Yes, well,' Niall said flatly, then added, 'Adrian coming too?' He spoke without enthusiasm. Adrian McConnell was a sardonic, smart-ass accountant he'd fallen out with over the extension to the marina years ago and the man never lost the opportunity to put the boot in. Truth to tell, his own ill-advised response to Kim's overtures last year probably had more to do with private revenge than anything else, and it didn't compensate for her personality which, once the novelty was over, affected him like nails scraping on a blackboard.

'Not till tomorrow, with Kelly and Jason for the half-term week.' She pushed back her hair and gave him a sidelong glance. 'I'm all by my wee self tonight.' Then she added, with an unenthusiastic glance towards the car, 'Well, apart from him, unfortunately.' She gestured towards the child confined in the car, whose protests were starting to sound tearful. 'He's such a crabby little sod.'

'Yes. Look, Kim, I'm sorry – I've got to get on. It's the trials tomorrow, and this bloody dog doesn't seem to know its business.'

Kim gave a throaty gurgle. 'Oh, Niall, you never learn, do you! Glutton for punishment!' she giggled. 'But don't you worry, pet, I'll be there, cheering you on. I never miss it – I always think the trials are the proper start to a Drumbreck summer. Come here and I'll give you a big hug, just for luck.'

Niall, with resistance in every line of his body, submitted. Kim embraced him, then patted his cheek.

'Well, I suppose I'll need to get on with heaving all this stuff up into the cottage. It's so hot, though – really sticky!' She looked at him hopefully, then, as no offer of help was forthcoming, said, 'You know what? The marina should be hiring out porters. There's a real business opportunity.'

Niall had turned away already. Sulkily, Kim went back to the car, where the child had started wailing.

'Oh, you just shut up, Gary!' she snarled. 'You're not going anywhere till I get all this dragged upstairs, so you may as well get used to it.'

Scowling, Niall Murdoch turned away. Stupid bitch! He'd have to get free of her somehow. Not that he suffered from pangs of conscience: given his home life he reckoned he was entitled to do whatever he liked. His wife wouldn't care, and his daughter treated him like something she'd found on the sole of her shoe.

But Kim McConnell, unfortunately, wasn't the sort graciously to accept a hint that time had moved on; she had a big fat mouth and a spiteful nature. He didn't appreciate her comment about the sheepdog trials either, even if he knew people laughed behind his back.

Jenna had seen to that. 'Face it,' she told him, with the sort of brutality you shouldn't have to take from your wife, 'you'll never train dogs like your father did. You haven't the personality for it. And even if you did win, you wouldn't be proving anything because he's been dead these past six years – remember?'

Niall had actually believed that once the old man wasn't there, putting a hex on him with his critical eye and mocking his failures, he'd have the confidence to win. It mattered; somehow his father, rot his black soul, had instilled this into Niall's consciousness as a measure of the man.

It was hardly asking for the moon. All Niall wanted to do was take the crown, just once, in the piddling little kingdom of the local sheepdog trials which his father had for a decade made his own. Then he could retire gracefully, but despite his best efforts at training a number of dogs, years of humiliation had followed, particularly unpleasant in this glossy world where all that mattered was material success. This was his last throw of the dice: he'd borrowed an exorbitant amount from the business to buy Findlay Stevenson's champion, Moss.

Findlay, overstretched by borrowing himself, had lost his farm during the foot-and-mouth epidemic. Since then, he'd travelled the countryside with Moss, winning trials wherever he went, to boost his new business of training up working dogs and selling them. It had taken five thousand pounds to part the dog and his master.

Niall hadn't mentioned the loan to his business partner. Ronnie Lafferty wouldn't react well. A Glasgow scrap metal dealer, he looked like a bullfrog and had manners to match; he had a trophy wife, the lustrous Gina, and he had no interest in anything except the bottom line. His sole reason for taking a half-share in the sailing school and marina along with Niall was that with it came automatic membership of the exclusive Drumbreck Yacht Club. He'd been turned down once before, and he hadn't liked that one little bit.

Niall was frankly afraid of him. Lafferty hadn't made a fortune in his sort of business using sweet reason and goodwill, and if he found out . . . But he wouldn't have to, Niall had reckoned; given another title to its name he could sell the dog on, probably for more than he had paid for it, in the next couple of days . . .

The only problem was that the dog wasn't living up to its reputation. Niall was beginning to suspect, with a sick feeling in the pit of his stomach, that he'd been conned. The dog must be past its best; if it couldn't manage to put in a decent performance under these conditions – a relatively small paddock, sheep that were accustomed to being handled – what was it going to do on the full-sized trial course, with unpredictable sheep? If this was how it showed tomorrow, Moss would be practically worthless. Niall would have to kiss goodbye to the money, or rather the business would, and then what would Ronnie say?

They'd spent a hell of a lot on expanding the marina, in the teeth of some forcible local opposition, which had cost them in planning applications and legal fees, and it was expensive to run: business had been diabolical during the foot-and-mouth and still hadn't recovered. It was all right for the farmers, raking in the compensation now, but no one was going to sub Niall a penny. The marina was only just keeping its head above water, to coin a phrase; five thousand would make a dangerous hole in the balance sheet and if Ronnie found out he'd go berserk.

And then there was Davina coming back as well as everything else . . . He'd thought he'd never see her again. He'd done as she asked, sent her the information she wanted eighteen months ago, but his subsequent letter to the address she'd given him was returned, marked 'Gone away'. After that, nothing – until now.

But he couldn't afford to think about her, not until tomorrow was over. Until then he had to be totally focused. He must practise, practise and practise again. Niall squared his shoulders and immediately the dog, which had been lying watching him warily, sat up pricking the ear that wasn't permanently pricked. A gesture brought it to his side.

The five sheep were clustered at the bottom of the paddock, dropping their heads and grazing now. With another gesture, Niall sent the dog on the outrun, meant to gather up the sheep and drive them calmly towards him through one of the sets of gateposts he had constructed in the middle of the field.

The dog took off, fast and low to the ground, making a wide, sweeping arc to bring itself round behind the sheep. It was well done: the sheep hadn't noticed it yet. They were still grazing and the trick was to lift them and begin the drive without alarming them. Cupping his hands, Niall gave an imperative whistle, then as the dog seemed to him too slow to respond, another, and it changed course obediently. The sheep spotted it; they looked from one to the other nervously, and the sheep in front broke into a run.

'Come by!' Niall yelled furiously. '*Come by!* No! *No!*'

The sheep were all running now, heading in disorder to one side. The dog, confused, started to come in at their heels, alarming them further, and none of Niall's increasingly furious instructions seemed to have any effect.

The sheep missed the gate altogether, heading off to one

side. His face purple with fury, his master yelled at the dog to come back and cowering, tail tucked between its legs, Moss obeyed, afraid to come yet even more afraid not to.

Marjory Fleming, smiling to acquaintances as she made her way along the crowded High Street, caught sight of her husband Bill before he spotted her. He was standing at the Raeburns' stall, laughing at something Hamish had said: a pleasant-faced big man with a countryman's complexion. Viewing him at a distance she saw with a pang that he was looking older: his fair hair was beginning to show the first signs of grey, and definitely wasn't as far forward on his forehead as it used to be. The problems of the last few years had taken their toll, but at least the compensation money had come through now and the prospects for farmers who had survived the bad times were better than they had been for years – not that you'd ever get a farmer to admit it. Optimism was a cultural taboo.

Still, the atmosphere in the market today was cheerful, almost festive, and Marjory's own lips curved as she came within earshot of Bill's hearty laughter.

'What's the joke?' she demanded.

'Marjory! Oh, you don't want to know – one of Hamish's worse efforts,' Kirsty Raeburn greeted her. 'Lucky to be spared it, really. Gosh, it's hot, isn't it? I'm melting, standing here, and the flies are driving me mad.'

'It feels as if the weather's on the turn,' Marjory agreed. 'I came out for a breath of fresh air but it's almost worse outside. We could do with a good burst of rain to clear it.'

'I didn't expect to see you this early. Playing truant?'

'Sort of,' Marjory admitted. 'Business has been slow this last bit.'

Bill put his arm round her waist. 'Kirsty, we've even had Marjory's home-cooking for the last couple of weeks and we're whimpering for some real food from the chilled section.'

Grinning, Kirsty served a waiting customer as Marjory said bitterly, 'Ungrateful swine! I was going to pop along to Anne Kerr's bakery stall to buy a couple of her quiches for supper, but if you're going to be like that I'll get mince instead.'

'No, no,' Bill said hastily. 'Spitefulness is unworthy of you.'

Kirsty shook her head at him. 'You're pushing your luck, Bill!'

'Too right he is. Don't worry, he'll pay for it later.'

Bill struck his forehead. 'Doh! And here's me just going to ask for a favour. I take it all back, every word of it.'

'That's better,' Kirsty said, adding, with a wink at another customer, 'Should he be on his knees, maybe?'

'What favour?' Marjory's eyes narrowed in suspicion.

'Oh, it's just that Findlay Stevenson's coming out to the Mains this afternoon to put in a bit of practice with the sheep before the trials tomorrow and I was going to offer him his supper, if that's OK.'

There was only a fractional pause before Marjory said heartily, 'Yes, of course. No problem. I'll buy an extra quiche and if Anne's got meringues I'll be back for cream, Kirsty.'

Hamish was taking the money for a dozen of Marjory's eggs and a pot of their own crowdie cheese. 'How is Fin?' he asked, over his shoulder.

Bill grimaced. 'It's tough. He's scrabbling along with temporary work – helped me out with the lambing and some fencing this year – and he's sold a few of his trained collies. There's a big demand and people are prepared to pay fancy prices, but it's not easy to get in the work on them when you haven't your own fields and sheep to do it with.'

Findlay Stevenson was badly down on his luck. The whole farming community, with a 'there-but-for-the-grace-of-God' feeling, had rallied round, but you couldn't give the man his farm back, or even give him a job if there wasn't one.

Marjory was happy to do her bit. Of course she was! And

Findlay knew his business; he'd been a real help to Bill at the busy times of the farming year. It was only the relationship with Marjory that was a problem. The long shadow of foot-and-mouth still hung over them, when the Stevensons had refused entry to the slaughter teams, and Marjory had been on duty during the protest they had organized against it. Forced to submit, his wife Susie had spat in Marjory's face, and neither she nor Findlay had ever really forgiven Marjory for what they saw as her part in their tragedy.

Marjory had hardly set eyes on Susie since. She had a job now in a smart clothes boutique of the sort that made Marjory feel inadequate just passing by on the pavement, so their paths didn't really cross. Findlay was always polite when they met at Mains of Craigie, but there was a certain constraint which made social occasions uncomfortable. Marjory could only hope something would come up at work this afternoon to give her an excuse not to be there for supper, and that her edgy feeling that a storm was brewing somewhere related only to the weather.

'Are you putting your Meg in for the trials tomorrow?' Kirsty was asking. 'She's always been a star.'

Bill shook his head. 'I haven't the time these days to give her the polish she'd need, and I wouldn't like to humiliate the dog. She always knows if she hasn't matched up.'

'We're going to watch, though,' Marjory put in. 'And Laura's coming. She thinks it would be good for Daisy to have some role models that do what they're told without arguing.'

Laura Harvey, a psychotherapist who had been involved in Marjory's first case, had settled in Kirkluce and was now the fond owner of Meg's daughter, Daisy.

'Actually, she's doing better with Daisy than I thought she might,' Bill admitted. 'I was worried she'd maybe let her get out of hand.'

Suddenly, his wife stiffened. 'Oh Lord! There's my Super,' she said, catching sight of Donald Bailey's bald head bobbing in the crowd further down. 'I'd better go.'

Kirsty regarded her with amusement. 'Marjory, you're all grown up. Surely you're allowed a lunch hour? He's having one, after all.'

'Yes, but we've both taken off early to do our shopping. It sort of means neither of us has enough to do. He'll be embarrassed if I see him and I'll be embarrassed if he sees me. Trust me – it's a sort of police thing that we're all invariably at full stretch.'

She ducked away round the back of the stall, leaving the Raeburns and her husband as she had found them, roaring with laughter.

Standing at the kitchen sink, watching her husband talk to Kim McConnell, Jenna Murdoch raised one varnish-stained hand to push back a strand of mousy-fair hair, lank with sweat, which had escaped from the elastic band confining it at the base of her neck. It caught painfully in the crack beside her thumb-nail and she winced. There was a time when she'd had pretty, well-cared-for hands, with nails that were lacquered instead of broken, and well-kept hair, too. She even used to put night-cream on her face but it hardly seemed worth it, these days. She didn't like looking in the mirror anyway and seeing the hatchet-faced woman with a sour expression who seemed to have taken her place.

It had all seemed so promising, when Niall got the money from the sale of the farm, with planning permission on a couple of fields. He'd never wanted to be a farmer, least of all alongside his father, a right old devil who had obviously driven his wife into an early grave, and this would be a brand-new life where Niall could be happy and fulfilled. She'd blamed his dissatisfaction for turning the man she'd married – a good-looking hunk, famous for his pulling power – into a curmud-geon like his father. But now the only time Jenna saw the charm that had attracted her was when he was chatting up some woman he fancied.

She'd actually been pleased when he bought a half-share in the marina at Drumbreck with its sailing school. Yachting and water sports were becoming more and more popular, it was well-situated and it looked like a sound business opportunity. Even when he told her that, without consultation, he'd snapped up a big house nearby, to stop it coming on the market, she had, God help her, been pleased. She worked in a bank and she knew all about the inflated values of Drumbreck properties.

That was before she saw it. Rowan Villa was a huge, ugly, jerry-built house which was effectively a demolition job. It had every problem known to surveyors: dry rot, subsidence, nail-sickness, crumbling plaster, dangerous wiring, primitive plumbing. Only, of course, these hadn't been known to surveyors, because Niall hadn't commissioned a report before committing himself.

'Lucky I could write a cheque on the spot,' Niall told her, proud of his business acumen. 'He'd a Glasgow entrepreneur sniffing around, he said, and with the Scottish blind bid system we'd never have got it if it went on the open market. And it's a little gold mine. Once we do it up, we can have two, even three holiday lets – another business to run alongside the marina. Or if we don't want to do that, we can do it up and sell it on for a serious profit.'

The trouble was that Niall, in the days when he had come in and collapsed in front of the flickering screen after a long day's physical labour, had seen too many property programmes from which he had absorbed the message that, with a quick lick of paint and a few interiors copied from the pages of a design magazine, you could find some idiot punter prepared to pay way over the odds. What he didn't realize was that the idiot punter role had already been more than adequately filled.

Niall couldn't get a mortgage. Well, of course he couldn't. When he'd insisted she pull strings with her boss at the bank, it had been embarrassing. 'Jenna, I can't. Not even for you. You know I can't,' he had said unhappily, and Jenna had been forced to agree.

So, with all the money locked into either the business or the property, they'd had to face it that they couldn't afford a professional conversion. 'We can work on it together,' Niall had said. 'Then, once we have properties worth a cool couple of million you can go back and move our account. Show that smug little sod the business opportunity he's missed.'

That word, 'we'. It was normally held to indicate more than one person, but it didn't seem to have the same meaning in Niall's dictionary. Jenna had given up her work at the bank; she wasn't earning enough to pay for a tradesman to do the sort of unskilled work she could do herself, and somehow the house had become her single-handed project. She'd learned to deal with basic plumbing, joinery and decorating; after grudgingly paying for rewiring, about a third of the house was habitable now. But with almost no money for major repairs, particularly with the recent downturn in the business, she'd had to concentrate on those areas, and the rest of the property was even more derelict than it had been when they bought it.

It had taken her independence, her youth, her looks. She had invested her whole life in the bloody house, so however bad the marriage might be she couldn't afford to walk away. That was all that kept her going: the thought that she could leave him then and force a sale which would leave herself and Mirren comfortably set up for a new life elsewhere.

And the first of the flats was all but ready now; she was going to put another coat of varnish on the floors this afternoon. Oh, they wouldn't get top dollar for it with the rest of the property in a mess, but folk from outside were desperate for a foothold in paradise and selling it wouldn't be a problem. In fact one of the locals who'd been causing trouble at the marina had made an offer – like they were going to move him in on their doorstep, even if it hadn't been pitiably under what they were looking for!

Once that was sold, there'd be money to move the project along a lot faster, and every day with a workman employed was one day fewer to wait for her freedom. She just had to keep things ticking over until then.

Niall's little escapades didn't bother her. He'd always had an eye for the girls and for some reason, which she had understood at one time but certainly didn't now, they seemed to fall for him too. But Jenna hadn't considered anyone a serious threat for years and she viewed the busty blonde now chatting him up over the wall with the same weary contempt she had felt towards all the others. Set in the balance, she was comfortably certain that her value to him as a free tradesman far outweighed any romantic consideration, and she hadn't been worried.

Until the phone call yesterday. She knew who it was immediately when she'd picked up on the top landing just as Niall answered it downstairs.

'Voice from the past!' Husky, with a touch of laughter – it was unmistakable. 'I've a new project, Niall. Meet me today, usual place, two o'clock?'

'God – Davina?' Niall sounded stunned. 'What – where are you?'

The only response was a mocking laugh, and the line went dead.

When Niall had put down the receiver, Jenna dialled 1471, but the mechanical voice told her that the caller had withheld the number. Of course.

She said nothing about it to Niall, who had been edgy and

preoccupied at lunch. Jenna would do whatever she had to do to make sure Niall did not wreck her precious future, but today, by the looks of things, he seemed to have nothing on his mind beyond his obsession with proving something to a dead man.

Niall was shouting at the poor dog now. He'd ruined it already; when he got it, it had been a cheerful, confident animal and now it was a mass of nerves with an uncertain temper. Mirren, whose love for animals was so passionate that she'd become a vegetarian five years ago when she was only eight, had been bitten the last time she'd gone to comfort it for being chained up outside. She had come in crying, for the dog not herself, having no doubt at all where the blame lay, and flown at her father with a sort of cold fury that was quite unnerving. Niall hadn't taken it well, and the relationship was now as bad as his own had ever been with his father.

Jenna heard a sudden yelp of pain from the dog and winced, looking at the clock. The schools were finishing early today for half-term and the bus from Wigtown would be dropping Mirren back any time now. If she saw that . . .

A moment later, the door flew open and Mirren burst into the room. She was thirteen, a thin, sharp-featured, awkward thirteen, still childish in some ways but with all a teenager's intensity. She was white with fury, her dark brown eyes wide and brimming with tears.

'He's hitting poor Moss now! I wish I could hurt him like that – I hate him, I hate him! He should be in prison!'

'Come and sit down. I'm just going to make you some pasta.' Getting drawn into her daughter's histrionics was never constructive.

'I'm not hungry!'

Mirren, starting to sob, ran out of the kitchen and slammed the door. Jenna sighed. Niall would be in any minute, also in a dramatically bad mood, and suddenly the job of varnishing floorboards seemed curiously attractive.

'And what, may I ask, are you doing with that thing indoors, on my clean kitchen floor?'

Gavin Scott, on his knees before the god of his idolatry – a new mountain bike – looked up with a start. He'd meant to get it out of the kitchen before his mother came home from work, but what with polishing it and oiling it the time had passed without him noticing.

'I'm just seeing it's ready for tomorrow,' he said defensively. 'I'm doing some of the forest tracks up above the Queen's Way, so I'm needing to be away first thing.'

Mrs Scott sniffed. 'Away to break your neck on that stupid thing, more like. Don't say I didn't warn you. And if there's a mark left on that floor . . .' Leaving the threat unspecified, she went out.

Gavin pulled a face at the shut door. He was nineteen, too old to be living at home still. It was cheap, that was all you could say for it, but now he'd saved up and bought his bike he could afford to rent a room in a flat somewhere. He might make more friends that way, find some other guys who liked mountain biking too. He enjoyed it anyway, but it would be more fun in a group.

With one last, loving polish to the machine, he stood up and prepared to carry it reverentially out to its place in the shed.

The Yacht Club bar was busy this evening, with the official start to the sailing season next day and the first race on Sunday. The schools' half-term week had started too, and the tables by the bar's low windows looking out over Drumbreck Bay were crowded, even if the view was less appealing now with the tide out. The decibel count rose to discomfort levels as acquaintances from previous years, not yet jaded by over-familiarity, brayed enthusiastic greetings. Children were bunched round a pool table at the farther end of the room, already establishing a pecking order which would condemn the unconfident, the unathletic and the seriously uncool to a summer of miserable isolation. A plump boy with spectacles was even now hovering uncomfortably on the fringes.

Niall Murdoch made his way directly to the bar, looking neither to right nor to left. He hated having to do the glad-handing bit; it was all very well for Ronnie to tell him that chatting up the buggers was part of the job, but he wasn't the one on the spot. Every time Niall spoke to one of the punters it seemed to turn into a moan session about some problem with the marina – broken decking on a pontoon, a dispute about moorings, vandalism by some of the disaffected locals which had meant they'd even had to hire a night watchman, a retired policeman, at great expense. And there were one or two people he was quite anxious to avoid, Kim and her husband in particular. But she'd said Adrian wasn't coming until tomorrow, and she'd be stuck in the house looking after the youngest kid, with any luck.

And the alternative was staying in the house, where Mirren kept looking through him as if he weren't there and Jenna, saint and martyr, was spending the evening drilling – deliberately, he reckoned – in the room next door to the sitting-room. And he'd engaged a rather tasty new water-ski instructor for the summer season – ah, there she was!

Niall bought a pint and made his way to the corner of the bar where she was standing with a group of young men, a couple of them his own workers from the marina. She welcomed him into the group enthusiastically, having seen nothing but his charming side as yet, and amid the banter and laughter his concerns about the trials tomorrow, the money and Davina slipped from his mind.

'Niall!' His partner's voice was an unwelcome surprise.

Murdoch turned and looked down from his six foot one at the squat man with prominent eyes, bulging now with temper, and three layers of chin below a jaw thrust out pugnaciously.

'Ronnie! I didn't know you were coming down this weekend.'

'I'll bet you didn't,' he said ominously. 'I wasn't, till I clocked the printout from the bank. Outside!'

Feeling faintly sick and with a feeble smile at his companions, Niall set down his glass and followed Lafferty's swaggering passage between the chatting groups and into the reception hall. It was empty at the moment; as the heavy glass door shut on the bar the noise diminished to a hum.

Lafferty squared up to him. 'Taken up embezzling, have you? What a moron – didn't even cover your tracks! Did you think I didn't check?'

Murdoch gulped. 'Ronnie, it's not like that! Just a temporary loan, that's all.'

'The marina's not in the money-lending business.' Lafferty took a step closer, jabbing at Niall's chest with a stubby finger. 'See, you – I want that money put back, right now. I don't care how you get it. OK?'

'Sure, sure.' Murdoch was sweating now. 'I'll sell the dog again whenever the sheepdog trials are over. I could have the money by tomorrow night.'

Lafferty's hand dropped, along with his jaw. 'You spent that on a *dog*? What are you – gormless or something? Oh, they saw you coming, boyo! You'd have done better backing one down the tracks.'

Stung, Niall protested, 'They're valuable, champion collies! And with another title to its name—'

'With you running it? That's a joke!' Lafferty laughed rudely. Then he shrugged. 'Not my problem anyway, is it? We'll need that money for wages at the end of the week. Where's it coming from?'

Murdoch flinched. He'd never quite allowed himself to articulate the fear that he would fail; Ronnie's naked contempt made it seem all too real. Inevitable, almost.

'Thanks. That's a great help, undermining my confidence,' he said bitterly, then, emboldened by self-pity, added, 'Anyway, what's five thousand to you? You could pay that out of your back pocket.'

'Five thousand!' Lafferty's roar of rage earned a startled look from the couple just leaving the bar on the way out. 'I could pay *fifty* thousand out of my back pocket! But I'm not going to. You've stolen money that's mine – just ask around what happens to people who try to cheat Ronnie Lafferty!

'Tomorrow night, you said? I'll be expecting to see it lodged in the account on Monday morning.' He turned and went to the door, shouldering his way past the couple who were still standing transfixed.

'Are you – are you all right?' the woman said hesitantly.

Niall, his face sickly pale, tried to smile. 'Just a little difficulty between friends. Flies off the handle – he'll calm down now he's got it off his chest.'

'Fine, fine!' The man's response was hearty and he put his arm round his wife's shoulders, urging her towards the door. 'Come on, Shirley – we'd better go. Babysitter, you know!'

As they left, with obvious relief, Niall put his hand up to his head. It would be a miracle if he won tomorrow, or even if Moss performed in a way that would make anyone want to buy him, and then there would be nothing he could do to raise the money. Chewing his lip, he walked across the hall. Then, at the door, he stopped.

Unless, unless . . .

Marjory and Bill sat on at the supper table in the kitchen after Findlay had left, lingering over the coffee cups. The children were upstairs, hopefully engaged in homework though more probably, in Cameron's case, finding elaborate ways of not doing it. Catriona mercifully seemed to be back on an even keel, eating normally, and wasn't for the moment at least a source of anxiety to her parents.

'He's in a bad way, isn't he, poor Fin!' Marjory shook her head. 'He couldn't talk about anything but the trials tomorrow. And if I had a fiver for every time he said, "If I just hadn't had to sell Moss!" I could afford to buy one of his dogs myself. I know he needs winners to boost his reputation, but he seems a bit paranoid – even if they lose to Moss, everyone'll know Fin trained him.'

'That's not what it's about, really,' Bill argued. 'It's personal. It's as if we were forced to sell Meg.'

The dog, curled up beside the Aga, looked up at the mention of her name.

'Don't listen to him, Meggie. We'd starve first,' Marjory said soothingly, and the dog put her head back down and shut her eyes. 'Oh, I can see it's awful for him. And even if he gets offers for both dogs tomorrow, it's not exactly a living wage, is it? He doesn't have another two he can sell next month.'

'No.' Bill shifted in his seat. He was playing with his teaspoon; he looked up and said, 'Marjory, I've been thinking.'

'Oh dear! I thought I heard a grinding noise.' She spoke lightly, but her eyes were suddenly wary. She knew her man, and she had a sinking feeling that the storm her tension headache had been signalling was just about to break, even if outside the evening was warm and still.

'You know this compensation money? I thought I'd go back to fattening cattle for the market again, the way I used to.'

'Good idea!' Marjory said enthusiastically. 'It'd be nice to have calves around the place again. But Bill, if you do you've got to have proper help—' She stopped. 'Oh.'

'It's obvious, really, isn't it? Fin needs the work, he's a good man and a hard worker, knows everything you need to know—'

'And you get on with him. OK, OK.' Marjory sighed. 'It's only the past history with me that's the problem. I can forget it but I'm not sure he can. I can hear him thinking about it whenever I'm around.'

She paused, drumming her fingers on the table. Bill said nothing and at last she sighed again.

'Of course you must. I know that. When you've got a job to offer and he needs one so badly, it would be wicked not to do it. He'll get used to me eventually, I suppose, and anyway I'd hardly need to see him, would I? I'd be out at work all day and he'd be gone by the time I came home.'

Bill still said nothing and she looked at him sharply. 'He would, Bill, wouldn't he? You're not thinking – oh Bill, no!'

'He didn't mention it this evening, but they're worried sick. With the tourist market recovering, their landlord would rather have holiday lets, so he's raised the rent to get them out. He's within his rights – it was only a six-month contract – but they've had to move in with Susie's parents. And our cottage is standing empty—'

Marjory sank her head into her hands. 'Bill, please don't do this! Fin's just awkward but Susie really hates me. I saw her in the street the other day and she didn't just blank me, she gave me a death stare.

'Of course I'd been thinking you might expand the farm again, take on a man. And I had hoped you might find someone with a wife who'd like a job giving a hand in the house. It's been quiet lately but when things were busy I was finding it really tough to cope before, now Mum can't do anything except look after Dad—'

'I know, I know. Maybe Susie could—' But even with Bill's optimistic nature he couldn't finish that sentence.

'No. Exactly. And she'll hate me even more when I'm in the farmhouse and she's in the farm worker's cottage.' Marjory was fighting a rearguard action, and she knew it.

'It's a big ask, sweetheart.' Bill put his hand on hers. 'But it's the right thing to do, isn't it?'

Marjory withdrew her hand. 'Of course it bloody is, and of course I'll do it, and I'll get new curtains for the cottage and see it's nice and clean and welcoming, and maybe she'll be pleased and won't hate me any more. But I reserve the right to be fed up to the back teeth.'

Bill smiled, leaning forward to kiss her reluctant cheek. 'That's my girl! Feel the pain but do it anyway.'

She laughed dutifully and got up to start clearing the table, but her throat was tight with misery and her head was pounding now. Her home had always been her refuge, the place she came back to with a lift of her heart. How would it feel when she couldn't so much as go out to feed her hens without knowing there were hostile eyes watching her?

3

The sun was still shining as Gavin Scott toiled up the steep, stony, rutted forest track early on Saturday morning, but it was oppressive and there were bruise-purple clouds boiling up ahead. With sweat trickling uncomfortably down inside his Lycra cycling gear, he gritted his teeth and bent forward over the handlebars of his mountain bike, forcing the pedals round and trying to ignore flies swarming about his helmet with no apparent purpose other than to increase his discomfort.

Still, it couldn't be too far to the top now, with its spectacular view out over the forest above the Queen's Way which links New Galloway and Newton Stewart. It would be good if he could get there before the rain started and after that, going back down on one of the smaller, more rugged tracks, he'd be sheltered better by the trees. He hoped he could find it again; he'd done it once before and it had been a scary, thrilling ride, with twists and turns and pot-holes and unexpected boulders. And with any luck, the rain would get rid of the effing flies.

With renewed vigour, he pedalled on.

'All right, you two? Anything to report?'

Marjory Fleming plodded through the forming puddles in her heavy black rubber boots, the hood of her well-worn waxed coat pulled up. She was making her way in the teeming rain across the field designated as a car park towards Jon Kingsley and Tansy Kerr, on plain-clothes duty after a report that car thieves might be targeting the Windyedge Sheepdog Trials.

Jon had dressed for the part in a flat cap, navy weatherproof hooded jacket and green wellies. Tansy, in a pink pearlized zip-up jacket, stone-washed jeans and trainers, with her bizarrely coloured hair plastered to her head by the rain, hadn't. Marjory reflected that at least she didn't look like a police officer; she was more likely to be stopped on sus if there were uniforms around who didn't know her.

'Nothing so far,' Kingsley said. 'We're just wandering round and – er – trying to blend in.' He gave an ironic sideways glance at Kerr as he spoke, which Fleming ignored.

'Fine. I'll be—'

'Marjory! Oh good, I was just wondering how to find you.'

With Daisy, her collie, prancing on the lead, Laura Harvey was coming towards them. She was always clever with clothes: her cream waterproof jacket and dark trousers were practical enough but her blonde hair was bundled up into a wide-brimmed hot-pink rain hat and her wellies had a jazzy pattern.

Marjory performed the introductions and patted the excited dog. Tansy barely greeted Laura before crouching down to make a fuss of Daisy; Jon, though, held out his hand, looking at her with some interest.

'Laura Harvey! You're a byword down our nick, you know that?'

Laura laughed. 'I hate to think what for! Are you here for duty or pleasure today?'

'Duty, theoretically. But the pleasure element has just started to kick in.'

Smooth bastard! Marjory gave him an old-fashioned look, but Laura was amused.

'I like that! Do you mind if I write it down? I'm making a collection of chat-up lines.'

'That was just off the cuff. I'm sure, given notice and opportunity, I could improve on it.'

'Oh, I think that one goes down as well.' She was enjoying herself, her grey-blue eyes sparkling.

'Laura, I'm just going back to watch now,' Marjory cut in. 'They were nearly finished with the brace class when I left so they'll be starting the singles any time now. Coming?'

'Yes, of course. Bye!' Laura smiled at Jon, and Tansy gave Daisy a final pat. As they squelched off she murmured to Marjory, 'Mmm! Quite fit, isn't he?'

'Mmm,' Marjory echoed. Jon Kingsley wasn't exactly handsome but he was undeniably attractive, slim-built and a little above average height, with fair hair and a narrow, intelligent face. It really wouldn't be fair to tell tales out of school and pass on her reservations about him.

A few trade stands, selling pottery and tweeds, honey and aromatic oils, had been set up in open tents lining the way to the arena. The largest tent had a café and a bar, well-filled at the moment as people took refuge from the rain.

'There's no point in that. You might just as well get wet right at the start,' Marjory said fatalistically as they negotiated the sea of slippery mud in the gateway to the field where the trials were being held. 'This looks as if it's on for the day.'

Bill was standing beside the commentary box, a good position right behind the point where the competitor would stand to direct the dog through the long-distance manoeuvres of driving the sheep through gates, and close to the shedding ring where the flock must be separated into two groups and the pen where they must be finally enclosed.

That was the stage they had reached at the moment, the man holding the gate wide on a rope and banging his crook on the ground to try to persuade the sheep in while his dog crouched, eying them and daring them to break free.

'How's it going?' Marjory asked as they reached him.

Bill didn't turn his head. 'Fine, fine. Hi, Laura!' At his feet Meg, too, ears pricked, was watching with total concentration as if she might be giving marks for performance. A klaxon sounded and a groan of sympathy went round the crowd.

'Timed out. That was bad luck,' Bill said and turned round. 'Sorry, Laura – very rude of me not to say hello properly.' He kissed her cheek.

'Not at all. The flower of courtesy, compared to Meg.' Laura indicated the dogs: Daisy was pushing her nose under her mother's chin and licking at her mouth while Meg tossed her head irritably, her attention already on the five sheep being driven in at the farther end of the field for the next competitor.

'How did Findlay get on in the brace class?' Marjory asked.

'Pretty well. Not first – there was a farmer up from Cumbria who's a national champion with a very experienced pair, but second's good enough for his purposes with two young dogs like that. And he'll be hoping for great things from Flash in the singles – brave dog with a very good eye.'

The tannoy announced the next competitor – a woman this time – and she took up her position with her dog for their fifteen-minute attempt. The klaxon sounded and an arm movement sent the dog streaking off on its outrun.

Marjory watched, her mind on Laura's encounter with Jon, feeling faintly ashamed of herself at terminating it so ruthlessly. She had nothing against the man, really, except that he was a bit cocky and too nakedly ambitious to be a team player. He was good at his job though and he was certainly quick-witted and amusing company. It was just that it was always a pity if a close friend took up with someone you didn't gel with.

And Laura was more than a close friend: as a psychotherapist with a growing reputation from her writing and broadcasting, she was someone Marjory relied on professionally for discreet advice which had proved its worth again and again.

Of course, she was running ahead of herself there. Jon and

Laura had barely exchanged two words; it wasn't as if he'd asked her out or anything. But, Marjory thought gloomily as she applauded the herding of sheep through the first gate, she'd put money on it that he would.

It was drier under the trees now Gavin Scott had begun on the descent. The track was just as hairy as he remembered it being; he braked hard as a boulder loomed up and skirted round it, then, grinning, speeded up again with clearer ground dropping away sharply below him. Thrilling, it was, hovering on the edge of disaster with the wind of speed in his face. He was the man!

The rain was getting heavier, though, and beginning to force its way through the canopy above him. Its coolness was welcome but it had begun to put a slick of moisture on the stones; he'd need to watch it. There was a nasty moment as he felt the tyres lose adhesion slightly and his stomach lurched in fright, but he corrected it and went on a little more cautiously.

He didn't even see the smooth, flat slab of stone in the path until he turned a corner and was on it. A couple of trees had died back and here the rain was falling straight through, converting the stone surface to a patch like wet glass.

He had no chance. The bike slid, hit a rock and reared up, throwing him to the ground before smashing its front wheel against a tree trunk.

Gavin lay for a moment, half-stunned. His head had hit the ground with some force, but his helmet had done its job of protection. He hurt all over, though: his back, his elbows, his knee . . .

Gingerly, he sat up to assess the damage. His back only felt bruised, though his elbows were scratched and bleeding, there was a tear in his shorts and a gash in the thigh beneath, but his knee – that was seriously painful.

Clutching at a nearby tree stump, he managed to lever

himself to his feet. The knee was swelling already and he yelped with pain as he put his weight on it. And the bike, his brilliant bike, was a write-off. He groaned, looking about him helplessly.

It was still a hell of a way down to the road. He was sure he couldn't walk that far; he'd end up shuffling on his bum for hours. He'd have to get help.

Gavin hobbled across to the bike and was reaching into the saddle-bag for his mobile when a picture suddenly came into his head, a picture of the mobile, sitting on the kitchen table. He'd left in a hurry, hearing the old girl on the move upstairs and keen to escape without her yakking on at him again. He checked the bag, like you always do even when you know it's pointless, but of course it wasn't there. Stupid or what?

It was a bit heavy, being injured and miles from anywhere. The air seemed sort of muffled by the soft steady downpour, like even if you shouted it wouldn't make a noise. The only sound he could hear was water running nearby, and what he did have in his saddle-bag was a towel; maybe if he soaked it and wrapped his knee it would help. He couldn't think what else to do.

It wasn't far to the burn, but picking his way over the roots of trees and the uneven ground was really slow and painful. At last he reached it and found a rock by the edge where he could sit; he sank down on it with relief and soaked the towel in the clear brown water. He cleaned his grazes, then soaked it again to bandage his knee. It was very cold, almost like an ice-pack. Perhaps it might work, in time.

Then he heard it: the ringing of a mobile phone, its tinny tune sounding in his ears like the bugles of the US Cavalry. 'Hello!' he called eagerly. 'Is there someone there?' Self-consciously, he added, 'Help!'

There was no reply, only the continued ringing of the phone. Then it stopped and there was nothing but the burbling of the burn and the persistent whisper of falling rain.

He called again, but there was no response. He frowned. The noise had definitely come from further downstream, across the burn to his left. He listened, then stood up to look, but he couldn't see any sign of movement.

If it had been answered he'd have heard someone speaking. So perhaps someone, a forester, maybe, had dropped it and didn't know where it was and was phoning to try to find it. They might even be hunting for it now, getting closer . . . He shouted a couple more times, then waited for it to ring again, but it didn't.

So perhaps it had just been lost. It was like some kind of torture, knowing it was there somewhere, but not how to find it. Needles in haystacks had nothing on this.

Willing it to ring again, he listened, but it remained obstinately silent. If he waited much longer, with this weather it'd soon be too dark to see his way down off the hill, and he seriously didn't fancy a night out here. Or he could head in the direction the ringing had come from and hope that his luck might turn. About time!

The compress had fallen off as he stood up, but it didn't seem to be doing much good anyway. There was a sturdy branch he could use as a stick lying at the edge of the burn, and leaning on it, he splashed across, heading downhill when he reached the other side. He had hoped for a path but there wasn't one, and negotiating tree roots, rotting logs and hidden rocks was agony. Cold sweat was standing out on his forehead when at last he reached a sort of clearing where several trees had fallen together.

Gavin slumped down on the trunk of one of them with a groan. He wasn't going to find the bloody thing, was he? He daren't go deeper into the forest and risk getting lost; he'd have to go back across the burn to the path and work his way down somehow. He was getting thoroughly soaked now and with the pain and the cold he was beginning to shiver. He'd better keep moving.

It was the flies he heard first, a curious low, muttering buzz. At first he thought it might be wasps with their byke built in the shelter of the fallen tree roots; they made their nests in places like that. He stood up to peer over the bank which the roots had formed.

At first Gavin thought she was asleep. Then he saw the flies, clustered together . . . He stared for a moment in disbelief, then turned aside and was violently sick.

It was a nightmare, right? He was dreaming this, in his bed, and he'd wake up any minute to go off on a ride on a sunny morning. But he wasn't. She was there, and she was dead, and he was alone and injured.

It was too much. This was nothing to do with him. He felt almost angry, aggrieved at being dragged into a mess that wasn't his mess. His own was bad enough, for God's sake, without this. The police – this was their job, not his.

Never one around when you needed one, like they said. Then he paused. It must have been her phone – what else?

He'd have to look at her again, touch her, even. Bile rose in his throat, but he swallowed hard. A moment's disgust, or hours crawling down a hillside in rain and dark to reach the road, and no guarantee when he got there of much passing traffic? And they'd come quick enough when they heard what he'd found. Then it would be someone else's problem.

It was, mercifully, in her jacket pocket. Shaking, he took it and withdrew, then dialled the emergency number.

The plump boy with spectacles who had been hovering on the fringes of teenage society in the Drumbreck Yacht Club sat gloomily by himself on a damp bench. James Ross's specs were misting up in the rain but he couldn't be fagged to wipe them since, frankly, at fourteen did anyone give a monkey's about a lot of wet sheep and a stupid dog chasing them? He'd only come with his parents because he hoped he might be able to latch on to the group of kids who always hung out together and who'd been talking about coming last night.

It wasn't quite as easy as that. He'd seen them and made his way over to join them, but everyone ignored him and eventually he drifted off to sit on a bench nearby.

Kelly McConnell was at the centre of the group, giggling and play-wrestling with one of the boys. At fourteen Kelly was the image of her mother Kim, with a well-developed bust and blonded hair. She had teenage acne and she'd tried to conceal it, not very successfully, under a heavy layer of pancake make-up, but that didn't seem to put any of the boys off. She wasn't wearing a coat; the short turquoise T-shirt which exposed a roll of puppy-fat round her midriff was soaked and clinging to her curves, which seemed to be the source of the jokes.

James sighed, then looked glumly back to the field where the sheep seemed to be having a fine time racing around all over the place, fat woolly rumps bobbing, with a dog after them and the man at the top of the field yelling.

'Hey, guys!' he heard Kelly say. 'We're needing to watch this one. My mum was saying this is always, like, the comedy act. Look – the dog's pants and he's tragic.'

'Who is it?' someone asked idly, joining in the laughter at the antics going on round the course.

'Murdoch – you know, from the marina. Dad says he couldn't find his backside if they painted a big arrow.'

'Watch out, Kelly,' one of the girls warned. 'That's Mirren there, see?'

'So?' Kelly said indifferently.

James followed the gesture. Murdoch's daughter was standing just to his left, a thin figure in a brown hooded cagoule with her shoulders hunched up almost to her ears, clutching the boundary rope. Her hands were wet and red with cold but he could see the white of her knuckles showing through. He didn't think she'd heard what Kelly said because her face was all screwed up and her lips were moving, saying something he couldn't hear.

He edged along the bench towards her, listening, but she wasn't talking out loud. The klaxon went for out of time and he saw her shoulders sag. When she turned away she was crying.

'What's the matter?' he said, more in curiosity than in sympathy.

She hardly seemed to see him, knuckling the tears away. 'Did you see what he's done to poor Moss?' she said savagely. 'Dogs like that know when it's all gone wrong, and he's really clever. He'll be feeling it's all his fault, and it isn't, it isn't! And my father will probably beat him now.'

'Oh,' James said feebly.

'He'll get rid of him, likely sell him to someone who'll treat him even worse.'

The conversation had attracted the group's attention. One of the boys sniggered.

'Who'd buy it? That dog's only fit for the knacker's yard.'

Several others tittered but Mirren Murdoch turned on him, her eyes blazing.

'If he kills Moss, I'll kill him,' she said, then ran away across the muddy field.

'Hey, lighten up!' a boy called after her, but still there was a slight feeling of unease.

'Poor kid,' one of the girls said, but Kelly, irritated at having lost their attention, tossed her head. 'Just having a kiddie tantrum,' she said. 'Anyone getting tired of this? Let's go to the tent and get a burger.'

'He's ruined that dog, hasn't he?' Marjory watched with some dismay as Niall Murdoch, his face set, looped a rope leash round his dog's neck and half-dragged it out. There had been a spattering of embarrassed applause; now it died in a wave of stony disapproval.

'Not the ideal start for Fin,' Bill agreed. 'Worse than if Moss had done brilliantly. He'll be devastated, and if he can't put it out of his mind Flash will pick that up. And I'll tell you another thing – there's a black sheep in with that lot. Fin's got a thing about black sheep – says they're always thrawn.'

'And are they?' Laura asked. 'Always supposing I knew what thrawn meant.'

'Stubborn, with a bit of perversity thrown in. And I might agree with him,' Bill admitted. 'They're different, you see – probably had to struggle for acceptance in the flock right from the start.

'Here he's coming now.'

A silence fell as Findlay Stevenson was announced and came forward to take up his position, the dog, a black-and-white collie with a rakish black patch across one eye, at his knee, staring up into his master's face.

Laura looked at Findlay with interest: he was in his late thirties, perhaps, and he was bare-headed so that his dark red hair looked almost black with the rain. She saw him shrug as if to dispel tension, then pause before he sent the dog off on the outrun. Living up to his name, Flash looked like nothing more than a streak of movement, low to the ground, speeding round the very edge of the field.

Laura had found the trials fascinating to watch. On safari with her ex-husband Brad she'd watched hunting-dogs in Africa do flanking movements just like this and then, as Flash was doing now, dropping to the ground then inching forward, raising one paw and freezing, a step at a time. Over how many tens of thousands of years had that extraordinary relationship between man – or woman – and working dog been developed?

On a perfectly timed whistle, Flash rose and, as they said,

'lifted' the sheep; they moved off smoothly, unflustered, with the black one leading, and earned a round of applause.

'Nice,' Bill approved. 'Very nice.'

The drive went well, gates neatly negotiated. It was only when they came back up to the shedding ring that the dominant ewe began to show a nature as black as her fleece.

Benefiting from Bill's instructions, Laura knew that with the handler standing by, the dog was supposed to separate two sheep from the others, within the marked ring, and then control them. 'In here!' she heard Fin call, and the dog moved swiftly into a gap in the flock that had opened up. The black sheep, however, was having none of it. She turned back towards the others, yellow eyes defiant, then even made a little rush at the dog, stamping her foot.

Bill drew in his breath. 'If the dog gives way, he's had it. But if he comes on too strong, he's had it too.'

But Flash, with encouraging noises from his master, held firm, staring down the sheep with his own steady gaze. The ewe became visibly uncomfortable as he inched forward with relentless authority until she turned and trotted off in the right direction, tossing her head nervously. Laura could almost hear the collective sigh of relief as applause broke out again.

Penning was the final challenge. The black sheep seemed almost bent on revenge for her humiliation as they were shepherded into position, stamping angrily, breaking away round the side of the pen between man and dog and unsettling the others. A white one followed and then the rest rushed away from the pen to join the rebels.

'It's like those puzzles where you have to get all the metal balls into the holes at the same time,' Laura said, though the others hardly heard her.

'He was quick on the drive, so he's got time in hand,' Bill muttered, and Marjory seemed almost to be holding her breath.

Flash had rounded them up again. Findlay had the gate wide open, spreading his arms out and reaching out his crook to cover the biggest area possible.

The first of the sheep went in, then another, and another. The fourth hesitated on the threshold and then the black one, bringing up the rear, stopped. When she turned, ready to break again, the crowd groaned. At a command from Findlay, Flash, belly to the ground, edged forward again. The ewe stamped. He raised his head, fixing her once more with that steady, unnerving stare. The clash of wills between the animals was all but audible.

Then she lowered her head, looking round uncertainly for support, and finding none scuttled to join the others. Findlay slammed the gate shut. It was done.

As the crowd clapped, Flash frolicked round his master in the comfortable knowledge of a job well done, and was given his reward of approval. Bill said, with some relief, 'He's home and dry. There are a couple more but I know the dogs and neither of them will come close.'

The exit from the arena was just by the commentary box. As the next competitor was announced, Findlay and Flash came out. Bill hailed him.

'Well done, man! What a performance! You've a brave dog there.'

Flash, ears pricked and head held high, looked up intelligently as if pleased at the praise, but Findlay did not have the expression of a man savouring success.

'Where is he?' he said tautly. 'Murdoch, I mean? Did you see what he's done to Moss?'

'I know, I know.' Bill patted his arm. 'The man's useless, but the dog's his now. There's nothing you can do, Fin.'

Findlay was not a big man, but he was square-shouldered and physically fit. Like most redheads his skin was pale, but now it looked unnaturally white, the freckles on his cheeks standing out in stark contrast.

'Oh yes? We'll see. If you see him first, tell him I'm looking for him.'

He strode off to put Flash back in his battered pick-up along with the other dog, leaving Bill and Marjory exchanging troubled glances.

'Maybe you should go after him, Bill,' Marjory urged. 'He's spoiling for a fight.'

'Susie's around somewhere. She'll talk him down. And Murdoch's probably gone home by now. I'd crawl away if I'd made a spectacle of myself like that.'

Marjory was doubtful. 'I hope you're right. It wouldn't be a very good start if I ended up having to arrest him for brawling.' She turned to Laura. 'He's coming to work on the farm with Bill next week. He and his wife are moving into the cottage.'

'Oh, that'll be nice for you!' Knowing nothing of the background, Laura was innocently pleased. 'Will she give you a hand in the house? I know you were wanting someone.'

'Not exactly.' She didn't elaborate, but Laura, professionally expert at hearing what people didn't say, left it there.

'I see. Listen, I think I'll go now. The rain's trickling down my neck and I reckon the drama's over.'

'Fine. I'll call you—' Marjory was beginning when her phone rang. Pulling a face, she answered it, and Laura, with a pantomime of farewell, set off for the car park.

Just as she reached it she heard a car alarm sounding, but it was only as she drew nearer that she realized, with embarrassment rather than anxiety, that the car flashing its indicators was her own. Daisy had rapidly become cold, bored and restless and Laura had brought her back to the car some time ago; her movement would have triggered the alarm and this had probably happened at regular intervals since.

To her further embarrassment, DC Kingsley was standing beside it, waiting for her. 'Is this your car, madam?' he said with mock severity.

'Sorry, sorry!' Laura cried, clicking her key to switch it off. The noise stopped, apart from Daisy's excited barking. 'Oh dear, I wish I could just click her off as well!'

He laughed. 'Don't worry about it. It's the only bit of excitement we've had all afternoon. Tansy's gone to warm up with a cup of coffee in the tent – she wasn't really dressed for the weather.'

'No, not exactly. Your turn next?'

'Doubt if I'll bother. There's a steady trickle starting to leave now and once there are enough people around in the car park we can knock off. What I need is a hot bath and then I fancy finding something a bit stronger than coffee to warm me up. Care to join me?'

'The drink, yes. Call me old-fashioned, but I think on such slight acquaintance I'll go home for my hot bath.'

'Don't miss a trick, do you?' he was saying, as Tansy appeared outside the tent, waving frantically.

'Jon! Fight in the tent – get over here!'

He swore under his breath. 'Phone number?' he said urgently, and she gabbled it as he took off.

Laura got into her car wondering if this would have scuppered the plans for the evening. She was well aware of what the problems of going out with a policeman might be, but this was an excessively early start to them.

Perhaps that had been what Marjory's phone call had been about too. She might give her a ring later tonight, if she hadn't heard from Jon.

Or perhaps she wouldn't. It hadn't been lost on Laura that Marjory had been suspiciously quick to break up their conversation. She remembered when Jon – English, a graduate and with a reputation as a high-flier – had joined the Galloway Force from Edinburgh, Marjory had been worried about Tam MacNee's reaction to him, and Laura had thought privately that it was not beyond the bounds of possibility that Marjory had felt threatened too. Since Jon joined her team she had been professionally loyal but somehow Laura had a feeling there wasn't much love lost.

Still, Marjory needn't know about what had been, when it came right down to it, the most casual of invitations.

'Bill, I have to go,' Marjory said urgently. 'I'll need the jeep. Do you think Fin and Susie would give you and the kids a lift home?'

'Someone will. Here – take the keys.'

Blessing him, as always, for his unquestioning support, she hurried back to the car park and jumped into the old jeep. She was driving across to turn right on to the main way out when she realized there was a commotion going on back down to her left, around the beer tent. She stopped to look, then gave a gasp of dismay.

Findlay Stevenson, dishevelled and with a graze on one cheek, was being frogmarched towards a police car, there on crowd duty, between Jon Kingsley and a uniform, with Tansy Kerr bringing up the rear.

There was nothing she could do. This would never even reach her level and at the moment she had more important – much more important – matters to deal with. She drove on with a leaden heart. As if things weren't bad enough already with Fin and Susie! And poor Bill would have to find someone else to give him a lift home.

4

'*How* far?' Marjory Fleming said blankly.

'About a mile, ma'am. Maybe a wee bit more. Uphill.' The PC at the foot of the forest track where it emerged on to the A712 not far from Clatteringshaws Loch was trying not to look as if he enjoyed giving that answer. Standing in the rain logging visitors to the site might not be much fun but at least he could sneak into the car when there was no one around, which was definitely better than scrambling up a winding rocky track in rain and fading light.

Fleming looked ruefully at her rubber boots, ideal for ploughing through muddy fields but pretty much guaranteed to give you blisters if you were daft enough to go hiking in them. An unappetizing prospect, and with that leaden sky, it was getting dark already too, even if it was only just after six o'clock. She went back to the jeep to fetch a torch, saying bitterly to the constable, 'All right for some!'

There were half-a-dozen badged vehicles of different types parked by the road, as well as a couple of ordinary cars, one of them Tam MacNee's. If they were lucky, the other might be the police surgeon. However dead the body might obviously be, no one could do anything until he'd said it was.

Fleming set off up into the shadow of the trees. It was much darker here, with a sort of greenish, unearthly light, and very, very quiet. There must be all of a dozen people not that far away, but the trees muffled sound so effectively that she could have been the only person for miles around. There was something about forests, with the towering trees that almost seemed to be crowding you and the deadening hush, as if – something – was holding its breath. A childhood memory came to her: a so-called friend who had told her as they played in a wood one day, 'Trees move, you know, when you're not looking.' She'd somehow never felt entirely comfortable alone in dense woodland since.

It was too dark to see clearly, but she found herself oddly reluctant to switch on her torch, as if the light might, well, draw attention or something – oh, for goodness' sake! She wasn't nine now. Annoyed with herself, she snapped on the torch and directed its light on to the path ahead. It might have the effect of further deepening the darkness round about but it did at least make it less likely she'd break her ankle tripping over a rock.

There was plenty of time to consider what lay ahead as she climbed. The report Fleming had been given was unspecific: the body was that of a female, but there was as yet no indication as to whether this had been natural, accidental or violent death, or how recently it had taken place. A body could lie undiscovered in a place like this for months – years, even.

The rain was going off now and in the light wind which had sprung up the trees were starting to sway and mutter. As she walked on through the shifting shadows, Fleming saw at last light shining through the trees, greeting the sight of it with a certain shamefaced relief which wasn't entirely because she could feel a blister forming on her left heel.

As she got closer, she could see other lights too – torches like her own, bobbing about. They must have managed to heave a generator up, since the main light, which she could see now lighting up the sky, was so strong and steady. She could hear its low, electronic hum and then, when she was about a hundred yards away, the buzz of human voices.

She must have been spotted; one of the bobbing lights came down towards her and she heard Tam MacNee's voice. 'That you, boss? They said you were on the way up.'

'Tam! You were quick off the mark.'

MacNee grunted as they walked up together. 'Sitting duck, that was me. There in front of the telly, Rangers 2–1 down, and Bunty takes the message and says no problem, I'll be right there.'

'Bad luck. Maybe it saved you seeing them lose.'

He glared at her. ' "*Your pity I will not implore, For pity you have none!*" '

'None at all,' she agreed. 'So what's the situation?'

'I'll give you a clue. She didn't bash herself over the head and wander up here looking for a quiet place to die.'

Fleming felt a jolt of shock which was part alarm, part excitement too. 'She's been killed? Recently?'

MacNee was leading the way off the path and down a slope towards a narrow, stony burn. 'Recent enough. Carstairs is here, grumphing as usual.'

The police surgeon, whose most common duty was attesting to the proper treatment of drunks held in police cells, was Arthur Carstairs, a small, self-important man with rimless spectacles, a prim mouth and a decided preference for making the worst of even the best of circumstances. Since the wildest optimist would have to concede that this assignment, in damp darkness and rough terrain, was far from ideal, Fleming resigned herself to having to work to placate him. Police surgeons were hard to come by, what with doctors getting a huge increase recently – apparently to reward them for declining to work nights and weekends. She should be so lucky!

Lit by powerful lamps on either side, Carstairs, in a white protective suit, was on the farther side of the burn, crouching in front of what looked confusingly like a wall of ropes. It was only by shading her eyes and looking beyond the pool of light that Fleming could see the shadowy shapes of the fallen trees whose roots had tangled together to form this sheltering bank. Nodding an acknowledgement to the other officers grouped around, waiting for official confirmation of death, she splashed her way across the burn to stand beside him.

At her approach Carstairs straightened up, glaring at her as he stripped off his rubber gloves. 'This really is the outside of enough! When I agreed to accept this post there was no indication that *mountaineering* would form part of my duties!'

'Of course not,' Fleming agreed soothingly as she reached him, resisting the temptation to add that they would, of course, issue an immediate directive that no one must die above sea level. 'Very difficult, I know. Have you had time to come to any conclusions yet?'

'Well, I can certify death. Obviously.'

Fleming looked down. The woman was lying on her back, her head turned to one side. She had been smartly, quite expensively dressed; she had a small diamond in her nose and a chunky gold earring in the ear that was visible. She was young, and the sickening injury under the matted mass of long dark hair was, indeed, eloquent proof.

'And equally obviously,' Carstairs went on, 'the fatal injury was not self-inflicted. With the evidence of extensive bruising to the face and the absence of any possible agent of accident in the vicinity, I think we can risk assuming that we are talking about unlawful killing.'

Fleming jerked her head at MacNee, who had been a silent observer. He nodded, then, signalling to one of the uniformed officers who was holding a radio phone, retreated with him out of earshot. That gave them all they needed to summon the pathology team.

'Any estimate of time?' Fleming asked.

Carstairs pursed his mouth. 'Not without a much more detailed examination than I am paid to do. But with the usual provisos about variations in temperature and so on, we might surmise from the absence of rigor mortis that death took place at least thirty-six hours ago.'

'And at most?'

'My good woman,' he said witheringly, 'if I could establish that, on the basis of the most cursory examination in semi-darkness, I would set up as a psychic.'

'Mmm,' Fleming said. When you were compressing your lips to prevent a tart response from escaping it was about all you could say.

'What I can tell you, with a tolerable degree of certainty, is that the body was moved here after death. No sign of blood, for a start.

'Now, perhaps I may be permitted to return home? We are having a dinner party tonight and my wife is relying on me to make my special dressing for the salad.'

'See and give your hands a good wash first.' MacNee had returned, earning himself a jab in the ribs as he muttered this in Fleming's ear.

'Of course, doctor,' she said smoothly. 'Thank you very much for dealing with this so promptly.'

Carstairs grunted ungraciously, packed up his bag and picked his way back across the burn, uttering an expletive as a stone shifted under his foot and his shoe filled with water.

Fleming turned to look again at the body. It had been protected from the worst of the rain by the overhanging roots, but even so the clothes were damp. She had been pretty, probably, before some brute beat her up and death slackened the skin of her face. She'd been young, anyway – late twenties, perhaps. Untimely death, however it came, always hit you hard, and now she felt horror, too, that someone's rage –

fuelled, more than likely, by drink or drugs or both – could reduce an attractive young woman to the sad remains lying before her now.

Behind her, she heard one of the officers laughing, and almost swung round with a reprimand. But that was how they worked – how they had to work, if they were not to be overwhelmed by the tragedies of life that were police business. She was guilty of callousness herself; they all were. It sounded better if you called it professionalism, but they were both names for the protective distance you had to keep if you wanted to sleep at night.

'Cover her up meantime – those flies!' With a grimace, Fleming turned away. 'Poor creature!' she said sombrely. 'How do you suppose she came to this? Who found her, anyway?'

'The lad up there.' MacNee pointed.

Gavin Scott, swathed in a silver survival blanket, was sitting morosely on the ground further upstream, his arms clasped round his knees and his head bent. A woman officer was crouching beside him.

'George Christie dealt with it – he'll tell you all about it. George!' MacNee raised his voice and beckoned to a uniformed sergeant who was giving instructions about taping off the site.

Fleming knew him slightly, a neat man with a dapper moustache based at Newton Stewart. He gave her an account of Scott's 999 call, made on his victim's mobile phone. 'I've got it here,' he said, unbuttoning his pocket to take it out in its plastic evidence bag. 'It's only the lad there who's touched it directly – we'll need his prints for elimination. But should we be using it now to try to establish identity?'

'Give it to Tam,' Fleming directed. 'I'm going back to set up the major incident room at Kirkluce after I've seen the pathologist – it'll be time enough then.'

She looked around, assessing the scene. The sky was starting to clear as the freshening wind tore the clouds apart. It would give them perhaps an hour of better light before sunset.

'The obvious route to the site is up the path and directly across the burn, of course – the way we all came. We may have destroyed evidence already, unfortunately, but tape it off now. And just in case, seal off the area beyond the fallen trees and the access from downstream. It's possible the killer may have carried her across below and walked up but it should be safe enough to assume at least that he won't have come down from above. So make sure everyone crosses upstream and approaches from there.

'There's not a lot we can do before the photographer arrives and after that the daylight will have gone. Just finish taping off, sergeant, then send away anyone who isn't needed. The fewer people we have stamping around here the better, and—'

The ringing of a mobile phone cut across her. 'It's this one,' MacNee said, startled, taking it out of his pocket and holding it out to Fleming.

She hesitated for a second then took it. Half-unwrapping it, she pressed the answer button through the plastic and held it a little way away from her ear.

They all heard the man's voice. 'Natasha! Thank God! What the hell are you playing at? I didn't know where you were – I kept calling and just got the frigging answer service. I've been going mental! Where are you?' Raw anxiety was overlaid with the anger of relief.

'I'm sorry.' Fleming's voice was carefully neutral. 'Who was it you wanted to speak to?'

'Natasha Wintour.' His tone sharpened. 'Who are you? What are you doing with her phone?'

'Police. The phone has come into our hands. Who am I speaking to?'

'God, has she lost her phone again? Typical! This is Jeff Brewer. Where was it found?'

'I'm sorry, sir, I'm not at liberty to give that information. Can you give me your address, please, and Ms Wintour's?'

'It's the same. We live together. Or at least we did, until four days ago when she suddenly took off without a word to me.' He sounded bitter.

At a gesture from Fleming, MacNee took out his notebook and wrote down the address as she repeated it.

'Thank you, sir. We'll be in touch.' Fleming ended the call then, with her lips pursed in a silent whistle, and replaced the phone carefully in its bag. 'Manchester! That's a surprise.'

Tam bristled. 'What's she doing here? Started trying to reduce their crime statistics by dumping their bodies on us, have they?'

'Even for you that's paranoid. Like the boys in blue in Manchester have a disposal squad going round Scotland looking for likely sites? Anyway, I'll have to contact them tonight to ask them to go and break the news to Brewer. We may find ourselves having to work quite closely with them, Tam, so you'd better stop reading Burns until this one's out of the way. I blame him for your rabid nationalist attitude.'

She turned to Christie. 'Someone'll have to work out how to get that poor lad down off the hill – we needn't keep him any longer. What about getting him a piggyback? I'm sure you've some young, strong constable who's blotted his copybook in the last few days.'

'Oh, indeed I do. I've one who put a dent in his patrol car yesterday. Brown! I've a job for you!'

'What's happened to you?' Jenna Murdoch, putting a vegetable curry into the microwave for her daughter, turned to stare at her husband as he came in. He was sporting a livid bruise on one cheek and his lip was split and swollen.

'I was attacked, that's what happened.' He was in a state of barely suppressed fury. 'Stevenson went for me like a madman after the trials. Not content with conning me over the dog, he comes up when I'm having a quiet drink at the bar and has a go at me.'

Jenna tried to conceal a smile. 'Do I take it you and Moss didn't cover yourselves with glory?'

'What could I do? The dog's past it, and Stevenson knew it. Who's going to buy it now, I said, and he started yelling at me. Then, when I told him if I didn't have a decent offer – from him, preferably – within the week, I was going to have the useless beast put down.'

Taking a stew out of the oven for their own supper, Jenna froze, waiting for Mirren's reaction. She had come in just before her father and gone to sit at the kitchen table, saying nothing; she'd probably start throwing crockery at any moment, having inherited her temper from her father's side of the family.

But she didn't even speak. Turning, Jenna saw that her daughter's face was white and drawn and her dark eyes, burning with hatred, were fixed on her oblivious father.

The microwave pinged. Relieved to have an excuse to break the tension, Jenna said, 'Here you are, Mirren. It's ready now.' She scooped the food on to a plate and put it in front of her daughter.

'I'm not hungry.' Mirren didn't drop her gaze.

'Can't say I am either,' Niall said. 'What is it – stew? If it's your usual watery muck, I'm not sure how much I fancy it, with my lip being sore.'

Jenna's lips tightened. She helped herself, then sat down at the table with her own plate. 'Seems like I'm the only one who's eating,' she said lightly.

Niall was taken aback. 'Well, that's nice, isn't it! I've been beaten up, and all my wife can do is sit and stuff her face. I would have thought I might have been entitled to a bit of sympathy and consideration.' He glanced towards his daughter, as if expecting support, then, encountering her unblinking, accusatory stare, snarled, 'And you can stop looking at me like that, too!'

He jumped to his feet. 'I wouldn't like you to worry about my supper,' he said to Jenna with heavy sarcasm. 'I'll get something to eat at the Yacht Club.'

'I'm surprised you're prepared to show your face there,' she returned with saccharine sweetness, 'looking like it does.'

Niall stormed out, slamming the door behind him so hard that the room shook.

Jenna set down her fork. 'Oh dear, I don't think I'm particularly hungry now either.'

Mirren's thin body was still rigid with tension and Jenna's heart went out to her spiky, passionate daughter. 'Mirren,' she said gently, 'please try to eat something.'

The girl's eyes were bright with tears. 'I can't. It would stick, here.' She touched her thin throat. 'He mustn't kill Moss, he mustn't!'

Jenna sighed. 'It's a working dog. It's not a pet. And if it can't work—'

'Moss only can't work because *he*'s useless. When Moss came, he was fine. It's *him* that's the problem. He should be put down, not Moss.'

When was the last time her daughter had called her father Dad or Daddy, or indeed anything but 'he', spoken with contempt? Jenna had been absorbed in her own daily struggle with the brutal demands of restoration work; she hadn't spared time or energy to attend to more than the basic physical needs of her family and she was long past concern about her own relationship with her husband. Now, looking at the sad child in front of her, she experienced terrible guilt.

She'd known, of course, that Mirren was something of a loner at school. Well, that was just Mirren. She'd never made friends easily, but she was a self-sufficient child, keen on wildlife and passionate about her Green causes, to the point where she was a pain in the neck about conservation. Jenna had been reduced to smuggling bottles into the bin after Mirren was in bed to reduce the glass mountain in one of the sheds; who had time to drive into Wigtown regularly to recycle them?

It was only recently that her mother had begun to feel uneasy. She'd heard a programme on the radio which she always had on while she was working. It had caught her attention, because the speaker was someone who lived in Galloway: a woman psychotherapist who wrote for the newspapers and had published a book about problem situations in family life. On this occasion, what she was talking about was the relationship of teenage girls with their fathers and the importance of paternal approval and encouragement to the development of self-confidence.

That was something Mirren notably lacked, which was another problem that could be laid at Niall's door, but on the other hand, her own dismissive attitude to her husband, while perfectly understandable, could only have made things worse. She had taken pleasure in cutting him down to size in front of her.

'Mirren,' Jenna said unhappily, 'I know how upset you are. But Dad's had a bad time. He'd set his heart on doing well in the trials.'

Her daughter's face was still stony. 'You see,' her mother went on, 'Granddad always made Dad feel a failure because he didn't win. And I know you find it hard to accept it, but Moss is only a dog—'

'Only a dog? Only a *dog*?' The tears started to spill over, fat tears, splashing down Mirren's face. 'There's nothing special about humans, you know – all they are is nasty animals.' She stood up. 'But I'm going to stop him. I don't care what I have to do.'

A moment later, Jenna was alone at the table with the plates of uneaten food and her uncomfortable reflections.

The rain had stopped by the time Niall had flung himself out of the house and the first pale stars were beginning to appear between clouds chased along by a stiff breeze. Jolly boating weather, he reflected acidly, as he walked out towards the far end of the marina's pontoons, beyond the lights and out of sight. It was always quiet there and you could be sure of being alone once sailing was over for the day.

Around the bay, behind the lit windows the smart set were having dinner parties, no doubt, and on some of the moorings, warm yellow light glowed from the boats' portholes, showing where some keen sailor was drying out equipment after today's outing, or preparing for tomorrow's. From the Yacht Club he could hear the sound of music, voices and laughter.

He couldn't bring himself to go in. Some of the laughter was probably at his expense and even the consolation of knowing that Findlay Stevenson could be behind bars by now didn't compensate for his own public failure and humiliation.

And anxiety. He'd still hoped, when he went to hang around the bar after the trials, that despite the disaster of Moss's performance, someone would come up and make him an offer on the basis of the dog's previous reputation. But he'd been drinking alone when Stevenson came in and started slagging him off. He'd lashed out with the deadliest weapon in his armoury – killing off the dog – and there had been considerable satisfaction in seeing the pain in the man's face. Niall had even managed to land a punch or two in self-defence before Stevenson was dragged away.

His big problem was Lafferty. Ronnie had scared him last

night, but if he went ahead with the rescue plan that had occurred to him, Davina would be furious and she was a bad person to cross. Then again, did she need to know? She'd said she was only passing through . . .

'Hey, lover!' The voice that spoke at his shoulder made him start, but when he looked round it wasn't the woman he was thinking about who stood there. He hadn't heard her approach, with the wind stirring the boats into clinking movement and the creaking of the pontoons.

Gina Lafferty stood smiling at him out of the darkness, the full mouth inviting as ever, the flirtatious eyes glinting and the plunging neckline of her dull gold silky top an arrow pointing to the dark hollow below. Lust on legs, he had called her once: the ideal woman, someone whose appetites matched his own, and who had an even greater vested interest in discretion.

Niall stood up, glancing nervously over her shoulder. 'Gina! I didn't know you were down this weekend. I thought Ronnie was here this week on his own.'

'He was. But then I thought, hey! Why don't I come down too? Especially when the office phoned the Glasgow house to say they were looking for him – some sort of minor crisis. I got here last night; he left this morning. And tonight – well, I felt like playing with fire and I came along to see if I could find someone to light the flame.'

It had been a bruising day, in every sense of the word. He'd have to be crazy to take a risk like this, but it was balm to his wounded spirit. So Lafferty was richer, more powerful? In one direction at least he was a loser, big time. How could Niall resist?

He took a step closer, smiling at her. 'Oh, I think I could just about manage that.'

Gina put out her hand and touched soft fingers to his sore lip. 'I hear you've been in the wars. I'll have to be gentle with you, won't I?'

'You go back,' he said thickly. 'I'll drift along when the coast's clear.'

'You're awful quiet this evening,' Rab McLeish said. 'You've barely touched your breezer.' He sounded faintly impatient as he looked down at the dark-haired girl sitting alone at the small corner table next to the bar.

They were a curious pair. Rab was big, self-confident and loud and she was a quiet little thing – mousy, in the opinion of some of his friends, though they never said it to his face. They'd been stepping out for nearly two years and Rab was daft about the girl; certainly she was pretty enough, with the soft blue eyes and pale skin that often goes with dark hair in Scotland.

Tonight she seemed even paler than usual and he was immediately concerned. 'You feeling OK?'

'Not – not brilliant.'

'Are you wanting home? I'll need to stand my round first, but—'

'No, no,' she said hastily. 'I'll be fine just sitting here for now. You get away back to the lads.'

Rab hesitated, but didn't argue. He was having a good time; this evening there were a lot of the regulars in the country pub just outside Wigtown and she watched him slap one of his mates on the back with a remark that made the group laugh. He wasn't good-looking, but she liked the way he looked: big-built and heavily muscled, thanks to his obsession with weight-training and keeping fit. Just as well, really, considering you didn't get much exercise driving a lorry. He'd been a barman before but that wasn't a lot healthier, and at least the money was better.

She was reluctant to break up the party. She hadn't seen him relaxed and happy like this since he got the dusty answer about the flat – which she always knew he'd get – from Niall Murdoch.

He'd come back then in a towering rage. Cath wasn't scared of him; she was serenely confident that he would never lay a finger on her, but she did worry that his fixation with Drumbreck would get him in trouble.

Cath could understand, in a way. He'd lived in Drumbreck when it was just a hamlet at the back of beyond, like generations of McLeishes before him. His parents' long-term tenancy of a cottage at the far end of the bay had been terminated when the gentrification of Drumbreck started ten years ago, and being offered a council house in Wigtown they'd moved out without making a fight of it. Rab's mum, at least, had been happy enough to go; she liked having central heating instead of a coal fire with a back boiler, and being able to pop out for a wee daunder round the shops in the town when she felt like it.

Rab, though, had been in his early teens at the time, just the worst age in Cath's opinion. If they'd stayed there longer he'd most likely have got sick fed-up of having nothing to do in the evenings but as it was he'd been left with a kind of storybook idea of the place. He was unbalanced about it.

That was Rab's problem. He wasn't good at balance. He saw things black-and-white and with his temper he didn't always see them straight. And he'd friends that didn't help: to him the Drumbreck thing was sort of like a religion but some of the others saw it as a bit of fun, baiting the toffs with their flashy cars and boats. Cath had heard rumours about vandalism and damage that made her very uneasy.

When he'd heard the flat was coming up on the market, he was elated. 'The rest of the property's a tip. They can't be expecting an incomer will offer for it, with the place looking like that. And I'm making good money – I can give them a fair price.'

Cath's heart sank. She wasn't anything like as sure as he

seemed to be that other people wouldn't see its potential and there were plenty folk in Glasgow with silly money to spend just gagging to get in there. Murdoch wasn't daft.

The worst thing was, Cath had been hoping to persuade him just to get somewhere in Wigtown. It would be handy for her, with her job there in one of the bookshops, and it would be better for him too. You couldn't take a great lorry down that road and park it outside your door when you'd an early start in the morning.

But once Rab had an idea in his head he was stubborn. He'd this picture of them getting married and giving their kids the childhood he'd had. Cath wasn't sure it would work like that; Drumbreck with half the houses shut up except at weekends and no shop or anything would hardly be the same. But she wasn't caring about where it was, just when. She'd had enough of living at home, with her parents worried and angry when she came in late, looking all flushed and rumpled. She just wanted somewhere they could move in together, and sort the rest out later.

And until this week, she had almost been winning the argument. She might look a wee mouse of a thing but she was strong-minded in her quiet way, and mostly Rab would let her have what she wanted if she dug her toes in. When he got caught up in the Drumbreck fantasy again, though, she was powerless. He was talking wildly about making the Murdochs change their minds, and she'd been really scared that he and his friends – the ones Cath didn't like him hanging out with – would do something crazy to the property to put people off.

But what Cath had to tell him tonight would bring him down to earth with a bump. A bump! That was a sick joke. She had made up her mind, and once she'd done that, she could match Rab any time for stubbornness. She was giving him a choice.

He could drop his daft notions about Drumbreck and find somewhere sensible now, or she could get rid of the baby. She hated the thought, but what she wasn't going to do was brazen it out living at home with her parents taking out their feelings of humiliation on her.

It was up to Rab.

5

Mirren slipped quietly out of the house. Her father was out somewhere and she could hear the sound of her mother's electric drill as she made for the big open shed across the yard where Moss was kept chained up. He was lying dozing on some straw in one corner, with a couple of bales providing a bit of shelter from the wind, but the second she approached he sat up, eying her warily.

'It's all right, Moss,' she whispered. 'I'm not even going to try to touch you because I know you're scared. I know you don't trust me – you don't trust anyone now, because of what he's done to you.

'But look—' She reached for the tin bowl lying on the floor and taking a squidgy plastic bag out of her pocket, emptied it in. 'Here's the stew they didn't eat – you'll like that.'

She pushed the bowl towards him and he sniffed the savoury smell; the tip of his feathery tail tapped the ground and he moved cautiously towards it, eying her all the time. He wolfed it down, then retreated to his corner again.

'That's better, isn't it? But oh, Moss! I don't know what's going to happen!' Her eyes prickled as the dog put his head to one side, both ears cocked, listening, as if trying to work out what she was telling him.

'Anyway,' she went on fiercely, sniffing and wiping her nose on the back of her hand, 'I'll see it's nothing bad, whatever I have to do.'

It was almost completely dark when she went outside. The bay looked pretty and cosy with all the houses lit up and the lights from the Yacht Club and the marina, with the night watchman standing on the dock talking to someone. Inside the house, the noise of the drill had stopped and she could hear the television. Her mum was probably watching *Who Wants to Be a Millionaire?*; Mirren liked that, and she was feeling quite hungry now too. She could get a packet of crisps and join Mum in the cosy sitting-room.

But she had work to do. She let herself into the darkened house and, shivering a little, bypassed the sitting-room and went down a corridor beyond. Here there had been little restoration and the walls were rough brick, with wires looping down from the ceiling. She hated these parts of the building. They always made her feel creepy, but this was where her mother had a sort of office, with a computer.

She never told anyone when she went on the internet like this, choosing a time when no one would be using the phone and dialling up, straining to hear any movement that would warn her someone was coming. Not that Mirren wasn't allowed to use the computer; her mother positively encouraged her to use it for schoolwork, but she wouldn't approve of what Mirren accessed on these quiet evenings.

As the familiar Google window appeared, she typed in the chatroom address.

'I'll need to speak to the Fiscal first,' Marjory Fleming was saying as she and Tam walked up the steps of the Kirkluce Police Headquarters. 'He's been notified, but I have to check if he wants to go up to the site. I'd be surprised if he does – he's usually happy enough to leave it to us and he hasn't exactly got the figure for hillwalking.'

'You could say,' MacNee agreed. 'He'd be asking for a hoist.' The Procurator Fiscal, a portly gentleman, was coming up for retirement, and his idea of being in charge of a murder inquiry – as indeed, legally, he was – consisted of delegation of the 'Carry on, chaps' variety, which suited them just fine.

'Then I'll need to—' Fleming broke off as she pushed open the door and went into the entrance hall. Her heart sank. There, in the reception area, was Susie Stevenson and with her a small child – her son presumably. Fleming knew there was a seven-year-old called Josh; she'd spent the morning cleaning the cottage and hanging Cammie's discarded Superman curtains in the second bedroom. But this was hardly the place for a child! The Stevensons had been staying with Susie's parents – surely one of them would have been prepared to babysit?

Fleming turned to Tam. 'I'll have to speak to her. You go on and set the wheels in motion.'

She walked towards them but before she could get there they stood up and she saw Susie murmur something to the boy and urge him forward.

Josh was a particularly angelic-looking child, with his mother's curly fair hair and his father's dark eyes. He was white with tiredness and strain and his eyes widened with alarm as he looked up at Fleming's tall figure. He glanced nervously back at his mother, who nodded encouragement.

He bit his lip. 'Please – please will you let me have my daddy back home?'

It was obvious that he had been coached to say this. Fleming felt cold with dismay. She looked across the boy's head at his mother.

'Susie, what is this?'

Susie came to stand beside Josh and put her arm round his shoulders. She was a bit above medium height, fair-haired and sharp-featured with a discontented mouth; tonight her eyes were swollen and she was very pale.

'I knew you wouldn't listen to me if I asked you to use your influence. But I thought you might take pity on a little boy who only wants his daddy.'

Josh's chin began to wobble. Without replying to Susie, Fleming bent down to his level, signalling at the same time to the duty officer behind the desk. Mercifully it was PC Bruce tonight, the mother of young children herself.

'Don't worry, Josh,' Fleming said as reassuringly as she could. 'I'm just going to have a little talk with your mum and see what's been happening, and this lady here's going to find you some juice and a biscuit.'

'No problem,' Bruce said cheerfully. 'Come on, pet – we'll away over to the desk and you can help me phone the canteen. What kind of juice do you like?' She held out her hand and Josh, with another anxious glance at his mother, allowed himself to be led away to the other side of the hall.

Fleming turned to Susie. 'Let's sit down, shall we?' Her voice was taut with anger. 'I don't think it was very kind to put Josh through that, do you? I know nothing about this, beyond the fact that I happened to see Findlay being taken into custody as I left the trials. What was it – a fight?'

Susie nodded sullenly.

'Then it will be nothing to do with me. Someone else will be dealing with it and will make any decisions necessary. It won't even cross my desk.'

'But you're the boss, you could order them—'

'No, I couldn't.' It really cost her to sound calm and reasonable. 'That's what is known as perverting the course of justice and it's a criminal offence.'

Susie looked at her with loathing. 'Oh, you're enjoying this, aren't you? Getting your own back . . . But I would have thought even you would want to spare poor little Josh!'

She wailed the last words and Josh came running back to

put his arms round her and looked up at Fleming accusingly. PC Bruce came hurrying across.

'Do you want me to take over, ma'am? I know you've a lot to deal with—'

Fleming managed to smile. 'Thanks. In a minute.' She turned back to the Stevensons. 'The only thing I can do is find out what Findlay's situation is at present. Who was dealing with it, constable?'

Armed with the information, she made a call from the desk, listened with some relief to what she was told, then came back to speak to the child.

'Well, Josh, I'm happy to tell you Daddy's fine and he'll be back in a minute.' Josh's woebegone face brightened, and Susie managed to find a smile.

'You see, Josh? I told you – and now say thank you to Mrs Fleming. And I suppose I have to say thank you, too, for arranging that.' Her expression was more indicative of satisfaction than gratitude.

'No, Susie, I didn't arrange anything,' Fleming said, calling on her dwindling reserves of superhuman patience. 'It just so happened that when I phoned he'd been charged and was about to be released on an undertaking to appear in court.'

'Charged?' Susie's face changed. 'You mean – but it wasn't his fault! That awful man pushed him beyond the limits! Surely you could have—'

Fleming had had enough. More than enough. 'No, I couldn't,' she said flatly. 'And now, if you'll excuse me, I have a murder to investigate.'

She walked away briskly. She'd wasted too much time on this already and if Susie wanted to make things difficult for herself, it was her privilege. By the time Fleming reached the major incident room, the problems of the Stevenson family were far from her mind.

★   ★   ★

Adrian McConnell stood at the back of the narrow hall of their cottage, a small, slight man whose most distinctive feature was his dark-rimmed glasses. He was wearing a fixed smile and his physical detachment emphasized his distaste for the spectacle of his wife, strapless sequined top only just decent, draped round their male guest's neck and fluttering her heavily mascaraed eyelashes at him as she said goodnight at the front door. She was oblivious both to the killer looks she was getting from the man's wife and to the fact that her mascara had run into streaks all round her eyes.

Kim making a fool of herself was nothing new. 'Give her a drink and she's anyone's,' he would say mockingly, without really believing it. He always comforted himself with the thought that if she was doing it in front of him, she wasn't doing it behind his back.

Adrian needed to believe that. He couldn't bear humiliation, his sensitivity a legacy from schooldays when he'd been a weedy little four-eyes, useless at football and with an unhealthy interest in studying, the butt of every oaf in the class. He'd had the last laugh, of course: who was on the dole with a drug habit, and who was a partner in a big accountancy firm, rich and successful, with two houses, a Mercedes and a Discovery for the wife and kids? And soon, if nothing went wrong, perhaps even a seat in Parliament. He'd paid his dues to the Labour Party – enough to buy a grin and a handshake from Tony Blair himself – and only a selection panel of people he'd been cultivating for years stood between him and a safe seat.

Kim released her victim at last, waved her guests down the steps leading to the road, then came back in a little unsteadily and shut the door.

'God, I'm exhausted!' She slumped against the wall. 'I don't think I can face the clearing-up.'

'You're not exhausted, you're drunk,' Adrian said coldly.

'And if you don't do it tonight, it will still be there in the morning, and I should think with the hangover you're going to have, you'll feel even less like it then.'

'So?' she pouted. 'Come to bed, pet. Jusht – just leave it. Kimmie wants a cuddle.' She undulated towards him.

He wasn't in the mood. All he could feel at this moment was revulsion and his response was cruel. There was a big brass porthole mirror on the wall, in keeping with the nautical decor Kim had chosen, and he took her bare shoulders and swung her round to face it. 'Look at yourself. How do you imagine anyone could fancy that?'

Kim screwed up her eyes, blinking blearily at her reflection, then, as it came into focus, screamed in dismay.

'Jeez! I look hellish! Why – why couldn't you have t-told me?' she hiccuped, starting to cry. 'You're such a sod! That bitch will be laughing at me all the way home.' Her maudlin tears were making pale tracks in her bronzing make-up and puddling the streaks of mascara as she tried ineffectually to wipe them away.

He really couldn't take one of Kim's dramas. 'Just go to bed,' Adrian said wearily. 'Sleep it off. I'll put what I can in the dishwasher.'

Still sobbing, though he would bet that she no longer knew why, she started to climb the steep wooden staircase, hauling herself up on the white rope looped through brass fixings on the wall. He could hear music playing in the children's rooms and could only hope it would cover up the noise of their mother's drunken distress.

Returning to the kitchen/dining-room they had created out of two rooms, a lobby and a coal-shed at the back of the house, Adrian looked at the dirty plates, glasses and empty bottles with disfavour. This would be only the first of many evenings spent at this table, and at other similar ones all round the bay: the same faces, the same conversations about sailing, house prices, schools and their neighbours, the same performance from Kim, getting smashed and flirting inappropriately.

Drumbreck brought out the worst in Kim. It was, he had once said to her bitterly, the Torremolinos syndrome: what you did away from home didn't count. She was a total airhead – not exactly the perfect political wife, but in Glasgow she was mercifully constrained by the demands of their more sedate lifestyle. He had no illusions, but he liked the sex – usually – and he still got a kick out of her effect on people who had expected, from his own quiet and unglamorous appearance, that he would have a correspondingly mousy wife. The Labour councillors always looked at him with new eyes after meeting Kim, and whatever you said about her, she was good at chatting them up.

But Drumbreck! This was only the start of the summer season and he was sickened by it already: the incestuous atmosphere, the virulent gossip, the scandals, the not-so-secret affairs. They'd come originally when it wasn't so expensive and they couldn't afford anything more exotic, but he'd wanted to get away from the place for years now, putting it all behind him. He dreamed of a villa in Tuscany, elegant, peaceful, with an open loggia and a view of some little hill town, framed by the spears of cypress trees piercing a hard golden sky . . .

But Kim wouldn't hear of it, of course. Who wanted to spend holidays cooped up with just your family, when all your summer friends would be here? And now Kelly had her own little gang – and what went on there he just didn't want to think about – and she was equally addicted to the Drumbreck experience. Jason at ten was besotted with his very own Mirror dinghy and Gary – well, Gary didn't really count. Gary would whinge wherever he was.

Perhaps, if things had been different four years ago . . . but he mustn't think of all that now. It was too late now. Much too late.

Marjory Fleming's mind was buzzing with plans and arrangements for the next day as she drove the five miles home to Mains of Craigie. It was only as she turned in at the farm gate that she remembered the Stevensons, and cringed. Tonight she was going back to, most probably, a quiet, darkened house – it was after eleven and Bill, with his early start, would be in bed – and she could stand outside for a moment when she got out of the jeep, refreshing her spirit by looking at the stars and the shadowy outlines of the soft hills, breathing the cool fresh air in a silence broken only by the occasional bleat of a sheep or the stealthy rustles of the creatures of the night, going about their secret business. Next week, if she did that, the thought that eyes filled with hatred might be watching her unseen from the cottage two hundred yards away, would taint the atmosphere like a foul smell.

To her surprise, the lights were still on in the sitting-room, which ran from front to back of the old farmhouse on the right-hand side of the front door – never used – and when she parked at the back and came in through the mud-room, she found Bill dozing in his chair in front of a dying fire. He started awake as Meg jumped up from the hearthrug to greet her mistress.

'Goodness, love, you should be in bed!' Marjory scolded him, but her mood lifted as she came into the warm, lamp-lit room.

Bill got up to kiss her, then went over to the tray where a bottle of Bladnoch stood waiting beside two heavy crystal tumblers. 'I thought you might need this,' he said. 'Findlay's been on the phone.'

Marjory sank gratefully into the embrace of her arm-chair, which was sagging and under permanent review for replacement, but somehow always got a reprieve. She rolled her eyes. 'Oh God, Susie! You wouldn't believe that woman!'

'Fin told me what she'd done.' Bill came back with their drinks, then threw another log on the fire and sat down. 'He was terribly embarrassed. I think they'd had a row about her dragging Josh into it. He certainly sent his apologies.'

'His, but not hers, I take it.' Marjory sipped her malt and sighed. 'She seems to think we can drop charges on a whim to do a favour for a friend. The only reason I didn't was because I am a spiteful and malevolent monster.'

'I know, I know. The woman's a nightmare.' Bill was visibly crestfallen. 'And I've wished her on to you – I feel really bad about that. I just thought it was being under so much stress at the time and she'd get over it, but I got it wrong, didn't I? I suppose we could say that in the circumstances moving into the cottage wouldn't be appropriate—'

'And have her tell everyone who'll stop to listen that I had them thrown out on to the street?'

Bill grimaced and she went on, 'No, I'm just going to have to ignore it. I ought to be used to unpopularity by now and I minded it a hell of a lot more when it was people I liked who wanted nothing to do with me. Susie's a nasty piece of work and I don't like her any more than she likes me. And to tell you the truth, I haven't given the woman a thought all evening.'

It was the truth, even if it wasn't exactly the whole truth, about her feelings. But she wasn't under oath, and Bill looking less miserably guilty was some reward. He was a good man who'd tried to do the right thing and it wasn't fair to make him suffer for it. Anyway, Marjory prided herself on her tough-mindedness and her pragmatism, so what option did she have?

She filled him in on the new case as they finished their whisky. 'It probably won't be very much to do with us. She was killed elsewhere – Manchester, probably, where she lived – and the killer drove her up here and dumped her body in the most isolated place he could think of. If they manage to finger him, we'll probably find he has some previous connection with the area – came on holiday with his bucket and spade when he was wee, or something, but until then it'll be mainly forensic stuff around the site and putting out an appeal to see if anyone spotted a car in the area.

'The partner would usually be prime suspect, but I'll be gobsmacked if the man I spoke to on the phone had anything to do with it. You see—'

Bill tried, unsuccessfully, to stifle a huge yawn, and Marjory got up, saying remorsefully, 'Oh – sorry. Come on, you need your sleep and so do I.'

Meg trotted to the door and Marjory collected the glasses as Bill put off the lights. He paused in the doorway.

'Just one thing – tell me you won't have time to cook tomorrow. I like to go to sleep with something to look forward to.'

The trees were singing tonight in a rising wind. The man in the loft bedroom lay awake, eyes wide upon the darkness, barely seeing the shadows of the agitated branches whose wild movements so closely mirrored the turbulence of his own thoughts.

When he did shut his eyes he kept seeing her, lying in the base of the tree roots – strangely, since he had taken particular care not to look as he left her there. Had she been sheltered from today's downpour, or was her battered face wet with rain, like tears?

As if it mattered. Already the stealthy work of dissolution had started. At this very moment it was separating flesh from bone . . .

A qualm of nausea swept over him and he fought against it until it subsided. He'd got up earlier to be sick but could only retch painfully: he had eaten almost nothing since yesterday morning.

Fear. Questions. Memories. Questions. Fear. Memories. The thoughts chased one another round and round, the sequence changing but always coming back to memories and, like a stuck gramophone needle, repeating them over and over and over again.

6

'DI Fleming? The Wintour case – you're Senior Investigating Officer, right?' It was a man's voice, pleasant-spoken, very assured – or perhaps that was just the English accent? Receiving confirmation, he went on, 'DCI Chris Carter, Manchester CID. I'm SIO here and I was hoping you could brief me on the situation at your end.'

Fleming had been expecting his call. 'Of course. What do you have already?'

'Body found dumped in woodland, right? And a mobile phone on the body established the link with Wintour. We can confirm she's been missing since Thursday and that the description your people sent down ties in with her appearance. We contacted the boyfriend last night – distraught, apparently, for what that's worth. They're always distraught, in my experience—'

'Extensive, I'm sure,' Fleming cut in, feeling she was being bounced into endorsing an unwarranted assumption. 'But as it happened, I was the person who spoke to Brewer last night on the phone. Obviously I didn't disclose how it came to be in our hands, and his reaction seemed innocent enough to me. He said he'd been phoning her regularly to try to find out where she was – there'll be records of that, of course – but his attitude suggested that he was unaware anything had happened to her.'

'Well, it would, wouldn't it?'

It was a dismissive response and she reacted sharply. 'My distinct impression was that when he thought initially that he was talking to her, he was both anxious about her and annoyed. And at that stage there was certainly no reason for him to suspect it was a police officer at the other end.'

Carter was still unimpressed. 'Might have worked out what was likely to happen, if he left a body lying around. Anyway, we've brought him in for questioning and of course we've swung into the usual routine – establishing her contacts, asking questions, listening to what people have to say . . .'

Only people at that end, evidently. She listened politely as he gave her a lecture on How to Conduct a Murder Inquiry, by One Who Knows. Eventually, taking advantage of a breathing pause, she jumped in: 'Does Brewer have any connection with Galloway?'

He clearly wasn't used to having anyone ignore the lead he had chosen to give. There was a brief, disapproving silence. 'Not as far as I know.'

'Have you asked him? The site where the body was found wasn't exactly at the side of the road, you know.'

'At the moment we're more concerned to establish his relationship with Wintour.' Carter's tone was cool. 'You'll have your opportunity to ask when we bring him up to identify the body—'

'You'll need to have two people to do that.'

He was startled. 'Two? What on earth for?'

'Scots law always demands corroboration. It means we have very few miscarriages of justice because of a false confession.' She didn't add, 'The way you have,' but she thought he was smart enough to get the subtext.

She heard him sigh. 'Oh, I dare say. But all we're talking about here is identification, for goodness' sake – what possible point is there in driving someone hundreds of miles, just for the sake of saying, "I know her as well"?'

Fleming made sure he heard her sigh too. 'OK, for the sake of argument, suppose some guy's murdered his wife. An unknown woman's body turns up, drowned or in an accident, say. He sobs, swears it's her and he's off the hook. Sorrowing widower, big funeral, sympathy, insurance, the whole jing-bang. No one goes out looking for a shallow grave.'

'Far-fetched, I'm sure you would agree. It doesn't happen, in my experience.'

'Are you sure?' It slipped out; she shouldn't have said it and she could almost hear his lips tightening. She went on hastily, 'It was only an example. Anyway, the SOCOs are up at the scene today. I'll forward their report to you whenever it reaches me and then perhaps we can liaise over bringing Brewer up here.'

'I was thinking that we might send up some of our own forensic people. They're experts, of course, with a lot of experience, and it might help your people out.'

Fleming bristled. She didn't have to read between the lines: this was being spelled out in screamers just under the mast-head.

'That would be a matter for the Procurator Fiscal's Office, which directs all murder cases in Scotland, but I think you'll find we can manage,' she said, ice forming on the words.

That got through. As if he had flicked a switch, when he spoke again his voice was charmingly apologetic. 'Oh look, I'm sorry about the way that came out. Did it sound patronizing? I didn't mean it to.'

'I'm so glad. I'd hate to think it was deliberate. Such an unhelpful attitude, I always find.'

'Well – er, sorry, as I said.'

She'd managed to put him off balance. Good! 'Don't worry about it. Keep me in the picture about Brewer, and we'll fix up whatever you need.'

'Fine. Thanks. We'll be in touch.'

He didn't seem keen to prolong the conversation. With a

certain grim satisfaction Fleming returned to her work, planning briefing notes and details for the following day.

It felt all wrong, though, like being in a phoney war. There was a woman lying dead, a woman who had been brutally assaulted first, and there was almost nothing to be done about it, at least as yet. Fleming had two duty officers out taking Gavin Scott's statement; another couple were knocking on the doors of the handful of houses along the Queen's Way road in the forlorn hope that someone might have happened to notice a car parked in the area, but there was no reason to bring in off-duty officers today and run up the bill for overtime. Any fingertip search that was needed could happen once the SOCOs were clear of the area.

She'd already commissioned roadside signs to appeal for information, which would be erected tomorrow at either end of the relevant stretch of road – in her opinion the best chance of getting eye-witness evidence of a parked car – and once these reports came in they might have something more to go on. She doubted if the autopsy which she would reluctantly have to attend, tomorrow probably, would tell them anything they didn't know.

The only thing that niggled away at her was the question of the killer's links with the area. You live in Manchester, you're looking for an out-of-the-way spot to leave a body and Scotland seems to fit the bill. Unless you've been there already, are you likely to think of Galloway, so many miles off the main road north, instead of the better-publicized wilderness of the Highlands? Galloway's unspoiled beauty of quiet hills and wild, empty moorlands – and huge forests – was one of the best-kept secrets of scenic Scotland. There had to be a connection of some sort.

Fleming was glad that the demands of identification would mean they'd get a chance to question the boyfriend directly. Even if Brewer had nothing to do with it – and it would take quite a lot to convince her that he had – he might be able to shed some light on that. And the second ID witness could be useful too, if it was a close friend, as it was likely to be.

It would be good to have the answer to that and get it out of the way, then hand over the whole package to the overbearing DCI Carter to do with as he chose. She couldn't think that the sum of human happiness would be increased by any prolonged co-operation between the two of them.

'Phew!' DCI Chris Carter set the phone down reverently, running his hands through his thick, iron-grey crop. 'And wipe that grin off your face, Tucker!'

DS 'Tommy' Tucker, who had come in just as Carter began his phone call and parked himself on the edge of the desk, failed to comply with the order from his superior officer. 'Got a right one there, haven't you?'

'God, I can just see her! One of these terrifying females who've been submerged in the job so long they've got barnacles on their bottoms, and they're ready to savage anyone who sets a toe on their territory. And typical Scots – chip on her shoulder the size of a hod of bricks. Kept trying to push her angle and got all frosty when I dared to suggest she might welcome some help from our boys.' He stretched out in his chair, his hands behind his head in a characteristic pose: at six foot three he always felt cramped in the standard office chairs.

Tucker gave him a sardonic look. He wasn't bad as guvnors went, but they'd missed out the listening-skills section of his primary education. 'You're losing your touch,' he said. 'Spreading on the charm like tarmac after you've bulldozed them flat used to work.'

'Cheeky sod,' Carter said without rancour. 'And anyway, what's a Procurator Fiscal?'

'I don't know. What *is* a Procurator Fiscal? Is there a punchline?'

'That may become apparent later. He seems to be someone who's in charge of ops up in Scotland. We may yet be grateful for our Chief Constable.' He paused. 'Well, perhaps not.'

'What's the score? Someone got to go up there? I'll volunteer – I fancy a short break in rural Scotland.'

'You may just have to. Anyway, did you come in for anything, apart from a good laugh?'

'Just to give you a sit-rep. The bar Brewer manages is called Cosmo – one of those minimalist, poncey places that can't serve a decent pint. Wintour's been employed there as a barmaid for a year – a bit over, maybe, and they've been shacked up together most of that time. Brewer doesn't seem to know if she's got family, parents, that sort of thing, but he's been quite happy to agree to searches of the flat and his car. Says he's nothing to hide.'

'Maybe he doesn't. Maybe we need to be looking for one of the regulars in the bar. That woman – Fleming – was adamant his reaction was genuine.'

'Maybe she's right. But one of the team who interviewed him said to me he reckons there's something there, at least. Brewer's brief was very protective and Brewer himself was definitely edgy.'

Carter made a face. 'Could be something unrelated. Black market booze, trousering the profits . . . it'll emerge.' He got up. 'Keep me posted, Tommy. I'm due in a briefing about that non-fatal shooting yesterday.'

'I didn't think you'd be free today, after what you said on the phone last night about the body in the forest.'

Laura Harvey, her cheeks pink with the wind and a blue woolly hat pulled well down over her ears, was on board Jon Kingsley's *Blackbird*, a smallish boat with a blue-painted hull and white sails and superstructure. An Achilles 24, he told her, although, knowing nothing about sailing, this meant little to her.

'It's kind of weird,' he agreed. 'You'd expect we'd all be swinging into a major operation, but in fact the boss seems to be reckoning it's not a lot more than a macabre sort of fly-tipping. Even so, we'd better not stay out too long in case there's a summons. It takes a bit of time to put my baby to bed.'

'Fine.' Laura wasn't about to argue. The weather had definitely broken and today, though it wasn't raining, the sky was heavy, and in the stiff breeze vicious little waves were slapping against the hull, making the boat buck as they clipped along, and she wasn't entirely sure that the croissant she had had for breakfast was happy in its new home.

They were a good way out in the bay now, tacking across it while keeping clear of the line of yachts pursuing one another in a race out into Wigtown Bay and then, so Jon said, round a fixed light buoy and back. More to take her mind off her stomach than anything else, Laura asked how long he'd had his boat. 'And why *Blackbird*? Did you choose the name?'

Jon laughed, his face glowing. He seemed almost high on the exhilaration of the speed and the wind in his face. 'Black bastards – that's what the Scottish criminal classes call us, from the colour of the uniform and – well, I leave the rest of the explanation to your imagination.' He broke off to make some fine adjustment to the sails and looked at his passenger. 'You all right? Not too cold or anything?'

Laura shook her head and he went on, 'So I changed her name to *Blackbird* because she was – is – the only woman in my life. At present.' He gave her a glancing smile. 'Anyway, I came down to Galloway sailing a few times with friends from the Uni in Edinburgh, sometimes on the west coast in Portpatrick and sometimes here. I got hooked, and was lucky enough to hear about someone selling her cheap for a quick sale and managed to snap her up. When I was in Edinburgh, I sailed out of South Queensferry, but the east coast sailing isn't as good.'

'Was that what tempted you away from the big city?'

He considered that. 'Partly, I suppose. And it was a chance to do something different, make my mark perhaps in a smaller place. It's not for ever, of course. I'm working for my sergeant's exams and I can see me heading back to Edinburgh, if I make rank.'

Ambitious, Laura thought, but that wasn't a crime. Being a young man in a hurry didn't endear you to everyone, though; she could see Tam and even Marjory being unsympathetic to someone with an eye possibly more to his prospects than the job in hand. Still, much as she loved Galloway herself, you could hardly blame someone for wanting a faster-paced life.

Jon was doing something clever that made them come about and now they were sailing towards the marina and the Yacht Club. Laura didn't dare to hope it meant they were heading in.

'Are you a member there?' She pointed.

'In my dreams! Not since it was a shack, before the country club makeover. Now the committee's all second-homers and they've raised the subscription to make sure they're the only people who can afford to belong. And even if I could find the money, as a humble copper I'd probably be blackballed.'

'They sound a charming lot.'

'The locals were upset about it too. It made Drumbreck even more fashionable, which of course had its effect on house prices, and it's ripped its heart out. Most of the houses are shut up half the year and the little general store they had was forced to close – no business during the winter, and even when they come for weekends they bring in their supplies from Tesco.'

It was sad, but a far from unusual scenario in the more picturesque areas of the countryside. 'You do lose any sort of community then, don't you? And all there seems to be here is a sort of glossy magazine fantasy.'

'And a pretty unhealthy one at that,' Jon agreed. 'Sodom-on-Sea, they call it. I tell you, I thought I had some free-wheeling friends but the morals in this place would make an alley cat blush.

'Oh, hold tight – here's one of the motor yachts. We're going to catch its wake.'

Laura, interested in the conversation, had almost managed to take her mind off her stomach, but as the smaller boat bobbed up and down she had to swallow hard.

Seeing her face, Jon grinned, though not unkindly. 'Having problems? It's a bit blowy today, I suppose. I'll take you out next time when it's a flat calm and you'll get used to it, but we can head in now, if you like.'

'I'm not going to argue with the last part of that, anyway.' Laura took comfort from the rapidly approaching shore. It would be a pity if what looked like a promising relationship foundered on his obsession with 'the only woman in his life'.

All hell had broken loose when Marjory Fleming came into the police headquarters on Monday morning. She stopped in amazement at the sight of the crowded entrance hall and the officers going to and fro, clearly under some kind of pressure.

Sergeant Jock Naismith was on the desk this morning and she caught his eye. He was dealing with a voluble lady with the high colour of indignation in her cheeks who was laying forth about some perceived deficiency in police operations. With some relief he excused himself and came across to Fleming.

'If looks could kill, you'd be skewered like a kebab,' she told him as the lady, even more indignant now, directed a dagger look at his broad back.

He grinned. 'Like enough. It's a wee bit lively in here today.'

'What on earth's going on?'

'What isn't, more like. Three break-ins in neighbouring council houses in Clapperfield Road. Third one, the wifie

disturbed them and ended up being taken in to the hospital
with a suspected heart attack. That's her sister there, giving me
my head in my hands and my lugs to play with.

'Then there was a robbery at a petrol station on the A75 –
not sure yet if the gun was real or replica, but the boy at the till
didn't like to argue the toss. Oh, the lads had quite a night of it,
seemingly.'

'Nothing to the day they're going to have,' Fleming pre-
dicted gloomily. 'Where were our regulars all last week, when
we'd have welcomed a wee diversion? No, don't tell me –
having a holiday and topping up their tans, and now it's back
to business as usual with a backlog to make up.'

'The Super's in. He said he'd be wanting a word.'

'You don't say!' Leaving Naismith to return to the desk and
take his punishment like a man, Fleming took the stairs to her
office two at a time.

'It's all simply a question of priorities.' Superintendent Donald
Bailey was leaning back in his chair, his hands together as if
forming a tent over his spreading stomach. 'Think triage,
Marjory, triage!'

This was a word Bailey had recently discovered – probably
from one of the TV medical programmes he liked to watch –
and as always when he had a word that was a novelty, he liked
to play with it as a child plays with a new toy.

'Of course.' Agreement always kept him happy, and what
did it cost her to pretend that arranging tasks in order of
urgency wasn't something you automatically did every day of
your working life? 'We have three major cases. Break-ins only
come up near the top if the heart attack is serious. Gun crime –
replica or otherwise – has to be high on the list. And then of
course we have the woman's murder.'

Bailey was inclined to dismiss that. 'As you said, it's nothing
to do with us, really.'

'That's not quite what I said,' Fleming protested, but he paid no attention.

'Sooner it's handed over to Manchester, the better. Have the SOCOs finished up in the forest? We don't exactly have unlimited numbers and we need people at the other sites this morning.'

Fleming glanced at the notes she had brought with her. 'They seem to think they've done the bulk of it. There'll be a couple of them finishing up today, and we'll need to detail uniforms to do a fingertip search after that.'

'I suppose that's necessary? Oh well, once we get it out of the way, we can give proper precedence to the local issues. The gun has to be at the top of the list – unless, God forbid, the poor woman dies.'

Fleming conceded that, but when he went on to assume she would be taking charge, demurred. 'I'm SIO on the murder, Don. There's a couple of loose ends I have to tie up on that first, but with any luck it may clear my desk today.

'They've just notified us that there's a detective sergeant and a PC driving up from Manchester at the moment, escorting Jeff Brewer, the boyfriend, and a woman who worked in the bar with Wintour to do the ID. I'll have to go to the autopsy and then I'll need some answers from them before I hand over to the Manchester police. Tam MacNee can meet them and deal with the formalities.

'I'll get out myself to the other scenes this morning with Greg Allan and he can take it from there.'

Bailey looked restive. 'Marjory, I'm not sure I'm happy with that. Allan may be MacNee's equivalent in rank but we both know he isn't exactly dynamic. I want some highly visible progress on the local cases. After all, a press statement about the woman's body went out yesterday and all it got in the Press this morning was a paragraph on an inner page. An armed robbery and three break-ins, with possibly the gravest of outcomes – the *Herald* could have a field day with that, never mind about the *Scottish Sun*. If you won't take charge yourself, I'd prefer MacNee to handle it.'

Fleming was stubborn. 'I want the Manchester officers to get the best possible impression of our effectiveness at this end. As you said yourself, Allan's not dynamic.'

'Mmm. I take your point. Well, what about young Kingsley, then? He might put a bit of pep in it. He wants to go for sergeant, after all, and this would give him a chance to show his mettle.'

'I could send him along with Allan,' Fleming offered. 'And Tansy Kerr can handle the heart attack situation – she's got a good touch with people.'

Appeased, Bailey said, 'That's better. And of course you and Tam will be free to take it on tomorrow once this Manchester business is sorted out.'

She got up. 'If Kingsley hasn't solved it first. He's got his reputation to think of, after all.'

Her tone was dry, and Bailey tutted. 'He has his faults. But we mustn't hold back the ambitious young. It's one of the failings of middle age which I flatter myself I haven't succumbed to, but you must fight it, Marjory, fight it!'

'Tooth and nail, Donald.' Fleming left, muttering under her breath.

She hit her office like a whirlwind, sending e-mails and making calls. The briefing on the Wintour case would have to be postponed, but that was no bad thing; the picture should be quite a bit clearer by the end of the day. She rescheduled it for nine the following morning, then summoned Tam MacNee.

'The most important thing is keeping our end up,' she told him. 'Everything has got to run like clockwork so those snotty buggers don't look down their noses at us poor teuchters.'

MacNee smirked. 'Someone got your dander up? Where's

your "sweetness and light to our southern brethren" campaign now?'

'If I tell you that DCI Carter almost had me quoting Burns myself, you'll get some idea of the provocation. Maybe his subordinates won't be so bad, and anyway, all being well we should be able to get shot of it in twenty-four hours.

'They're on their way now with Brewer and a barmaid called Mandy Preston – should be here – what? Late morning? Fix up an immediate appointment with the mortuary – the autopsy's early this afternoon and we want the ID done before that.

'And remember, Tam, cool and dignified. Hang on, I'm not sure you do dignified. I'll settle for civil. Just don't let the side down with DS Arnold Tucker.'

'*Arnold?* What kind of a man would have a posh name like that?'

'Probably a very superior being. And if you start quoting "*A man's a man, for a' that,*" it's a disciplinary matter.'

7

The dining-room in the Mackenzie household was a silent place this morning. Jennifer Mackenzie, Susie Stevenson's mother, was trying so hard not to give vent to her fury that the atmosphere was as thick as the porridge her grandson Josh was unenthusiastically pushing round his bowl. His father, the graze on his cheek now surrounded by a large and livid bruise, had been stirring and stirring at his tea as if totally unaware of what he was doing.

At last his mother-in-law snapped. 'For heaven's sake, Findlay, you'll wear a hole in the bottom of that cup.'

Findlay, who had been avoiding her eyes since he came in, coloured, looked up briefly, muttered, 'Sorry,' and set down his spoon.

Jennifer's lips tightened and she fussed with the collar of her Alexon blouse. They had been sorely tried, she and Derek, these last few weeks, having their pleasantly ordered lives turned upside down with three extra people living in an executive villa designed for a retired couple with only occasional visitors. She really thought that if it weren't for the en suite she would have gone mad, and Derek was seriously restive about his BMW being parked in the drive, now that the garage had become some sort of squalid kennels for Findlay's wretched dogs.

They'd been perfectly happy when Susie married him, but at the time he'd been a respectable farmer, well able to support her in proper style. Since then, he'd reduced their daughter first to being a shop girl, and now, as if *that* wasn't bad enough, a common labourer's wife. And Jennifer, with her high blood pressure, just didn't dare to let herself think about this latest humiliation he had brought on the family.

Susie, at the other end of the table, was drooping and red-eyed, making a production of her misery.

'Have some toast, Susie. You're not eating anything.' Jennifer spoke bracingly; her supply of sympathy was running low. Findlay was Susie's husband, after all, and she should never have permitted him to get himself into this sort of mess. If Derek had shown signs of stepping out of line – which, to be fair, in thirty blameless years of banking he never had – Jennifer would have brought him up so short he'd have pitched on to his nose.

'How can I?' Susie said tragically. 'With all this – and the move today—'

'If it's still on.' Findlay spoke without raising his eyes.

Jennifer stiffened. 'Still on? Why not?' She couldn't bear to think what Derek would say if she had to tell him that the garage wouldn't be ready for thorough cleaning to-night.

'Ask your daughter.'

The ready tears came to Susie's eyes. 'My fault now, is it? If you hadn't—'

Her mother rose majestically. 'Come, Josh,' she said to the child who had been a silent witness, looking from one parent to the other in anxious dismay. 'Mummy and Daddy have something they need to discuss together. *Quietly.*' It was an instruction. 'It's time you went up to tidy your room anyway.'

Obediently Josh went out with his grandmother, who shut the door behind them in a marked manner.

Susie, aggrieved, wasted no time in springing to her own defence. 'I was only doing it for you, Fin. And they released you, so it worked – you can't say it didn't.'

'I can, actually.' Findlay had the temper that went with his colouring; he was having to struggle to keep it under control. 'I had been told I was free to go before the phone call from Marjory came through. And I can't believe what you inflicted on poor Josh.'

'Then you should have thought of that before you got into a fight.' Her expression was mulish.

'I know, I know,' Findlay said impatiently. 'But I told you what that bastard's threatening to do to Moss—'

'Moss is a dog, remember?'

'A dog who's brought us in the money that we needed, just to scrape along. If I hadn't built a reputation on his cleverness, I wouldn't be getting the prices for the trained pups that I am now. Don't you think I owe him something – life, at the very least?'

Susie pouted. 'Oh, in an ideal world . . .'

'This is far from an ideal world.' Findlay's voice rose. 'In an ideal world, I wouldn't have lost the farm. In an ideal world, I wouldn't have been forced to sell the best collie I'll ever have. In an ideal world, I wouldn't have a wife who was dumb enough to antagonize the very people who are offering us a job and a home that would get us out of this awful situation.'

'My parents' house isn't good enough for you? And I'm not good enough either? Is that what you're saying?'

For a moment they glared at each other, then Findlay dropped his head into his hands with a groan. When he looked up, he said tiredly, 'They don't want us here, Susie – you know that as well as I do. We need a fresh start, need to get back to being a proper family again. It was fine before all this, wasn't it?'

She hesitated, then sighed. 'Oh yes, it was fine before. And of course the Flemings won't withdraw the offer – how could they? It would make them look terrible.' She brightened. 'And you got a good price for Flash yesterday. Once you have a paying job, and we're living rent-free, we can use that as the start of the fund for a better future—'

'That money's going to buy back Moss.'

'*What?* Are you mad?'

'I'm going to offer it to Murdoch,' Findlay said stubbornly. 'It's three thousand less than he paid me, but I can't see him getting a better offer.'

His wife jumped to her feet, too angry for her usual tearful response. 'You don't care about us, do you? Not about me, not about Josh, not about what you've put us both through since you lost the farm. We've been forced on to my parents' charity and even now you haven't been able to find a decent job.

'Well, you can choose. Do that with the money, and you can forget the idea that Josh and I will come and live with you in the miserable hovel that Her Graciousness Marjory Fleming has been kind enough to offer. Get out, and take your stupid dogs with you. We'll stay here.'

'Fine.' In the pallor of his face, the bruise stood out among the freckles more vividly than ever. 'I'll do just that. And you can suit yourself about whether you come or not.' In a pantomime of indifference he picked up his cup with a shaking hand and, without even noticing, drank the stone-cold tea.

Closing the door with a vicious slam, Susie marched across the hall to the kitchen.

Putting dirty plates into the dishwasher, Jennifer heard the slam and she compressed her lips again. She straightened up as Susie came in and looked at her daughter with disapproval. 'Good gracious, what was all that about?' she asked coldly.

'That was me, telling Findlay to get out. I'm staying here, with Josh.'

Jennifer looked at her with consternation. 'But Susie, you can't—'

'Oh, can't I? He's going to throw away all the money he got yesterday on buying back his stupid Moss!'

'But that doesn't mean you can just walk out on your husband!' She recognized the signs: Susie was having one of her temper tantrums again. And she'd seemed to be more strung up than ever for the last couple of days. This was going to call for desperate measures.

'Sit down, Susie.' She took her daughter's hand and led her to a chair by the little breakfast table where, in happier times, she and Derek used to have breakfast and read the *Daily Express* in companionable silence. 'Now, first of all, is the offer of somewhere to live still there?'

'Of course it is!' Susie was scornful. 'Findlay was just making a point.'

'Then you must go with him,' her mother said firmly. 'You and Findlay have things you need to sort out between you, and that can't be done at a distance. Remember, a child is entitled to a home with his mummy and daddy – we brought you up to believe that. You took a sacred vow, and marriage isn't something to be tossed aside because you've had a tiff. You have to grow up, Susie, and accept that sometimes you have to work at it.'

Susie stared at her in hurt disbelief. 'You're not saying – you don't mean we *can't* stay on with you?'

'For your own good, dear, no, you can't,' Jennifer said piously. 'It would be quite wrong for us to encourage you in any way.'

Susie sprang up. 'Let me get this straight. You're throwing me, and your grandchild, out of this house?'

Jennifer tittered. 'Oh dear, that's so like you, Susie – over-dramatic since the age of three! It may have got you your own way then – we used to laugh about you being such a headstrong little thing – but I'm not about to allow you to throw away your future. And little Josh's too, don't forget.' The words had a fine moral ring to them. 'Now, away you go back to your husband and say you were just upset. I'm sure he'll be very sympathetic.'

As an indication that this was her last word, she returned to stacking the dishwasher.

Casting a look of fury at her mother's oblivious back, Susie went back to the dining-room where Findlay was still sitting at the table.

'She won't let me stay.' Her whole frame was rigid with resentment. 'We'll have to come with you.'

It was his chance to get up, take her in his arms and tell her how relieved he was. He didn't.

'Fine,' he said. 'I'll phone Bill and check that it's still on.'

He went out, leaving Susie staring after him, her eyes narrowed and her hands clenching, unable to decide who she hated most: her husband, her mother, or Niall Murdoch, who had been the cause of this whole thing.

'Arnold? Tam. Tam MacNee, DS.'

Summoned by the duty officer, MacNee held out his hand to the man who had detached himself from the little group waiting in reception. With a warily professional eye, MacNee noted greying brown hair, a boxer's nose and eyes that were now undoubtedly assessing him in much the same manner. Tucker was heavily built, with a look which suggested he had seen it all before, and dealt with it. He was short, though, very little taller than MacNee himself, which got him plus points: so often, in MacNee's view, big blokes confused height with superiority. And the man probably hadn't much say in what he'd been christened.

Indeed, at the mention of his name, Tucker winced. 'Make

that Tommy,' he said, shaking hands. 'Nickname I've got. Can't think why.'

His deadpan delivery struck a chord too. 'Random, these things are sometimes,' MacNee said with matching solemnity, and, heartened by this exchange, walked across to the two civilians, waiting uncertainly with a policewoman. He greeted them with a formal expression of sympathy, made his inspector's apologies and led them to a room where PC Langlands was waiting with a coffee tray.

Mandy Preston, a plump woman, in her late thirties perhaps, had red hair with an unnatural purplish tinge and metallic silver nail polish. She looked a bit confused, but Jeff Brewer seemed to be still in shock. His eyes were red and he was shivering occasionally, though the hall was warm enough.

Leaving Sandy Langlands to make soothing noises as he ushered them to their seats and poured out coffee, his normally cheerful face creased into sympathetic lines, MacNee withdrew with Tucker to the corridor outside.

Tucker jerked his head approvingly. 'Lovely little mover. See the way he's being mother – real class, that.'

'Know these PAT dogs, go around hospitals cheering up the patients? He's ours. We've had to stop the punters giving him doggie treats.'

Together they observed the little group through the open door. Mandy Preston was visibly brightening under Langlands' solicitude, but Brewer's movements seemed mechanical, as if he was hardly aware of raising the cup to his lips. He was wearing a cheap suit with an open-necked black shirt, which did nothing for his sallow skin. The pallor of exhaustion and strain had given it an almost greenish tinge.

MacNee nodded towards him. 'Prime suspect?'

'My guvnor thinks so. But yours doesn't, seemingly. Bit of a dragon, is she?'

'Big Marge had a go at him, then?' MacNee, remembering

what Fleming had said, was amused. 'She seemed to have taken a scunner to him, for some reason.'

'If that means what I think it does, it was mutual. He's not exactly noted for his tact. JCB, we call him – has the same effect as heavy machinery.'

'Knowing Big Marge, I'd put my money on her. I'd like fine to see the two of them have a square go. Any chance you could get him up here?'

Tucker pulled a face. 'Not much. He'll just want reports. He's a lot on his plate – gangland killing a couple of weeks ago that's given us a bit of bother. And we're not expecting to get a lot here. The action'll be in Manchester.'

'Right enough. Bit of a doss, really, this end. We're going through the motions, but once the reports are in it'll be over to you.

'Anyway, the mortuary knows to expect them. Langlands and your constable can handle that while I take you up to the crime scene. The boss has the autopsy this afternoon, then she wants to give Brewer a grilling and see what Preston can tell her, but I'd guess you'll be heading south again tonight.'

Tucker looked disappointed. 'Couldn't spin it out a bit longer, could you? I could do with a break and I can always tell Carter you do things slowly up here.'

'Say that in front of Big Marge and you're dead meat. We're to show you lads what serious police work's all about.'

'Scary, is she?'

'Has her moments. Still, she won't be back till mid-afternoon. There's this wee pub, near where we're going – you're not an arrows man, by any chance?'

'Pound a game?'

In perfect accord, they saw the others leave, then set off for the Queen's Way, MacNee smugly contemplating his moral superiority to his boss in the 'hands across the Tweed' initiative.

*   *   *

Fleming returned from the autopsy in sombre mood, as she always did on these occasions. Despite the cold impersonality of the clinical surroundings – the stainless-steel tables, the harsh light, the antiseptic which didn't quite mask the underlying smell but at least stopped you gagging – it was never easy to maintain professional detachment. The chilled body might have a waxen look, but the narrative of injuries, which told of a violent quarrel and a terrified woman overpowered and battered to death, made it all too vividly human.

There had, John Brownlee the pathologist pointed out, been five separate blows to Wintour's face, delivered open-handed but with some force.

'Someone was very, very angry. A man, most likely – it usually is, given a situation like this – but it's not impossible that a woman in a rage could do it. Wintour was small and slight, and we've seen a lot more woman-on-woman violence lately.'

The aggressive ladette had certainly started featuring quite prominently on the charge sheet after drunken brawls. Fleming nodded. 'Did she fight back?'

Brownlee picked up first one limp hand, then the other, and studied the nails. 'Doesn't look like it, but we'll check.' He nodded to an assistant who, in a macabre parody of a manicurist, began taking samples.

Fleming averted her eyes. 'Could she have been knocked off her feet and accidentally hit her head as she fell?'

After another careful examination, he was positive in his reply. 'No. Oh, the first injury – yes, it's just possible. But look' – Fleming was again obliged to take a quick glance – 'it's clear she was struck again after that, twice, perhaps three times more. With something hard and heavy and roundish – something more like a rock, say, than a club. But you'll have to wait for the tissue analysis before we can give you that sort of information.'

Dutifully, Fleming had stayed for the rest of the ritual desecration which the interests of justice demanded, without any other significant information emerging. They might get some more useful pointers about where she had died once the analysis of clothes and shoes was complete, and the SOCO's report from the scene of crime should be on Fleming's desk today or tomorrow.

Driving back, she planned out the rest of her day. Getting the interviews done and the Manchester contingent despatched back south came first: you never knew when Tam would be inspired to re-enact Bannockburn. Then she could see what was happening on the local front; she'd just have to take care to dodge the Super until she had. And somehow she must make time at the end of the day to call in to see her parents.

But as she passed the desk, the duty officer hailed her. 'DS Allan and DC Kingsley were wanting a word as soon as possible, ma'am.'

'Right,' she agreed hollowly. She'd have to see them; Bailey had spelled out that whatever her priorities might be, the local issues were his and she couldn't afford to be seen quite openly ignoring them. Still, getting their report shouldn't take that long, and she'd been going to the CID room anyway to find Tam to sit in on the interviews.

The sound of laughter and cheerfully raised voices could be heard right down the corridor. Through the open door, Fleming could see that Allan and Kingsley, clearly in high good humour, were the centre of a small group which included Tam and a man she did not know – Tucker, presumably, his oppo from Manchester.

Allan swung round at her approach. 'Hey, boss! Great news! Jon's done it again!' Greg Allan, in his fifties, stockily built and balding, with small dark eyes in a wide, round face which had more than once been unkindly compared to a currant scone – and not to his advantage – was hugely impressed by his sharper subordinate.

'Really?' Fleming glanced at Kingsley, now composing his features in a modest smirk. *No*, she chided herself, *be fair. If it was someone else you'd call it a smile.*

'The hold-up at the garage – well, you tell her, Jon.'

Kingsley shrugged. 'It wasn't rocket science. It happened when the garage shop was empty, of course, and the boy behind the till gave us a description that could have fitted any man under the age of thirty. Claimed he'd been too scared to notice clearly, all that sort of stuff.

'But we'd a female witness who'd seen him coming out, and the first thing she said was that he was wearing a red striped beanie hat, and you'd think that was something it would have been hard to miss, however scared you were. So we'd a chat with some of the uniforms and it turns out the one working in the shop has a pal who's come to our notice once or twice before. And as luck would have it, when we went round he was even wearing the beanie hat. We've got him downstairs, and once we got the search warrant a fairly unconvincing toy gun and a remarkable amount of cash turned up under his bed.'

'Congratulations, Jon – that's good work,' Fleming said with genuine admiration. It might not, as he said, be rocket science, but she was wondering unkindly whether Allan on his own would have put two and two together when the man said, 'I'd never have worked that out, not until we'd started running background checks.' She caught sight of MacNee's sardonic smile, but pretended she hadn't, turning instead to the man standing beside him.

'You must be DS Tucker. I hope Tam's been looking after you. Did you find it useful?'

'Yes, ma'am.' It was a very correct response; she couldn't read from his expression what he was thinking, but it had occurred to her as she glanced at the two men that their body language suggested their association had been at least relatively harmonious.

She looked back at Allan. 'Any word on the woman in hospital?'

'Good news there too, boss. Panic attack, rather than a heart attack, and she's being discharged today. We've got a couple of SOCOs checking out the houses and Tansy's off making inquiries.'

'Excellent.' That would keep Donald happy; heart attacks were news, mere house-breaking wasn't. 'Tam, I want to talk to Brewer and the woman – Preston, is it?' Turning back to Tucker, she said, 'That would let you and your constable take them back tonight, sergeant. You'll be keen to get back, no doubt – I'm sure you don't have manpower to spare in Manchester.'

She had said it tongue in cheek, but he only said, 'No, ma'am,' sounding rather wooden, and she was surprised when MacNee said, 'Maybe Tommy could sit in on the interviews, give us a different perspective?'

'Of course. And you might pick up something that would be useful to DCI Carter. Supposing he's interested.'

She didn't see MacNee look at Tucker, and both men grin as they followed her out.

'This is DI Fleming, Mandy. She's just going to ask you a few questions, all right?'

Tucker made the introduction reassuringly. The inspector was still an unknown quantity; he hadn't sussed her out, beyond reckoning he wouldn't choose to take liberties with her, but on the whole female guvnors liked you to show your feminine side in police work, even if Mandy wasn't exactly the type to need putting at her ease and drawing out. She might have been a bit uncertain in the morning, but by now she was thoroughly relishing her starring role in the drama.

'Gave me ever such a turn, seeing her laid out there,' she told Fleming, woman-to-woman, with an elaborate shudder. 'Horrible, it was.'

'Indeed,' Fleming said gravely. 'We're very grateful to you for agreeing to come all this way to do it.'

'Oh, it was my—' Tucker almost heard the automatic 'pleasure' that was about to follow, but she stifled it with her hand, giving a giggle. 'If that isn't me all over! Only open me mouth to change feet! No problem, anyway.'

'Was she a very good friend of yours?' Given the woman's insouciance, Fleming's question seemed hardly necessary, but its effect, Tucker realized, was to shed a light on Mandy's reliability as a witness: she was torn between truth and self-importance but in the end truth won, if only by a short head.

'We weren't exactly *close*,' she admitted, then went on hastily, 'but of course we did see each other every day. It's just, well, you know – working in a bar you don't get much time for girlie heart-to-hearts, with all the punters bellowing for drinks.'

Fleming moved on. 'How long had she been working there?'

'Ooh, don't know, do I? Before me, anyhow, but I've only been there six months. When I came, she was Jeff's girlfriend.' Mandy sniffed. 'Supposed to be, anyway.'

Tucker stiffened, like a hunting dog which has spotted a movement in the undergrowth, and realized the others had done the same.

MacNee spoke first. 'Supposed to be?'

Mandy lowered her eyes and looked coy. 'Well, wouldn't like to speak ill of the dead . . .'

Tucker knew the type. 'Course not. But think of it this way, Mandy – you'd be letting her down if you didn't give us any help to find her killer. Having a bit of a fling with someone else, was she?' He got a look of approval from Fleming.

Mandy didn't take much convincing. 'Oh, if it's for

Natasha, I suppose it's different. Well, not anyone special, I wouldn't have said.' She gave another little giggle. 'Just, any-one, really.'

'Is that not a barmaid's job?' MacNee's tone was provo-cative and Mandy bridled.

'There's ways and ways. I enjoy having a bit of a joke with my regulars, but she liked to get them going. Cheap, I call it, the way she went on.'

Tucker watched with interest the way the Jocks worked as a team, Fleming leading her on, MacNee needling her just a little; Mandy had plenty more to say, but nothing very useful.

When she had gone, Fleming said thoughtfully, 'Hard to know what to make of that one. Is she jealous that a younger, more attractive woman got all the attention, or is this going to give us the key to the whole thing? The regulars – now, they ought to be able to give a bit of perspective on that—'

'SEP,' MacNee said laconically, and as Fleming looked taken aback he rubbed it in. 'Someone else's problem.'

'Yes – yes of course. Sorry, sergeant – your case.'

Tucker grinned. 'Thanks for letting me sit in on this, ma'am. I'll pass on what she said to DCI Carter. Would you like me to fetch Brewer now?'

The man was looking even worse than he had been in the morning, so exhausted that his eyes were drooping and it looked as if it was taking him all his time to put one foot in front of the other. When Tucker ushered him in and indicated a chair, he collapsed into it.

'We'll try not to take up too much of your time, Mr Brewer,' Fleming said crisply, which took Tucker by surprise; there was an unexpected edge to her voice, now she was dealing with a suspect. 'I've no doubt the Manchester police will have a lot of questions they'll want answered, but I have a couple relating to my brief.

'Have you ever been to this area before?'

Brewer hardly seemed to focus on her. 'Never been to Scotland before.'

'Never? Not even as a child, say, on holiday?'

'No.'

'Right.' His response seemed to satisfy her and she moved on. 'Did Natasha have any connection?'

'Na-Natasha?' He had difficulty saying her name, swallowing as if it had formed a lump in his throat. 'I don't know. She never said.'

'Where did she come from, originally?'

Brewer shook his head. 'Never talked about it.'

'Never? What about her family?'

'Didn't have any, as far as I know.'

'She told you that?'

'Just never said.' He was shifting in his chair.

Fleming's voice had become harsher; now she gave him a sharp look. Taking his cue from her, MacNee said roughly, 'Come on, pull the other one. You lived with her, and she never mentioned her mother, brothers and sisters—?'

'No, she never.' There was no doubt that he was uneasy.

They were like sharks smelling blood on the water, Tucker thought, starting to circle closer and closer.

'She didn't talk about her family. At all. Or so you say.' That was Fleming again. 'Where did she work before she came to work in the bar?'

'Don't know. She—'

'– never said,' MacNee finished mockingly. 'You employed her, right? So you must have known.'

Brewer had begun to sweat. 'Not – not exactly.'

'But what about—?' Tucker began, but Fleming cut across him. 'Look, Jeff, I believed you were innocent. I started questioning you hard on the basis that I wanted my belief confirmed, but at the moment you're having the opposite effect. You're acting shifty.

'If there's something that you're covering up, and it's not that you bludgeoned Natasha Wintour to death, I'd strongly advise you not to muck us about.'

The young man crumpled, putting his head in his hands. 'She – she wasn't employed officially. She didn't have the right documentation, she said – she wouldn't tell me why – and I fiddled it so I could pay her without it going through the books.'

Tucker eyed Fleming with some respect. The team in Manchester had picked up on this unease, but hadn't got anything out of him. Admittedly he'd been softened up by strain and exhaustion, but even so it was impressive.

'Was she an immigrant?' Fleming pursued.

'I don't think so.'

'She never said, I suppose,' MacNee put in. 'Had she an accent, maybe?'

'Sort of, a bit. Irish, Welsh, Scottish – something like that.'

'Scots? If it was, where would it be from?'

Brewer looked blank. 'How the hell would I know? I'm sorry, I can't tell the difference. Look, there's no point in asking me about her before she came to work in the bar. It was about a year ago – more, maybe, I can't quite remember. She didn't talk about the past. She wouldn't.'

MacNee sneered at him. 'So she just came in off the street one day and said she wanted a job and by the way, she'd no references, no national insurance number and she didn't want to pay tax on her wages so naturally that was OK?'

'Yes,' he said simply.

'Why?' Fleming had fixed him with her eyes – unusual eyes, Tucker had noticed earlier, clear hazel.

Brewer met her gaze. 'You never saw Natasha when she – when she wasn't dead. There was something about her, something that made you want her desperately. To tell you the truth,' he was defiant now, 'I'd have done worse than that, to get her.'

'And would you have done worse than that to keep her?' Fleming's questioning was merciless. 'You told me, when I spoke to you first on the phone, that she'd just walked out, without telling you where she was going, or even that she was going at all. Did she go – or did you discover she was planning to leave and decide that if you couldn't have her, no one else could?'

'No, no! I swear it! I wouldn't have harmed a hair of her head – oh God, her hair!' He collapsed forward in his chair, sobbing uncontrollably.

Fleming got up. 'Tam, find someone to sit with him till he calms down,' she said and went out. The two men followed, Tucker reflecting that perhaps he hadn't needed to worry about showing his feminine side after all. As Tam left, she turned to him.

'I should really apologize, sergeant – as Tam didn't hesitate to point out, I was trespassing on your territory.' She didn't sound all that apologetic. 'I have to say, I'm not as convinced he's clean as I was when I spoke to DCI Carter yesterday. Perhaps you could pass that on to him.'

'Yes, ma'am,' he said demurely. 'I'll be able to say you got more out of him than our guys did, anyway.'

Fleming smiled. 'Oh, we have our methods.'

MacNee reappeared with the policewoman from Manchester who went into the waiting-room. He was holding an envelope which he handed to Fleming.

'Here's the photo of Wintour you asked for.'

She pulled it out and glanced at it. 'Good clear one – that's great. I'll put it up in the incident room for the briefing tomorrow.

'But it looks as if it's over to you now anyway, sergeant. Pity – I was just getting my teeth into it.' She shook his hand. 'Good luck!'

★   ★   ★

Returning to Mains of Craigie after her visit to her parents, Marjory was feeling depressed. Her father had been having one of his bad days, confused and angry, and Janet had been so distracted she could hardly speak to her daughter, who could only wonder how long it would be before he was actually beyond her control. For once she had been wise enough not to raise the subject with her mother, knowing it could only upset her more, but it was a conversation they would have to have one day.

Then, when she reached the farm, she saw the elderly pickup and the car parked outside the cottage. There was smoke coming from the chimney too. The Stevensons had moved in.

Marjory got out of the car, not even noticing the apple blossom foaming in the orchard below, or the evening sun warming the stone of the old farmhouse to honey-gold. She didn't hear the hens muttering contentedly to one another as they scratched about under the old trees, or the blackbird giving a recital from the rowan on the lawn as with a heavy heart she went inside.

8

They were all talking about it. When the truck stopped at the cottage in the clearing to take him to be dropped at his working area, it was the other men's only topic of conversation.

He sat on one of the rough benches in the back, composing his face into an expression of suitable interest, holding his hands clamped between his knees to stop them shaking and hoping they couldn't hear the pounding of his heart.

A woman's body, they were saying. Police cars. Signs on the Queen's Way road asking for witnesses. Someone from down south, apparently, just dumped here – this from someone whose brother-in-law was a policeman.

He cleared his throat. 'Funny, that,' he said, and to his surprise his voice sounded quite normal and no one turned a head to stare. They all just nodded and talked on.

Reaching the destination, the truck lurched to a standstill and they all jumped down. He was still working on restoring a path which had become worn away with use; there wasn't much more to do to that section and he'd be working on his own. It would give him time and space to collect his thoughts, to plan – if there was any plan he could make, with the thoughts whirling round in his head so violently that he felt as dizzy as if their movements had been physical ones.

Gina Lafferty woke at the first of a series of muffled crashes downstairs. Her eyes shot open and she sat up, her first instinctive reaction a glance towards the other side of the king-size bed. Reassuringly, it was empty, the pile of goose-down pillows in their white Egyptian cotton covers plumped up and pristine, without the indentation of her husband's – or anyone else's – head.

Of course not. As she shook off sleep, she remembered: Ronnie was still in Glasgow and, last night at least, she had retired early and alone. She glanced at the clock. Quarter to eight! She sank back on her pillows with a groan as the sound of a vacuum-cleaner, wielded aggressively, assailed her ears.

Bloody woman! Eight-thirty, Gina had told Mrs Aitcheson, was the earliest she could come in to start her cleaning duties, but she had treated this as she always treated Gina's instructions: she said, 'Mphm,' and did precisely as she chose.

Ronnie was forever pointing out that she was lucky to have anyone at all, cleaning ladies in this middle-class enclave being even rarer than women whom Gina could call her friend. Mrs Aitcheson only came because Ronnie had made it clear that her husband's job as night watchman at the marina depended on it, and she resented that.

And 'Mrs Aitcheson'! That was another irritation. Gina had been charmingly democratic when they first met, saying winsomely, 'I'm Gina. And you are—?' only to get the repressive reply, 'Mrs Aitcheson'll do.'

She didn't scruple to call her employer 'Gina', though, using it as a weapon in the tacit psychological warfare waged between them. It annoyed the hell out of Gina, but she'd never discovered the woman's first name – her husband Brian always referred to her as 'the wife' or 'Mrs A' – so couldn't even retaliate in kind. She'd have told the old cow that she'd prefer to be called 'madam', if she hadn't known it wouldn't make any difference and that ten minutes later the story would be all over Drumbreck, with everyone sniggering behind their hands.

She hadn't a hope of getting back to sleep now and the day yawned ahead of her. It was tempting to go right back to

Glasgow but Ronnie had said he was coming down today and wanted to spend another week here, for some reason. And what Ronnie wanted, Ronnie got. It would be wrong to say she was afraid of him – or perhaps it wouldn't, exactly. Gina certainly didn't trust him; she had a secret deposit account which was coming along nicely in preparation for the day when he changed his mind about his second wife just as he had about his first. But it wasn't big enough yet for her to be anything other than very serious about keeping him sweet. Gina had tried poor and she'd tried rich and she knew which one she preferred.

There was still the rest of the day to fill in. She could spend a bit of time working out at the club, and the bar at lunchtime was always better than it was in the evening when the families came in, the teenagers being a pain and the wives giving her the sidelong looks that explained why Ronnie had needed to buy half the marina to get membership. She'd egged him on, believing, God help her, that this would give her entrée into a social elite; it was only once they were members that she realized there was more to it than that. Once a scrap merchant, always a scrap merchant, even if you were richer than most of them. The ones prepared to be friendly, like Kim McConnell, were, frankly, white trash and Gina did have standards.

If only she could have persuaded Ronnie to sell up here, buy in to one of those luxury developments in Spain! Heaven knew she'd tried, but Ronnie liked Drumbreck, where he'd the most expensive house, the largest luxury cruiser and the glossiest trophy wife – oh yes, Gina knew her status – but if they went somewhere more glamorous and cosmopolitan he would be a small fish. Here, however little they liked him, whatever they said about him behind his back, he couldn't be overlooked, and that was important to Ronnie; thwarted, he turned nasty. She'd never forget his insane rage when he was blackballed by the club.

Gina lay for a while contemplating the problem, then got up and opened the curtains. Beach House, a handsome Edwardian villa, had the best position in Drumbreck, looking straight down the bay to the marina and the Cree estuary and Wigtown Bay beyond. This morning again the water was shimmering in the sunshine and the usual group of small dinghies was having a sailing lesson. It didn't look settled, though; there was heavy cloud gathering on the horizon and Gina pulled a face as she turned away to get dressed.

'Morning, Mrs Aitcheson!' she called with determined cheerfulness as she went downstairs and passed the open door of the lounge where the Dyson was being propelled about with a fine disregard for the legs of tables and the edges of chairs.

Mrs Aitcheson was a short, powerful-looking woman in her fifties with a weathered complexion and coarse grey hair badly cut in a straight fringe which did not quite cover a scar running from her temple to her cheekbone on the left-hand side. She was wearing her own Day-Glo orange overall, as she always did. The more tasteful navy one in the cleaning cupboard hung ignored; Gina had accepted that, short of wrestling the woman to the ground and forcibly dressing her in it, the cupboard was where it was destined to remain.

Pretending that she couldn't hear for the noise of the vacuum-cleaner was another of Mrs Aitcheson's little games. Gina's smile vanished as she received no response to her greeting; she went in and stood in front of the other woman, who grudgingly turned off the machine.

'Mr Lafferty's coming this afternoon,' Gina said, pointedly using the formal name. 'Could you clean the study, please, and iron the shirts in the laundry.'

Her dark eyes cold as pebbles, Mrs Aitcheson said, 'I'll see if I've time, Gina.' Then she switched on the Dyson again, moving it in a wide sweep which gave her a reason to turn her back.

Gina was just leaving the room when a gap on one of the shelves caught her eye, a gap where a small silver box had stood. The other objects on the shelves had been moved closer together. She swung round.

'What's happened to the silver box, Mrs Aitcheson?'

Mysteriously, Mrs Aitcheson's hearing seemed to have improved. Switching off the motor once more, she turned round, her face blandly innocent. 'I couldn't say, Gina. I noticed it wasn't there. Maybe Ronnie moved it – there hasn't been anyone else in here, has there?'

This time it was Gina who turned away. Her face flaming, she went to the kitchen. She knew Mrs Aitcheson was lying; she lied whenever it suited her, and small items and sums of money were always disappearing. But Ronnie wouldn't hear of her being sacked and Gina had for some time had an uneasy feeling that part of the woman's duties was checking up on his wife's activities when Ronnie wasn't here.

She knew she'd taken a risk, bringing Niall back the other night. But sometimes a sort of madness seized her; she knew all about the advantages of being married to money, but often the price seemed high. She was pretty sure that yesterday, when Mrs Aitcheson didn't come, she had removed any traces that could have given her away.

At least, she hoped to God she had.

'You're going to have to call the police,' Jenna Murdoch said flatly. 'I don't care what it does for community relations – they've got to put a stop to it. It was petty vandalism before, but this is more than that. I've put up with you telling me they'll get tired of protesting for long enough, and next week the flat goes on the market. I'm not going to spend my morning scrubbing it off and pretending it hasn't happened.'

She was standing with Niall looking at the obscene graffiti

which had been spray-painted in red across the stretch of wall beside the entrance to the newly renovated flat.

'I'm not asking you to,' Niall snapped angrily.

He seemed to have been angry for days now. Jenna was feeling much the same herself. 'So what are you going to do, then?' she snapped back.

'Oh, I'll phone the police before I go to the marina.' He cast an irritable glance across the yard to where the collie lay at the end of a chain, watching them with head on paws. 'You'd think the sodding dog could have barked, or something – it's no good for anything else.'

'It's not a watchdog,' Jenna pointed out, then, reminded, asked, 'Is Findlay going to buy it back? You didn't tell me what he said when he phoned last night.'

Niall snorted. 'Thought he could get the brute back for less than half of what I paid for him. I've told him he can think again.'

'Reckon you'll get a better offer from anyone else?' His wife gave him a pitying look. 'Take the money and run, is my advice.'

'Damned if I will. I've told him he'll have to come up with the full amount. If he doesn't, the dog's dead.'

'And somehow, that will solve the problem?'

Niall chewed at his lip. 'No. But neither will what he's offered me. I've another plan anyway . . .'

'Care to share it?' There was an edge to Jenna's voice. Niall had flatly refused to discuss the financing of his purchase but she couldn't see where the money had come from. These dogs were expensive, and it hadn't come out of their joint overdraft – she'd checked.

'No. I'll go and phone the police from the office.' He went into the house just as Mirren came out. Ignoring him, she walked past her mother too and spoke to the dog, which sat up as she approached. His tail gave the faintest twitch, and with a pang Jenna saw Mirren smile. How long was it since she'd seen a smile on her daughter's face?

'You're pleased to see me, aren't you, Moss?' she was saying, bending down and speaking softly, but not trying to touch the animal. She produced a piece of toast from her pocket, which was accepted warily.

'Mirren, for goodness' sake, your pocket will be full of crumbs,' Jenna scolded with transferred distress, but her daughter paid no attention, still talking to the dog.

'You'll be all right, Moss, till I come back. I promise.' Now she did look at her mother, her expression fierce. 'You won't let him do anything to Moss if I go out for a walk, will you?'

'Of course not.' There wasn't the faintest chance of anyone stopping Niall if he made up his mind in a fit of vindictiveness, but saying that wouldn't help. If the worst came to the worst, she'd just have to cope with Mirren's reaction when she heard. It would be a considerable relief when, one way or another, it was all over.

More or less satisfied, Mirren left and Jenna went back inside. Today she was decorating the new flat. She always enjoyed decorating; the instant transformation which paint brought about was all but magical. There wasn't much else in her life to encourage her belief that a better future – her only hope for herself and Mirren – might actually be possible, that the day would come when all the sacrifices would have been worth it, when she could concentrate on her daughter and make up for all the neglect and indeed, she reflected uncomfortably with their most recent conversation in mind, the lies of the past. She sorted out the paint, trays and rollers she would need with pleasurable anticipation.

When the doorbell rang, Jenna was up a ladder, reaching awkwardly over her head with a roller to paint a ceiling. She swore, then set the roller back in the tray and climbed down, easing her aching shoulder. Her face and hair must be covered with flecks of white paint but it hardly mattered, since it was most probably the police.

It wasn't. It was a tall, heavily built young man whom she recognized, after a moment, as Rab McLeish, who had come before and made a laughable offer for the flat.

'Yes?' she said, without enthusiasm.

He ducked his head in greeting. 'I was hearing you'd been having a wee bit of trouble,' he said, indicating the lurid message along the side of the house.

Jenna's eyes narrowed. 'As you see.'

'I was just thinking, it's maybe going to be a bit of a problem for you, selling the flat, when there's people not happy about it. It'd fairly put off any buyers from outside, thinking they might get their windows broken next.' He was visibly nervous; he put his hand up to his mouth before he went on, 'I was thinking, you see, I could maybe do us both a bit of a favour. I know you were looking for a better price than I offered, but I could see my way to upping it a bit.'

It was blatant. The nerve of the man! Jenna couldn't decide whether that was more astonishing, or his naivety. She could actually see a little smudge of red paint on the side of his hand. Oh, she was going to enjoy the phone call she'd make to the police when he was off her doorstep, but she wasn't stupid.

'Well, I'd like to discuss it with you, of course,' she said sweetly. 'But I'm afraid my husband wouldn't hear of it. He's phoned the police and I'm sure they'll see to it that this sort of thing doesn't happen again. Sorry.'

As she shut the door and saw the look of black rage which crossed the young man's face, she congratulated herself on the wisdom of not telling him precisely what he could do with his miserable offer.

Findlay hadn't been meant to start work until next week. After all, Susie had taken time off to get the house straight and it wasn't as if there wasn't plenty that needed doing: unpacking boxes, moving furniture, replacing curtains – since there was of course no way she was going to live with the second-hand rubbish Marjory Fleming had hung at the windows.

But when Susie woke, there was no sign of Findlay. Going downstairs to make breakfast for herself and Josh, she found a half-empty mug of tea with a cold film on top; he must have gone out hours before.

While Josh ate the Sugar Puffs he had negotiated as compensation for the porridge he'd had to eat at his grandmother's, Susie went outside, shading her eyes against the watery sun and looking round for her husband.

Outside the farmhouse, Marjory Fleming was getting into her car. She raised a hand in greeting but Susie pretended not to see, swinging round to scan the fields.

She saw him almost immediately, just below, standing by a dry-stone dyke with a stone in his hand. He bent forward to tuck it into a gap, then stood back to assess its effect, dusting his hands. Satisfied, he turned away and plodded up the field in her direction, his head down.

'Findlay!' she called, making the name an accusation, and he looked up.

'Oh – I'm just coming in for some breakfast.'

She'd have liked to say, 'Are you, indeed? And who do you think's going to make it for you?' but she wasn't going to give Marjory the satisfaction of seeing them brawling on the doorstep. Susie walked back into the house, poured herself a mug of tea and sat down beside Josh. There was no place set for Findlay.

He came in, looked at the table with its unspoken message and went to the fridge, taking out eggs and a packet of bacon.

Josh's eyes brightened. 'Oooh, can I have some?'

'Of course you can, son,' Findlay replied at the same moment as Susie said, 'You won't have time. You're supposed to be going to play with Peter and I'm far too busy to hang around waiting for you today. Go and fetch anything you're taking with you.'

Findlay exchanged a complicit glance with his son. 'Run upstairs now, Josh, and get everything together. It's in the pan now – it'll be ready when you come down.'

Josh needed no second telling. Susie, with exactly her mother's mannerism, compressed her lips, but she knew when she was beaten. 'I thought we agreed you would be here today, helping sort out the house,' she said coldly.

'I know. I'm sorry, but I'd a chat with Bill last night. He's keen to buy in some stirks as soon as possible and there's quite a bit of maintenance needing done first. It was the least I could do – there's plenty time for the house when I finish this afternoon. You only need to make a list of what you'd like me to do.' The bacon was sizzling now; he cracked a couple of eggs into the pan.

'If you're at all interested in knowing what I want you to do, you can put giving up your stupid idea of getting Moss back right at the top of the list. Murdoch gave you your answer yesterday; now you need to forget about the whole thing.'

Findlay prodded the contents of the pan with unnecessary violence. 'No, Susie, I won't. I've told you how I feel, and I've made up my mind.' He turned to face her. 'If he won't settle for what I've offered, I'm just going to have to borrow the rest. I don't care what you say. It's a matter of principle.'

'Borrow!' Susie screeched, setting down her mug with a bang. 'After all the trouble your borrowing got us into before, reducing us to – this?' She gestured round the small, cheaply furnished kitchen. 'Over my dead body, Findlay Stevenson. I'll do whatever it takes to stop you. I'm not going to let you ruin our lives even more than you have already. Think about poor little Josh, if you don't care about me!' She finished on a wail, bursting into tears.

Josh, returning at speed, opened the door, then stopped in dismay, looking from his sobbing mother to his father's white, furious face.

Findlay lifted a plate and tipped the contents of the pan on to it. 'There you are, Josh, it's all yours. I'm not hungry any more.'

He walked out, leaving Josh staring uncertainly from the mountain of food – half a dozen rashers of bacon, two eggs – to his mother.

She was no comfort. 'Well, you'd better eat it,' she sniffed. 'You wanted it.'

Then Susie got up and walked to the window, looking after her husband's retreating back with an expression of loathing on her face. It was going to drive her mad. She had to stop this, somehow.

There was a curious atmosphere in the Incident Room where officers had gathered for the morning briefing, Marjory reflected. Six months ago, after the Knockhaven lifeboat had been deliberately wrecked on a stormy October night, she had entered to a silence so strained that she had almost felt she had to push her way through it; today it took a moment for the talk and even laughter to die down as she made her way to the board which ran along the side of the room. Someone Else's Problem indeed, as Tam had said.

He was there, in the front row, with Tansy sitting beside him. The other members of the CID, Fleming noted uneasily, were all sitting together in the centre of the room further back, grouped around DS Allan, who had saved a seat beside him, for Kingsley, presumably. Jon wasn't there: he'd had a meeting with the Super earlier which had obviously overrun.

'These are the facts as we know them,' Fleming began, and took them through what they had: Natasha Wintour lived in

Manchester with her partner Jeff Brewer, she had been dead at least thirty-six hours – possibly more – before the body was found and she had been murdered with repeated blows to the head, probably from something like a stone. She had been found lying on her back, but from the evidence of post-mortem lividity the pathologist had been able to confirm that her earlier position had been lying on her side.

'Not surprising, really; it was obvious she'd been moved and we've been assuming that the body would have been brought in a car, and whether it was covered up on the back seat or placed in the boot, it wasn't likely it would have been lying flat out, as we found it.

'I've got the SOCO's report now too, but all they've really come up with is negatives: they confirm that she wasn't killed at the scene, which we knew already, and that it wasn't raining when the body was put there, but given the time of death we knew that too. They can't find anything to indicate how the body was transported – you have to remember the ground was baked hard after the heatwave so you couldn't expect foot-prints, for instance. But there's nothing to suggest that our hypothesis, that it was brought up the track here from a car parked by the road, is wrong.' She traced its course with her finger on the large-scale Ordnance Survey map fixed to the board.

'The Manchester police are pursuing the investigation at their end. Our job is simply to check here for any possible sightings of the car and of course get on with a fingertip search of the area. Yes, Ryan?'

One of the younger PCs had put his hand up. 'Is it a popular spot, ma'am?'

Fleming shook her head. 'Not at all, so it's pretty clean. Probably almost the last people walking round there would be the foresters planting the trees twenty years ago or so. Any-thing at all that is found is likely to be significant.

'The other thing we're hoping for is info from the public, but as I understand it there hasn't been much – right, Jock?'

Sergeant Naismith, detailed to bring a record of calls, said gloomily, 'Couple of nutters and the usual attention-seekers. Nothing useful.'

MacNee had been looking thoughtful. 'I've just been wondering – can we be sure she was dead when she arrived in the area? If she was killed in Manchester and dumped from a car, the chances are no one saw anything. Middle of the night – you could go hours without a car passing along the Queen's Way.

'But if she was alive – well, she was a wee smasher. If we circulated the photo round hotels, bars, petrol stations, someone would remember her.'

Tansy Kerr chimed in, 'And if we didn't have a sighting after all that, we could be pretty sure she wasn't alive when she got here.'

'Right,' Fleming approved. 'I've got the photo here.' She took it from its envelope and put it on the board beside the map. It was a shot which had clearly been carefully posed, showing a glamorous young woman with a cloud of dark hair and long-lashed, dark brown eyes, half-turned and smiling back provocatively at the camera.

There was a muted 'Phoo-arr!' from somewhere in the group around Allan and a few sniggers. Fleming frowned. 'Think of her with a hole bashed in her head and you won't find it so funny. You'll see the video and stills tomorrow,' she said tartly, but she was aware that, though faces had straightened rapidly, one or two sidelong looks were exchanged. There was a situation developing in the CID that she was going to have to tackle sooner or later, and she wasn't temperamentally suited to later.

Capitalizing on what she knew to be a widely held belief that when Big Marge sounded sweet she was at her most dangerous, she said silkily, 'Greg, I'd like a word with you afterwards,' and saw the man sit up nervously as he said, 'Yes, boss.'

'So, Jock,' she went on smoothly, 'can you arrange for copies of this to be run off and distributed? Thanks. And I'm just posting a detail now for the fingertip search, but in view of the fact that we want to get this cleared off our patch as quickly and efficiently as possible, I think we can spare a few detectives to help. With the robbery wrapped up and the house-breaking lower on the priority list, there's nothing that won't wait. You'll get overalls when you arrive.

'OK? Any questions? No? Fine.'

Fleming scribbled the extra names on the list and stuck it up, aware of the sullen silence in the centre of the room, but aware, too, of discreet amusement among the uniforms. It wasn't exactly a secret that detectives considered mundane physical police work beneath them, and it would give them a lesson about the unwisdom of tangling with Big Marge. She was heading for the door when it opened and Jon Kingsley came in, stopping as he saw her.

'Oh – you've finished! Sorry, boss. The Super kept me talking about the petrol station case.'

She did wonder whether Donald Bailey, a stickler for proper procedure, had been made aware that Kingsley was expected elsewhere, but said only, 'All right, Jon. I was just assigning details for the investigation of the Natasha Wintour case, but you'll see the list up there.' She indicated. 'All the signs are that once we finish the search at the scene of crime we can hand over to Manchester.'

But Kingsley was looking past her to the board where the photograph was displayed. He said blankly, 'What's that doing there?'

'It's Natasha Wintour.' Fleming was puzzled by his reaction. 'Jeff Brewer brought it.'

He looked uncertain. 'Is it not Davina Watt? Lives in Wigtown – or at least she did, a few years ago.'

A silence had fallen on the room. Fleming said, 'Are you sure of that?'

'Well,' he took another look. 'She'd short hair then, and I didn't know her very well, but I'm pretty sure . . . I think she worked for a solicitor – they'd be able to tell you definitely. But yes, I'm sure it's the same woman.'

With hypotheses crashing about her ears, she acted decisively. 'Right. Tam, Tansy, Greg – my room. Come on, Jon.' She swept out, hearing the buzz of astonished speculation rise in her wake.

9

'It's only him that's standing in my way,' Rab McLeish said exultantly. 'I reckon she'd be willing to talk. And maybe after another couple of wee hints—'

'Rab,' Cath Dunsire said despairingly, 'you're mental! You'll get in trouble with the police.'

They were standing on the doorstep of the bookshop in Wigtown where Cath worked. The shop wasn't busy; it was still too early in the day for the visitors who made Scotland's Book Town a place of pilgrimage, and there were only a few people browsing among the yards and yards of shelves.

Rab laughed. 'You think they're going to want folk to hear there's a problem? You know all the things that have happened already – kept quiet enough about them, haven't they?'

'You're pushing your luck. And anyway, there's no time for a campaign.' She produced a copy of the *Galloway Globe*, folded open at the 'To Let' page, where she'd circled an advertisement in red. 'There's this one in Station Road – it's not big, but it's all we would need. And then later—'

He was shaking his head stubbornly. 'Later's no good. If we let up on them, later only means they would sell for so much that the next one'll go for far more than I could ever pay, and then we'll never be able to get back. I want the best for my kid, not some rubbish flat. And I'm making good money – you know that.'

'I never said you weren't,' she cried. 'But it's not the sort of money they can make in Glasgow just by picking up the phone and making a deal. I know, I know,' she went on as he opened his mouth to release a tirade, 'it's not fair. It's not as if they had to work for it, like you do. They can go into a posh office and sit there all day and come back to their family at night when you're sleeping behind your cab with two more days before you see your own front door again. But get real! There's nothing – *nothing* – you can do about it.' She was shaking.

Rab grinned, the macho male making light of the little woman's worries. 'Oh yeah? Stick around!' He walked away to where the lorry was parked on a double yellow line.

'I meant exactly what I said, Rab,' Cath said quietly.

He turned as he swung himself up into the cab. He was still smiling. 'Trust me! I'll be back tomorrow.'

Cath stood on the doorstep watching him drive away, her hands folded miserably across her stomach. She had been sick this morning, as quietly as she could, but even so she thought her mother had given her a strange look when she came in for breakfast. Fortunately the phone had rung and she'd managed to empty a pot of yoghurt and a cup of coffee down the sink without her father, watching the sports news on breakfast TV, noticing what she was doing. She couldn't rely on that every day.

It wasn't going to work out, was it? She'd tried to get through to Rab and she'd failed. If she, and their future child, counted for so little compared to his stupid obsession, it wasn't going to be much of a relationship. It was as if she'd been wearing distorting spectacles and now she had taken them off she could see the whole thing clearly.

He was totally unaware of what he had just done. He'd be back tomorrow evening, and she'd tell him then that this was the end. Of everything. And no matter what he said, she wouldn't change her mind.

Cath went back into the shop. 'Would it be all right if I took a few days of my holiday leave?' she asked the owner.

'Sure. It's still early enough in the season – we won't start getting really busy for another couple of weeks. But I thought you and Rab were going to Tenerife next month?'

'Not any more,' Cath said bleakly.

'Right, Jon. Tell us about it.' Fleming had a pad in front of her on the desk and a pen in her hand.

Kingsley was looking faintly bemused, which, to be fair, was hardly surprising. He hadn't been in on any of the discussions earlier, hadn't even heard the theory that there had to be some connection with the area for the body to be dumped here, so suddenly seeing a photo of a bonny girl you'd once known and having it sprung on you that she was the corpse would give anyone a bit of a shock.

MacNee and Allan had taken the two chairs in front of the desk and Tansy Kerr was perching on the table behind. Kingsley himself was standing like a teacher in front of a class, with them all gazing at him expectantly.

'I – I don't really know where to begin.' He spoke with uncharacteristic diffidence.

'How did you come to know her?' Fleming prompted.

'It was years ago, while I was still a student at Edinburgh. I got keen on sailing through some mates of mine who came from down this way. One of them was a member of the Yacht Club at Drumbreck when it was just a wooden shack and had some great weekend raves.

'But the Glasgow mob muscled in and decided it wasn't posh enough for them and they'd raise money to demolish it and rebuild, and after that we took to going to Portpatrick instead. There was some big fuss though – can't remember the details because I wasn't around but there was a scandal about the Hon. Treasurer embezzling or something. He was Davina's boss. Imrie – no, Ingles. That was it – Ingles.'

That rang a bell. MacNee said, 'Hang about – Keith Ingles! He was jailed for robbery with violence.'

'That's right,' Allan chimed in. 'Took money from the Yacht Club, bashed the cleaner over the head when she caught him at it. Got three years, as I remember it.'

'I vaguely remember hearing about it at the time,' Fleming said, 'but no more than that. Tansy, can you nip down to Records and see if you can get the file? Thanks. Go on, Jon. Davina Watt.'

'Ah, Davina!' He gave a half-smile, then sighed. 'Davina was – something else. She was a considerable cut above the usual local totty. When she came into the bar every man in the place would suddenly start trying to look cool.'

'Fancy her, did you?' Allan gave a suggestive leer.

'Too right. Who didn't?' Kingsley had no hesitation. 'But it was one of those "in your dreams" things. She wasn't about to waste her talents on a student whose idea of showing a girl a good time was buying her a pint of lager.

'Drumbreck was, and still is, full of people with so much money that they think – how shall I put it? – that the usual constraints don't apply.'

'Do you mean there's a lot of screwing around?' MacNee said with deliberate coarseness. Kingsley's talent for putting plain facts in frilly drawers fairly got up his nose.

'If you want to put it crudely, yes.' Kingsley, leaning back against the radiator now with his ankles crossed, looked down at MacNee. 'Davina was reckoned to put it about a bit – got herself quite a reputation for choosing targets with an eye to the main chance.'

'A wee hoor, was she?' MacNee seemed to have a mission to lower the tone.

'More on a ruthless hunt for a meal ticket. Problem was everyone knew that; you'd hardly break up your marriage for her when she'd be off like a greyhound after an electric bunny if a better prospect turned up.

'The last time we were down here there was a lot of talk about her and her boss – she'd moved in with him. Boring old git, he was – ticked us off once for having a pie fight in the bar – and he probably couldn't believe his luck. But she wasn't going to get the lifestyle she wanted to become accustomed to on a solicitor's salary. Could be why he took the cash.'

Fleming had been scribbling notes as she listened. 'He must have done his jail term, given remission. Anyone know where he is now?'

Kingsley looked blank; the other two men looked at each other then shrugged.

'We can find out. When did Davina leave Wigtown?'

Again, Kingsley couldn't help.

The door opened and Tansy came in. 'Here you are, boss.' She put a bulky file down on the desk.

Fleming looked surprised. 'That was quick!'

Kerr simpered modestly. 'There's a new guy in Records. He was boasting in the pub the other night about this brilliant system he's introduced so I told him to put his money where his mouth is.' She paused. 'I might also have suggested that a seriously brilliant response might just make you more sympathetic when it came to budget allocation. Not that I suppose it will.'

'Bad things happen to people who tell wicked lies,' Fleming warned her. 'So you can go now and find out where Keith Ingles went on release. Shouldn't be difficult – he'll be under restraint until October so they'll know where he is.'

Muttering that there was no gratitude, Kerr pulled a face and left.

Fleming riffled through the pages, then stopped to pull one out. 'This is Davina Watt's police statement. Pretty damning. Wouldn't back up his alibi.'

'Can't have made him happy,' MacNee said. 'He'd be

thinking that when she was his bidie-in she wouldn't go into the box against him. What happened to the money?'

Fleming flicked through to the end of the file. 'No recovery. You might wonder . . .'

'Aye, you might,' said MacNee.

'I wouldn't put it past her,' Kingsley admitted.

Allan had been frowning, deep in thought. 'Here!' he said suddenly. 'You don't think it could be her took the money, after all that? She'd maybe have got him to do it for her, then let him take the rap and went off with the money!' He looked round with a smirk of satisfaction at being one step ahead.

'Mmm,' Fleming said, just as the phone rang.

MacNee couldn't quite make out the words at the other end, but he could certainly hear the volume at which they were being spoken. Fleming was doing a lot of 'Yes sir-ing', and when she put the phone down she got to her feet.

'That was the Super. Some bastard who was in the briefing-room has tipped off the Press and he's just had a request for a statement about the revised identification of the body. I'm just off to the lion's den.'

'She's for it now,' Allan said with undisguised satisfaction as the door shut.

Kingsley grinned. 'Maybe he'll ask us to give her a few tips on effectiveness, Greg.'

'Very funny,' MacNee said. 'As far as I can remember, your name was on the fingertip search detail. If there's nothing else you can share with us about your acquaintance with Davina Watt, you'd better get out there now.'

He had the satisfaction of watching Kingsley leave with a very bad grace.

Donald Bailey did not move when Fleming came into the room. He had old-fashioned manners and his remaining seated was a bad sign. If she had needed any more pointers, he was scowling too, and tapping his fingers on the desk.

'I'm sorry, sir,' she said, before he could say anything.

'So well you might be! What is it coming to, when I learn about major, indeed crucial, developments in a murder case from a secretary on the telephone, courtesy of the *Scottish Sun*?'

'I was just gathering the information to bring to you, Donald—' She tried to explain, but there was no stopping him.

She let it all flow over her. Was it the great J. P. R. Williams who had said that finding himself at the bottom of a rugby scrum, he just lay there and thought of happier times? Cammie would know . . . She barely heard what he said, though she was aware that the words 'protocol – breakdown in communication – unsatisfactory – discourtesy' featured. Still, better out than in.

Eventually he ran out of accusations and subsided, glaring at her. 'So what have you got to say for yourself?'

She explained, and saw the glare fade. At the end, he said, a little uncomfortably, 'Oh, I suppose, in the circumstances . . . perhaps I overreacted, Marjory, but you can understand why.'

'Of course, Donald. I'd have been livid myself.'

'So what are you going to do to find the officer concerned?' Bailey seized on the chance to redirect his indignation. 'It's quite intolerable! Disgraceful behaviour. Put him on a charge!'

'First catch your hare,' Fleming said ruefully. 'There's nothing I'd like better, but unless you can get authorization for me to apply red-hot needles under their fingernails, the paper isn't going to tell me and whoever's doing it isn't going to confess. It's a problem we've had before – a nice little earner for someone.'

'Harrumph!' Bailey said.

He was the only man she had ever heard utter that word,

usually to signal his reluctant acceptance of defeat. Fleming moved on.

'At least we now seem to have a clear line of inquiry. We'll need people, probably from the office where she worked, to confirm that Kingsley's right and do an official ID, of course, but it would hardly be surprising if Ingles bore her a grudge, particularly if she did in fact go off with the cash.

'We'll have records of what happened after his release, with luck might even pick him up for questioning today. I sent Kerr down to check it out. In fact, she may even have some info by now, if I can use your phone?'

They found Kerr for her. 'Tansy? Did you get anything on Ingles?'

Fleming listened with growing satisfaction. 'I see. Very, very interesting. Thanks.' She put down the receiver and Bailey looked at her expectantly.

'Well, you never know. This just might be one of the quickest wrap-ups on record. He's working for the Forestry Commission, renting a house in the forest up above the Queen's Way, less than a mile from where the body was found.'

'Excellent, excellent!' Bailey rubbed his hands together. 'Press conference later this afternoon, once we've made the arrest?'

'Hey, whoa!' Fleming protested. 'We may not be able to pick him up just like that. But if we get to him before any of this appears in the media, he'll still think we're assuming it's someone from Manchester and the safest thing to do is to carry on as normal and not arouse suspicion.'

'I certainly hope so. This is very good news, Marjory, very good indeed. I won't keep you, then. Well done.' He got up to escort her to the door. 'And it was young Kingsley who made the connection, was it? Smart lad – and working for his stripe, he tells me. Very promising young officer.'

She longed to point out that happening to have recognized the victim wasn't exactly a mark of professional expertise, but managed to smile and say, 'Absolutely,' then with her brain buzzing went back to her office.

They'd have to get in touch with the Forestry people, find out where Ingles would be working and send a team up there to bring him in. And Davina's family – they'd have to trace parents, siblings to let them know before they saw it on the news. That was the other priority, obviously. Then a warrant would need to be sworn out so they could go through Ingles's house . . .

But she mustn't forget to have her little talk with Greg Allan. If this was somehow going to be put down as another triumph for Kingsley – and she had a nasty feeling it was – she'd have to make sure that Allan remembered where his duty lay.

Susie Stevenson picked Josh up from his friend's house and hurried away, refusing the invitation to stay for coffee and admire Peter's mother's wonderful new kitchen, all gleaming Corian and exotic dark wood, which had undoubtedly cost more than she and Findlay together had earned over the past year.

The injustice of it all made her so angry she could feel the pressure building inside her head. And Findlay was all set to make things even worse! Raging at his stubborn stupidity, she'd come up with a plan – a long shot, certainly, but Susie always had great confidence in her power to get her own way when she put her mind to it.

She looked at Josh as he climbed into the Fiat hatchback. 'What on earth have you done to your hair? It's standing on end.'

'Don't know,' the child muttered.

'Here's a comb. Tidy it up. We've got to go and see somebody.'

Josh looked sulky. 'Aren't we going home?'

'After we've done this.'

'But I wanted to watch Tracy Beaker while I had my tea,' he protested, but it was no use.

'Well, you can't, that's all.' She started the engine.

'Where are we going, anyway?' he demanded as they set off in the opposite direction to the farm.

'We're going to see a man who's been really mean to Dad. You know Dad's dog, Moss, that he was so fond of? This man says he's going to have Moss put down. Isn't that terrible?'

Josh agreed politely, and his mother's voice sharpened. 'You know how fond you were of Moss?' she prompted.

'I wasn't, actually,' Josh said, with a child's brutal honesty. 'He didn't pay any attention to anyone except Dad.'

'Oh, nonsense, darling!' Susie laughed. 'You adored him! Don't you remember the fun you used to have, throwing the ball for him?'

'Not really.'

Susie clicked her tongue in exasperation. 'Josh, this is something you have to do for Dad. It would make him really happy to have Moss back, and he's no use to the other man because no one will buy him. He won't listen to Dad because they've quarrelled.

'But I used to know him quite well, a long time ago,' she gave a little giggle, 'and if he knows it's just that a little boy really misses his pet, and Moss isn't going to be going off winning trials again, I'm sure he'll be more reasonable. And Dad would be really pleased.

'You know how well you did, talking to Mrs Fleming—'

Josh's face darkened. 'That was horrible. And Dad said he was just going to be allowed to come home anyway.'

'Nonsense!' his mother said again, savagely this time. 'Your father is embarrassed about it, that's what *that*'s about.

'Now, all I'm asking you to do is tell Mr Murdoch how

much you miss Moss and how fond you are of him, and then say, "Please will you let me take him home with me?" really nicely and politely. For Dad!'

Josh didn't reply, slumping sullenly in his corner, and they drove most of the rest of the way in silence. As they turned into the narrow Drumbreck Road, Susie glanced in the mirror.

'You've got a dirty mark on your face, Josh. Here – lick this and wipe it off.' She handed back a tissue. 'And put away that sulky face. No one wants to do anything for a boy who looks all scowly and bad-tempered.'

She parked at the marina. She wasn't sure which was the Murdochs' house but at this time of day Niall was most likely to be at work. She asked a young man who was sorting out sailing tackle, and he directed her to an office at the side of the big storage shed.

Niall Murdoch was alone, frowning over some papers that looked like accounts; when he saw his visitors a slow, unpleasant smile spread across his face.

'Well, well, well! Sent in the heavy mob, has he? Or have you come to up the offer for that useless dog?'

It was with some difficulty that Susie managed to say coquettishly, 'Oh, Niall! What a way to greet me after all these years!'

Niall looked at her, derision in his eyes. 'I'm *so* sorry, Susie. I hadn't realized this was a social call. After all these years, I'm touched that a couple of smoochy dances at the Young Farmers' ball could have inspired you with a desire to renew the acquaintance.'

Susie's face flared. 'It – I didn't mean that. I just expected common courtesy.'

'Well, I think you've had that now. Can I revert to my question – have you come to up the offer?'

'I wish I could.' She was proud of her self-control. 'I know you've turned down the offer Findlay's made, and that really was the last penny we could raise. You know the foot-and-mouth simply wiped us out – you can imagine what it was like, being a farmer yourself.'

'Ah, but I had the sense to get out, didn't I?' He laughed. 'Poor old Fin – never the sharpest knife in the drawer.'

It was hard to believe that this sneering and unpleasant creature was the young man all the girls had fancied when they were young together. The first part of her plan had clearly failed; she could only try the second, though with a sinking heart.

'It was Josh who made me come, actually,' she said. The child, standing silent and unhappy at her side, gave her a startled look as she went on, 'I'm sure you realize that Moss is finished, professionally. You haven't been able to sell him as a working dog. But Moss was one of the family. Josh can hardly remember him not being around and he's been grieving for him ever since he had to be sold. And I thought that, even if you couldn't agree to it on a business basis, you wouldn't be cruel enough to kill a little boy's pet. He's no use to you, anyway.

'Go on, Josh.' She nudged the child.

'Please, Mr Murdoch, may I have Moss back?' he said without conviction.

Niall threw back his head and laughed. 'Dear, dear! Was this Fin's idea?'

'Of course not!' Susie was indignant.

'You would say that, wouldn't you? Well, whoever thought of it, it was bloody silly. You can go back and tell Findlay he knows my price. If he wants the dog, he'll have to find it – that's all. Tell him I'll be phoning to make the appointment with the vet.'

Then he bent down to the child. 'But I tell you what, Josh. If you like, you can go to the house over there, where Moss is,' he pointed, 'and say goodbye to him. Give him a nice big hug to show him how fond you are of him. But I warn you, he just about had my daughter's hand off when she tried to pat him.'

He roared with laughter at the look on Josh's face.

She wasn't going to budge him, after all. He was going to go back to Findlay and Findlay was going to plunge them into debt all over again. Susie felt real panic at the thought of it. She wanted to walk out, hurling insults at him, but she had to have one last try.

'Niall, I know what Findlay's able to pay would leave you out of pocket. But surely even two thousand pounds is better than nothing?'

He looked at her oddly. 'No, I don't think it is, really,' he said. 'Fortunately I'm in a position now where it doesn't matter so much. Findlay cheated me, and I'm going to see he pays me in full, one way or another. It's up to him.'

'But Niall—'

'Heaven knows,' he went on, interrupting her, 'I always had you down as a bit of an airhead, but I never realized you were dumb enough to think I'd fall for a pitch like this.

'And what on earth's happened to you? I remember you as moderately fit, but you've fairly let yourself go, haven't you?'

Susie felt physically sick with rage. 'Oh, did you fancy me? Now I always thought your eyes were too close together.'

It was childish and ineffectual, but it was all she could think of to say. She grabbed Josh's hand and stormed out, with Niall's laughter following her. The young man who had directed them earlier, on his way into the office, had to jump back to let them pass.

Back in the car Josh said, in a small voice, 'Do I – do I have to go and say goodbye to Moss?'

'Of course you don't. Don't be silly,' she snapped unfairly. 'And you're not to say a word to your father about this. Knowing what Mr Murdoch said would only upset him.'

★   ★   ★

It was five o'clock when the phone rang in Marjory Fleming's office with the unwelcome news that Keith Ingles wasn't at the location where he was supposed to be working. He wasn't at home either. He had fled.

10

'DI Fleming? You've been trying to contact me.'

Marjory Fleming glanced at her watch. It was six o'clock; she had first phoned with an urgent message for DCI Carter to contact her at half-past eleven this morning, and then again at two o'clock this afternoon.

'Oh yes,' she said coolly. 'I was anxious to brief you on developments at this end in the Natasha Wintour case.'

'I gather from Tucker that you're a bit more prepared now to accept my theory that it's domestic.' He sounded bored.

'Not exactly.' The man had a serious talent for irritating her. 'The situation's changed radically and I didn't want your team to waste time investigating a false trail. Or getting sued by Jeff Brewer for wrongful arrest.' She shouldn't have said that.

He didn't react. 'To be honest with you, we haven't been able to do much about it yet. We've a couple of Yardie gangs who seem hell-bent on mutual destruction and we've just had our fourth fatal shooting in a fortnight.'

My body count's higher than your body count? Oh, please! 'Then you'll be relieved to know that we think it's more likely to be our case than yours,' she said crisply. 'We've identified her as a local woman called Davina Watt. She went to Manchester and changed her name, but we suspect it's linked to a robbery with violence here some years ago. We're looking for confirmation but at the moment it looks as if the killing didn't take place in Manchester after all.'

'Fine, fine!' he said heartily. 'Good to know. Over to you, then.'

Fleming could readily appreciate his eagerness to wash his hands of it, but she had a job to do too. 'We would need to have someone talk to Brewer again and to the regulars in the bar in the light of this new information. If we could establish what happened to her after she left home here—'

She heard another phone ringing at his end. 'Excuse me,' he said, 'I'll have to take this call. I'll put you on hold.'

It was several minutes before he came back to her. 'I'm sorry. Something's come up. I'm going to have to go.

'We'll do our best for you, naturally, but I can't promise any very speedy action on your request. It may be hard for you to understand what it's like in a city like this, but we're fire-fighting crime at the moment and it seems to be taking hold. Liaise with Tucker – that would be best.'

The phone abruptly went dead. Trying very hard to be reasonable, Fleming put down the receiver at her end.

Of course she understood. The man was under a lot of pressure, obviously, and perhaps his voice had been weary rather than bored. He was right, she didn't know what it was like to be in a position like that, and since the killing wasn't on his patch, why should he make the priorities of the Galloway Constabulary his? It was his tone and his attitude that she found hard to take.

She had seen Davina Watt's broken body left in a hollow in the ground and lying on a mortuary slab. She was a woman who had died violently, and that was important too. Death in a quiet rural area was no less horrifying than death in the squalid streets of a city, even if Carter was afraid there would be another death tomorrow in a way that she wasn't.

They might, anyway, be better off working through Tucker. She'd liked the look of him, and he and Tam, amazingly, seemed to have developed a good rapport. If Tam had a chat with him they might get a better result.

Fleming looked at her watch again. She was going to be late tonight; there were patrols out looking for Ingles and others going round pubs and hotels with Davina's photo and she wanted to get at least some of the reports before she packed it in and went home.

She'd phoned Bill earlier to tell him what was happening; she rang him again now. He and the children had gone to see Janet and Angus, he said, so there would be no need for her to build in a visit. Angus had been quieter today but Bill was worried by Janet's obvious exhaustion.

Weren't they all? Marjory sighed. Working on a murder case might have its problems, but you could at least hope for a successful conclusion. In her parents' case, the only possible outcome was bleak indeed.

Tam would still be in the building. She'd asked him to familiarize himself with the Ingles case; if he wasn't committed to being home for supper they could discuss it at the Salutation over a pint and a sandwich. Or perhaps, if her resolution failed, one of their Scotch pies, guaranteed to give a nutritionist heart failure at ten paces.

Mirren Murdoch was eating the mushroom omelette her mother had made for her supper. She wasn't hungry, but eating it was easier than explaining why she didn't want to.

Mum was doing the usual mumsie bit, asking questions about what she'd been doing today and stuff, but Mirren had conversation-killing down to a fine art now; if you just said 'Yes,' 'No,' and 'Whatever,' it usually worked.

Mum had given up quicker than usual tonight and had started talking to HIM (she refused even to think of him as Dad) about the swear words someone had sprayed on the house. Mirren was on that person's side; anyone who hated

HIM couldn't be all bad. But Mum was saying the police had been and someone was going to be arrested. Pity it wasn't HIM.

Mirren had finished. They were still eating, but when she asked if she could go Mum sighed and said, 'Oh, all right, if you want.'

She went out and shut the door, marched on the spot for a moment or two, then stood listening. It was a habit of hers, the way she learned what was really going on. And sure enough, after a moment or two her mother started.

'Niall, I need to talk to you about that dog.' Jenna spoke in tones of exasperation. 'For God's sake, will you settle for what the man's offered you, or else if you're set on cutting off your nose to spite your face, give it away? What's the point of having it put down – you'll only be landed with a bill from the vet.'

'Hand it back to Stevenson – or his stupid wife – as a present, you mean, with a bow round its neck and a card saying, "Best wishes, Niall"? You're joking!'

'Not exactly. And don't sneer at me like that. There are plenty of charities that find homes for unwanted dogs.'

There was a pulse ticking at the corner of his eye. 'Stevenson fleeced me. He buys back the dog for less than half of what I paid for it, and I've been taken for a sucker. If you think he's going to go away smirking, you've got another think coming.

'He put me through it over that dog – could have caused me serious grief if I hadn't thought of a way round it – and he's not getting away with it. The way I see it, killing his dog is fair compensation for him making a fool of me in public.'

'You didn't need him to make a fool of you at the trials. You've been doing that unaided for years,' Jenna said spitefully. 'But you could just think for a moment about your daughter.

'I'm seriously worried about Mirren, Niall. She's besotted with Moss. I don't know what she'll do if she finds out you've killed it. Is your relationship with her not bad enough already? You're prepared to go ahead and break her heart?'

'Too right I am! It's about time she grew up. All this touchy-feely-veggie nonsense – and you're only encouraging it by pandering to her. Give her proper food and she'll eat it soon enough when she's hungry.

'And if you reckoned this was the way to persuade me to change my mind, you're not very bright, are you? It's had the opposite effect.'

Niall pushed back his chair angrily and stood up. 'The sooner that bloody animal gets the chop the better.'

She stared after him as he went out. The marriage was dead; she knew that. But was it rotting now, and spreading contamination?

As she heard the chair scrape across the floor, Mirren fled as silently as she could, her hand pressed to her mouth to stifle her anguished sobs.

She went down the dingy corridor to her mother's office, shut the door quietly behind her and switched on the computer. She knew what she had to do.

Tam expressed himself delighted to join his boss in the Salutation. Bunty, it seemed, was away staying with a sister in Glasgow, leaving Tam resentfully home alone.

'It's the livestock,' he said bitterly. 'With her away, it's like being in charge in a cat-and-dog home. I've had to miss my lunch break, going home to let them out.'

Bunty was famous for her tender heart, and the MacNee villa in Kirkluce was seldom without its complement of war-weary tomcats and stray dogs. 'How many have you got at the moment?'

'A three-legged mongrel, a puppy that doesn't know what a newspaper's for, a tom with stitches where he's had the chop and three females, one of them expecting.' He took a sup of his pint of Special. 'Last time I counted, that is. But then, I haven't been home since eight this morning.'

Marjory laughed. 'You'd miss them if they weren't there. Under that black leather jacket you're just a big tumphy.'

Tam glowered. 'A softie – me? Listen, if I wasn't feart for what Bunty would do to me I'd let the lot of them out to play in the traffic. She's left a list of what they all like to eat, and a stack of "healthy meals" for me. How come they get to eat what they want, and I'm to have "healthy meals"?' He said the words with loathing, then brightened up as the barman appeared with their pies and beans. 'Thanks, Donnie.'

'Right,' Fleming said, lifting her knife and fork. 'Tell me about the report on the robbery.'

'Three inches thick, for a start. My bum's numb from sitting all afternoon. But it's interesting, I will say.

'The prosecution case was that there'd been five thousand quid, give or take, with some cheques as well, put in the safe after the sponsored events. It was one of those old-fashioned efforts – they probably built the old club round it. Weighed a ton, with a couple of locks to open it. Not much kept there, usually, just the bar takings and a couple of silver cups.'

'So who held keys?'

'Duplicate set at the bank. The other set, somewhere on the bar premises, but on the Saturday they didn't open because of some posh gala do they were having in Newton Stewart that night, and it was closed then on Sundays. So Ingles as Hon. Treasurer put the money away on Saturday afternoon and kept the keys.

'Story was, he went back at around eight on the Sunday, let himself in, opened the safe and took the money, cleverly breaking a window to suggest an outside job.'

'And it couldn't have been?'

'Broke the window from the inside, didn't he?'

'Ah. Not an experienced villain.'

'You could say. Sad, really. He was just leaving when the cleaner arrived.'

Fleming raised her eyebrows. 'Kind of late, wasn't it? Her usual time?'

'I couldn't tell you, but no one picked up on it. Ingles probably didn't know the routine.

'In her witness statement she says he called, "Who's that?" and when she told him he said, "It's all right, Mrs Aitcheson, it's only me putting something in the safe." Then as she went to the cleaning cupboard he came bursting out holding something in his hand and assaulted her. Laid her out – lucky she survived.

'Used a marlinspike, apparently. What the hell's a marlinspike?'

'Don't ask me. Is it the sort of thing you'd use in the office of a yacht club?'

'More likely just leave it lying around, from the sound of it. Anyway, she survived to give ID evidence against him.'

'Corroboration?'

'The rest's circumstantial, but solid stuff. The keys were in his possession, and they found a couple of the cheques in a drawer in his house. Open and shut, really. And then he tried to get Davina to swear out an alibi for him and she testified against him instead.'

'Ah.' Fleming pounced. 'You could be just a wee thing peeved if the woman you'd done it for shopped you.'

'Particularly if she'd gone off with the goodies. Lack of recovery didn't do him any good when it came to the sentencing.'

'Right enough.' She sat back, frowning, and her empty plate caught her eye. She pulled a rueful face. 'Every time I eat one of these things I regret it afterwards.'

'Now that's a funny thing. I don't. I should have made it a double while I was at it.' Tam's glass was empty too. 'The other half?'

Marjory shook her head. 'I've to drive later and I've not finished this one.'

A few officers had come in now and were propping up the bar. There was a lot of banter as Tam waited for his pint, but rapt in thought she barely heard it.

When MacNee, with a last sally over his shoulder, came back, she said, 'So what's the scenario? Why does she come back here? She was scared enough to leave the locality and change her name – what possesses her to come back and see him?'

'Ah, there you have it – as Rabbie says, "*one point must still be greatly dark – The moving 'Why?' they do it.*" Unfinished business?'

'Or looking for a truce, so she could come back home?'

'Didn't sound as if she liked it much when she was here,' MacNee pointed out. 'Jon said she'd run through the existing talent, got herself a reputation – you'd think she'd have reckoned Manchester would give her a bit more scope.'

Fleming sat up suddenly. 'Hang about! Suppose she didn't. Suppose he got on her trail somehow, went down to Manchester, killed her there, then brought the body up here for disposal?'

'He'd think it wouldn't be found for years.' MacNee was impressed with the theory. 'You wouldn't guess you'd have such bad luck.'

She fished out a pad from her bag and began scribbling notes. 'I'll want his work records, car registration – might get something from CCTV. Dig out his mugshot – someone might have seen him in her locality.'

Then she stopped, and swore. 'So of course, that means involving Carter again, who thinks deaths that don't come in multiples don't count. We'll get stick for an unsolved murder while he sits on his backside doing nothing for us as long as he possibly can. Spelled it out when I spoke to him today.'

MacNee looked shocked. 'Dearie me, that wouldn't be you showing politically incorrect racial prejudice, would it?'

'Nothing to do with race,' she retorted defensively. 'He'd be a pompous, patronizing bugger if he was a direct descendant of William Wallace.'

'Now you see, me and Tommy Tucker are just like that.' MacNee held up smugly crossed fingers. 'Would you maybe like me to try some telephone diplomacy instead of you putting the heid on the man? As you say yourself, you catch more flies with honey than with vinegar.'

She gave him a withering look. 'Time I went back to work, *sergeant*. What about you?'

'Me, ma'am? Oh no, I have starving animals that need me. But you know where I am if anything breaks. I could be tired of their conversation by then.'

Shaking with impotent rage, Adrian McConnell went into the little sitting-room overlooking the bay, picked up his *Herald* and opened it with a crack, though with the red mist in front of his eyes he was unlikely to be able to read it for some time. The window was open; he could hear his daughter talking to her friends as they went down the steps to the road.

'So he goes, "When will you be back?" and I'm like, "Hello-o? You think I know?" and he goes, "Ten o'clock!"'

'Ten o'clock!' one of the others squealed. 'Is he out of the Ark, or what?'

'So I go, "I am so-o not going to do that!" and suddenly I'm thinking, ohmigod, he's going to ground me! And then you guys ring the bell and I'm like, I'm out of here!'

Peals of girlish laughter followed and their voices died away as they went off, trouble on the hoof.

Adrian found he was grinding his teeth, a bad habit his dentist had spoken to him about before. Kelly was getting completely out of hand and there was nothing he could do about it.

And Kim was no help – on the contrary. The row had started at the supper table: Kelly hadn't come in till almost two last night and he'd wanted to know what she was doing. All he got was the evasive, 'Stuff,' and when he tried to tell her she wasn't going out this evening until she answered, he got no support from his wife.

They'd both been round at some friends' for sundowners after the day's sailing; he'd no idea how much Kim had drunk but she'd certainly been knocking it back. And by the time she'd had a couple of glasses of wine over supper she was definitely the worse for wear. He'd pointedly taken water himself at the meal, which was a tactical error, since once Kim had laughed at him and opened a bottle, it left her with it all to herself, and once she started she wouldn't stop.

So when he'd confronted their daughter, Kim had made it all worse. 'You do look silly when you're cross, Adrian,' she had giggled. 'Doesn't he, kids? Just because he doesn't know how to have a good time doesn't mean we all have to be boring, does it, Kelly pet?'

Kelly shot a triumphant look at him, Jason a pitying one. 'We were just, like, mucking about,' she said airily. 'Didn't notice the time. How about you chill, Dad?'

He knew when he was on a loser. He subsided in silent fury until he had the child on her own, away from her mother, but then she had just walked out on him, shutting the door on what he was saying when her friends arrived, all of them looking, like Kelly, as if they were heading for a street corner to tout for trade.

The door slammed again and he looked out to see Jason leaping down the steps. His father had no idea what he was doing either. And if Gary wasn't safely upstairs asleep in his cot he'd probably be off to a toddlers' rave somewhere too.

Anger drained out of him and he could only feel sick with despair. Everything had gone so terribly, terribly wrong recently.

Kim's heavy drinking worried him – would he be able to get her back to more normal consumption when they went home? – but in a way Kelly's goings-on worried him even more. It was like a gathering boil, with foul matter accumulating until, sooner or later, it must burst.

He hadn't read a word of the article he was staring at concerning the latest idiocy of the Scottish Parliament. He put down the paper and got up. Kim was on her own, and if he was to get any sense out of her it had better be now before she had a chance to finish the bottle.

She was well through it already. When he went into the kitchen, she was still at the table with a glass in front of her. She patted the seat next to her invitingly.

'Come to keep me company, pet? 'Sboring through here all by my wee self.'

He pointedly went back to his own place at the other end of the table. 'Kim, we need to talk about Kelly. Seriously.'

His wife pouted. 'Kimmie doesn't want to.' She sloshed the last of the wine into another glass and pushed it towards him. 'Let's go through to the front room and make out on the sofa like we used to when we were kids. Better than the back of your car.' She giggled.

Kim always got amorous when she was drunk. It was beginning to put him off sex completely. He tried again.

'You're her mother – doesn't the prospect of a gymslip pregnancy worry you at all?' It worried the hell out of him: what would the Press say about a political candidate who couldn't bring up a teenage daughter with proper standards?

'Silly! She's been on the pill for ages.'

'On the pill? *What?*'

'Oh, you're just so *square*! They're all on it nowadays. They're not stupid – not like we were.'

He didn't like to be reminded of the reason for their own marriage. He scowled.

She had reached the belligerent stage. 'If I'd been as smart as Kelly, I wouldn't be married to a boring stuffed shirt who only gets excited about politics. I'd be with someone like Niall – oh, I know you look down on him because he works with the boats and you're a fancy "accountant",' she put mocking quotation marks round the word, 'but I tell you he's got it over you where it counts.'

Adrian froze. 'Wh-what?' he stammered stupidly.

'Oh, you may not want me but you can't complain if someone else does.' She smiled triumphantly.

There was water left in his glass from supper. He picked it up and threw it in his wife's face. She gasped with shock.

'Do you mean you're having an affair with Niall Murdoch?' he said very quietly.

The cold water, and her husband's face, white with burning eyes, sobered her to some degree. 'Well – sort of. Last year. But it didn't mean anything, not really.' She took refuge in tears.

'Niall.' He repeated the word through clenched teeth. 'And I suppose you've told everyone about this – it's all over Drumbreck?'

'No, no, of course not,' she hiccupped, but he knew she was lying.

He didn't say anything more. He walked out of the room, leaving Kim staring after him and dabbing ineffectually at her wet face with a paper napkin.

'Are we going down to the club tonight?' Gina Lafferty asked her husband as they sat at their glass table in the dining-room which overlooked the patio and the garden at the back of the house. Ronnie didn't like to eat in the kitchen; Gina suspected that it reminded him of his Glasgow tenement childhood when the bathroom was a shared lavvy on the stairs and personal hygiene, such as it was, centred on the kitchen sink.

He looked across at her with his frog's eyes. 'No. Haven't seen my lovely wife for a few days. Thought I'd have her all to myself tonight.'

There was something about the way he spoke that made her uneasy. But she was wrought up already; perhaps she was imagining it. 'Goodness!' she said, her tone light and mocking. 'Whatever will we find to say to each other?'

'Oh, I'm sure we'll find something,' he said blandly. 'I called in at the marina earlier – had a good chat with Brian Aitcheson. Now *there's* a man who's happy in his work.'

The protuberant eyes were fixed on her. 'That's nice.' Her voice sounded hollow, even to herself, and her mouth was dry.

'And then I had one with Niall.'

She took a sip of water. 'How is he?' What else could she say?

'Oh, surprisingly chipper, for someone who's owing me money. It's not often my creditors take it as casually as he seems to be doing. Must be something making him happy too.'

The chicken she was eating seemed to have turned to sawdust in her mouth. She had to drink some more water to swallow it. 'That's good!'

'Yes, isn't it! And later I bumped into Mrs Aitcheson as well – very chatty, she was.'

She wasn't going to play mouse to his tormenting cat. 'Oh, there was something I was going to tell you. That woman's nicked the little silver box you gave me for our anniversary. Can't I sack her? For all we need here, I could do the house myself. I haven't enough to do when you're in Glasgow.' She saw her mistake as soon as the words were out of her mouth.

'Satan finds mischief for idle hands, eh?' Ronnie's smile wasn't a pleasant one. 'You could have a point there. But Brian'll sort it out. He knows her little ways. I don't choose to have my wife scrubbing floors, and where would we find someone else with Mrs Aitcheson's – er – talents?'

It was intolerable. Gina looked at her watch and jumped up. 'Oh, it's time for *EastEnders* – can't miss that. Coming?'

She went out but Ronnie did not follow her. He sat looking into space, his froggy mouth turned down in a hard line.

He had found himself curiously calm. When the truck dropped him where he was to work, Keith Ingles had simply set down his tools and walked quietly away through the trees. No one would think anything of it when he didn't appear at noon; sometimes he joined the people working nearby to eat his sandwiches, sometimes he didn't.

Fortunately, he was only a couple of miles from home. If he could reach it before the alarm went up, he would at least have a chance of escape. He could collect his passport, driving licence and bank card; if luck was on his side he could withdraw cash before they stopped his bank account and be on the boat to Ireland from Stranraer before they alerted the ports. And if, as his co-worker had said, they were concentrating on the Manchester end, it might give him a couple of days' grace before they homed in on him. As, sooner or later, they most definitely would.

When he reached the cottage, it was as quiet and peaceful as when he left. The birds, busy about their parental duties, were almost silent, but there were butterflies flitting among the nettles. He paused for just a second to look round the place which had been for him such a blessed haven, then, grim-faced, went about his preparations.

He changed his working boots for proper walking ones and packed a rucksack with clothes and such food as would travel:

cheese, apples, biscuits, a bottle of water. He folded up a thin blanket too, and stuffed it in. He'd be sleeping rough tonight; it must be at least forty miles to Stranraer and he dared not attract attention by taking a bus or hitching. Even if they weren't looking for him now, they soon would be, and he must not leave a trail for them to follow.

Keith knew a lot more than once he had done about the underbelly of society. Prison gave you the sort of education a law degree couldn't match and he was confident that once in Ireland he could take a Ryanair flight to a new life wherever he chose and find work, no questions asked. Relations between the British police and the Garda meant there was bound to be a time-lag.

It made sense to follow the main road, but he had taken paths alongside wherever he could. He didn't allow his sense of urgency to translate itself into suspicious speed, walking with a steady, swinging stride, just another rambler out for a pleasant hike to anyone who saw him. He had covered the ground; Keith reckoned he must have done at least thirty miles by the time the sun went down.

As light lingered in what Scots call the gloaming, he had seen a filling-station where he got money from an ATM, bought crisps, a bottle of milk and a pasty heated up in the microwave and ate as he walked. It was almost dark now and he was very tired, so it was a relief to see a tumbledown shed, still half-roofed in a field by the side of the road. It would give him shelter from the chilly night wind which had sprung up and though it had rained a couple of times during the day, he'd had time to dry out and at least it wasn't raining at the moment. He climbed over the fence and went in.

It was dank and cold, the ground damp and covered with fallen stones, rank grass and nettles. His spirits sinking, he did his best to clear the most sheltered corner, then took off his waterproof jacket and spread it out. Shivering in his shirt sleeves, he piled on layers of clothes and wrapped the blanket round him, then, using his rucksack for a pillow, lay down and shut his eyes. It would be light not much after four, and he could get on his way then. With luck, he'd reach the ferry by lunchtime.

He couldn't sleep, though. His legs twitched and his mind seemed to twitch too, in spasms of fear. Cold and wretched, he huddled in his corner waiting for daybreak.

11

It was raining this morning, with that fine silvery rain which feels soft on your face but can soak you to the skin in minutes. Thick cloud was hanging low over the hills opposite the Mains of Craigie farmhouse and Marjory Fleming, huddled in her hooded waterproof jacket as she fed her hens, was feeling low too.

The hens didn't like it any more than she did, stumping round unhappily with wet feathers. There had been a major squabble at the feeding trough when Cherie, the alpha hen, launched an unprovoked attack on one of her meeker sisters, and even Tony, the rooster, wasn't strutting around as smugly as usual.

Marjory wasn't tempted to linger. She checked for eggs, then collected up her pail and plodded up through the orchard to the farmhouse. She didn't glance at the Stevensons' cottage but as she crossed the yard she saw Findlay on his way to one of the steadings, a young collie at his heels. She called a greeting, which he returned. Fin wasn't the problem.

He didn't look happy though. Well, Marjory probably wasn't looking too cheerful herself. She'd stayed at work late last night hoping for a breakthrough, but despite all the hours of police time nothing useful had emerged. Ingles had vanished, and though the usual alerts had gone out to ferries and airports, she was all too aware that if he just had the sense to lie low until the heat was off, they would have a problem. And his house, on the initial search, had given them no leads. It almost seemed to be deliberately impersonal: no diary, no address books, no letters, no photographs. The forensic team would be gutting the place later today: if Davina had been there, they'd find the evidence, but that wasn't a lot if the killer remained at large.

Showing Davina's photo around had turned up several people who'd known her years ago – which had at least produced the information that her parents were dead and she was an only child – but they still hadn't found anyone who had seen her recently. Still, formal identification had been done by a solicitor colleague of Ingles's and one of the secretaries from the Wigtown office, and the photo would appear in the *Scottish Sun* today so the calls would start. Perhaps there would even be one or two that were in some sense useful.

As she reached the back door Marjory could hear their own phone ringing and, kicking off her rubber boots in the mud-room, she hurried along to the kichen just as Bill, with a piece of toast in one hand, was putting the receiver down.

'That was Donald. He wants you to call him back.'

Marjory collapsed on to a chair. 'What now?'

'The Chief Constable disturbed Donald's breakfast and he seems to be working on the pay-it-forward principle. Apparently the *Scottish Sun* is favoured reading in the Menzies household and he was tweaking Donald's tail.'

'That's all I need.' Marjory's gloom deepened. 'There isn't any good news and today will mainly be a waiting game, whereas what Donald will want is Action. Lots of Action! Action even if it means chasing our tails until we're dizzy, just so we look as if we're doing something. Still, I suppose I'd better phone.'

'Good luck!' Bill said, finishing his toast and heading out to get on with the day that had started at six.

He was looking for binder twine in a drawer in the mud-room when she came looking for him. He turned round and saw the look on her face. 'Oh dear! What's he said now?'

'The man,' Marjory said tautly, 'is unbelievable. I had to tell him that until we had reports and preferably picked up Ingles, there wouldn't be much to announce at the Press briefing today. Then, like a fool, I told him that Carter in Manchester was dragging his feet, and he went ballistic. Tam and I, if you please, are to go right now to Manchester for a couple of days, while Bailey contacts his oppo and pulls strings, so that when we arrive we'll be about as welcome as a heavy cold. And meanwhile Greg Allan is to take charge of developments here. And we all know what that means.'

'Don't worry about this end anyway. We'll cope. It's a lot easier now I have Fin, and Cat's a dab hand with the frozen peas. Even Cammie's mastered the art of putting things in the oven.'

'Thanks, love. I'll have to phone Tam right away.'

She tried, but the line was engaged – probably Bunty checking on the livestock. She took the phone with her as she went upstairs to throw some clothes into a suitcase and change into her posh trouser suit. She didn't want to have people pointing and staring at the bits of straw when she reached the big city.

Laura Harvey was just stripping off her outer layers after taking Daisy for a damp morning run when her own phone rang.

'Hello? Oh, Jon – you're an early bird this morning.'

She was pleased; he hadn't contacted her since their sailing day and she had more or less decided that this had been a test which she, with her land-lubber tendencies, had failed.

'Just wanted to touch base before I went on duty. I don't know if you've spoken to Marjory, but there have been big developments in the murder case and there have been a couple of other local problems I've been involved in too, so it's going to be a busy spell. I didn't want you to think I'd forgotten about you.'

'No, no, of course not!' she protested, crossing her fingers.

'I'm not sure how I'll be placed over the next bit, but would it be very cheeky to ask if I could drop in when I have time, and pick your brains? I know you've given Marjory good advice in the past on motivation and so on, and it could be a great help to me.'

'Yes, I suppose so.' She was a little taken aback; this wasn't what she had expected him to say.

'Thanks. I'll have to go now. Our prime suspect's done a runner so we're going to be spending the day trying to catch up with him.'

'Good hunting!' Laura put the phone down, then, in response to increasingly frantic prancing, went to give the dog her breakfast with a furrowed brow.

She wasn't entirely comfortable. It was odd, surely, that one of Marjory's constables would want to consult her like that when presumably it was his boss who was in charge of the direction the case would take. She'd picked up vibes from both Marjory and Tam which suggested that neither of them was Jon Kingsley's biggest fan, but she'd chosen to ignore that. Now she couldn't help wondering if he was trying to steal a march on them, and if this was part of some sort of undermining operation, she wanted no part of it.

On an impulse, she picked up the phone again and dialled Tam's number. It rang for a long time and she was just on the point of hanging up, thinking he'd left for work, when Tam's harassed voice snapped, 'MacNee.'

She could hear a dog yapping in the background. 'Sorry, Tam, it's Laura. Sounds like a bad time. Shall I call again?'

His voice warmed immediately. 'No, no, Laura. It's just the bloody dog's eaten the cat's food and – but never mind. What can I do for you?'

'Would you be prepared to tell me what you think about Jon Kingsley?'

There was a silence at the other end. Then Tam said, 'Not without using words you shouldn't even know.'

'What's the problem?'

She knew Tam would be honest. Now he said, very fairly, 'He's a good officer. He's clever, and he's got a feel for it. He should have stayed in the big city, probably. He wants to get ahead quickly, and he's got every right to. It's just that in a place like this it doesn't all happen like that, and he's frustrated.

'So what he's doing is trying to show the rest of us up, Marjory and me in particular. If we look bad, he looks even better. He goes over Marjory's head to the Super, who's not savvy enough to realize what he's up to. And what's happening is that he's splitting the CID team. Marjory's going to have to tackle it soon; if we're not working well together in a big case like this, it's going to go pear-shaped. And it's not exactly difficult to work out who gets the blame.'

'Oh dear.' Laura's heart had been sinking at this recital. 'I don't quite know what to do. He was asking if he could consult me, but if he's trying to use me to get one up on Marjory, he can forget it. I'm her friend, first and foremost.'

'You're a wee stotter!' High praise, indeed, from Tam! 'Here – you don't think you could just tell him a load of rubbish and then we could watch him fall on his face and have a good laugh? Oh, maybe not – but it's a nice idea.'

Laura laughed. 'I can certainly make it clear that anything I tell him I'm going to pass on to Marjory, and tell her that he's asked me. That way it's out in the open.'

'Yes. But could you maybe not lead him on a wee bit, find out what he's planning, first?'

'We-e-ell, I'll think about it.'

She did think about it, a little sadly. She'd really fancied the bloke; when he'd kissed her goodbye on Sunday she'd been more than happy to respond. It was lowering to suspect that his chatting her up was only because he thought she might be useful to him later.

The headline 'Cops' Blunder' hit Keith Ingles with the force of a blow. He was buying a sandwich in a filling-station on the outskirts of Stranraer; when he saw it, with Davina's photo underneath, on the front page of one of the newspapers in the rack by the door, it was all he could do not to run blindly out of the place. But it was her photo, not his; it could have been worse, he told himself, and soon it will be. He forced himself to pick it up and pay for his purchases calmly, then, with the paper tucked under his arm, walked on until he saw a low wall in a side street where he could sit and read it.

There wasn't much in the report. But they had established who she was, which made it a foregone conclusion that they would be looking for him. They had his mugshot readily to hand, and they would have alerted the ports, particularly this, the nearest one. He had missed his chance.

Perhaps he should have gone sooner, when the nightmare began. But he had no reason to suppose the body would be found for another twenty years, more, even. And by then, who could have identified her? Leaving his work suddenly would have raised questions, which was the last thing he needed. Or not quite, as it turned out. The very last thing Keith needed was to be the focus of a nationwide manhunt.

He found another cash machine, and with a useful amount of money now in his wallet walked, more or less aimlessly, towards the ferry. And yes, he had been expecting them, but the sight of the two police cars at the entrance to the terminal brought on a lurch of panic. Again, there was the guilty urge to run; instead, he turned into a quieter street and headed back.

What was he to do now? He couldn't get anywhere quickly,

on foot. He needed either a boat or a car. It would be too obvious to try to hire a boat here, but if he hired a car then drove to the Lake District it wouldn't be difficult to get one from a marina there. He'd sailed across to Ireland more than once in his yacht club days.

He definitely couldn't hang about the place. Even if the papers didn't have a photo yet, the patrol cars would – and there was one, turning the corner ahead. He ducked swiftly into the nearest shop.

There were no other customers; the man behind the counter was happy to tell him where he could find a car hire firm and thanking him, Keith headed off. The police car had disappeared and he hadn't far to go, just a few hundred yards in the direction of the port. Looking towards it, Keith could see another police car joining the two already stationed there. He gave a twisted smile. They must think he was *very* stupid.

'There he is,' Jon Kingsley said suddenly. 'Look, that's him, isn't it?'

'Too right,' Allan said, unbuckling his seat-belt. 'He's nicked!'

'Hang on a minute.' Kingsley, at the wheel, put out a hand to restrain him. 'Let's trail him, see where he's going.'

The unmarked car nosed out. It wasn't difficult, in this busy street, to edge along, keeping Ingles in view. After about ten minutes he turned into a garage yard where there was a hire cars sign.

'He's realized we've got the ferry staked out.' Kingsley parked the car a little further along the road. 'But we've got him nicely now. Less chance of him making a run for it. And I tell you, if we can get him arrested and charged before Fleming and MacNee get back tomorrow, it'll show who does the real work in the CID, won't it?'

Allan's heavy face brightened. 'About time too. Good thinking. Let's go!'

The two men walked briskly down the street and into the little office where the girl behind the desk was asking questions indifferently as she filled in a form. The man, not small but slimly built, with greying fair hair, wearing a waterproof jacket, jeans and hiker's boots and with a rucksack at his feet, didn't turn his head to look at them as they came in.

'Keith Ingles?' Kingsley said. 'I am detaining you on suspicion of the murder of Davina Watts. You do not have to say anything . . .' He recited the caution.

Even now Ingles didn't turn. The girl was gaping and shocked, but he stood as if the words had turned him to stone.

Susie Stevenson kept eying the clock nervously as she emptied yet another of the boxes from the removal. Findlay always looked in to grab a mug of coffee and a sandwich around ten, and the bank hadn't rung with their answer to his application for a loan. Perhaps they would say no, but if not, and if Findlay got a chance to speak to them . . .

She bit her lip, looking from the clock to the phone as if will-power could persuade the loan manager to call. But there was Fin now!

He usually fended for himself but today Susie, willing the phone not to ring now, had his snack ready for him. No, she said, they hadn't phoned. She took an unusual interest, too, in what he was doing today – cleaning out the steading – and emphasizing how keen Bill must be to get on with buying the new stock. He didn't linger, and she saw him out with a sigh of relief.

It wasn't a moment too soon. She snatched the phone up at the first ring, afraid he might hear it as he crossed the yard. The loan manager announced himself and asked to speak to Mr Stevenson.

'I'm afraid he's out. But I take it this is about the loan he wanted to arrange through our joint account?'

The man hesitated. 'My assistant who took the message when I was out yesterday said I'd be dealing with Mr Stevenson. But since the account is in joint names, I think it will be all right to tell you that his application has been approved.'

'That's very kind. But in fact, we've decided not to go ahead with it just at the moment.'

The man was taken aback. 'Oh? I understood Mr Stevenson was very keen—'

'We've discussed it, naturally, and we've decided that we don't need a loan quite yet, but perhaps we may come back to you at some later date?'

'Of course. So I should simply destroy the application form?'

'I'm sorry if this has put you to extra trouble,' Susie said graciously, 'but that would be best. Thank you so much.'

She set down the receiver, then, with another nervous glance out of the window – Fin was so anxious that he might look in at any time to see if there was news – she picked it up again.

'Niall? Susie Stevenson.'

She hated the way he laughed, really hated it. 'Findlay come up with the money after all, has he?'

'No,' she said coldly. 'No, he hasn't. In fact, he's decided to withdraw his previous offer. You can do whatever you like with the dog.'

That surprised him. 'Really?'

'Yes, really.'

'Fine. Then I shall. You can tell him I've made an appointment at the vet's tomorrow.'

When Findlay came in at twelve o'clock for lunch, Susie met him with a very grave face.

'I'm so sorry, dear – two pieces of bad news. The bank said

no, and Niall rang to say that even if you do come up with the full amount, he's not interested. He's not prepared even to discuss it any more.'

Fleming and MacNee made the eleven o'clock train to Manchester with only minutes to spare. It was a good service; they would be in Manchester at around quarter past one and Tam had checked, with due circumspection, that they would at least be expected if not welcomed at the North Manchester Divisional HQ in Bootle Street in the afternoon, once they'd dropped off their cases at the nearby Thistle Hotel where rooms had been booked.

They'd done their moaning in the car on the way to Carlisle.

'I've had to phone Bunty's sister in Newton Stewart,' Tam grumbled. 'Her that's married to the bank manager, and treats me like sweepings off the street. Sticks in my throat to have to ask a favour, specially since it's not me wants the house full of the minging things. And she'll report back to Bunty that I've not done the dusting and there's too many bottles in the bin.'

'I've had to give up my week's egg money to get Cat to look after the hens. She used to do it for fun but she's got very grasping lately. Still, I drove a hard bargain – she can clean the henhouse at the weekend for that.'

Afterwards they had taken turns to cast aspersions on the character, acuity and general effectiveness of their superior officer so, with grievances thoroughly aired, they didn't talk much on the train. Fleming had her laptop and MacNee, who still felt that thought travelled from brain down his arm to pencil to paper, had a notepad, a small bundle of police notebooks and a couple of files. They were lucky enough to get a table to themselves and they worked fairly steadily, with only occasional glances at the countryside as they whirled past.

When the trolley came round at half-past twelve, Fleming

leaned back and stretched. 'I got quite a lot of useful admin done there. What about you?'

'Seven reports written,' MacNee said with some satisfaction. 'Here – there's something to be said for a day out now and again. Fancy a beer and a sandwich?'

As they settled to eat, Fleming turned to the topic of the case. 'We'll need everything absolutely cut and dried. They'll be irritated enough; we're not wanting to give them the chance to accuse us of wasting their time.

'First, Jeff Brewer. Will you take him or will I? We've not the time to do interviews together.'

'You better. You had him like a hen on a hot griddle last time, so at the sight of you he'll crack if he's anything new to tell you. Anyway,' he took a pull at his beer and winked at her, 'someone'll need to chat up the regulars and it's not fitting for a lady like you.'

'That was no lady, that was your boss. Still, you might as well. You're a more convincing bar-fly than I am.'

'Years of practice. So I'm trying to trace someone who can fill in some of the blanks, right? When she came to Manchester and why. Why she wanted to come back, if we get lucky.'

'Try to avoid that Preston woman. Davina clearly wasn't a friend of hers but she likes the limelight and you could waste a lot of time that way. See if there's someone around who might be one of her mates. I'll find out from Brewer if he knew of any girlfriends.'

'And Brewer's definitely off the hook? We're assuming Ingles is our man, right, and we flash his photo about too?'

'Right. We get through that asap and hope to be out of Carter's hair and on the ten o'clock train tomorrow. I'm not comfortable with Greg being i/c under the Super while I'm away.'

'If he is,' MacNee said darkly.

They were travelling now through the outskirts of the city.

Watching the spreading mass of streets and houses in drizzling rain, Fleming's mind was elsewhere. She had spoken to Allan about the rift that seemed to be opening up in the CID, but he was the hardest type of person to deal with: he apologized where that seemed to be called for, agreed with her points, expressed himself full of good resolutions and left. He would then go on in precisely the same way.

It was all making her very uneasy. She had long ago come to terms with being a woman in what was still resolutely a man's world; she could be as tough as any man when it came to it, but there was still a subtle male conspiracy which someone – Jon Kingsley, specifically – could tap into, encouraging a sort of jokey, patronizing condescension which was fatal to authority. Donald Bailey, though he would have given a shocked denial, was part of it too, and she was feeling very vulnerable just at the moment. And being away from the action at this stage was seriously bad news.

'Could you put me through to DI Fleming, please?'

'I'm sorry,' the telephonist at the Galloway Constabulary Headquarters said, 'I'm afraid she's away today. Should be back tomorrow afternoon.'

'Oh.' There was a pause. 'I've got something to tell her that came up in the forensic examination at Keith Ingles's cottage. We haven't completed it, but this is information we felt she should have as soon as possible. Who's in charge, then?'

'DS Allan. Shall I put you through to him instead? I know he's in the building.'

'That might be best. Thank you.'

The hotel room was very large, very bare and, with the triple-glazing on the windows, synthetically quiet. Marjory could hardly remember the last time she'd had a night away in a hotel on her own.

She opened the door to the neat en suite bathroom, with pale stone tiles and shiny taps. The towels, white and fluffy, were in two piles on a rack; she had almost forgotten that towels in bathrooms came like that, instead of crumpled on the floor where people hadn't picked them up. There were dinky little bottles too, with shower gel and body lotion. She could quite happily spend the entire afternoon in here.

Sadly, Tam would be waiting for her in the foyer and there wasn't even time for a quick shower. She patted the smooth cover of the huge double bed and cast an affectionate eye on the large TV you could watch from it. 'I'll be back,' she murmured as she went out.

When Fleming got out of the lift Tam was standing with his back to her talking to another man, of around his own height though more heavily built, and she recognized DS Tucker. That, at least, was good news. As the two men swung round with one movement to face her, she greeted him warmly and apologetically.

'I'm sorry we're treading on your toes like this. We have a Super who suffers from a sense of urgency. Your DCI can't be very happy at having us wished on to you.'

Tucker grinned. 'Oh, better today than yesterday, ma'am. We persuaded one of our little canaries to sing and the uniforms are out hoovering up most of our current problems right now. There'll be another one along in a minute but at least that's something wrapped up.'

'Congratulations. I wish we could say the same.' She turned to MacNee. 'I don't know if you've had time yet to fill Tommy in on what we're wanting to do?'

'Roughly.'

'He's sketched it out.'

They spoke together. Standing there side by side, they could, with a slight adjustment for girth, be Tweedledum and Tweedledee, Marjory thought with secret amusement as Tucker went on, 'There's a car and a driver been allocated, and I've seen to it that Brewer's expecting you – at his flat, OK? Then I thought I'd tag along with Tam – two heads better than one.'

'Good. I'd appreciate copies of interviews that have already been done too, if you could organize that. The other thing is car hire firms. Davina would have needed a car and we've someone checking out Carlisle, just in case she started out by train, but could someone run a check to see if she hired it here? Probably under her own name since we know she didn't have documentation as Natasha. All right? Thanks. Shall we go, then?'

'Oh, I've arranged for you to see DCI Carter first, ma'am. I know you've spoken on the phone and I thought you'd want to say hello.'

'It'd be rude not to,' MacNee added.

A sudden suspicion crossed Fleming's mind, especially as the two men, looking like superannuated schoolboys, were regarding her with identically bland and innocent expressions.

'That's good,' she said with all the enthusiasm she could muster, given that she would have preferred being told they were popping into the alligator pond at Manchester Zoo so that she could extend the hand of friendship to its inmates. 'He's expecting us now, is he?'

They were following her to the door when her mobile rang. As she fetched it out of her shoulder bag they withdrew to a polite distance, though they were inevitably within earshot of her side of the conversation.

'Yes? No, really? That's excellent news. Thanks for getting it to me at once, Greg. Congratulations!' She was getting a lot of practice in feigning enthusiasm today; she'd be quite good at it shortly.

She hadn't expected her new talent to be in demand again quite so quickly. Allan was still talking, giving her the news from the forensic team.

'Do they really think so? That's an amazing breakthrough, if they're right. We'll have to wait for official confirmation, of course, but that may just tie it up.

'And of course you'll ask Ingles – yes, yes, of course. You'd better go then. Thanks.'

Switching off the phone, Fleming rejoined the others. 'That's good news. They picked up Ingles in Stranraer this morning. And the forensic team have found what they're pretty sure are bloodstains on a tarpaulin at the back of a shed by Ingles's cottage.'

'Mmm.' Tam didn't feel obliged to sound upbeat. 'Who brought him in?' he asked, then, looking at his boss's face, added, 'Don't tell me.'

She refused to be drawn. 'Yes, Jon and Greg have done a good job on this, and he tells me they have everything under control. He was just hurrying off to question Ingles.' She smiled ruefully at Tucker. 'Makes all this down here a bit redundant, from the sound of it. I hope we won't waste too much of your time.'

Fleming led the way out of the hotel. From her personal point of view, it could hardly be worse; by the time she got back, Ingles would have been charged and her role in the case would be reduced to rubber-stamping. It wouldn't do her any good, just at a time when she was feeling her authority so shaky. It was hard to decide whether what she would most like to do to Donald Bailey would involve boiling oil or red-hot pincers.

DCI Chris Carter glanced at his watch and frowned. His time was precious and there were about twenty-five things he'd rather do than donate ten minutes of it to an old battle-axe with heather in her hair who'd stooped to using coercion from above when he wouldn't twitch into line. His Super had more years of service than he did and in Carter's opinion held the job for that reason rather than on merit – as if seniority made a fool anything other than an old fool. He had been delighted to play Handsome Harry in response to the Scottish Super's request, and ordering Carter to comply was the icing on the cake.

Big Marge, they called the woman, apparently, which told you all you needed to know. Tucker had been unusually silent about her, only rolling his eyes and saying she was 'quite a lady'. But he'd been determined that Carter should meet her and not leave him to cope with her on his own.

'The Super said we'd to show them every courtesy,' he'd pointed out. 'He wouldn't be pleased if she complained.'

This unusual attention to official decrees suggested that Tucker was keen to spread the pain around. He'd pay him back for that later, Carter vowed as the knock came on the door and he got up from his desk, bracing himself.

The woman who came in was totally unexpected. She was tall, certainly, and not slight, but well-proportioned. You wouldn't call her pretty, or even handsome, exactly, but she had the sort of face you could enjoy looking at, intelligent, with a humorous mouth and very clear hazel eyes. She was wearing a pale grey trouser suit which was at least as well-cut as the suit he'd bought for best from Austin Reed. She was also some years younger than he was.

Not only that, but she began by saying sorry.

'DCI Carter? Marjory Fleming – Marjory. I can't apologize enough for the situation you've been bounced into. I'm deeply embarrassed. All I can say in excuse is that it was my Super's initiative: I did my best, but there's no stopping him when he gets the bit between his teeth.'

She had a pleasant, low-pitched voice too, with a soft Scottish accent. What could he do, faced with such underhand tactics? 'Not at all – our pleasure,' he managed. 'Come and sit down.'

He led the way to seats round a coffee table in one corner of the room. Tucker and MacNee had followed in on her heels – looking, he suddenly realized, expectant. Tucker must have known perfectly well that he was giving a misleading impression of the woman; was this a set-up? The demure expression of the two men was all the evidence he needed.

He could do charming too. 'Good to meet you, Marjory. Look, I'm uncomfortably aware I've sounded a bit short on the phone. It's no excuse, but we've been under pressure lately. Anyway, I'm sorry.'

Fleming met him more than half-way. 'I'm sure I've been extremely annoying,' she acknowledged, with almost cloying sweetness. 'Let's admit we both have despicable character faults and forget it.'

She had a very warm, attractive smile. He smiled back. 'Forgotten. So what are we to do for you?'

'This is the most embarrassing part. I've just had a call to say our chief suspect has been detained and we may even have the evidence to charge him. I'm horribly afraid we're taking up your time needlessly, but since we're here anyway we'll go on with the programme Tommy has set up, just to tie up the loose ends, and then with any luck you'll get rid of us.

'My only concern is that it could be possible that instead of the woman travelling to Scotland, our man may have come and killed her here, which would of course change the emphasis. But we may be able to establish that one way or the other in the next few days.'

'Right.' He digested that; he'd mentally dropped the murder from his caseload. 'On the balance of probabilities . . . ?'

Fleming made a see-sawing motion with her hand. 'You never know, we might even pick up something conclusive today. I'll keep you informed.

'But you're a busy man.' She got to her feet and the men

rose too. 'Tommy tells me you've just had a good result. Congratulations!'

Carter ran his hand through his hair. 'Hopefully. Still a lot to tie up, of course.'

'We won't take up any more of your time. Thanks for your help.'

She held out her hand. He took it, saying with a glance out of the corner of his eye at Tucker, 'Good luck with your inquiries. I've enjoyed meeting you. I'll make a point of seeing you again before you go.'

There was no mistaking the look of disappointment on the sergeants' faces. In a spirit of pure mischief Carter said, 'Had a bet on, did you?'

Tucker and MacNee looked at each other in consternation, stammering denials. Fleming burst out laughing.

'You spotted it too! They're so bloody obvious, aren't they? Sorry to disappoint you, gentlemen, but your cocks won't fight. And some of us have work to do, once Tweedledum and Tweedledee have stopped playing silly buggers.'

She swept out, the two sergeants following sheepishly in her wake. Still smiling, Carter went back to his desk.

12

The flat Jeff Brewer had shared with Davina, or Natasha as he still called her, was a one-bedroom box in a twenty-year-old block. The furniture was cheap, chain-store stuff and the place showed signs of recent neglect, with dirty mugs and plates, empty crisp packets and full ashtrays littering the smeared and dusty surfaces. The vase of expensive-looking silk flowers in one corner, the only feminine touch, was out of keeping with the cheaply framed Manchester City posters on the walls. The woman had lived here for well over a year; did this lack of input suggest, Fleming wondered, that she only ever saw herself as passing through?

Brewer himself, in jeans and a beige V-necked T-shirt, was looking better than when she had last seen him though he was still pale, with dark circles under his eyes. He was also pitiably nervous and Fleming could see his Adam's apple bobbing up and down as he showed her in and asked her to sit down.

At least she could set his mind at rest. 'Jeff, the first thing I have to tell you is that someone has been detained in Scotland on suspicion of murdering your girlfriend.'

He stared at her for a long moment as if she had spoken to him in a foreign language. 'You – you haven't come to take me in? Who is it?'

'I can't tell you that at the moment. But I can explain that the reason I've come is to ask for any help you can give us.'

Jeff burst into tears. He was very young – probably not much more than twenty-five or six – and Fleming waited sympathetically until he gulped, 'Sorry – stupid. Just – such a relief.'

'Of course. Now, I'm very short of time. I'm hoping you can offer me some short cuts.

'First off, is there anything more you've remembered, anything that would give us some idea of what Natasha did before she got together with you, or after she left?'

But he had nothing to add to the story Fleming had heard already. The woman hadn't wanted to talk about her past and he hadn't been interested.

'Did she say anything about going? Leave a note?'

He shook his head. 'Only knew she'd gone when I saw she'd taken a suitcase and clothes and things were missing.'

If she'd packed a suitcase, it definitely suggested that she'd gone to meet Ingles, not the other way round. That would be good news for DCI Carter.

'Has she left anything behind?'

'Oh God, yes, most of her gear. I guess she took sort of what would do for a few days. You want to see?'

Fleming followed him through to the bedroom. It had a grubby cream carpet and a divan bed with a fake leather headboard. The only other furniture was bedside tables and a couple of chairs; there were built-in wardrobes down one side with a section in the middle acting as a dressing-table.

On it was a muddle of bottles and jars, and sticky rings which showed where others had once stood. Fleming's eyebrows rose as she examined them. You didn't buy large bottles of Patou's Joy – one of the world's most expensive perfumes – on a barmaid's wages, and the rest of the cosmetics also came from the most expensive ranges.

It was the same story when she opened the wardrobe: good designer labels were mixed in with Top Shop and Florence and Fred cheap 'n' cheerful stuff. There were empty clothes hangers too, but one hanger still held an Armani jacket – proof positive, surely, that Davina/Natasha had intended to return. What woman would abandon an Armani jacket?

She opened the drawer below the dressing-table which held underwear – La Perla as well as standard M&S knickers. It didn't look as if she had taken a lot with her – enough, perhaps, for a week or a long weekend, as Jeff had said. She shifted them with her hand and noticed, on the bottom, a page from a newspaper folded so that it showed a small item, circled in red ink.

Fleming pointed. 'Do you know what this is?'

Brewer peered over her shoulder. 'No. She wasn't much for reading newspapers, Natasha.'

'Did she get many letters? Did someone send her this?'

'Never got any letters since she moved in, far as I know.'

Looking closer, Fleming saw with interest that it was a page torn from the *Galloway Globe*, her own local paper. It dated from last October and the encircled article was headed 'Rogue lawyer freed': it gave the briefest of accounts of the robbery and assault at the Yacht Club but beyond that said only that Keith Ingles had been released on licence. Had Davina asked someone to warn her when he came out of prison, someone who at the time at least, had known where she was?

'Have you touched this?' she asked, and when he said no, dug in her shoulder bag for one of the plastic evidence bags she always carried, and a pair of tweezers. She picked it up carefully, tucked it in and put it away.

'Does she have any papers anywhere? Passport – that sort of thing?'

He shook his head. 'Never saw any.'

'There was nothing at all on her when we found her. Presumably she had a handbag, but we haven't located it. Would you know what it looked like?'

Wordlessly he indicated a shelf at the top of the wardrobe where there were more than a dozen bags of varying size and colour including some even Marjory recognized as seriously expensive. 'She changed bags all the time. I wouldn't know what's missing.'

The only lead he could give her was the name of one of the other barmaids. 'Natasha and Jax used to go for a girls' night out together every week. Maybe Natasha talked to her, like girls do.'

'Will she be in the bar today? My sergeant's there now.'

'No. Day off. But I can give you her mobile number – can't remember the address but I don't think it's far from here.'

Fleming scribbled it down. 'Are you at work yourself to-day?'

'No. Took the week off – just in case.'

She smiled. 'So at least you have the rest of the week to relax.'

As if the word were a trigger, the young man's shoulders sagged. 'I suppose so,' he said dully. 'I just feel shattered. Can't take it in, know what I mean? It's kind of like some sort of weird dream, like she might come walking in any minute. But . . .' He hesitated. 'What's going to happen – to her, I mean?'

'You would like us to notify you when the body's to be released? We have no record of next-of-kin.'

'Yes. Yes, I would.' His eyes had filled again. 'I wouldn't want her to be – you know – just left there. You see, I really loved her. Whoever she is, whatever she's done.'

From the sound of things, he was a lot more than she deserved. 'We'll do that, then,' Fleming said gently. 'There's just one more thing. Can you think of anything that might have prompted her suddenly to do this?'

He didn't say anything for a moment, and when he did speak it was as if the admission was physically painful. 'Yes, suppose I do, really. I just didn't want to admit it, even to myself.

'You see, my gran left me a bit of money. Not a lot, just a few thousands. But Natasha wanted to do things – expensive things – like we took a holiday cruise in the Caribbean, and another time we went to Bali. And, well, the money was running out.'

'And her clothes and so on didn't come cheap either.' Fleming felt very sorry for him.

'Oh no, she paid for all that sort of stuff out of her wages,' he said naively. 'But when I told her we couldn't go on living that way any more, she went sort of cold and angry, like it was my fault.'

As Fleming left, he said, 'I know she made a fool of me. But you know what? I'd do it all over again, even now.'

If ever there was a woman asking to get herself murdered, it was Davina/Natasha. But it wasn't this poor innocent who had done it.

And the man who, it seemed, had? As she went down the stairs, Fleming glanced at her watch. They'd be questioning him now – Allan and, no doubt, Kingsley. She regretted bitterly that she could not be there for the crucial six hours of questioning before they had to charge or release him.

She knew what Allan would want. Allan would want a confession, a nice neat confession followed by a guilty plea. That was what they all wanted, after all, but Fleming liked to hear what they had to say first, even if she then with painstaking ruthlessness tore the story apart until they cracked and admitted it didn't stand up. Allan didn't care, just so long as they signed at the foot of the page.

She was never sure about his methods either. Since the advent of meticulously recorded interviews, you couldn't use a rubber hosepipe on your suspects, but it was surprising what pressure a powerful and aggressive man could bring to bear in the confines of an interview room. The point sometimes came when a man would put his name to anything, just to get the questioning to stop. And she didn't trust Kingsley to restrain him.

Jon had worked closely with her, but somehow he had never wholly accepted her principles. Law courts might be purely and simply about proof: on the basis of the evidence presented, you were guilty or not guilty, though she had always believed the verdicts of 'Proven' or 'Not Proven' gave a more accurate picture of the process. As a police officer, you could see it as your job simply to find evidence that would satisfy a court, but if you didn't also believe it was to find out the truth and deliver justice as best you could, sooner or later grave injustice would be done. Kingsley believed in the quick fix.

Fleming had little doubt that Ingles was guilty, but she wanted even that small doubt removed and she was far from sure that Allan's questioning would do it. But he'd been on his way to the interview room when she spoke to him and there was nothing she could do about it.

Oh yes there was! She got out her mobile and scrolled to the Kirkluce HQ number. 'Get me DC Tansy Kerr. As a matter of urgency.'

Keith Ingles was waiting in the interview room, sitting at the table with his head bent over his clasped hands. He looked up as the two officers came in, giving them a veiled look from hooded blue eyes. He had an outdoor complexion, weather-beaten rather than tanned, and there were deep lines about his mouth. With his greying hair he looked considerably older than forty-three, the age given on the charge sheet.

Jon Kingsley went to fiddle with the recording machinery while Greg Allan sat down on one of the two chairs opposite, leaning back and crossing his legs in a pantomime of assurance.

'Well, well, well,' he drawled, 'some old lags just can't keep away, can they? Looking forward to meeting up with the boys again?'

Ingles lowered his head again, saying nothing, then jumped in shock as Allan brought both hands flat down on the table with his full force.

'I asked you a question!' he roared. 'When I ask you a question, you answer! Got that? Now, when I ask you a question, what do you do?'

'I have the right to remain silent . . .' The response hung in the air, but the man who could have said it had done time and had learned the futility of that sort of response. Ingles licked his lips. 'Answer.' He had a slight lisp, a sort of thickening of the 's' sound.

' "Answer, *sarge*." '

The old bully's trick. 'Answer, sarge.'

'That's better. Now, what was the question again? Oh yes, looking forward to another spell inside?'

'No . . . no, sarge.'

Allan leaned back again, beaming. 'Now, that's what I like to see. Co-operation. DC Kingsley likes that too, don't you, Jon?'

'Yes – *sarge!*' Kingsley said cheekily and they both laughed.

'Right.' Allan turned back to Ingles. 'Now. We're just going to turn on the tapes and do the formalities. Then you're going to tell us about how you murdered Davina Watt.'

Struggling for composure, Ingles said, 'Would it make any difference if I said I didn't?'

Allan pulled a face. 'Means it would all take longer, that's all. Waste of everyone's time. Give us a confession and we can be out of here in half an hour. You'd like that, wouldn't you?'

There was no reply from Ingles, and Allan raised his voice. 'I said, wouldn't you?'

'Yes.'

'Yes what?'

'Yes, sarge.'

'That's better. OK, Jon, get us started.'

Kingsley recited time and names, adding that the subject

had been cautioned and informed of his rights, and Allan began.

'Keith Ingles has stated his intention of making a confession.'

Ingles sat up in his chair. 'I didn't!' he protested. 'I said no such thing.'

Very coolly, Kingsley said, 'You expressed your wish to do it and be finished.'

'I – I didn't! You asked me – I can't remember exactly what you asked me.'

'DS Allan asked you if you wanted to make a confession and you agreed. Do you mean you now wish to change your mind?'

'Yes – no – I mean, I never said that.' Sweat was beginning to appear on Ingles's forehead.

'Sweating already!' Allan said with marked enjoyment. 'You're going to have to do better than that. It usually takes a lot longer to break someone down. So let's cut the cackle. How did you kill her?'

Ingles shut his eyes and drew a deep breath, then another. Allan gave Kingsley a hopeful glance and they waited in silence. But when the man spoke again, it wasn't what they were looking for.

He seemed to have pulled himself together. 'I wish to state that I did not at any time suggest that I wished to make a confession. I am innocent, and I am now aware that these officers are trying to coerce me into making a false confession.'

Kingsley stiffened. Allan's doughy face turned bright red. 'Are you accusing us—?' he began, but Kingsley cut in.

'There must have been some sort of misunderstanding. DS Allan and I were both of the opinion that you had expressed your intention of making a confession. However, we are applying no coercion and the last thing any of us wants is a false statement.

'But it may help you to decide that truth is in your best interests if I tell you that there is forensic evidence proving your guilt.'

'I didn't kill her.'

'Oh no?' Allan sneered. 'So how come her blood's been found on a tarpaulin at your house? And that won't be all, believe me, once these boys get going. But for starters, maybe you'd like to explain how it got there? She cut her knee, maybe, so you wrapped her up in a tarpaulin to make it better? Tell that to the jury – they always like a bit of a laugh.

'Come on, Ingles, you're wasting my time.'

Kingsley leaned across the table. 'Shall I tell you what happened? She did the dirty on you over the money you stole from the Yacht Club. Then she turns up again, wanting more. You've still got quite a bit of cash tucked away somewhere, haven't you – you must have! You were a solicitor, you'd a house, a car.

'What did she do, Keith? Did she come wheedling round you, sweet-talking you, thinking you'd fall for it all over again? But she'd got you wrong, hadn't she? You hated her, because she wouldn't lie for you when you'd done it all for her. Can't say I blame you. It's a natural reaction.

'You've been here before, Keith. You know the score. You didn't accept the evidence the last time, and it did you no good, did it? We've got an open-and-shut case here. Have a look at the tariff. Probably you didn't even mean to kill her, it was an accident, and with the reduction you'd get for an immediate plea it could mean you'd be out in four years – three, even.'

Still Ingles did not speak.

'Cat got your tongue?' jeered Allan. 'Can't find anything to say? Too hard to explain away, just like last time? Some people never learn!'

'I can explain.' Instead of being worn down, Ingles was

gaining in confidence. 'But there is no point in talking to you. I'll save it until I can make a statement through my lawyer.'

The officers' frustration was evident. Kingsley looked coldly furious and Allan's face darkened in temper. 'You'll talk,' he blustered. 'Oh, believe me, you'll talk.'

'We've a long time left.' Kingsley's voice was tightly controlled. 'You'd be surprised how difficult it is to stay silent all that time, knowing that at the end of it you're going to be charged. As you will be.'

After three-quarters of an hour, in which Allan and Kingsley between them had bullied, reasoned and even sat in silence themselves, Ingles had said not another word. At last, with a jerk of his head to his subordinate, Allan rose and left. As Kingsley joined him, he instructed PC Jack, waiting outside with an expression of lugubrious resignation, to keep an eye on the suspect.

'Not working, is it?' Allan said in frustration. 'So where do we go from here?' He looked hopefully at Kingsley. Jon didn't like it when things didn't go his way; maybe he could come up with something.

'Stubborn bastard!' Kingsley's annoyance was obvious. 'Not much point in waiting another couple of hours like this – I've better things to do.'

'You reckon we should charge him anyway? Haven't got much to put in a report. And then that accusation about forced confession – we just have to stick to it that he said he wanted to confess.'

'Of course he did.' Kingsley didn't hesitate. 'Changed his mind, clammed up.'

'Right, right!' Allan was saying, when DC Tansy Kerr and PC Sandy Langlands appeared in the corridor.

'Hey, lads! Having a breather? Has he told his uncle Greg nicely what a bad boy he's been?'

Allan looked at Kerr sourly. 'He's in there, thinking about it. What are you two wanting?'

'I'm to take over for a bit. Boss's orders. She wants me to have a wee chat with him.'

'And I'm telling you, there's no need for that.' Allan was outraged. 'We've talked to him already, he's denied it, and he's decided he's not saying anything till he's got his brief. I'm in charge here – I'll speak to Marjory later.'

'I've had my orders.' Kerr wasn't giving an inch. 'Anyway, is there any reason why not?'

She could tell what he was thinking: *because you might succeed when we had failed.* Allan turned anxiously to Kingsley for backing. 'Jon?'

Kingsley shrugged. 'You never know, Greg, the woman's touch! I'll come in and support you, Tansy.'

Allan gasped in outrage at this shameless determination to be on the winning side, but Kerr was having none of it. 'No, no, Jon, it's all right. The boss suggested I took in Sandy to do his hand-patting act. See what a bit of sweet-talking can do.'

Langlands grinned, and they went into the interview room, leaving the other two outside.

'Well, thanks a lot for backing me up!' Allan snarled and stalked off down the corridor without waiting to see if Kingsley had followed.

Jax Jones was something else. She had agreed warily to a visit and Fleming found a taxi to take her to a run-down terrace in the Northern Quarter of the city.

Jax was a skinny bottle blonde with her hair tied on top of her head in what looked like a chimney sweep's brush. She was wearing turquoise leggings and a yellow crop-top which exposed the tattoo of a pink rose on her hip. She was made up like a teenager, with green glitter on her eyelids and fingernails, but Fleming guessed she'd be lucky to see thirty again. She was chewing gum, and her accent was so strong that it took Fleming a minute or two of saying, 'Sorry?' before she got her ear in enough to understand what the woman was saying.

Jax led her upstairs – 'All bedsits, innit?' – to a room where the bed in one corner was almost completely covered with soft toys of lurid hue and indeterminate species. There was a sagging curtain across another corner, a portable TV and a floor cushion as well as a chair covered in a purple throw.

'You better sit there, I s'pose.' Jax indicated the chair and curled herself up on the cushion, chewing rhythmically. 'Watcha want, then?'

'Jeff Brewer tells me that you and Natasha Wintour used to have a girls' night out once a week?'

'Believed that, did he? Well, that's a laugh!'

Fleming blinked. 'You didn't?'

'Nah! Used to buy me a drink, then I'd do my thing and she'd do hers, no questions asked.'

'Was she on the game?' Fleming asked bluntly, leaving aside the question of what Jax herself did in her spare time.

'Nah!' she said again. 'She'd a better scam going – chose some bloke from the bar, didn't she, then he'd show her a good time and give her "presents". Nice work if you can get it, right?'

Reluctant to be drawn into discussion of the finer points of what did, or did not, constitute being on the game, Fleming moved on. 'Was this usually the same man, or a series of men?'

'Same man, for a bit. 'S what I mean, see? Always looking for some rich punter to take her on, but never stopped putting it about, in case she missed a better one. Then they'd twig and we wouldn't see them in the bar again in a hurry. So she'd have to move on to another one. Told her once, didn't I? "You watch it, my girl, stick to one while you still got your looks." Don't last long, do they?'

Jax pulled a rueful face and Fleming realized she was older than she had thought, possibly nearer forty than thirty-five.

'Did she ever tell you how she came to be in Manchester?'

'Not really. Oh, said she'd been living with some old geezer but he threw her out – up to her old tricks, I'd reckon.'

'And she never told you she was going away?'

Jax looked down, picking at a chipped nail. 'We-ell, couldn't say it was a surprise, know what I mean? Not with Jeff always on about money, and her looking at him like he was dirt. Thought she'd just do a bunk, if you want to know, minute she got a better offer.

'But here – what happened to her? You hear all sorts. Done you a favour, talking to you, haven't I, so I want to know. Was it one of them in the bar did it? Got a right to know if I'm safe.'

She sounded truculent, but Fleming recognized the aggression of fear.

'No, I think you're all right. I can tell you that someone in Scotland has been detained on suspicion of her murder.'

'What's that, when it's at home?'

Resorting to TV speak was the best chance of communication. 'Our prime suspect's in custody.'

'Oh. Well, that's all right, then. Just never know, do you?' She digested that. 'So – a Scottie, was she? Sounded like you, any road. What was her name?'

'You knew it wasn't Natasha?'

'Do us a favour – Natasha, her? And Wintour – well, told me, didn't she? Some fashion woman.'

'Anna Wintour?'

'Could of been. Didn't like her own name, whatever it was.'

'Davina Watt.'

Jax sniggered. 'Yeah, well, not quite Natasha Wintour, was it?'

No, it wasn't. As Fleming took a taxi back to the Cosmo bar, she thought about Davina Watt's aspirations. She'd read herself somewhere about Anna Wintour, the editor of American *Vogue*, so icy and elegant that she was known to the media as 'Nuclear' Wintour. An aptly chosen name for Davina, who had created devastation in her own small world.

'That's that Rab at the door,' Cath Dunsire's mother said without enthusiasm as she came back into the sitting-room where she and her daughter, just back from work, were having a mug of tea.

The blood drained from Cath's face. 'Fine,' she said, with marked reluctance. 'I'd better go and speak to him.'

Jess Dunsire looked at her in surprise. 'Here – what's wrong, pet? Is there a problem? Your dad's out the back – I could get him to tell him to go away.'

'No, I've got to speak to him.' Cath went out, but Jess did not sit down, looking at the closed door and listening with some concern. Just lately they'd been getting really worried. Rab McLeish had always been a bit of a problem and he was in with a bad crowd too. Cath was a good girl and she deserved better than that.

Jess could hear the sound of voices, but not what they were saying: Cath's quiet voice, doing most of the talking, then Rab's, loud and getting louder. Then he was all but shouting, and her hand was on the door-handle ready to rush out and protect her child, when she heard the front door close and Cath came back into the room, looking white and wretched.

Immediately, the bell began ringing and there was a pounding on the closed door. 'Ignore it,' Cath said, 'he'll give up in a minute.' She picked up her mug in a show of indifference but her hand was shaking so much she had to set it down again.

'Whatever's happened?' Jess asked sympathetically, but with hope in her heart.

'I've told him I've finished with him. He's upset.'

'Oh, I'm so thankful, dearie! Your dad'll be pleased – never thought he was good enough for his girl. And if he doesn't stop this nonsense, I'll phone the police.'

'Don't do that!' Cath cried, alarmed. 'He's got problems enough already. The police had him in earlier about some vandalism at Drumbreck when he got back from his latest trip.'

That confirmed her parents' worst fears. 'You're well rid of him,' she said firmly. 'I'll just have to go myself then – no,' as her daughter protested, 'I'm not feart for Rab McLeish. I kent him when he was a wee boy, and I could sort him then and I'm going to sort him now.'

The ringing stopped. After a brief exchange, Jess came back in. 'That's tellt him,' she said, with some satisfaction.

Cath was crying quietly. Before her mother could go to her, she got up. 'I'm just away upstairs,' she said and went past her to the door, her manner forbidding sympathy. She opened it, then turned.

'I'm taking a few days off. Thought I'd go to Glasgow and stay with Lisa.'

'That's a nice idea, pet,' Jess approved. 'Lisa's a good friend. She'll cheer you up – you'll come back feeling much better.'

Her daughter's face, as she went out, was tragic, and Jess, picking up her mug again, shook her head, smiling. These young folk! You always took everything so seriously at that age. Oh, she wouldn't be young again, not for anything.

Time for *Neighbours*. She clicked the remote, refilled her mug and settled comfortably back in her chair.

13

Keith Ingles had got up and was standing by the small barred window, looking out, his arms wrapped across his chest like a protective shield. He turned as Kerr and Langlands came in.

'OK, Kevin,' Kerr said to the constable standing guard. 'We're just going to have a chat with Mr Ingles.'

PC Jack nodded and stepped outside. Langlands set up the recording equipment as Kerr gestured to Ingles to sit down and took the seat opposite. She was quite clear about her brief. 'He's a professional man, a lawyer,' Big Marge had said. 'Greg and Jon will have gone in hard and either he'll have cracked or he'll have decided he isn't talking. If that's happened, it's your job to persuade him to open up. Try reason. Don't quote me, but I'm not sure that will have occurred to Greg.'

Kerr identified them for the tape, then began. 'Mr Ingles, I gather you've stated that you don't want to say anything till your brief is with you.'

Ingles, she realized, was staring at the green streak in her hair. Perhaps it hadn't been such a good idea after all. 'Mr Ingles?'

'Yes, yes,' he said hastily.

'Would you let me tell you why you'd be smarter not to wait? We've evidence that pretty much drops you in it—'

'The tarpaulin,' he muttered.

'DS Allan told you? Yeah, that's right. But look at it this way. How do I know what you did? Maybe you killed her, maybe you didn't. Maybe you think we don't care either way, but that's not true. If you're innocent we'll try to help you prove it. So if there's an explanation, tell us. It could open up a new line of inquiry.

'And once you're charged, the balance shifts. Everything takes time. You have to talk to your lawyer, he has to talk to us, we have to agree to proceed – and the guys upstairs won't be too keen on providing manpower to prove we shouldn't have charged you in the first place. And in that time evidence can disappear. Can you understand that?'

Langlands, his cheery face unnaturally serious, urged, 'She's right, you know. We want the truth, just as much as you do. That's if you're innocent, like you say you are.'

Ingles looked from one to the other, chewing his lip. 'I – I can see that. But what guarantee have I that you won't simply distort everything I say?'

Kerr gestured to the video camera. 'That. And I promise I'll listen. We won't put words into your mouth.'

There was a long, long silence. Kerr could feel the man agonizing over the decision. Then Ingles began to talk.

The Cosmo Bar, all glass, stainless steel and subtle lighting, had a young, slick, city clientele with which Tam MacNee and Tommy Tucker didn't exactly blend. Tam's outfit of black leather jacket, white T-shirt and jeans might just have passed for minimalism despite the jacket being well worn, the T-shirt being from Asda and the jeans being unfashionable, but Tommy's ensemble – zip-up top, checked shirt and chinos – blew any chance of that. Sitting at one end of the bar, they couldn't have indicated 'police' more clearly if they'd topped off their outfits with a London bobby's helmet.

A sort of cordon sanitaire had formed, but even beyond the empty bar stools there was an uncomfortable atmosphere. The barman, a snake-hipped youth in a black shirt and tight black trousers, kept giving them dirty looks as customers finished their drinks hastily and left.

It had proved impossible to follow Fleming's suggestion that they avoid Mandy Preston. The woman worked here, after all, and they could hardly tell her to go home. She was determined to help things along by pouncing relentlessly as regulars appeared with a cheery cry of, 'Now *here's* someone you'll want to talk to!' Then, to her victim, 'It's the p'lice. About Natasha's murder.'

Even after Tucker had some fairly blunt words with her, she resorted to sign language which was almost more alarming to the hapless customers. It was a far cry from the quiet chats over a drink that MacNee and Tucker had planned.

The men selected had been variously angry – 'Sure I knew her. That's suddenly a crime?' – nervous – 'I used to chat to her sometimes – that's all right, isn't it?' – or flatly evasive – 'Natasha? Oh, was that the dark girl? Never spoke to her except to order a drink.' They gave their names with a bad grace.

In a desperate attempt to have a conversation to which the hovering Mandy was not a party, MacNee and Tucker experimented with taking them over to a table to talk to them instead, but that only seemed to make things worse. After three hours, the most unguarded remark they had on record was, 'She was very attractive.'

No one, it seemed, had ever seen her outside the bar and no one admitted that she was anything other than the most casual of acquaintances, despite helpful promptings from Mandy like, 'You remember that Thursday – you and Natasha were all chummy in the corner of the bar and I'd to tell her to come and help serve – d'you not remember?'

No one had shown the faintest sign of recognition when shown Keith Ingles's photograph either, and at last MacNee and Tucker were prepared to admit defeat.

'If you'd told me that I'd prefer to be at the station being hounded by JCB for a report I hadn't written than sitting in a pub for three hours, I wouldn't have believed you,' Tucker said morosely.

'If you'd told me I could nurse one pint of shandy for three hours—'

'Two pints, but who's counting?'

'Well, two then, and I don't even like the bloody stuff. And what have we got to show for it? We know she was a wee hoor from the way she was going on before she ever left Galloway and it's not our business if she'd decided to forfeit her amateur status and turn pro.'

'We weren't going to have got them to open up however we came on to them, Tam. They've all heard she was murdered. They're not exactly going to say, "Oh, that's right, she was my bit on the side," are they?' Tucker was resigned.

'Waste of time, all this, when we've got our man anyway. And God knows what that pair of jokers back home are doing with the questioning. More likely to take him round the back and fill him in to make him confess.'

'Maybe your Big Marge has turned up something.'

Tam pulled a face. '"Maybe aye, and maybe hooch aye." That's Scots for "Oh sure, that'll be right."'

'"That'll be right" isn't English either. But me having a talent for languages, I know what you mean.'

'Right, Tommy, since you're so smart, you can probably tell me where we go from here?'

Tucker groaned. 'Not as smart as that.'

It was half-past five and Mandy had gone off for a break ('Toodle-loo, boys, won't be long!'). There was a lull in custom and the barman who, when questioned earlier, had said that he knew Natasha only as someone whose bar shifts had sometimes coincided with his, came over to them, looking surly.

'What will it take to get you two out of here? Haven't had a tip all afternoon and at this rate the bar'll be empty all evening.'

Tucker was quick off the mark. 'Information.'

'Haven't got any. But—' He paused. 'If you want a hunch . . .'

'We'll settle for something your granny saw in the tea leaves, if it's useful,' said MacNee.

'She was a right little tart, we all knew that. But just lately, I wondered if she'd a new idea. Saw her having a couple of conversations that looked more like she was putting on the pressure than chatting them up – know what I mean? They weren't looking very pleased by the end of them. Not sure she was getting far, mind you. One guy burst out laughing and she flounced away in a huff. And I noticed after that a lot of the punters were backing off.'

'Names?'

He shrugged. 'Don't know their names. Don't want to. Wouldn't demean myself with that kind of thing – I've got standards, haven't I? Not like some.

'That's it. That's all. Now, will you effing get out of here? You've done enough damage for one day.'

'That's your guv now,' Tucker said suddenly as the door opened and Marjory Fleming appeared. 'Any chance she'll let us knock off and find a decent pub somewhere?'

When Kerr came back to the CID room, Kingsley was staring at a computer while Allan, his arms folded, was perched on a desk talking gloomily to one of the other detectives. They both looked round.

'Well?' Allan snapped.

'He gave us his version, anyway – found the body lying on the grass outside his house, was scared he'd be blamed, wrapped it in a tarpaulin and took it off into the forest to get rid of it.'

Allan guffawed. 'Oh, I like a villain with a talent for fiction! Nice one. We can have a lot of fun with that.'

'Obviously we have to check it out,' Kerr said and Allan stared at her.

'You're kidding! You're saying you fell for that? "I just found this body, officer – don't know where it came from but thought I'd get rid of it without telling anyone." Like you do.'

'No.' Kerr was annoyed. 'I'm not saying that. I mean what I said – we have to check it out.'

Hot colour came to Allan's face. 'And what am I supposed to do meantime? Release him on police bail without charge? And the next thing we know is a postcard from South America?

'No, I'm going along there right now to charge him. And I think you'll find the Super will back me on this. Right, Jon?'

Kingsley had got up and come over to join them. He was looking edgy and irritable. 'Let's get it over with, then. I've been dealing with the bastard all day and I've had enough of this. Charge him, and then I'm going on my break.' He turned to Kerr. 'There's no alternative, Tansy. You couldn't call it a convincing story, and he tried to do a runner before. With the evidence we've got – he's even admitted to you that it was her blood on the tarpaulin . . .'

Kerr could see that, of course. But the boss wasn't going to be happy. If Ingles had been released, she could have pulled him in later for further questioning. Once he was charged, the questioning had to stop.

Well, it wasn't her job to break the news to Big Marge and she'd take a small bet that Allan wouldn't either. It would be a nasty surprise for her when she got back.

MacNee and Tucker had given Fleming their report over beers which went down rather quicker than the shandies, then left. Fleming, finishing a glass of wine, sat on at the table by the window where they had retreated to be out of earshot of the rested and effusive Mandy.

This was a good time to catch Bill and she fished in her handbag for her mobile. But it was Cat who answered: Dad had had to go out and she wasn't sure how long he'd be. Yes, they were coping. Yes, they'd had supper. Yes, Cammie was remembering he had work to do on his project. Probably. No, he wasn't watching TV. Yes, she'd remember to shut in the hens.

'Tell Dad I'll phone him later.' Smiling, Marjory switched off the phone, seeing them in her mind's eye: Cammie, in his room, most likely reading a rugby magazine or else lifting weights, which was his latest obsession; Cat, getting down to work after checking that her make-up was suitable to the occasion; Bill, sorting out some problem with the sheep, which as every sheep-farmer knew had only one ambition – to die in some peculiarly inconvenient way.

For a moment she felt almost homesick, then she thought of the evening ahead. A long bath, with no one to rattle the handle of the door. Room service. *Room service.* She lingered over the delicious words. Later, bed and the telly. She loved her family, of course she did, but there were times when you needed a little break in order to appreciate them even more. She'd phone Bill for a chat at ten, before he went to bed.

And she felt she had at least something to show for the day's work. According to Tam and Tommy, Davina seemed to have been developing a little side-line in blackmail. And the newspaper cutting told her that someone in Galloway knew where she was, or at the very least, had known. Of course, if Ingles confessed, or if it really did turn out they had hard evidence, it would be of no more than academic interest, but when the defence started trying to break your case, you were as well to be in possession of the fullest possible explanation. God, she hoped he'd confessed! She didn't trust Allan if it came to anything more subtle.

Absorbed in her thoughts, Marjory hadn't noticed the tall figure of DCI Carter pass the window and glance in. She jumped as he spoke at her elbow.

'On your own? I thought you'd have Tweedledum and Tweedledee still with you. Another of these?'

He headed for the bar without waiting for her refusal. 'What was it?' he called over his shoulder.

How could she shout, 'I don't want anything'? 'Rioja. If you insist.'

He brought it back to the table, with a glass for himself.

'Thank you,' she said with heavy irony. 'Very masterful.'

Carter looked at her in surprise. 'Are you a one-glass woman or something?'

'No, of course not.' Marjory was annoyed to hear herself sounding defensive.

'Glad to hear it. Unhealthy, that. My old ma's ninety and she could see me off.

'Now, how did you get on?'

'I think we can safely say she's off your patch.' Fleming finished the first glass and picked up the second; the sooner it was empty, the sooner she could get back to the hotel. 'She packed before she went. I'd like confirmation of a car hire somewhere – your Tommy Tucker said he'd check that out – but everything points to Galloway.

'Mind you, she seems to have had quite a nice lifestyle on what one of the other barmaids described as "presents" from admirers.'

Carter raised a quizzical eyebrow. 'Presents?'

'Presents,' she said firmly. 'What else do you call it when you do a gentleman the favour of stepping out with him and he gives you something to show his appreciation?'

He was amused. 'Tricky call, that.'

'The only little kicker is that the boy behind the bar there says that latterly she may have been trying a spot of blackmail.'

Carter twisted round to look at him. 'The gay?'

'Is he?' Fleming was startled. 'How do you know?'

'Trust me. Was she having any success? Mmm – looks as if we'll have to send someone in to check on what goes on in this establishment, whether or not it's linked to the murder.'

'Don't send Tucker. He and MacNee didn't exactly fit in unobtrusively. Apparently they were the kiss of death to trade. The barman was all but offering them money to clear out.'

Carter leaned back in his chair, his eyes on her face. He had, Fleming noticed, very dark blue eyes. Police officers were trained to notice these details.

She went on, 'If that's her mindset, it makes me wonder if the sudden departure to Scotland was prompted by the notion there was money to be made there. For instance, what more does she know about the boyfriend who got sent down, that she might think was worth money? Was he on the fiddle or something – solicitors have a lot of temptations . . .'

Carter was genuinely interested, and then, somehow, the talk drifted to his recent case, and suddenly the glasses were empty. She stood her round; by then, they were discussing the particular difficulties of their level in the Force.

It was eight o'clock when he looked at his watch. 'Where are you going to eat? I know a good place, just round the corner—'

'Oh.' Fleming stopped short. The conversation had been an indulgence, a rare chance to talk shop with someone who knew all the problems but wasn't involved in her own professional life. But her luxurious bath – room service . . . 'I wouldn't want you to feel you had to entertain me. Don't you have someone at home who'll be expecting you?'

His face darkened. 'Not recently. And it was a mutual decision to call it a day, so there's no need to go saying, "Oh, I'm sorry!"'

It was unnecessarily savage, and she had no intention of being bounced into discussion of his personal life. 'It's all right,' Fleming said sweetly, 'I wouldn't have meant it, except in the most conventional and indifferent way.'

Carter blinked, and then the corners of his mouth twitched. 'You don't pull your punches, do you?'

'Not as a general rule. It only means having to hit harder later. Where's this restaurant, then?'

Jenna Murdoch looked anxiously at the time. That was the Channel 4 news coming on, and she'd told Mirren to be back at half-past six. She was normally fairly relaxed about Mirren's time-keeping, but with all that was going on at the moment she was on edge, and when the phone rang she answered it with uncharacteristic nervousness – was Mirren all right?

But it was her husband's voice she heard, telling her he wouldn't be in for supper. He had spoken civilly enough; her sharp reply, 'Oh, had a better offer then, have you?' was needlessly provocative. There was a short pause, then, 'Just letting you know,' he said, and put down the phone.

Taking her anxiety out on Niall wasn't exactly going to improve their relationship, she acknowledged wryly, but she was past caring. What was the point? Sooner rather than later, she was going to have to deal with the whole sorry mess.

It was with some relief that, after quarter of an hour of watching a news story of political chicanery without taking in a word of it, she saw Mirren appear unhurriedly up the path, pausing to talk to the chained-up dog on the way. She turned off the set.

Don't alienate your daughter the way you have your husband, an inner voice cautioned, and when the child came into the room she said lightly, 'You're very late, Mirren. What have you been doing?'

Mirren seemed surprised as she looked at the clock. 'Sorry, Mum.' She sat down at the table.

'What were you doing?' Jenna persisted.

'Oh, just kind of walking round,' she said. 'I didn't notice the time. Is it pizza? Oh good.'

Admitting defeat, Jenna put the pizza into the microwave and removed the place she had set for Niall. 'Your father won't be in for supper this evening,' she said, but her daughter didn't reply. Staring blankly out of the window, she seemed lost in thought.

Laura Harvey was on the phone to a friend at a little after seven o'clock when there was a knock on the door and the collie started to bark.

'All right, Daisy, that's enough. Someone at the door, Maggie – I'll call you back.'

Jon Kingsley stood on the doorstep. 'Sorry – is this a bad time?' he asked, as the dog sniffed round his feet.

'No, not at all. Come on in.' Laura stood aside to let him pass. 'This is a surprise! I thought that with all that's going on you wouldn't have seen daylight for a week.'

'*Was* going on,' he corrected her. 'All that *was* going on. We've got our man under lock and key.'

'That was quick! I did think you were looking very pleased with yourself. Coffee? Or would you like a drink?'

'Better be coffee. I've got the car and with the red-hot policing about here, you can't be too careful.'

Laura laughed. There was something very engaging about such childish strutting. 'Shall we have "Show and Tell" while I make your coffee?' she teased.

The kitchen was very tiny. With Daisy, as always, making herself Laura's shadow, there was room only for Jon to stand in the doorway.

'Actually, I'll have to go back in shortly. There's quite a bit of paperwork to process, but I needed a break and decided to pop in to see you.

'It'll be in the papers tomorrow. We've got solid evidence – better not say what it is, but it nails him good. And he didn't quite confess, but he had to admit to everything short of the killing. Greg Allan – my sergeant – is the Super's blue-eyed boy, and I got a great big pat on the back as well. Should be a step towards my stripe!

'Oh, Greg's a buffoon, of course – brain of a backward goldfish – but at least he doesn't muck about like some people.'

Laura, taking the lid off a tin and peering doubtfully at the shortbread inside, frowned. Slagging off your colleagues like that wasn't attractive. And it suggested, too, some sort of insecurity, as if the only way you could shine was by denigrating someone else. She was beginning to understand Tam's attitude to Jon.

She handed him a mug. 'Come on through. I can't vouch for the shortbread – it's a bit elderly, I think.'

They sat down and Daisy, bribed with a small piece, lay down at her mistress's feet.

'So do I take it this isn't a consultation?' Laura asked. 'Since you've got your man?'

He wisely refused the shortbread. 'I came for the pleasure of your company, of course – what else? But you were very kind to agree when I asked you. I pride myself on taking an in-depth view of the cases I'm involved in, though we're not going to have to do anything very subtle here. It's the sort of motive even a jury can't fail to understand – she did the dirty on him, he killed her when he got the chance.'

'Why did she give him the chance, though?' Laura wondered. 'The report in the paper today said she'd changed her name and gone to live in Manchester, which would suggest she'd had a guilty conscience and was avoiding him.'

'We did talk about that. But why she came back – who knows? Any ideas to put forward? It's a question someone's going to ask, isn't it?'

Whatever he might say, he was pumping her. But she was prepared to indulge him that far. 'It would depend on what sort of person she was. She might have wanted to make her peace with him – guilty conscience. Or she might just have got tired of the inconvenience of living under an assumed name. Or didn't like Manchester and wanted to come back.'

'Mmm. More likely the second, I'd guess. But thanks, anyway. Her motive isn't really our business, but it just could be helpful to be able to offer some sort of rationale.

'The big question, of course, is what Big Marge is going to say. She won't like it; she's been off in Manchester and she's going to come back and find we've got it all tied up and there's nothing for her to do. She's completely out of the loop, so how's she going to react? Is she going to try to rubbish what we've done? You're the psychologist, you know her – tell me that!'

Was this what it was all about? Laura looked at him with profound distaste. 'I think you're forgetting that Marjory is my friend. Not just that – I owe her my life. If you're playing some sort of dirty little game to undermine her position, I want nothing to do with it. Or you.' She stood up. Daisy, immediately alert to her mistress's tone, began to growl.

The expression of dismay on his face was almost comical. 'Laura, you've got it wrong! I didn't mean – it's just—'

In steely silence, she moved towards the door.

'Laura,' he tried again, 'I'm an idiot. Sorry. We had something going here – I don't want it to end like this. Please sit down again and let me apologize – explain . . .'

When she still said nothing, Jon smiled ruefully. 'They say you shouldn't do that, don't they? "Never apologize, never explain" – it's just supposed to make matters worse. But in this case, they seem to be about as bad as they can be. Please sit down.'

She hesitated, then, as he said, 'Please?' again, sat down on the edge of her chair, Daisy at her feet eyeing Jon watchfully.

'I know, I know, I'm a young man in a hurry.' He leaned forward, his elbows on his knees and hands together as if in prayer. 'You're a psychologist; perhaps you'll understand.

'My father was a very successful businessman and then one day everything went pear-shaped and he lost the lot. He was a man who'd told a hundred people what to do, and suddenly he was – nothing.

'So he needs me to be successful – for him, really, more than for me. And nothing I've done so far has been good enough. So I suppose I'm inclined to lose sight of everything except the need to prove to him what I'm made of.'

Interested against her will, Laura said, quite gently, 'You do realize, don't you, that whatever you do might not be good enough?'

'Of course. Even policemen have to know some psychology. But you see, if I'm a high flier, if I can make rank ahead of everyone else, I can look him in the eye and say, "I don't care what you think, Dad, I'm a success and I have the stripes to prove it." '

She doubted that. Reason didn't come into this; you couldn't argue it away. She said only, 'If you push too hard, and you try to do it by cutting other people down, it often backfires.'

'Like it just did. Sorry.' Jon looked down at his hands. 'I enjoy the job anyway – you know that? It's a great job, and part of the reason I want to get further up the ladder is because I know I'm good at it.'

He looked up, then grinned. 'And the money's a lot better, too.'

She found herself smiling back. Oh, he had charm; there was no doubt about that. 'All right, you've made your point. But lay off Marjory, OK?' She got up again and this time he did too.

'I promise. But I haven't blown it completely with you?'

'Not completely, no.'

But after he had left, she stood staring into space, thinking over what he had said. Daisy, unsettled by the tension there had been in the atmosphere, nudged her with her nose; she patted the dog absent-mindedly and went to sit down again.

Jon had promised. Did she believe him? She wasn't sure that it was even a promise he was able to keep. It was a textbook scenario – and curiously enough, one she had seen affecting Marjory as well. There could be breakers ahead.

It was a small Indian restaurant in a back street. They knew Chris Carter there, and Marjory felt embarrassed by the proprietor's attentions.

'I feel you should tell him that this is a purely professional relationship,' Marjory said as the man, beaming, led them to their table.

'Not a chance,' Chris said. 'You're doing wonders for my cred. I've eaten here alone too often recently. What about you? Significant other?'

It was strange to think of Bill that way. She told him, briefly, about the farm and her family.

He said only, 'Lucky you. Now, there's no menu here. They work out what you'd like, then bring it. Trust me – you'll love it.' Then he went back to talking about the job which possessed both of them, quite possibly to an unhealthy extent.

'The thing is,' he said, 'what other job is there that's so important? Being a doctor, OK. But short of that, you're dealing with the most vital thing in anyone's life – freedom.'

'And justice,' Marjory said eagerly. 'How would you have coped with the death penalty – if someone would actually die as a result of your investigation, whether you were right or wrong?'

They were off. The food, delicious, unobtrusive, appeared and was removed as they talked on. They talked about their cases: his, where there were firearms and multiple deaths, hers where an occasional death sent a whole community into shock.

'The stakes are probably almost higher, in a way,' Chris said thoughtfully. 'A gang death is a gang death, but they know the risks – they accept them at the initiation ceremonies. Mostly it doesn't involve anybody else unless they're caught in the cross-fire, so ordinary folk will just shrug. Within a community . . .'

'You're going to have to deal with another death tomorrow. With us, it'll all settle down again. We'd a quiet spell before this when quite honestly, apart from the usual trivial stuff, it was deathly boring. I thought of sending Tam out to mug someone, just for the sake of variety.'

'Now, why don't I find it as hard as I should to picture your sergeant in that role?'

Marjory smiled. 'I know. But he's invaluable. He's seen the other side, and decided against it. Or at least, his wife has seen to it that he decided. If I were asked who should run the penal system, I'd nominate Bunty.'

The supply of food had stopped. There were several bottles of Kingfisher beer on the table, and they were all empty. 'So,' Chris said, 'back to the farm tomorrow?'

'Oh God, what time is it?' Stricken, Marjory looked at her watch. 'Eleven – too late to phone Bill!'

'He'll be in bed already?'

'You don't stay up late, if you're up at half-past five – probably nearer five, as the light gets better. I hate going to bed without saying goodnight.'

Chris looked at her for a long moment. Then he said, 'It sounds idyllically happy. I envy you.'

'Yes,' she agreed, and then for no reason she could think of, apart from the number of empty bottles on the table, she started talking to him about the serpent in her Eden, the woman who had spat in her face and was now her nearest neighbour.

Chris listened, his elbows on the table, his mouth covered by his hands and his eyes never leaving her face. As she finished, he said, 'Bit rough, your husband inflicting that on you.'

And it was a bit rough. She did feel hard done by, and sympathy was very soothing.

'Yes, I know.' She said it, aware that she was being disloyal. 'It's tainting everything. Bill's a saint, but it would be nice if just occasionally he bore in mind that I'm not.

'Still, it's done now, and I just have to get on with it.'

Chris's eyes were very warm as he looked at her. 'You're quite a woman, Big Marge. If there's ever a vacancy, give me first refusal.'

Alarm bells rang. Marjory looked at her watch again, jumped up. 'Good gracious, look at the time!' She insisted on splitting the bill – somehow that seemed important – but when she got back to the hotel the luxurious bath wasn't as relaxing as she had hoped it would be. She hesitated as she went to switch off the main lights. Should she phone HQ before she went to sleep? She'd rather expected to hear from Allan . . . But it was late, she was tired and she'd find out soon enough. Marjory climbed into bed.

There was nothing on late-night TV that she could bear to watch, and she couldn't get comfortable with the pillows – somehow one seemed too low and two were too high. She tried not to think that her discomfort was anything other than physical.

Jenna Murdoch was suddenly awake. She didn't know why. She sat up in bed and looked at the clock. It was just after midnight; she was alone, and Niall's side of the bed hadn't been slept in.

There had been a noise – some sort of thunderous crash – or had she dreamed it? And there was a smell – smoke! Mirren! In a panic, she flung herself out of bed, but through a chink in the curtains a flicker of red caught her eye. As she went to tear them open she realized there was a crackling roar too, coming from that direction, the terrifying sound of a fire blazing out of control.

The bedroom window looked out across the yard to the stone-built open shed. It was well ablaze, the roof struts now nothing more than thin, charred sticks; it must have been the roof falling in that had woken her. Below, there was nothing but a boiling sea of flame.

The dog! That was where the dog was kept chained up, surrounded by bales of straw, unwanted timber, old pots of paint. All it would take to send that lot up would be a carelessly tossed cigarette end.

The dog, poor creature, would be dead now. There was nothing that could have withstood that raging inferno. Her main concern, as she dialled 999, was what that would do to Mirren. Devoutly hoping she was still asleep, Jenna pulled on a dressing gown and opened her bedroom door as quietly as she could.

But Mirren wasn't. She was out on the landing in her pyjamas. 'What's happening?' she demanded when her mother appeared.

'It's all right – something's gone on fire. The Fire Brigade will deal with it – it's not a problem. Just go back to bed,' Jenna said, not hopefully. But to her astonishment, for once Mirren obeyed.

'OK,' she said meekly and went back into her bedroom and shut the door.

Thank God for that! Jenna hurried downstairs, past the long, uncurtained staircase window. In the flickering light of the flames, lurid, unhealthy, she shivered. *Götterdämmerung*: her mouth shaped the word. The Twilight of the Gods, when the known world began to crumble.

A foolish thought! She snapped on all the lights and flooded the hall with comfortable, familiar electric illumination. Drawing her dressing-gown tightly about her, she went into the kitchen to put on the kettle. The Fire Brigade, they had promised her, would not be long.

14

Marjory Fleming woke just before seven, unrefreshed after a restless night and troubled dreams. The room must have been too hot. Or something.

She reached for her mobile. Bill was probably out by this time and the kids were always dead to the world at this hour, but at least she could leave a message.

Her heart gave a little skip of pleasure as she heard his voice. 'Oh, hello, love. Didn't think I'd manage to catch you. Sorry not to phone last night – I got tied up until it was too late.'

'No, it's all right. I knew that was what must have happened.'

His voice sounded flat and tired and she was immediately alarmed. 'Bill? Are you all right? The children—?'

'No, no, we're fine. But look – sorry to have to tell you on the phone, but there was a bit of a problem with your father yesterday. He'd a bad turn – got violent, started lashing out—'

'Oh no! Oh poor, poor Mum!'

'Yes, poor Janet. That's the worst of it, really. He hit her and she fell. No broken bones, just a mild concussion, so don't get upset. One of her neighbours – James Brodie, you know? – he heard the noise and went round and raised the alarm, and the services were brilliant. I took her to hospital in Dumfries and they're keeping her for observation overnight, but she's going to be fine.'

'Why didn't you phone me, Bill?' Marjory was almost in tears. 'I wasn't doing anything that couldn't be interrupted.'

'What would have been the point? I was quite glad you didn't phone, quite honestly, because I'd have had to tell you about it when you couldn't have got back anyway, and there was nothing you could do except have a wretched night worrying about it. Janet would have been furious with me.'

'I'd still have liked to know,' she protested stubbornly. 'And – Dad?'

Bill sighed. 'They've taken him for psychiatric assessment, to try to see if they can get him stabilized. But of course he can't go back home. Janet mustn't be left alone with him again.'

'Of course not. Even she must see that now. But I still feel I should have been there. Or known what was happening, at least.'

'It wouldn't have made any difference, Marjory. You were just doing your job.'

Having guilt added to shock and dismay didn't help. 'I'll get to the hospital the minute I can. We'll try and catch an earlier train and I'll go in on my way back. They can send a car to take Tam back from there.'

'She'll want to see you, but don't worry about anything here. We're managing fine. And you'll have quite a bit to do today. I heard on the radio the man's been charged.'

'With murder?' Her spirits rose. If he'd been charged, he must have confessed. They wouldn't have had time for lab results on the tarpaulin. Then she frowned, as Bill went on, 'Yes, that's right. Didn't you know about it?'

She certainly should have known. Was this another Allan/Kingsley machination? Marjory said slowly, 'I haven't been in touch since yesterday afternoon. But that's seriously good news – means we won't be under the cosh today and other people can handle it.'

She heard him yawn at the other end of the phone. 'Oh, Bill! What time did you get to bed?'

'Don't remind me! About two, I suppose. I didn't get up till gone six, though.'

'That's only four hours, and you're a man that needs his sleep. Tell Fin you're having the day off.'

'Well, the afternoon, maybe. He's a good man, Fin. When I went out earlier he was heading off to do the rounds on the hill. He's got a new dog – dead ringer for his old Moss, so he'll be happier now.'

'That's good. See you later. I'll phone when I know what's happening.'

Marjory sat down heavily on the edge of the bed and put her head in her hands. How sad, how awful it all was! And she hadn't really done anything wrong, of course she hadn't, except forget to make a phone call, but somehow she still felt miserably guilty about the whole thing.

By morning the fire had been out for some time, but a pall of acrid smoke hung in the damp air. The blackened timbers were still smoking and the ashes, though sodden, were still too hot even to rake through for the remains of the poor dog.

The fire chief was sympathetic but firm. 'Let the air in, and it could all flare up. Sorry about your lassie's pet, but you can tell her the smoke would have got it first. It's most likely true.'

'Yes.' Jenna looked anxiously over her shoulder, watching for her daughter coming down. She couldn't even guess how Mirren would react, but she would take it hard.

A little crowd of neighbours had gathered to make the usual expressions of sympathy, while satisfying their curiosity and assessing the threat to their own properties.

'It's just *awf'ly* worrying!' one lady with exquisitely modulated Glasgow vowels exclaimed. 'None of us are safe in our beds, Jenna! And what, might one ask, are the police doing about it?'

As if in answer to her rhetorical question, a police car appeared, nosing round the corner on to the narrow road around the bay, and at the same moment, Jenna realized that her daughter had appeared at the front door of the house. She was staring at the smoking ruins expressionlessly.

'Excuse me.' Jenna broke off the conversation to hurry across to her daughter and put her arm round her narrow shoulders to sweep her inside. 'Mirren, you're going to have to be very brave. The shed went on fire last night when we were asleep and I'm afraid poor Moss can't have stood a chance. The firemen say he wouldn't have felt anything, because the smoke would have reached him first – it would have been very quick.'

She was babbling as she took the child into the kitchen, and persuaded her to sit down. 'I know how upset you'll be, and I'm really, really sorry. I wish there was something we could have done . . .'

She had been expecting an explosion of rage, floods of tears, or – well, something. Mirren's calm was unnatural, unnerving.

'Oh, poor Moss! That's awful,' she said at last, but it was almost as if the words didn't mean anything.

She must be in shock. Jenna didn't know what to do. 'Well – I'll put the kettle on. Perhaps you should have some hot, sweet tea?'

Mirren made a face. 'Yeuch!'

'I'll put the kettle on anyway. The firemen might like some. They've had a long night.' And about five cups of tea as well, as witnessed by the dirty mugs on the draining board, but at least it gave Jenna something to do. 'Do you – do you want breakfast?'

'I'll get some Shreddies.' Mirren went to fetch a packet from the cupboard, then assembled a bowl, a spoon and a bottle of milk and sat down to eat composedly.

Her mother watched her helplessly. If she was in a state of denial like this, there was going to be a backlash later, and Jenna had no idea what form it would take, or how she would cope when it came.

'There's a policeman coming to the door, look.' Mirren gestured with her spoon to a figure in uniform passing the window on his way to the front door.

'Oh – right. I'll go and let him in.'

Jenna recognized him; he was from the police station in Newton Stewart and he'd come to see her yesterday about the graffiti.

'Come in, Sergeant Christie. I've got the kettle on – would you like a cup of tea?'

'No thanks, Mrs Murdoch. Too much to do today.' He was a neat, sharp-featured man with a small moustache and a permanent air of busyness about him. He followed her through to the kitchen. 'Nasty, this. A dog killed too, I understand.'

Jenna tried glancing meaningfully from him to her daughter, shaking her head, but he ploughed on. 'Sick sort of person who'd do that to a defenceless animal, in my opinion.'

She hardly dared look at Mirren, but she seemed not to have heard. Christie took a seat at the table, still in full flow.

'Anyway, I think we know where to look for our villain, don't we? Had him in yesterday to have a wee word about your problem, and there he was still with the smear of red paint you mentioned on the side of his hand!

'We charged him and he was released on bail yesterday afternoon, so our gallus fellow comes back here for his revenge – they've cheek enough for anything, these neds. But of course they're not very bright. Sometimes you wonder how they walk about without bumping into things. Or drive, in McLeish's case – not a happy thought, is it, him in charge of a juggernaut!'

He chortled, and Jenna smiled feebly.

'Now,' he went on, 'did you see anything suspicious last night?'

'Not a thing, I'm afraid. I was very tired and I went to bed early. Something woke me – a noise, or the smell of smoke, I think – but the shed was well ablaze by then.'

Christie had taken out a notebook and was scribbling down her answer. 'And what about Mr Murdoch?'

'My husband – wasn't here last night.'

'Away, is he?'

'That's – that's right. Away. Just at the moment.' Jenna was aware of her daughter's eyes on her. 'He'll be back shortly.'

'Fine. And you, dear?' Christie was just turning to Mirren when there was a tap on the kitchen door and a young constable put his head round.

'Sorry to interrupt, sir, but I've someone here who says she saw something.'

'Good, excellent! Wheel her in.' He winked at Jenna. 'Now we're getting somewhere!'

The constable stood aside and Kelly McConnell appeared. She had clearly taken some pains to prepare herself for the starring role of major witness: she was wearing a disco outfit of cropped top and rah-rah skirt, and the way she had applied her make-up hinted at a possible future career as a plasterer. She cast a scornful glance round the shabby kitchen, at Jenna and the thin, pale child at the table, then, homing in on Christie, favoured him with her mother's come-on smile.

Christie looked at her with some horror. He had daughters himself, two nice, well-doing lasses who would have been sent back upstairs to wash their faces if they'd come down looking like that.

'Kelly McConnell,' the constable told him, taking out his notebook in readiness.

'Kelly, fine. Right, Kelly, what have you got to tell me?'

Kelly moistened her lips. 'Well, last night I, like, came home from hanging out with – well, a friend—'

'Time?'

She looked put out at the interruption. 'Like – midnight, maybe? Didn't really notice.'

'Was anyone with you?'

'No. There was just me and Chazz Armour at his house. We – kind of lost count of the time,' she simpered. 'Like you do.'

'Where does this Chazz live, then?' Christie's distaste was evident.

'Just round the bay there. I got home and went upstairs – being quiet, you know, because Dad goes, like, mental sometimes if I'm after ten o'clock?' She giggled, looking up at Christie under her lashes.

He wasn't amused. 'Kelly, I'm a busy man. Can you get on with it and tell me what you saw?'

Kelly pouted. 'Like, I'm trying to. I was just getting ready for bed and my window looks on to the road – and there he was!'

With a dramatic pause, she surveyed her audience.

'Who?' Christie barked. She was sorely trying such patience as he possessed.

'This really, really scary guy, all in black. I couldn't see his face. I think he might have had something over it, you know, like a terrorist or something. He was standing out there in the road, just looking at this house.'

'Tall, short? Fat, thin?'

She hesitated. 'I – I couldn't say, really. He was down below me.'

'And then what happened?' Christie prompted her.

'Well, I don't know. Couldn't see, after that. He just disappeared. Probably went to start the fire, I expect.'

'So what did you do?'

'Well, I went to bed, didn't I?' Disappointed by the effect she had produced, Kelly was sulky. 'I was tired. Next thing I knew there were these fire engines and everything.'

'You weren't worried that there might be what you thought was a terrorist wandering about?' Christie's tone was sceptical.

'She's just making it up.' Mirren's shrill voice startled them all.

Christie spun round. 'What?'

Mirren gave Kelly a contemptuous look. 'I bet she didn't see anything at all. She's just trying to get attention. She's a liar anyway.'

'How dare you, you little cow!' Kelly's face contorted with rage. 'She's a total minger – always hanging around, all on her own, and she's jealous of me! I tell you, I did too see that man – and I know who's a liar, and it's not me. You going to let her get away with that?' She turned to Christie, glaring at him.

'Now, now, Kelly, calm down. The constable there's taken a note of what you said, and we're very grateful to you for coming forward. Someone will take a formal statement you can sign, tomorrow, probably.' Christie stood up, jerking his head to the waiting constable to get her out. She was most likely a total waste of time, this child. He found himself inclined to agree with the other one.

'Why do you think what Kelly said wasn't the truth?' he asked her.

'Because it's just the sort of story she would make up – terrorists and things.' Mirren's theory sounded entirely plausible. 'She always has to be the centre of attention, all the time.'

'And did you see anything, yourself?' Christie was interested.

'My bedroom's round the back. I heard my mum moving around and went out to see what was wrong.'

'Yes,' Jenna said. 'That's right. I told Mirren to go back to bed.'

'And I did.' Mirren went back to her cereal.

'Good, good.' Christie was hearty in his approval. He liked little girls who did as they were told. There weren't many of them about these days. 'Thanks, Mrs Murdoch. We'll be in touch later and a forensic team will be working with the fire department to see how the fire was started – you'll be amazed what they can find out.

'When are you expecting your husband back?'

Jenna hesitated. 'I'm not sure. He didn't say.'

Christie nodded and left.

Mirren had finished her cereal. She stood up. 'Can I go and see what they're doing outside?'

'Fine, but don't get in anyone's way,' Jenna instructed mechanically, but as Mirren left she was frowning. There was something odd about her daughter's response to this, something very odd.

Janet Laird was looking heart-breakingly frail, a small figure in the big hospital bed, with a great dark bruise on her temple which her soft white hair, pulled forward, couldn't conceal. She was dozing, propped up on her pillows, when Marjory came in, but when her daughter said softly, 'Mum?' her eyes opened and her face lit up in its usual sweet smile.

'It's you, dearie! Oh, what a shame you had to come, with you so busy. I'm to be away home today so you could have seen me there.'

Marjory sat down on the chair beside the bed and took her mother's hand. 'I'm just upset I wasn't here when all this happened. How are you feeling?'

'Och, I'm fine. They've been real good to me in here. But how's Bill? I was worried, keeping him so late last night.'

'I've told him he's to take the afternoon off. But look, Mum, I want you to come back to the farm. I don't like to think of you by yourself in the house.'

'Oh, I'll not be by myself! John and Mary Brodie are picking me up this afternoon and Aileen from number twelve is making our tea. And I'm needing to get back anyway, to sort things out . . .' Her voice faltered and Marjory squeezed her hand.

'It's awful, I know.'

Janet's faded brown eyes filled. 'He's been such a good man to me, your father. He didn't know what he was doing, didn't mean it—'

'Of course he didn't.'

'— and now it's like he's being punished, locked away in that place. We need to get him back, Marjory. They'll find some pills for him or something . . .'

'Mum,' Marjory began, with her old feeling of irritation at her mother's stubborn determination not to face facts, but Janet simply wasn't strong enough to be upset by being taken through the old arguments again. Once she'd had a chance to rest and to eat properly, without the strain of caring for Angus, it would be time enough to insist. She said instead, 'You do realize they'll have to keep him there for quite a while until they get his medication sorted out?'

Janet sighed. 'He'll not be happy. He likes his things about him, and I know his routine and what he likes to eat. I'll need to explain that to them. I was thinking, maybe the Brodies could take me in on the way home—'

'No,' Marjory said firmly. 'You probably wouldn't be able to see him yet anyway.' Then, cunningly, she added, 'You don't want to put the Brodies to any more trouble, when they've been so good to you. And if Aileen's making your tea, you wouldn't want it to get spoiled because you were late.'

It was a masterstroke. Janet's face clouded. 'Right enough, I wouldn't want to do that. Maybe I could ask them about tomorrow—'

'I'll phone the hospital and if we can see him I'll take you there myself.'

'Oh dearie, I don't like to ask you – but it would make a difference.'

'Mum, he's not just your husband, he's my dad too.' A sudden picture of her father as she remembered him as a child, tall and splendid in his police uniform, came to her mind and Marjory felt her throat constrict. Her relationship with Angus had never been easy, but there were those other memories too and it was hard to think of him as he must be now, just one more demented old man along with all the others.

'I know, I know.' Now it was Janet who was the comforter this time, and she produced a wobbly smile. 'We just have to keep brave and cheery for him, pet.'

Marjory smiled too, but it was with the melancholy thought that whatever they might do, Angus Laird would now neither know nor care.

She left, promising to look in on Janet at home later, and wishing that she could have taken her back to the farm and been a proper daughter, comforting and cherishing her mother at a time of such crisis in her life. But Janet would insist that Marjory's work came first – she'd been a policeman's wife, after all – and then, with the others out all day too she'd be lonely, and being Janet would probably set about cooking meals and doing the neglected housework. No, she was better off with the neighbours who had been her friends for thirty or forty years.

It didn't make Marjory feel comfortable, though. If Ingles had indeed pled guilty, Greg could wrap it up. He'd enjoy that, and given his success he was entitled, along with Jon, to get all the credit going. Then she could take some of her leave allocation, which had been piling up, and persuade her mother to come and stay for a few days while Marjory did all the proper daughterly things, and perhaps look for a home where Angus could be comfortable, if she and Bill could manage to convince Janet that there was no alternative. If!

The crowd had drifted away now, and only people passing on the way to their day's sailing stopped briefly to have a look. Mirren Murdoch, perched on the garden wall and shivering in a chilly breeze, watched the proceedings. The ashes were grey now, not glowing red, and the two fire engines had gone, leaving the fire chief to wait for the investigators.

He was standing, hands on hips, surveying the debris, when Sergeant Christie came over to him.

'Discarded petrol can there, look.' He kicked at the blackened, buckled object poking out of a pile of ash.

'Ah! that's good. Now, see and not let anyone touch it,' he instructed. 'Get it bagged up for Fingerprints when it's cool enough.'

He got a sardonic look in reply. 'I've seen more fire inquiries than you've had Sunday roasts. We know the ropes. But it's definitely arson, as if we'd any doubt. The team's on its way.'

Christie tapped his nose. 'Got our man fingered. Just radioed to have him lifted on suspicion of wilful fire-raising.'

Aware of a presence at his elbow, he turned. Mirren had left her perch and was standing beside him, staring at the can. It crossed his mind that the next discovery, when they started sifting through, was likely to be the charred bones of her deceased pet – not very nice. And anyway, the last thing he needed was a child having hysterics.

'Off you go now,' he said, not unkindly. 'You're better

inside with your mum. There's going to be a lot of coming and going here and we don't want any accidents.'

'I don't want to go.' Mirren stood her ground. 'It's our shed. I want to see what happens. And I could help – look, I could show you where the dog slept. There was straw all round – here.'

She ducked under the tapes and headed towards where the fire chief was standing. 'It was just where this can is—' She bent forward and was just about to pick it up when the fire chief grabbed her.

'Are you daft, lassie?' he roared. 'You'll burn your hand – and that's evidence, anyway. See those tapes – they're there to keep you out. Get back on the other side of them. In fact, do like the sergeant said – get back in the house. We're not needing you getting in our way.'

With a bad grace, Mirren allowed herself to be removed, then with a smouldering glance back over her shoulder went into the house. The two men were shaking their heads; she heard one of them say, 'What do they use for brains nowadays?'

Inside the house, she stopped to listen. It was all very quiet; there was no sound of drilling or anything. She tiptoed down the corridor leading to the office; the door was shut and she stopped to listen again, in case her mother was inside and on the phone, but she couldn't hear anything there either. Most likely she was upstairs working on the new flat; she'd said something yesterday about doing the painting.

It was a risk she had to take. She opened the door.

Jenna, sitting at her desk frowning over some papers, looked up. 'Hello! Are you looking for me? I'm just checking on the insurance.'

'I just wondered if you were going to be working in the flat today?' It was all Mirren could think of on the spur of the moment.

'I doubt it. There'll be too many interruptions to make it worthwhile. Did you want me to do something?'

'No,' she said. 'Not really.' She shut the door on her mother's anxious, 'Are you all right?' and stood chewing her lip.

There would be interruptions. Her mother would have to deal with them. And then . . .

The young constable came back from his round of knocking on the doors of the houses round the bay with nothing to report. The Drumbreck folk all seemed either to have been socializing until much later or else snugly tucked up in bed, and who was he to wonder, given the reputation the place had, whose bed that might be.

Christie had headed back to Newton Stewart, leaving him with instructions to check out everyone in and around the marina. There were cars parked, staff and family groups for the sailing, no doubt; it was a pound to a dud penny that this would be another couple of hours of slogging round with nothing to show for his efforts.

He glanced over his shoulder. There were plenty of places round here where you could lose yourself for a quiet fag. He walked very purposefully towards the marina and then round the corner to the end pontoon, where he was well out of sight and likely to be undisturbed.

Reaching into his pocket, he took out his cigarettes, lit one, and took a deep, satisfying drag. It was a rare morning now, with the clouds lifting and the sun starting to come through. There was a light breeze blowing, and the moored boats were moving gently and making a clinking sound. There were some wee boats clipping along, out into the estuary, having a fine time, and a sleek red-and-white motor boat came roaring past, shattering the silence. He looked after it admiringly; he'd like fine to have a shottie at that, sometime.

At peace with the world, for the moment at least, he turned towards the pleasant vista of Drumbreck, the neat houses, the trim boats at the pontoons – floating palaces, some of them. He took another drag, then choked on it.

There, trapped between the last two boats moored to the end pontoon where he was standing, a man's body was floating, face down.

15

Lurking in her office at the Kirkluce HQ would be e-mails, voice-mail and no doubt a message from Donald Bailey summoning her, but Marjory Fleming had no intention of finding them before she had a proper grasp of the situation. When she arrived she headed instead for the CID room.

As she went along the corridor towards it, DCs Wilson and Macdonald came out, heading towards her.

'Off on a job?'

It was Macdonald who answered. 'Fire in a shed over at Drumbreck. Nothing very exciting. How was the big city?'

'Oh, wild,' Fleming said dryly. 'Probably not a lot to show for it. You'd more action here, by the sound of it. Do you know where Greg and Jon are?'

'I don't know where Jon is, but Greg's in there. With – with Tam and Tansy.'

She registered that Wilson, a tall, skinny young man with a crooked nose and untidy fair curls, spoke with some constraint, but she only nodded and passed on. She'd find out soon enough.

When she opened the door, the tension in the atmosphere was palpable. Allan, high colour in his face, was confronting MacNee, who was saying, 'But for God's sake, man—'

'Tam!' Kerr, at his elbow, warned him. 'Here's the boss.'

As if she hadn't heard, Fleming said, 'Greg! You seem to be starring these days, you and Jon.'

Allan thanked her, but he looked uncomfortable rather than

smug, as she would have expected. What was this all about? She perched herself on the edge of one of the tables. 'I was – *surprised*,' she said, giving the word a cold emphasis, 'not to hear from you last night, but fill me in now. I want to know exactly where we are before I see the Super.'

The door opened and Kingsley spoke behind her. 'Oh, we've given him all the details. I was just talking to him and he was wondering when you'd be back. He's keen to see you.'

It was paranoid to worry about being the subject under discussion. 'You'd better brief me quickly, then. I take it Ingles confessed?'

A look passed between the two men. 'All but,' Allan said.

'All but?' Fleming was startled.

'He didn't confess,' Kerr chipped in. 'He specifically denied it.'

'But you charged him with murder? What evidence did you have?'

Allan shifted from foot to foot. 'The bloodstained tarpaulin – he admitted he used it to wrap the body while he moved it.'

'Not to you, he didn't.' Kerr, usually the conciliator, seemed to be spoiling for a fight. 'It was only when Sandy and I talked to him that he told us.'

Allan sneered. 'Oh, he spun Tansy some sort of cock-and-bull story about finding the body on his doorstep, being scared he'd be blamed and taking it off to where we found it. Knew a soft touch when he saw one. Before that, he said he wanted to confess, then changed his mind.'

It didn't sound good. 'I'll need to have a look at the tape,' Fleming said. 'I want to get this clear.'

Allan cleared his throat. 'Er – he didn't actually say that when it was running. He said it before, when we were getting everything set up, didn't he, Jon?'

'That's right.'

They were both looking uneasy. 'So,' Fleming said slowly,

'explain to me. What was your evidence for charging him with murder?'

'We only did it after Tansy came back to say he'd admitted – on tape – that he'd disposed of the body.' Kingsley was defensive. 'So there was no need to wait for analysis of the stains on the tarpaulin, or DNA linking him to it.'

'And he'd tried to do a runner already,' Allan added eagerly. 'Had his passport and a great wodge of cash on him, trying to hire a car. Couldn't release him to give him another chance at it, could we?'

'You didn't have to—' MacNee began aggressively, but Fleming silenced him with a look.

'Was there some reason why you shouldn't have charged him with attempting to pervert the course of justice by moving the body? For goodness' sake, the man hadn't served his full sentence so he was still under restraint – I told you that myself. On the admission he did make, he'd have gone straight back to serve the unexpired part of his sentence, just for a start.'

Allan's face turned crimson and Kingsley looked at the floor. 'I – I suppose it just didn't occur to us.'

'Playing for high stakes.' Fleming's face was grim. 'I'm sure you're right that he's our man, but we'll just have to hope for something a bit more conclusive from the SOCOs. Otherwise we're struggling.'

'That's the point. We're struggling already,' MacNee said sombrely. 'The report from them has just come in and I've called it up, here.' He pointed to the computer.

Kingsley looked startled. 'When did it arrive?'

'Five minutes ago.' Allan was running his finger round the inside of his collar as if, despite it being open, it was too tight. As the others clustered round the screen he pulled a face at Kingsley. 'Not good,' he muttered.

It was worse than 'not good'. They hadn't as yet checked the clothes he was wearing and had with him, but after an exhaustive forensic examination of Ingles's belongings, his house and the surroundings, there was nothing at all – not a fibre, not a hair – to suggest a connection with the dead woman. On the other hand, they had investigated the area just outside the clearing where he claimed to have found the dead woman, and it had produced a wealth of confirmatory evidence.

'I called them yesterday afternoon,' Kerr said, 'and asked them to check that out.'

'You had no authority—' Allan started angrily, then, at a look from the inspector, stopped.

Fleming had finished reading the report, but she sat looking at the screen for a little longer while she marshalled her thoughts. Then she rose, saying decisively, 'Right. Tansy, set up a screening of the tape. I'm going to see the Super, and we'll both want to look at it.

'Tam – car hire. Find out if Carlisle have done their checks, then get on to Tucker in Manchester and see if you can sweet-talk him into geeing up the searches there. And get someone contacting all local firms – since he hadn't a car, it's possible Ingles may have hired one too.'

Fleming turned to Allan and Kingsley. 'I'm keeping in mind that just because there's no trace of the woman in his house, it doesn't mean he didn't kill her. He could have killed her somewhere else then brought her there to dispose of the body. He's an intelligent man – he may well have worked out that a half-truth is always more convincing than a flat lie.

'I don't know what the Super will say.' Fleming sighed. 'But it will be better if you back off this and leave it to someone else. I'm taking you off the task force. Just finish whatever admin needs doing—'

'Done that. We thought that there'd be a lot more evidence that would need attention today so we stayed late last night, clearing it.' Allan was sounding sorry for himself.

Fleming sighed again. 'Look, I know you've put in a lot of work on this and I'll give you the credit for that. The Super has got to know the full story, obviously, but I'll do my best not to drop you in it.'

'Thanks, boss.' Kingsley was looking worried. 'I'm sorry – not very clever, was it?'

'Sorry,' Allan echoed.

'No,' she agreed, 'it wasn't clever.'

And now she was going to have a difficult interview with Donald. She could hardly suggest to him that his impatience was to blame for sending her off to Manchester, or that it was his inflated opinion of Kingsley that had encouraged the man to overreach himself and, no doubt, to egg on the feeble Allan. And Donald would be aware of that, and would be looking for someone to blame. As his subordinate, she knew her place: in the wrong.

There were a couple of men in white overalls picking their way through the rubble of the collapsed shed and sifting through the piles of ash when Sergeant Christie arrived with PC Neish, a sensible middle-aged woman who could be relied on to make tea and pat hands as required.

This was one part of the job he always hated – breaking bad news. He wasn't good at it. A fastidious man, he always felt uncomfortable round raw emotions: things always turned messy and there was nothing you could do to control them. As they arrived at the door, he straightened his diced cap and squared his shoulders. 'Right, Aileen?'

'OK, sarge.' Neish rang the bell.

Usually the sight of two police officers at the door, one a woman, is enough to set alarm bells ringing with the house-holder, so that the news is often delivered in the form of confirmation. Jenna Murdoch, expecting such a visit, would have to have it all spelled out.

She greeted them with a smile. 'Back again, sergeant?'

'May we come in?' Christie said, with appropriate gravity.

She didn't notice. Turning away, she led them to the kitchen. 'Cup of tea?'

They refused, suggested she sat down, sat down themselves, but even then she only looked at them with an inquiring smile.

At least the child wasn't there. Christie said heavily, 'I'm afraid I have bad news for you, Mrs Murdoch.'

Her brow furrowed. 'If it's the dog's bones, please just dispose of them quietly, before Mirren sees them.'

'I'm afraid it's not the dog. It's your husband. I'm afraid he's dead.' There wasn't a tactful way of saying it – not one he could think of, anyway.

Her face went blank. '*Dead?* Niall? In the shed?'

'No, no, nothing to do with the fire.' This was getting complicated. He looked hopefully towards Neish and she took over.

'Mrs Murdoch, they found your husband drowned this morning. Just by the marina.'

'Niall?' she said again. 'Drowned? He's dead?'

'I'm afraid so.'

This was always the moment Christie dreaded. You just never knew what they were going to do – scream, faint, go into shock . . .

Mrs Murdoch got up and walked away from them, and stood with her back to them, looking out of the window. 'What happened?' she asked quietly.

He was on safer ground here. 'We don't know, as yet. It may be an accident. He could have tripped and hit his head as he fell into the water. He was between two boats, out at the further end of the pontoons. We'd a couple of CID officers here anyway to investigate the fire, so they have it all in hand.'

'When did it happen?' She still seemed very calm.

'Perhaps you can help us there. You said he was away – where was he?'

She turned, showing for the first time some sign of emotion. He wasn't good at reading that sort of thing, but somehow it looked more like embarrassment than anything else.

'I'm afraid I was – economical with the truth, don't they call it? To be honest, my husband and I hadn't been getting on for some time. He wasn't there when the fire broke out last night so I assumed he was – elsewhere,' she gave a wry little smile, 'and to be perfectly frank, I didn't want to be humiliated. So I told you he was away.'

Christie's first thought was relief that this made it unlikely that there would be any awkward manifestations of grief, his second that here was a very cool customer.

'So where would he have been, then?'

'Oh, I wish I could tell you, sergeant! There were a number of – ladies, shall we call them, though it's not the word that springs to mind, who shared his occasional favours.'

He'd heard Drumbreck called Sodom-on-Sea before now, but even so Christie was taken aback by her offhand reaction. He retreated to safer ground. 'So when was the last time you saw your husband?'

'Let me think. He had breakfast here yesterday, but he didn't come back for lunch. He phoned to tell me he wouldn't be in for supper.'

There was no love lost between this pair, that was for sure. If it was foul play – and there was a nasty bash on the back of the man's head – and if Christie hadn't been quite sure that in the circumstances Rab McLeish was their man, he'd have wondered if it wasn't the old story of the woman scorned.

'Can you remember when that was, Mrs Murdoch?' Neish asked.

'I can, actually.' She pointed to a portable TV in the corner of the kitchen. 'The Channel 4 news was just starting.'

'Seven o'clock,' Christie nodded. 'That's very helpful. And—'

The kitchen door opened and Mirren Murdoch came in, looking suspiciously at the visitors. Christie directed a meaningful look at Neish, whose services had not so far been needed, and she nodded reassuringly, sitting forward a little on her chair in readiness.

For the first time, Jenna's face softened. She crossed the room to put her arms round her daughter, who stood stiffly in her embrace.

'Mirren, I'm afraid the police have come with some very bad news.'

The child's face flushed and her eyes, over-large in her pinched face, went from one to the other in fright. 'What – what?'

'It's Dad. I'm sorry – he's dead. Drowned.'

Pushing her mother aside, Mirren sat down heavily on one of the kitchen chairs. 'I didn't know he was dead,' she said oddly.

Jenna sat down beside her and took her unresponsive hand. 'No, dear. They've only just told me.'

It seemed that this one wasn't going to have hysterics either. She sat at the table like a zombie, not even turning her head as her mother prattled on about being brave. 'We'll manage, don't worry,' Jenna kept saying.

Further questions would have to wait. Christie and Neish got up; Neish asked if there was anyone they would like contacted, but Jenna assured her, yet again, that they'd manage.

'Well, takes all sorts,' Neish said as they walked back across to the marina.

'Couple of cold fish, if you ask me. Losing your husband, losing your father, and not a tear between them!'

'I suppose, with him and his bits on the side, it's understandable.'

'It's not so much her – it's the daughter. Even if there was trouble between the two of them, you'd expect a child to show some natural feeling.'

It quite upset him. He would hate to think of his own daughters displaying such wounding indifference on being told of their father's demise. But then, of course, they wouldn't. They were decent, well-brought-up girls who could be relied on to feel just as they should and do whatever was proper. That was a great comfort.

'There's the police surgeon, look,' Neish said, pointing to a man with rimless glasses and carrying a doctor's bag, talking to one of the detectives.

'I'd better have a word with him, since I'm the man on the spot.' Christie bustled off, past the frontage of the Yacht Club and the marina office and the boat shed, through the crowd of gawpers and round the corner to where the blue-and-white tapes were fluttering along by the end pontoon.

'But Marjory, I didn't realize! This could be disastrous, disastrous!' Bailey's jowls wobbled in consternation.

'I'm not going to give you an argument.' Fleming stared glumly at the now blank screen.

'That accusation – the suggestion that they were trying to force a confession—'

'They probably were.'

'Yes, I know, I know,' he said tetchily. 'But to try to bounce him into it in that crass way – whatever were they thinking about?'

'A quick result. They were quite sure he did it – and I'm not saying they're wrong – but they misread their man. As I told Tansy Kerr before she went in, remember he's a lawyer. He's not one of our usual clients.'

Bailey sat back in his chair. 'You're going to tell me this is all my fault, sending you and Tam away, aren't you?' He looked deflated, the balloon of his usual pomposity pricked.

It was an admission she hadn't expected, and as always – on the rare occasions when it happened – his unexpected honesty disarmed her.

'Now, how could you think I would say a thing like that?' she wondered innocently. She had her pound of flesh; it was all that needed to be said.

'Still, Manchester.' He perked up a little. 'Tell me you got something useful.'

He wasn't getting off the hook that easily. 'It could all have waited. I'd have been more useful here, but there were a couple of pointers. Tam picked up a hint that Davina had turned her talents to blackmail, so it's just possible she thought she could get money out of Ingles – knew something about his dealings, maybe, that could get him into more trouble.

'And I discovered someone had been in touch with her since she left, at least once. She had a cutting from the *Galloway Globe* about Ingles being released from prison. I've sent it for fingerprinting.'

Bailey looked disappointed. 'Interesting, certainly, but does it get us anywhere?'

'If she was blackmailing him, it might show up in his bank records,' she offered, but he looked at her impatiently.

'Unlikely, if she came to get it in person, and he killed her for asking.'

Fleming had to concede that. 'It seems an odd thing for her to do, I have to say, when she could have contacted him by letter.'

'Asking for trouble, you'd think. She must have been very confident.'

'Over-confident, from the sound of it, certainly about her own effect on men. But our best hope has to be tracing the car she probably had to hire to come here. Ingles didn't have a car, so unless he hired one, she may have picked him up in hers; he could have killed her, then used it to transport the body up to his house, where he'd be able to dispose of it in the expectation that it wouldn't be found for years. Then he'd have to abandon the car, in which case it won't be far away.'

'Get on to that, Marjory. Throw everything you have at it – for once I won't be nagging you about costs!' Bailey was recovering.

'Done it already.'

'I knew I could rely on you. Now, anything else?'

Fleming got up. 'I've taken Allan and Kingsley off the case. I'll handle it myself, with MacNee and Kerr.'

'Good, good.'

'The only problem may be the Fiscal. Is he OK about this? Prosecuting's his decision, after all.'

'I spoke to him myself yesterday. Told him what we'd got – what I thought we'd got,' he corrected himself, 'and he was quite happy then. What he'll say when he hears this—'

They were both silent for a minute, then Fleming said, 'He won't be dropping charges at the moment, obviously, since he couldn't raise them again after that if more damning evidence emerged. Legally he's allowed 110 days before he must proceed to indictment, and by then we may well have a case to present that he'll feel can stand up in court. We've a lot of lines to pursue.

'The downside is that I can't talk to him now without jeopardizing the whole case. Kerr did a good job as far as it went, but I can think of a dozen things I'd have liked to ask him once he'd started talking.'

'Yes, yes.' One helping of humble pie was quite enough for one day. 'Pity. Still, there it is. Just have to see—'

The mobile in Fleming's pocket rang and he gave her permission to take it with a gesture.

'Wilson, yes?'

She listened, her eyes widening. 'He says *what?*'

Again, there was a long explanation at the other end, while Bailey watched her with increasing impatience. When at last she said, 'Right, I'll be there,' he demanded, 'Well, what was all that?' before she had switched it off.

'That was Wilson. He's at Drumbreck – do you know it? Sailing place, just north of Wigtown on the Cree estuary. There's been a man drowned – Niall Murdoch, used to be a farmer but part-owns the marina there now. The police surgeon's just said he was bashed on the back of the head before he entered the water.'

The two police cars, lights flashing, drew up outside the yard which had 'Dickson and Sons – Haulage' on a board beside the gate.

Christie, with Neish, got out of the first one, then, flanked by the two men from the other car, strode across the yard between lorries and truncated cabs waiting to be hitched up and walked into the office.

The young woman at the desk, speaking on the phone, looked up, startled.

'Dickson in?' Christie demanded, gesturing towards the door on the other side of the room.

'Yes, but – oh, wait a minute.' She laid down the phone and jumped up. 'You can't—'

Christie ignored her. With a perfunctory tap, he opened the door and marched in.

Dickson, working at a computer with a cigarette in his mouth and his eyes screwed up against the smoke, was overweight and ill-shaven; he was no stranger to the police over the matter of tachographs and he eyed them sullenly.

'What are you wanting this time? Everything's in order. You've got nothing on me.'

'Where's Rab McLeish?' Christie barked.

'McLeish? Oh, he's in trouble, is he?' The lightening of his expression suggested that his statement had displayed optimism rather than confidence. 'At home, probably. Sent him back this morning – came in with the sort of hangover that would send your breathalyser up in flames.'

'Flames.' Christie seized on the word. 'Funny you should say that. Where was he last night?'

'Down the pub, from the look of him.'

'So he wasn't away on a job?'

'Got back yesterday afternoon.'

Christie turned. 'Right, lads. On our way.'

As he went out, the receptionist said resentfully, 'Rude sod!'

Following him, one of the uniforms winked. 'Thinks he's on *Taggart* – that's his problem.'

Back in her office, Fleming sent for MacNee and Kerr. Her prospects of getting to grips with the Ingles case seemed doomed; she'd be forced once again to leave her subordinates to deal with it, even if this time they were the ones she trusted. She didn't feel comfortable about that, but she couldn't be in two places at once.

The irony of it all had not escaped her. She could hear her own voice saying to Chris Carter, 'You're going to have to deal with another death tomorrow. With us it will all settle down again.'

And as she thought of it, his name caught her eye, in the list of e-mails she had called up to check if any was urgent. She scrolled down and opened it.

It was very brief. 'Great evening. Good hunting. Keep in touch. Chris.'

MacNee's knock on the door came as she was still looking at it and she closed it with a guilty start, feeling idiotic and hoping she wasn't looking flustered as he and Kerr came in.

It didn't help that MacNee's first words were, 'Here!

Manchester's got nothing on us, eh, boss? Tell this to DCI Carter!'

'You've heard about it, then?' Fleming said quickly.

MacNee gave her a pitying look. 'Well, what do you think?' They took their seats.

'I've got to get along there now, obviously,' Fleming told them. 'It sounds as if it should sort itself out fairly quickly. According to Wilson it's pretty straightforward – local man, Rab McLeish, with a grudge against Murdoch. Been charged with vandalism already and was the prime suspect for arson on Murdoch's property last night anyway. The body was floating face down with a smash on the back of the head – if it didn't kill him, it would have knocked him out. Looks as if he confronted Murdoch, lost his temper, picked up whatever came to hand and let him have it. May not even have meant to kill him.'

'Sounds OK,' Kerr said, but MacNee snorted.

'Going to be sorted in a couple of days, is it, just like the last one? Funny we've suddenly two murders in the area, both with a connection to Drumbreck.'

Fleming looked at him, aghast. 'Don't say that, Tam! This is straightforward stuff – McLeish has a grievance, probably takes a drink, gets into an argument and lashes out—'

'Aye, likely.' MacNee wasn't convinced.

'But if it wasn't him, it certainly wasn't Ingles,' Kerr pointed out. 'So what you'd be saying is that this would suggest Ingles didn't kill Davina either.'

'Yes, I noticed that too, funnily enough,' Fleming said sarcastically. 'You don't think, Tam, that this could have anything to do with your belief that Allan and Kingsley couldn't come up with the right answer to two plus two, when someone was holding up "Four" on a prompt card?'

' "*If honest Nature made them fools*," ' he quoted, unabashed. 'And I'll tell you the other thing – I wouldn't trust them not to come up with new "evidence" that proved they were right all along.'

'Tam, shut it,' Fleming said firmly. 'You didn't hear that, Tansy. Anyway, they're off Ingles's case. If we need more manpower at Drumbreck they can pitch in there with Wilson and Macdonald.

'Anyway, any progress on the hire cars? Did you manage to get hold of Tucker?'

'Ah!' MacNee gave a self-satisfied smirk. 'Not only did I get hold of him, my old pal Tommy came up with the goods. They were going to notify us that Davina Watt hired a blue Corsa just over a week ago – last Wednesday. She was supposed to take it back last Saturday – the firm's a bit put out that it hasn't appeared.'

'That's brilliant. Tell Tommy he's a star. You've got the registration?'

'Of course. And I've sent out an alert to all patrols.'

'Trying to be teacher's pet? Take Tam away and give him a sweetie, Tansy. And what I want done now is to go back through the old case and make a list of who gave evidence and who might have something more to say about Davina. Who might even have sent her the cutting about Ingles's release – Tam will brief you on that, Tansy. It's with Fingerprints just now.

'The other thing I'd like you to find out is whether the partners in Ingles's law firm in Wigtown were unhappy about him. These firms don't like scandal; they'd probably have swallowed a loss to stop questions being asked. See if there's something Davina could have latched on to. And find out who knew her – Drumbreck, Wigtown. Find out if she contacted them in the last couple of weeks. See if they knew of any reason for her to return.

'Tansy, I want you to concentrate on the Drumbreck end. Tam, Wigtown.'

He scowled at her. 'What if there's a link?'

'Then Tansy will find it, won't she?' Fleming said blandly.

But after they had left, she thought about what Tam had said. What if Ingles's story was true after all? What if someone had tried to incriminate him, knowing that with his history he would be the obvious suspect?

Who?

Christie was on a roll, driving through Wigtown at excessive and unnecessary speed, with lights and sirens.

In the car behind, proceeding a little more decorously, one of the constables said, 'What's he on? Never seen him like this.'

'High on his own importance,' the other sniffed. 'Bets that he's got it wrong?'

But Christie wasn't in any doubt. He hammered on the door of the house where McLeish lived with his parents, then, as there was no immediate reply, hammered again.

At last McLeish opened it, looking so ghastly that even Christie paused. His eyes were red as if he had been weeping, his face was haggard and unshaven, and he looked as if he had slept in his clothes.

Christie recovered himself. 'Police,' he said unnecessarily, flashing his warrant card. 'Can we have a word?'

'What is it now?' His breath made the officer recoil.

'We want to talk to you about last night.'

McLeish seemed to be finding it hard to focus. 'Oh.' He thought about it. 'Better come in, then.'

He was an incongruous figure in the neat sitting-room, with the smell of Pledge furniture polish in the air and doilies on the side tables. He sank down on to the tweed sofa.

Christie remained standing, Neish at his side and the other two men standing in the doorway. 'Where were you between the hours of seven last night and midnight?'

'Drinking.'

'So I would imagine.' He had no sympathy: drunks were the bane of his life. 'Anyone with you?'

McLeish drew his hand down his face. 'Yeah. People. At the pub. Did I do something?'

Christie pursed his lips. 'You tell me.'

McLeish gave a short laugh, then winced. 'You tell *me*.'

They were definitely getting somewhere now. Christie said, in his most soothing voice, 'Well, why don't we take you down to the station and talk it through? You help us, and we'll help you and see if we can try to piece it together? All right?'

McLeish made no resistance. 'Fine,' he said dully, and walked to the door, where he turned. 'Are you arresting me for something?'

Christie sounded positively avuncular. 'No, no, laddie. Not yet.'

16

It was a twenty-five-minute drive from Kirkluce to Wigtown, if you weren't hurrying, and today Tam MacNee had a lot on his mind.

He wasn't happy. It had given him a wee bit of a lift, right enough, to see Kingsley with his tail between his legs, but that wouldn't last long. It was all just going to get dirtier. Kingsley was smart, that was the problem, smart and nasty, and he had it in for Marjory. Sooner or later he'd trip her up. The atmosphere around the place was changing already, and Tam didn't like it.

Oh, he knew fine his hatred of change was pathological, all but. And why wouldn't it be? As a kid, change never meant better: from indifferent father to abusive stepfather; from poor housing to worse housing, then to a downright slum. His professional life here and his marriage with its comfortable certainties seemed to him a sort of miracle, precious and far beyond his deserving. Any change was alarming; the change that Kingsley was trying to engineer was a threat.

Recently attitudes had begun shifting, with officers he'd worked alongside for years starting to question the principles of policing Marjory so firmly enforced. Even Wilson, a man he respected, had said the other day he thought she was old-fashioned. And there were no prizes for guessing who'd put that idea in his head.

Now Ingles had been arrested, they'd be going all out to find something to make the charge stick, as a matter of professional pride. At least Marjory had the sense not to let Allan and Kingsley back to the site, where the temptation would be just to give the investigation a wee nudge in the right direction. Even so, Tam wished he could be sure there weren't others who, if they were certain they had the killer, would be ready enough to give justice a helping hand.

Had Ingles killed her? On the balance of probabilities, certainly. Bailey was for ever yammering on about Ockham's razor, but fair enough, the simple answer was usually the right one. Tansy wasn't convinced, though, and she'd questioned the man. He rated Tansy.

So perhaps the best Tam could do was talk up the doubts. His colleagues were decent enough men who might jump to conclusions, but wouldn't want to bang up an innocent man.

Now he was going to have to go and talk to lawyers. That thought depressed him too. Tam didn't like lawyers. Either they were the criminal's friend, out to make life difficult for the polis, or they were charging him an hourly rate that should have bought a personal appearance by Claudia Schiffer to hand over the contract. Lawyers weren't in the business of giving you useful information, but he had his orders.

From reading the file on the robbery, the person he was really interested in was Euphemia Aitcheson. She knew more about what had happened than anyone except Keith Ingles and possibly Davina Watt, and he couldn't talk to either of them. She could tell him about the whole set-up in the Yacht Club – who was who, who did what. And probably also, given the reputation the place had, to whom.

Yes, a gossipy Euphemia could be key to the whole thing. Maybe it would all fall into place this afternoon. And maybe if Kingsley passed his exams he'd apply for a transfer and bugger off back to Edinburgh.

The thought raised his spirits. And though the straggling bushes by the side of the road were still blowing in a stiff breeze, the sun was coming out now, turning the peaty-brown waters of a little lochan across a field to a surprising deep navy-blue.

It wasn't all bad. Bunty would be home tomorrow and so far none of the animals had died or killed one of the others. At least, not when he left this morning.

Marjory Fleming could hear crowd noise before she opened the door of her car. She'd parked at the entrance to the hamlet of Drumbreck, in preference to weaving her way slowly through what looked like about fifty men, women and excited youngsters gathered outside the marina, discussing the dramatic events of the day.

DC Andy Macdonald, a solid, square-shouldered young man with a buzz-cut, had spotted her arrival and was making his way through the crowd towards her: 'Excuse me, sorry, thank you, could you get back there, please, excuse me . . .'

People yielded good vantage points reluctantly, their eyes following him to Fleming and Kerr getting out of the car.

'Sorry about this, boss,' Macdonald apologized. 'We hadn't reckoned to need crowd control in a place like this but maybe we should have.'

'Ah! Are you in charge here, then?' A grey-haired man wearing a navy-blue Guernsey and a discontented expression stepped into Fleming's path. 'Perhaps you would care to tell us what's going on? It's not good enough that we should be kept in the dark.' There was a murmur of support from those equally curious but less courageous.

'I'll be releasing a statement once I have had a chance to investigate the situation, sir. Which, you may have noticed, it is impossible for me to do while you are standing in my way.'

She stood her ground calmly and the man, still muttering, though under his breath, stepped aside. There were no more interruptions as she walked down to the taped-off area beyond the marina.

It was a bright day, with a breeze setting the halyards on metal masts clinking, and the boats seemed restless in the choppy waves. The tide was going out; there was still deep water around the pontoons but inshore the unsightly, khaki-brown mudflats were being exposed.

'No Press here yet?' Fleming asked Macdonald.

'Not so far, no. You'll have seen we've a car at the end of the road checking incoming traffic, and if you can authorize this statement we'll see it's given out whenever they arrive.'

He handed her a piece of paper and she skimmed the scribbled information: it was a bland statement that a man had been found drowned and the police were treating his death as suspicious. She OK'd it and he went off with it back through the crowd.

Niall Murdoch's body, covered with a plastic sheet, had been laid out on the dock. There were several uniforms in attendance and one, she saw with approval, was logging her name as a visitor to the scene.

'Good organization, Will,' she said as DC William Wilson came towards her, huddled into a windcheater and with his curly hair blown into bushy tangles. 'You and Andy have done well.'

Wilson grinned. 'Happy to take the credit, boss, but Sergeant Christie's a canny man. Does everything by the book, he tells me. Every "t" dotted and every "i" crossed – or something like that. He's away to pick up McLeish. His face fits, seemingly.'

Fleming looked around. 'The police surgeon's gone, has he?'

'Yes. He said he'd better things to do than hang about here. But he confirmed death, obviously, and said the wound on the back of the head didn't look like accidental injury.'

'Right. You'd better let me see him.'

Wilson pulled back the sheeting. The man was lying on his back on the dock, his head turned to one side, wearing sodden clothes – a checked shirt with the sleeves rolled up, a navy padded gilet and a worn trainer on one foot, though the other was missing. He was tall, over six foot probably; his face was bloated from immersion, and there was bloodstained froth inside the half-open mouth. His hands were deathly white, swollen and wrinkled, and on the back of his head his dark hair was matted with blood, though there was no depression to suggest a break in the skull.

'A stunning rather than a fatal blow, you'd think,' Fleming said. 'Delivered unexpectedly from behind, knocking him into the water unconscious – job would be done in a couple of minutes. Thanks, Will – you can cover him up again. Where was he found?'

'Floating here, face down, between the sloop and the ketch. His arm was caught in the sloop's moorings.' He indicated two boats, one with one mast, the other two. 'This is his, *Sea Sprite*.'

'You seem to know your boats.' Fleming, a landlubber to the core, was impressed.

'Used to sail a bit when I was a kid. Haven't the time or the money now, with two kids—' He broke off at the sound of an altercation behind them.

A short, fat man with a face like a malevolent cane toad, was swearing at the young constable who was refusing to allow him into the taped area. Two of the uniforms were hurrying across; Fleming reached him a second later.

'I would strongly urge you to moderate your language, sir.' There was a cutting edge to her voice, and making use of her superior height, she moved in closer so that she could look down at him.

He didn't like that. 'And who the hell are you?' He had a broad Glasgow accent.

'This is Detective Inspector Fleming,' one of the constables said.

He sneered. 'Part of the sex equality quota, are you?'

'Name?' Fleming snapped.

'Never mind that. I want some answers first.'

Fleming turned away. 'Take him in. Verbal assault on a police officer, obstructing the police—'

'You can't do that!' The man's eyes were bulging with rage to the point where she was almost afraid they might pop out of their sockets.

'I think you'll find I can. And if you don't co-operate I'll have you for resisting arrest as well.' She turned away.

'Wait – wait a moment. I'm – I'm sorry.' From the colour of his face, framing those words might bring on apoplexy. 'I'm Ronnie Lafferty. Niall Murdoch was my partner. Naturally I'm upset.'

'Naturally.' Fleming's voice was icy. 'You can tell us all about it back at the station.'

'This – this is . . .' He seemed lost for words, perhaps having appreciated that those which had clearly sprung immediately to mind were unwise. 'No one treats Ronnie Lafferty like this!'

'It'll be a steep learning curve for you then, Mr Lafferty.' She allowed herself to show amusement. 'Now, let me explain. We can do this two ways. My officers can take you out in handcuffs – which will, of course, give rise to all sorts of unfortunate rumours in Drumbreck – or you can walk out freely to the police car, a public-spirited citizen helping police with their inquiries. The choice is yours.'

Again, the effort to control himself seemed to be taking a physical toll. 'OK,' he said. 'Let's get this sorted out and drop this nonsense. I'm happy give you any help I can—'

'Good. I look forward to hearing what you have to say. Later.' Fleming jerked her head to the waiting constables and walked away.

She didn't turn her head until she was sure he would not see her do it, then checked to see what had happened. He was walking ahead of the two policemen, pausing now and again to speak to people in the crowd.

'Putting his spin on it,' Wilson observed.

'Seen sense, anyway.' Fleming was grimly satisfied.

'You certainly spelled it out for him, boss.' Kerr, who had been talking to the constable on duty with the log, was amused.

'Ah, Tansy! You're not here just to watch the sideshows, you know. We need the dirt on Davina and with so many of the natives handily gathered here you can start getting names and asking questions.'

'See you at Christmas,' Kerr said, assessing without enthusiasm the numbers involved.

'Andy will be back in a minute. He can help. And I'll review the situation once we know more about McLeish. I can always call in Jon and Allan if we need back-up.

'I'm just going to go across and have a look at the site of the fire. When the pathologist arrives, send someone to fetch me.'

Fleming walked past the now-thinning crowd in front of the Yacht Club, which seemed to be doing good business today, then headed along the road which skirted the bay towards the Murdochs' house.

There were no signs of activity outside it; the fire investigators must have done their job and gone. She had almost reached it when she became aware that there was someone hurrying after her, and turning round she saw a plump boy with spectacles and dark frizzy hair, about thirteen or fourteen, perhaps.

'Did you want to speak to me?'

He surveyed her. 'They said you were who's in charge?' he said rather doubtfully.

'Yes. DI Fleming. And your name is—?'

'James Ross. Is it right Mr Murdoch's been *murdered*?' he asked, with definite relish.

'It may simply be an accident. It's too early to say.'

He looked crestfallen, and she added, following an instinct which had served her well in the past, 'But was there something you wanted to tell me anyway?'

'Yes. You see, I'm sure he was murdered. And I can tell you who did it, too.'

She recognized the type. He'd always be the one who sought out the teacher to drop the culprit in it, the school sneak. 'If you can, James, that might be a great help to us,' she said gravely.

His eyes gleamed. 'His daughter. Mirren.'

Startled, Fleming said, 'His daughter? You think she killed him?'

'She said she was going to.'

'And when was this?'

'At the sheepdog trials – you know? Her father was in it with a dog called Moss.'

She did indeed know, but she had forgotten the connection with Niall Murdoch. As he talked about it, it all came back to her clearly: Murdoch's humiliation, his unpleasant display of anger with the dog.

'You see, Mirren said he was being cruel to it, and he was going to kill it if it didn't get it right. And she said, if he killed it, she would kill him. Lots of the kids heard her. She's completely mental when it comes to animals.' He had an expression of smug satisfaction.

'And did he kill it?' This sounded to her just the sort of thing kids said; if they always carried out the threat hardly a day would go by without a child in the dock for patricide. Or matricide, depending on who had said no to clubbing till three in the morning.

'He was going to. She told me yesterday afternoon. There wouldn't be much point if you waited till after he'd done it to kill him, would there?'

'Do you not think that might be a bit extreme?'

He picked up her scepticism and flushed. 'Not with Mirren. She's like that. But anyway, the dog lived in that shed that got burned up last night in the fire. So it's dead anyway.'

No one had told her that. Fleming glanced towards the ravaged shed with some dismay. 'That's very sad.'

'Yeah, well.' James shrugged. 'So she probably did it for nothing.'

'There are a lot of other things to consider. And as I said, Mr Murdoch's death may well be an accident. But thank you very much for your help, James. Do you live near here?'

James indicated a house across the other side of the bay and when she said that if they needed a statement from him, someone would come to take it, he smiled self-importantly. 'Oh, you will!' he said, then strutted back to a group of teenagers who, Fleming saw, had been watching their conversation with some interest.

Not a taking child. Sneaks, like the invaluable police grasses whose information was vital to the clear-up rate, weren't attractive people, but no doubt in schools they had their uses too. Still, somehow she didn't think she'd be seeing him as star witness in the trial of Mirren Murdoch.

But the poor dog! Miserable with its final owner, and then such a ghastly end. She walked into the yard to look at what remained of the shed. She could only hope that Findlay wouldn't hear the details; he'd loved the animal.

'Strachan, Macrae and Ingles'. They still had his name on the plate by the door, which surprised Tam. Perhaps they just hadn't got round to doing something about it; that would figure, with lawyers.

His warrant card produced raised eyebrows and a silent 'Oooh!' from the young receptionist, who then looked thoroughly confused when he asked to speak to Mr Strachan.

'You can't. He's dead!' she blurted out, with a helpless look over her shoulder to the older woman sitting at a desk behind her who rose and came over. She was fresh-faced and neatly and befittingly twinsetted.

'Mr Strachan was the founder of the firm,' she explained. 'Mr Macrae is now the senior partner – perhaps you would like me to find out if he could see you now?'

'Fine,' MacNee said. He had a problem with twinsets; their owners usually seemed to expect all police officers to wear a collar and tie.

The receptionist, at a nod from her colleague, picked up the phone. MacNee was about to turn away when the other woman spoke. 'This is to do with Mr Ingles, is it? I just want to tell you he's done nothing wrong. He's worked here since he qualified, and he's a kind, gentle, decent man. The last verdict was a miscarriage of justice, and now it's going to happen all over again, isn't it? It's wicked, wicked!' There were tears in her eyes.

She sounded so fierce that MacNee was positively relieved when the girl said, 'He'll see you now,' and got up to lead him through.

The firm of Strachan, Macrae and Ingles was housed in the main square in Wigtown and Macrae's office was high-ceilinged, with an elaborate fireplace and moulded cornice. The furniture, though, was surprisingly modern and there was a computer on the desk.

The man who got up to meet him was just what MacNee had expected – a stuffed shirt, and it was an expensive-looking shirt at that, thick cotton with collar points which lay absolutely flat. Tam found, on the occasions when Bunty forced him into a shirt, that the points always curled.

Macrae had wiry grey hair and unusually bright blue eyes behind his gold-rimmed spectacles. He did not look particularly welcoming as he waved MacNee to a chair.

'Keith Ingles,' MacNee said. 'I wonder if you'd be good enough to give me a bit of background, sir. Did you know he had been arrested?'

'We all know.' His manner was forbidding. 'And we heard it with great sadness. If there is anything any of us can do – my colleagues, the staff – which would be helpful to him as witnesses to his good character and probity, then we are happy to do it.'

A certain closing of ranks was to be expected; this level of enthusiasm was not.

'You think we've got the wrong man?' MacNee asked bluntly and got a wintry smile in reply.

'You're not one to beat about the bush, sergeant, are you? Yes, you have got the wrong man. Just as you did the last time. Keith could have had no need for a paltry sum like five thousand pounds.'

It didn't seem a paltry sum to MacNee. 'He'd an expensive girlfriend,' he pointed out.

Macrae's lips tightened. 'Ah yes, Davina. I had to identify her body, you know, along with one of the office staff. She worked here as a secretary – a very indifferent secretary, I may say. Now that was someone who might have found the money *very* tempting.'

The suggestion was obvious. Decent chaps didn't do that sort of thing. Blame it on the hired help.

'Come off it!' MacNee said with deliberate rudeness. 'There was an eye-witness—'

'Mrs Aitcheson. Oh, *very* reliable!' The words were loaded with sarcasm. 'There had been big problems with pilfering from the cloakroom at the Yacht Club and Ingles was asked to tackle her about it. Nothing was proved – though the thefts then stopped – but as you can imagine she bore him a considerable grudge.'

MacNee didn't trouble to hide his incredulity. 'You're really telling me she'd have lied about the person who nearly killed her, just to land Ingles in it?'

'I know, I know.' Macrae was silent for a moment, then, leaning forward, he said earnestly, 'Look here. If Keith had needed money, and were dishonest – which he was not – there were half-a-dozen trusts he administered which he could have bled discreetly for larger sums than that, with very little risk of discovery as long as he wasn't too greedy.'

'Are you sure he didn't?'

Macrae bristled. 'For the sake of client confidence, we commissioned a forensic audit of every one, and there wasn't a penny unaccounted for.'

Very scrupulous. 'You've a point there, I'll give you that,' MacNee conceded.

'You'll say, no doubt, about the murder, that when it comes to a relationship like his with that – that little trollop, you can't predict how a man will react. But if he did it, in a moment of blind passion, he would confess. And unless he has, you've got it wrong. He was set up the last time, and the person you're looking for is the person who did it.'

His emotion was such that MacNee almost thought he would see those collar points curl. He left, and could feel Twinset's eyes boring into his back as he went out of the door.

'Where is Inspector Fleming?' Sergeant Christie demanded. 'I need to brief her on the situation.'

The crime scene was quieter now: the crowd had mainly dispersed and the owners of boats not within the cordoned area were free to resume normal holiday activity. The detectives, with a couple of uniformed officers, were taking names and statements inside the Yacht Club; the forensic team hadn't arrived yet and there were three officers on duty by the blue-and-white tapes.

'Over at Rowan Villa, I think, sir,' one told him, and Christie trotted off self-importantly.

He found Fleming surveying the blackened debris of the Murdochs' shed, looking troubled. 'I've just heard there was a dog burned alive in there. Horrible thing to happen.'

'Ah!' Christie was delighted to find himself in possession of superior information. 'Now that's where you're wrong. They sifted right through the rubble this morning, and the fire chief assures me that there was no dog inside. The fire wouldn't have been hot enough at any time to do more than char the bones and there wasn't a trace. It must have escaped when the fire started, or perhaps the fire-raiser took pity on the poor brute and set it free.'

Fleming's face brightened. 'That's good news. Where—?'

He didn't let her finish, anxious to proceed to the description of his next triumph. 'More importantly, we've picked up McLeish. He's only the haziest recollection of his movements last night – I wouldn't like to guess his blood alcohol count, even now – but it turns out he wanted to buy the flat the Murdochs have been doing up, there –' he pointed, 'for him and his pregnant girlfriend. Murdoch laughed at his offer. McLeish sprayed graffiti on the wall on Tuesday – you can still see the red streaks. And now the girl's broken up with him and yesterday she told him she was getting rid of the baby.'

'Powerful motive for revenge, probably.'

'Definitely,' he corrected her. 'We're not in a position to charge him yet since he claims he was with his mates all evening. We're checking that out now.'

'Good. You've been most efficient, sergeant. And a copybook exercise at the scene of crime too.'

Christie smirked modestly as she went on, 'Presumably we won't have a time of death until we get the pathologist's report—'

'Ah!' Christie said again. He was really enjoying himself

now. 'As it happens, we do have some idea. He phoned his wife at seven; the night watchman comes on duty at nine. Now, someone may have seen him after seven and we haven't had a chance to talk to the night watchman yet, but it seems likely it happened sometime between seven and nine.'

There was no doubt about it; he'd impressed her. 'That's a very promising framework. Have you enough manpower to cover checking McLeish's alibi?'

'All in hand, ma'am.'

Fleming smiled. 'Then I can leave everything in your capable hands for the moment, sergeant. Thank you very much.'

She walked away, leaving him glowing. He was inclined to resent the promotion of women to senior ranks, but whatever you said about tokenism, you couldn't fault Big Marge's judgement.

It was the woman draped sobbing over one of the tables in the smart bar in the Yacht Club who attracted Tansy Kerr's attention immediately, even though the place was full of people.

She was a blowsy blonde. Her considerable bosom was more or less restrained by a bra with black straps under a strappy hot-pink top, unsuited to the chilly weather, but she seemed oblivious to the gooseflesh on her flabby arms. Her make-up had smeared; there was a box of tissues and an empty bottle of wine on the table in front of her and the glass she was clutching was almost empty too. Another woman, with mousy hair scraped back in a ponytail and wearing an olive-green golf shirt, was sitting beside her as if to offer comfort, but with her rigid posture screaming disapproval.

Kerr hung back as she heard her say severely, 'Kim, you really have to pull yourself together and stop making a spectacle of yourself. For goodness' sake, what will people say? Supposing Jenna came in? Or Adrian?'

'So what? I loved him, and I don't care who knows it. He loved me too. He didn't give a stuff for that frigid bitch—'

'That's quite enough, Kim. I'm sorry.' The woman stood up, pursuing her thin mouth. 'If you're going to talk like that, I'm not staying to listen.'

'No, Shirley!' Kim grabbed at her arm. 'You're my friend, my only friend! Don't leave me—'

With an air of desperation, Shirley looked around and spotted Kerr, notebook in hand.

'Here's a policewoman, come to talk to you.' She turned to Kerr. 'You'll want to talk to Mrs McConnell. She was a great friend of Mr Murdoch's.'

As Kim looked up blearily, Shirley made good her escape and Kerr took her place at the table.

'Mrs McConnell, I'm DC Kerr. You knew the deceased?'

It was, as she realized as soon as it was out of her mouth, an unfortunate term to choose. It provoked another explosion of tears and an incoherent jumble followed which was hard to make out but in which the words, 'loved each other' and 'bastard who killed him' featured prominently.

'You were having an affair with Niall Murdoch?' Trying to get the interview back on track, Kerr offered her a wodge of tissues.

'So crude – affair! It was love, that's different.' Kim scrubbed at her face, creating a fresh streak of mascara on her cheek.

'Did your husband and his wife know about this?'

'I told him. Bastard. I told him I was going to leave him, you know, and have a real life, instead of boring, boring, boring—' She emptied her glass, tipped up the bottle, and when only a dribble came out waved vaguely in the direction of the barman. 'Another one, Dave!'

Kerr would have to grab her chance before the woman was completely blootered, but despite doing her best to drag out some more concrete information, like when Kim had last seen him and what he had said, details seemed vague. As far as she could make out, Kim hadn't had more than the most casual contact with Murdoch for some time. Her recollections all seemed to relate to last summer, and at last Kerr gave up.

'Thank you, Mrs McConnell, you've been very helpful.' *Not*, she added under her breath as she turned to select a fresh victim.

To her surprise, Shirley, who had made such a sharp exit, was hovering, waiting for her.

'Shirley Clark,' she introduced herself. 'There's something I wanted to tell you.'

'About—?' Kerr discreetly indicated Kim, who having had no response to her gestures was weaving her way across to the bar.

'Kim?' Her scornful laugh offered a fine view of large, yellowish teeth. 'She's a fantasist. He dropped her long ago.

'Just in case no one's told you, Niall Murdoch saw himself as the local stud. Ready to screw anyone who stood still long enough.' There was something in her tone that hinted she might have been someone who had stood still to no effect. 'No, what I felt I should tell you was that when my husband and I were leaving the club last week we heard Niall having the most tremendous row with his partner, Ronnie Lafferty. You know him?'

Kerr shook her head.

'Oh, he's the most *ghastly* creature! Poor old Keith Ingles knew a bit about him and tried to keep him out of the club, but of course he just bought his way in and there was nothing any of us could do about it.

'Anyway, this was really *violent*. I was afraid they'd come to blows or something. Not the sort of thing you expect in a club like this.'

Interested, Kerr prompted her, 'What was it about?'

'It seemed to be about money. And Ronnie was threatening him, definitely. But I'll tell you something else – everyone knows Niall and Gina have been having a fling.'

'Gina?'

'Ronnie's wife. Oh, quite attractive, I suppose, in a vulgar, obvious sort of way. And if Ronnie found out – well, according to Keith he has some *very* dubious connections in Glasgow. He's a scrap metal dealer, you know – I should think he could probably take out a contract on someone's life with one phone call!'

'You've made a very serious allegation, Mrs Clark. Got anything to back it up?' Kerr enjoyed seeing the look of horror on her face.

'No, no! That's just, well, you know . . .' The sentence trailed away, then she went on more confidently, 'It's so unfortunate, that's all, having people like that around. The rougher element. And Niall's – activities,' she compressed her lips again, 'they simply give the place a bad name, which reflects on the rest of us. Oh, I'm sorry for his little girl, of course I am, but I have to say I think Drumbreck is better off without him.'

It was in a spirit of pure mischief that Kerr asked, very gravely, 'Mrs Clark, could you give me an account of your movements last night, please?'

The wind had dropped. Out in the Cree estuary, Adrian McConnell reefed the sails of his 25-foot Contessa and started the engine. The sun was almost too bright now; he screwed up his eyes as he headed towards Wigtown Bay, the boat bucking as it hit the edge of the waves and salt spray blowing into his face.

It was so clean out here, so clean and fresh and quiet, away from the sordid mess of his life. He had walked out of the house this morning, walked out on Kim indulging herself in hysterical grief, and on his furious daughter, yelling, 'Don't damn' well leave me with her! She's your wife! I've got better things to do.'

He was tired, that was the thing, so tired. Yet he couldn't sleep: night after night, as Kim snored drunkenly at his side, his mind had gone round, and round, and round.

Could he face going back, face the dramatic scenes and the accusations, the questions, the pretence? Had he the strength to cobble together something that would pass for normal life? Did he even want to?

Adrian cut back the engine. The movement of the grey-green waves was mesmeric, the mysterious depths below darker, blacker, an invitation to silence, oblivion. He savoured the word. His mind, his whole soul, ached for oblivion. And it was there, just one step away.

17

The house MacNee was looking for was one of half-a-dozen in a cul-de-sac on the outskirts of Wigtown. Duntruin Place had been cheaply built in the seventies; there were cracks now in some of the dreary beige pebble-dash walls and where plastic double-glazing hadn't been installed the window-frames were rotting. There was one with a 'For Sale' sign which looked as if it had been standing empty for some considerable time.

The Aitchesons' house was well kept, though, and the small garden at the front had some kind of wee orange flowers – Tam was no gardener – on either side of the slab path. He pushed the bell beside the metal front door with its frosted glass panes and heard it chime.

He wasn't optimistic. This was a bad time for catching people in, and unless her injury had forced Euphemia into retirement – and certainly, with a name like that, she couldn't be young – he'd probably have to call back later.

But that was the sound of footsteps, and the door opened and he found himself looking at the burly figure of Brian Aitcheson.

'Tam MacNee!' he hailed him. 'This is a surprise. Come away in, man – I've not set eyes on you these five years!'

MacNee was taken aback. Aitcheson wasn't an uncommon name in these parts, and with the assumption he'd made about Euphemia's age, it had never occurred to him to connect her with Brian – in his fifties, retired from the Force a few years back. He'd never worked at the Kirkluce HQ, but MacNee had had dealings with him on occasion and found him a decent enough lad.

'Good to see you again, Brian.' MacNee shook hands and followed him inside. 'It was really the wife I was wanting,' he said, and saw the man's shoulders stiffen.

'She's out cleaning. What were you wanting her for?'

It suddenly came back to MacNee: Aitcheson had taken early retirement when his wife was caught shoplifting. Very embarrassing all round.

He said hastily, 'It's about the attack on her during that robbery. You'll have heard Keith Ingles has been charged with murder?'

Relaxing visibly, Aitcheson led him through to the kitchen at the back of the house, an old-fashioned kitchen with beige Formica surfaces and oatmeal-coloured doors, clean and bare to the point of being uncomfortable. MacNee sat down at the matching Formica table while Aitcheson switched on the kettle and set out mugs.

'Oh, we heard all right. Couldn't happen to a nicer fellow.'

'What happened that night, Brian?' MacNee had read Euphemia's statement, but it would be interesting to know her husband's take on it.

'Bastard all but killed her, that's what. I tell you, if I'd not come in, he'd have finished her off.'

'You saw him too?'

Aitcheson shook his head. 'Heard him leaving out the side door. I'd given herself a lift to the Yacht Club that evening – she usually went in the morning, but they'd had a hoolie the night before in Newton Stewart and she'd to clear up there. I was driving off when I saw she'd left her pinny, so I went back – lucky for her!

'It was just a wee wooden building in those days, not posh like it is now. I went in the front and called to see where she was, but there was just that door slamming. I went in, Tam, and I tell you I damn near stepped on her – on the floor outside her cleaning cupboard, blood everywhere. Scared me out my wits – you can imagine.'

'I can imagine.' MacNee pictured Bunty lying in a pool of blood and felt sick. 'So – so what was he like? Would you have said he was violent?'

Aitcheson fished the teabags out of the mugs and brought them over, then fetched a milk carton, a bag of sugar and a couple of teaspoons.

'Didn't know the man myself, but he fairly had it in for Mrs A. Made all sorts of accusations – couldn't prove one of them. All lies, of course,' he hastened to add.

'Of course.' MacNee nodded gravely as he stirred his tea. 'I'll get a word with her later, maybe.'

'It's her night for the WRI – she'll be going straight from her work, so you'd maybe be better to wait till tomorrow. It's Friday, so she'll be at the Laffertys' for a couple of hours – Beach House, you know it? Biggest place on Drumbreck Bay?'

'I can find it. But what are you at yourself these days, Brian? Dossing about?'

'Hardly that! I'm on shifts – night watchman at the Drumbreck marina.'

MacNee, who had been leaning back in his chair, sat up. 'The marina? You'll have heard about the boss, then?'

'I'm not long out my bed. Which boss – bloody Lafferty or bloody Murdoch?'

'They found Murdoch drowned this morning. Suspicious circumstances.'

Aitcheson's jaw dropped. 'Murdoch – dead?' Then he added, 'Don't know why I'm surprised, really. If ever a man had it coming to him, it was Murdoch.'

'Someone had it in for him?'

'Someone? I'll tell you who didn't have it in for him – that'll be quicker.'

'I have all the time in the world.' MacNee settled back again as comfortably as he could in the flimsy chair.

'Got a problem, old man?'

Adrian McConnell jumped as the voice hailed him. A motor yacht, with a cargo of women, children and men showcasing varied interpretations of the nautical look, swept round in a curve and throttled back alongside.

'No, no.' He leaned forward to fiddle with the engine. 'Cut out, that's all.' He turned the key and it obligingly caught. 'That's it now. Thanks all the same.'

'My pleasure,' called the man at the wheel, touched his hand to his white skipper's cap, and roared away.

Adrian looked down at the water again, foaming now in the wake of the motor yacht. The moment had passed.

Feeling so weary that every bone in his body ached, he turned the boat and headed for the shore.

Fleming sat at her desk, her head in her hands. It was only six-thirty, but it had seemed a very long day.

She was depressed as well as tired. She'd called the hospital from her mobile to get the latest on Angus's condition, but the report wasn't good. They still hadn't got him stabilized; they were having to keep him mainly under sedation at the moment, the sister said, and suggested delicately that for his wife to come and see him at the moment might be distressing. With experience of psychiatric hospitals, Fleming had read between the lines: he would be being physically restrained, ill-shaven, unkempt – Angus, who had always had an almost military precision in his grooming – and the condition of his neighbours on the ward would be upsetting too.

It hadn't been easy to persuade Janet that she should leave it for a day or two until the news was a little better and she was stronger herself. When Marjory went in, she was in the sitting-room, dressed but looking egg-shell fragile, with the bruise on the side of her forehead now showing rainbow colours. She'd had a stream of people in to look after her all afternoon, she said, though Marjory wasn't sure that having to make the effort to be sociable was the best thing for her.

Janet brushed aside the notion that she should be in bed, though, and when her daughter sat down beside her, her first question was when they were going to see Angus; on being told that it wouldn't be for a day or two yet, she burst into tears.

Marjory had put her arms round her, of course, patting and soothing as she would have done with Cat or Cammie, but it felt unnatural, ineffectual. How could she comfort her mother, when comforting was a mother's job? How could she console for a grief even she, in middle age, was still too young fully to understand?

It was Janet who calmed herself down, found her hankie and tried to smile as she dabbed at her eyes. 'I suppose I'll just have to possess my soul in patience, won't I? And maybe it's all to the good if he's getting a proper rest – he got awful trauchled, sometimes, you know, with the confusion in his mind.

'And don't you go fretting, dearie. We'll get him home again when he's more like his old self.'

Sick at heart, Marjory had weakly agreed, lied about having had lunch, and allowed herself to be shooed away because she'd be needing to get finished up at her work and be away home to her man and the weans.

So here she was at her desk, finishing up. Or at least, she ought to be, but there seemed to be so many aspects to these two investigations that she couldn't sort them out. Was Tam right that they were linked? Or was Murdoch's murder, as the strutting Sergeant Christie would have it, a drunken revenge attack? There was something about what he'd told her that was niggling at her, but every time she tried to focus on it, it seemed to slip away again and puzzling at it only made it worse.

At least MacNee's appearance at the door gave her an excuse for stopping. He seemed in high spirits.

'Anything you want to know about Drumbreck, just ask. I'm the wee boy!' he proclaimed, then, as she looked up wearily, he frowned. 'Here – who's stolen your scone? You're looking about as cheerful as a wet weekend in Rothesay.'

'Oh – long day, I suppose. And I've just been telling my mother that the news about Dad isn't good.'

'That's a bummer.' Tam sat down. 'How is Janet?'

'Looks as if she'd fall over if you breathed on her, but she's doing her usual stoic bit. Chased me away after checking up to make sure I'd eaten.'

'And had you?'

'Well, not in that sense,' Marjory admitted. 'Not since breakfast.'

'No wonder you're looking so peely-wally. Come on, I'll take you down the pub.'

'I've stuff to do to be ready for tomorrow and I don't want to be too late home, after being away.'

'Canteen, then, even if you only take a sandwich.'

She realized that she was, after all, very hungry and got up, sketching a salute. 'Sir!' She followed him downstairs.

There were two people sitting in the big room, with at one end the canteen hatch with tables, and at the other some easy chairs and a TV, now broadcasting regional news. Jon Kingsley and Tansy Kerr were sitting watching at the same table, Fleming was glad to see; it looked as if the hostilities of the morning had been suspended at least.

'That's Drumbreck, look,' Kingsley said as they came in.

There were views of the marina, of a handful of people and of uniformed officers by the blue-and-white tape, followed by a shot of the burned-out shed.

'A spate of vandalism in this quiet village has caused problems recently,' an earnest young man was saying to camera, 'and there is speculation that Niall Murdoch was killed during the arson attack which left this shed in ruins. A man is helping police with their inquiries.'

Fleming, choosing a sandwich, turned. 'That's what was bothering me – of course! Christie was telling me he was fixing on a time between seven, when Murdoch phoned his wife, and nine, when the night watchman came on, but of course the shed wasn't torched as early as that. If it's the vandal he's fingering, he'd have to be considering a much later time.'

'Around midnight, according to the night watchman,' Mac-Nee, at the hatch, said over his shoulder. 'Bridie and beans, thanks, Sally. Turns out he's Euphemia Aitcheson's husband, Brian – used to be in the Force, maybe you remember? Didn't see a thing – quiet night, till the fire broke out, he said.

'But I reckon we're needing to take a wider look at it anyway. According to Brian, if you fancied taking out Murdoch you'd be told to form an orderly queue. His partner, Ronnie Lafferty—'

Fleming and Kerr chorused in unison, 'Oh, him!'

MacNee looked surprised, and Fleming explained that the man himself was probably even now upstairs awaiting release on an undertaking to appear.

'Serious bad news, Lafferty is. After what Brian said I gave a pal in Glasgow a call, and he says the man's got some very nasty wee chums.'

Kerr pitched in her account of the row between Lafferty and Murdoch, and the rumour of Murdoch's affair with Lafferty's wife.

MacNee agreed. 'Brian talked about that too. Said Murdoch was a brave man – that's brave, like, stupid. He didn't say so, but he seemed a wee thing embarrassed and if you ask me he's been reporting to Lafferty about Gina's activities.'

'And the horse-faced woman I talked to said that Ingles had

known stuff about Lafferty and tried to keep him out of the club,' Kerr said.

Fleming listened to it all, frowning. 'You know,' she said slowly at last, 'it all does seem to keep coming back to the Ingles thing. We'll need to keep a very open mind about this.

'Incidentally, the pathologist says he drowned. The blow on the head, with something small and round and heavy, knocked him out, but he was alive when he hit the water. So there'll be an argument there for the lawyers when we get our man.'

'There's always an argument for the lawyers,' Tam said bitterly.

Kingsley had been uncharacteristically quiet. Now he said, awkwardly, 'Look, I just want to say sorry. I've apologized to Tansy for things I said this morning, and I know we screwed up. I've talked to Greg and he still thinks Ingles is guilty. I think he may be, but with this other killing – well, I'm scared we got it wrong. Listening just now, I had an idea . . .'

He hesitated.

'Always ready to listen to ideas,' Fleming said lightly.

'We know Murdoch was still alive at seven. He must have been dead by the time of the fire, or surely he'd have come rushing. And why wasn't he going home for supper? If we knew where he was, who he was with, that might tell us something.'

'I bet the night watchman takes a break from time to time,' Kerr said shrewdly. 'And anyway, the body was out at the end of the pontoons and everyone in the place has a boat. If he was there to watch for vandals he wouldn't look out to sea.'

'All good points. There's a lot to consider.' Fleming got up. 'I'm going back to finish up. I'd appreciate reports as soon as you can, and Tansy, I'd be grateful if you could chase up Christie if his doesn't arrive tomorrow. Briefing in the morning.'

As she went to the door, she turned to Kingsley. 'I'll detail you to do interviews in Drumbreck tomorrow,' she said. 'But just don't make any sudden movements.'

He grinned. 'Thanks, boss.' Then he added, 'And if you see Laura, could you tell her I'm being a good boy?'

'Laura? Oh – yes, if it comes up.' Fleming left, with MacNee following her. She had forgotten all about Kingsley's meeting with Laura at the dog trials, and this wasn't entirely welcome news.

She did try to make her voice as neutral as possible as she said to MacNee, 'Are they an item, then?'

'Not that I know of,' MacNee said sourly. 'Laura's far too good for the likes of him.'

'Laura's too good for most people, but we mustn't be selfish. He's a bright lad – homed in on the question of where Niall was at suppertime.'

MacNee sniffed. 'Still wouldn't let him or Allan anywhere near the Ingles case.'

'I know, Tam. There's always a temptation to want to be right, especially when it's your career at stake, but at least for once he's prepared to admit he's been wrong.' She laughed. 'Laura's influence, maybe.'

But it wasn't a happy thought. How could she, in future, talk to Laura as freely and confidentially as she always had done, when it would mean asking her to keep secrets from someone she was involved with?

Gina Lafferty heard the front door close with such a resounding bang that she winced, half-expecting it to be followed by the sound of its glass panel crashing to the floor. Ronnie had returned.

Ronnie storming in could hardly be called a novelty, but this, from the sound of it, was going to be the kind of storm where you were advised to put up the shutters and leave town. She shivered. Ronnie's rages were indiscriminate: you could be caught up just by being in the wrong place. *Stay calm, stay calm*, she told herself.

She was opening the sitting-room door when he bellowed, '*Gina!* Oh – there you are. You heard? You heard what they did – to *me*?'

She took a step back as he pushed past her, heading for the built-in cocktail cabinet. Taking a water tumbler, he filled it to the brim with Scotch. She noticed, inconsequentially, that the missing silver box had magically reappeared on its shelf.

Ronnie's face was a murky purple, an unhealthy colour. It crossed her mind to suggest he call a doctor – but why? It would only provoke him further, and anyway, what was wrong with being a wealthy widow?

'Yes. Tony phoned and told me.' Tony was Ronnie's 'fixer' in Glasgow, the man whose job it was to see that things like this didn't happen.

From the torrent of obscenities which followed, she gathered that the Fixer of the Year title was unlikely to be coming Tony's way. 'I managed to put in a call, told him to see to it they dropped all charges, there and then.' Ronnie gulped at his whisky, sat down, then got up again to pace the room; he stopped in front of the fireplace. 'Told him to get Beltrami on to them – he's a top Glasgow lawyer, knows the score – and all the moron could say was that the busies have six hours to do as they like first. Nazis, the police in this country – Nazis!

'So surprise, surprise – they charged me – they sodding charged me!'

'Tony said you'd get a slap on the wrist, that's all,' she offered soothingly.

This had much the same effect as pouring oil into a blazing chip-pan. 'A *slap on the wrist!*' he yelled, smashing the glass in his hand down so hard on the marble mantelpiece that it broke. Whisky poured out along the surface, dripping on to the pale carpet, and shards of crystal fell to shatter on the hearth. He didn't even glance down. 'A slap on the wrist? Has the man gone doolally? Do you know what a "slap on the wrist" means? It means a criminal conviction. It means fingerprints and DNA on file. That's what it means.'

He glanced down impatiently at the debris at his feet, then walked back to the drinks cupboard to fetch another Scotch. He turned, his bullfrog eyes hot and red, glaring at her. 'Well? Say something!'

Frozen in uncertainty, Gina's mind raced through responses. 'Why does that matter?' was out, as was, 'Why did you throw your weight around in the first place, then?' Her last attempt at calming him down had been disastrous; get it wrong, and the next whisky glass could break in her face.

She changed the subject. 'They're asking questions about Niall's death.'

'Never!' he sneered, but at least he hadn't flared up again.

'And you should know this.' Gina edged backwards, nearer to the door, just in case. 'I met Shirley Clark, shopping in Wigtown this afternoon. She's told the police that you and Niall had a flaming row in the club last week. She said that it had been her duty to inform them. I think she enjoyed telling me that.' She held her breath.

He wasn't going to hit her. He went very quiet, alarmingly quiet. 'She did, did she?' The hand that wasn't clasped round the glass tightened into a fist, then slowly relaxed again. 'I don't like busybodies. Tell her that from me next time you see her.

'And naturally, when the black bastards turn up here, asking questions, we can be totally open with them, can't we, babe? I was with you all last night, and you were with me.'

'Yes,' Gina said. 'Yes, of course.'

Jenna Murdoch made herself another cup of coffee. She'd lost count of how many cups she'd had today; probably enough to ensure that she wouldn't sleep, despite having been up most of last night.

She didn't particularly want coffee, but it was something to do. Unless you were prostrate with grief, it was hard to know how to pass the time. After the police left, there had been the visits from neighbours, of course: people who had barely spoken to her in a year had come to her door to express their shock and sympathy, some using the fig-leaf of a ready-meal from their own freezers to cover their naked curiosity.

It still left a lot of hours to be got through. There was plenty of work needing done in the flat upstairs but it wouldn't do, exactly, for such a recent widow to appear with a paintbrush in her hand. And TV entertainment seemed callous when your husband was lying, presumably, on a mortuary slab. Jenna would, they had told her, be required to go and identify him tomorrow. She didn't want to dwell on that. She'd picked up a book, but her thoughts kept drifting.

At least the dog hadn't burned to death. The investigators had been quite definite: either the fire-raiser had taken pity and let it go, or in its panic it had managed to slip its collar and bolt. She wondered what had happened to the poor thing – living rough somewhere, presumably. She hoped, in a general sort of way, that someone would find it and give it a good home.

It was odd that Mirren hadn't been more concerned about that. She'd told her, of course, when she heard the good news from the police, but the child's reaction had been as muted as her reaction to the news of its horrible death had been in the first place. But then, shock affected people in very strange ways.

And there had been a lot for Mirren to cope with today. She had lost her father; whatever their recent relationship might have been, that would knock any child off balance. The thing was, though, she couldn't see any sign of it. Mirren had gone about everything quite calmly, watching the police activity, appearing at mealtimes to eat with good appetite. She had been silent, certainly, making only the briefest replies to Jenna's anxious inquiries, but that wasn't unusual.

There had always been a curious detachment about Mirren. She had been her own, self-contained person from the time she was old enough to free herself from an unwanted embrace and toddle away to something which interested her more. She was passionate about animals, of course; had her father's ill-treatment of the dog destroyed all the normal affection you would expect a daughter to have?

Children were, in any case, less developed emotionally than adults liked to think. Oh, everything being well, they responded to love and tenderness by returning it. But there were enough cases in the newspapers, when you thought about it, to show that when things went wrong, there was something in children, some instinct for self-preservation, perhaps, which allowed them to be astonishingly callous.

So perhaps Mirren, receiving so little affection from her father, had shut down her own response. It was logical enough; Jenna could perfectly understand it. Whether, in later years, Mirren would be lying on a couch somewhere, paying to have herself unscrambled, was a whole other question.

It was more her reaction to the dog that baffled her mother. Perhaps the fury and despair Jenna would have expected had only been postponed, but Mirren hadn't gone blank, hadn't seemed anything other than – well, normal. After supper just now she'd asked if she could go and play computer games, which seemed fair enough. They couldn't sit at the table staring at each other all evening.

Her coffee was cooling. She sipped it, pulled a face, and had just got up to pour it away when she heard her daughter's hurrying feet. She hadn't played games for long, then – and when Mirren opened the door it was clear she was in distress.

She was trying to conceal it, though, sniffing hard, wiping away tears with the back of her hand.

It was almost a relief that the backlash had started. Jenna came towards her. 'Mirren, dear—'

'Can I go out?'

Jenna glanced at the window, the lights inside making it a black square. 'It'll be dark soon! Of course not. Why do you want to go out anyway?'

The tears fell faster. 'It's Moss,' she wailed. 'He's out there somewhere. He must be lost and frightened. Something could happen to him – he might be run over, anything! I have to find him.'

Her mother was bewildered. 'Yes, I know. I told you he must have run away. The police know that too, and they'll have been looking out for him. He'll be miles away by now, probably. There wouldn't be any point.'

Mirren went to the door. 'But he knows me! He could be hiding somewhere, afraid to come out. If I called he'd come, I know he would.' She wrenched it open and ran out. Jenna could hear her calling, 'Moss! Moss!'

She hurried after her and caught her arm. 'I tell you what. We'll walk round together, along the bay, and then back the other way along the road for a bit, and you can call him. If he doesn't come, we'll see about putting up a notice and offering a reward tomorrow. All right?'

Mirren barely seemed to hear her mother. Shaking herself free, still sobbing, she trotted down the road. 'Moss! Moss! Oh, Moss!'

Marjory Fleming parked her car in the yard and got out, arching her aching back, glad to have reached the end of the long day. It wasn't dark yet, quite: it was a fine, mild evening and the landscape was still bathed in the soft gloaming light as the sun slowly took its leave. The first star, low in the sky, was just visible and as usual she walked across to look out over the quiet hills, taking a deep breath of the cool air. Below her in the orchard, under the pink and white blossom on the trees, a few of the hens were still enjoying their freedom before darkness brought danger.

The lights were on in the Stevensons' cottage. It looks pretty, Marjory told herself. The fact that Susie could be at one of those windows, watching her now with ill-wishing eyes, was no reason for not relaxing, enjoying this precious, peaceful moment at the end of the day.

And it didn't spoil it, not really. The silence could still calm her mind; she stood a little longer before, with a deep sigh, she turned away, fetched her case from the car and went inside.

'Bill!' she called as she came out of the mud-room, but got no response, and when she opened the kitchen door, there was only Cat, sitting in the broken-springed armchair beside the Aga reading a book with a cover whose colour could only be described as fluffy pink.

She looked up. 'Oh, hi, Mum! Did you have a good time?'

'Not *quite* how I'd put it.' Marjory set down the case and went over to drop a kiss on the top of her daughter's head. 'But the bathroom in the hotel was sensational.

'Where's Dad?'

'He and Fin went out with the dogs – some rambler phoned to say there was a sheep on its back in a burn.' She went back to her book.

'Where's Cammie?'

'Weight-lifting, need you ask?'

'Well, he might have been doing press-ups. Better than doing nothing except playing computer games, anyway.'

Marjory picked up the pile of mail on the dresser – cata-logues and bills – then put it down again, and looked round the kitchen for indications as to what might have happened while she was away. The most obvious of these – apart from a number of pans 'soaking' in the sink – was a home-made chocolate cake, with thick icing, sitting on the kitchen table. Or, to be more precise, what was left of a chocolate cake; the raggedness of the remains suggested that Cammie had been allowed a free rein with a blunt knife.

'Where did this come from?' Marjory asked.

With an almost audible plop, Cat detached her eyes from the page. 'Oh – that was Susie. She brought it across when she heard you were away.'

'That was nice of her,' Marjory said, neutrally, she hoped, but her daughter wasn't fooled. Cat's eyes narrowed.

'She said she was afraid you wouldn't like it, but it was a shame we should miss out all the time because you were always too busy to do fun family things, like baking.' Her voice had a reproachful note and Marjory, too tired to be sensible, reacted.

'Oh, did she? Well, as a matter of fact some of us don't think that baking cakes is vital to a happy family. There's nothing wrong with the kind you can buy – and at least they don't put the icing on with a trowel.'

She knew it was childish, and Cat, as she put down her book and came over, had a long-suffering look on her face. 'Look, Mum, Susie told me that you and she had a row. But she'd had really, like, a hard time with losing the farm? And of course having to live in the cottage, with you going, "I'm not going to forget about it" all the time—'

There was a tone in her voice which reminded Marjory of one of her schoolteachers who had never delivered a rebuke without making it a sermon. And Cat was continuing.

'You're always saying to us "Can't bear grudges, let by-gones be bygones, have to understand the other person's point of view," right? So why don't you do that? Susie's nice, she could be a good friend if you let her—'

Something snapped. 'You know absolutely nothing about it!

And when I need lessons in social conduct from my daughter, I'll ask for them.'

The crusading light in Cat's eyes died. 'Fine,' she said tonelessly. 'I was only trying to help.' She picked up her book and walked to the door. 'And you can shut up your stupid hens yourself.'

'Cat – I'm sorry. I didn't mean—'

The only response was the slamming of the door. Marjory sank miserably into the chair her daughter had vacated. Was she the worst mother in the world? Had her own mother ever said to her something she would have given anything to take back a moment later? Marjory couldn't remember it, if she had. Probably not; her mother, like Bill, was a saint. She was surrounded by frigging saints, and it got trying, sometimes. Perhaps that was why she had got on so well with Chris Carter, who had no aspirations towards beatification.

Susie Stevenson certainly was no saint. Susie was – but there was no point in letting this latest underhand attack get to her, and the hens needed shutting in.

She was in the orchard when Bill, with Meg at his heels, came across the yard and spotted her. He leaned on the dry-stone dyke and called down to her.

'Good to see you home, love. Tough day?'

'You could say.' But at the sight of him, her spirits lifted; it was a gift he had. 'I won't be a minute – just one chookie with suicidal leanings to round up, then I'm with you.'

'Thought Cat was meant to be doing that. Anyway, I'll get out the Bladnoch, shall I?'

'Oh, *what* a good idea!'

He laughed at her heartfelt tone, then disappeared. Marjory shooed the last hen safely home, then stuck her head into the henhouse to make sure they were all accounted for. Some were roosting already, some crooning drowsily, and she smiled as she bolted the door. Oh, Susie or no Susie, it was good to be home.

There was a light on in one of the steadings as she went back across the yard and she could see Fin putting some rope away. His younger dog was trotting round him; the new one was lying on the threshold, watching.

He was, as Bill had said, very like Moss, though Moss had had a white blaze on his nose, while this dog's muzzle was black. But he had the same wide head, and one prick ear—

Marjory stopped, a dreadful suspicion forming. Without attracting Fin's attention, she altered her course to pass close behind the dog. 'Moss!' she said softly and the dog's head immediately swivelled, eying her suspiciously. She walked away.

Bill had put the lamps on in the sitting-room, which meant that the dust didn't show, and with the summer fire screen concealing the ashes in the grate the room looked welcoming, even if Meg was making a loud silent protest about the lack of a fire. And the whisky Bill was holding out to her – that *did* look good. Marjory took the tumbler and sat down.

'Bill,' she said unhappily, 'tell me about Fin's new dog.'

Bill, filling his own glass, didn't turn. 'Oh, Flossie! Shaping up very well.'

'Flossie. Or Floss, as I expect he calls it when it's working, Flossie being rather an odd name for a male dog.'

He turned with the guilty expression of a schoolboy who knows rules have been broken but blames the rules not the perpetrator.

'Look, I know he may have kidnapped the animal, but I've played along. I know it probably legally belongs to Murdoch, since I know Fin's too short of money to buy it back. But you saw yourself what Murdoch had done to Moss; the man's not fit to own a dog. And Fin told me a couple of days ago that Murdoch was going to have it destroyed if he didn't get the money.

'I know you have to uphold the law – of course you do – but

can't you just turn a blind eye? No one else knows it's here. I bet the police don't waste too much time on prosecuting people who remove unwanted stuff from skips, do they?'

For the second time since she came home this evening, Marjory felt like an outsider. 'No, of course we don't,' she managed to say levelly. 'Have you watched the news this evening, Bill?'

He looked at her sharply. 'No. Did I miss something?'

'Only that Niall Murdoch has been murdered. Fin is on a charge already for having attacked him, the shed where Moss was being kept has been burned down and Moss – curiously enough – seems to have disappeared.'

Marjory took a certain bitter satisfaction in his stricken look. He sat down heavily in the chair opposite.

'You're not saying—'

'No, of course I'm not!' she said impatiently. 'I'm not making any assumptions of any kind. This is the very start of a murder inquiry. There are, quite literally, thousands of questions to be asked. There are other suspects – one of whom is even now "helping with inquiries", though I'm not convinced.

'But perhaps you'll understand if I say that I can't treat this in quite the same way as if Fin had helped himself to a suite of wicker furniture for his conservatory.'

Bill's head was bent over his glass. 'No. No, I see that.'

She let a silence develop. It was a family joke that Bill's mind, like the mills of God, ground slowly, but the finely processed result was often worth waiting for.

This time, what he said was, 'I understand what you feel you must do. But Marjory, please – can I ask that you aren't the person to question him? It probably isn't realistic to hope it can be presented in such a way that they don't realize where the information came from, but if you could at least be distanced from it in some way . . . otherwise things here will become intolerable.'

Marjory felt as if he had slapped her. Her voice was icy as she said, 'I don't normally go out on preliminary inquiries myself anyway. But you're making it sound as if, because he's living on my doorstep, I should somehow feel guilty because he's a suspect in a murder inquiry. Of course the position is intolerable. It's been intolerable all along, only you haven't noticed.' Her eyes were stinging as she took a gulp of whisky.

'Of course I've noticed!' Bill was impatient in his turn. 'Susie's a devious besom. I found her having a very cosy chat with Cat, which I didn't think was at all healthy. There's nothing I'd like better than to see Fin with a better job and them both off the premises. But I like the man, and he's someone who's had a very hard time that looks as if it's about to get even worse.

'Can I ask you – do you really think he's a murderer? Honestly?'

She wasn't going to cry. 'No, I don't think he is. But whether I do or not, it doesn't matter. I have a job to do – and there are times when it feels a bloody lonely job.' She drained her glass and got up. 'I'm sorry, I'm very tired. I'm going to bed. I'll do my best to take a back seat on this, but I think you'll find I'll be blamed anyway. See you upstairs.'

'Marjory—'

She shut the door. No one understood the job, did they, except other cops – the hard, painful, demanding, isolating job which was, even so, the only one she had ever wanted to do.

18

'I'm coming round to your way of thinking about the deaths, you know that?' Marjory Fleming said to Tam MacNee.

With little incentive to linger at home, she had been at her desk early this morning, and on it was a huge sheet of paper with, at the centre, two names circled, other names round about and a lot of annotations and arrows.

She tapped the paper. 'Davina Watt. Niall Murdoch. She's the local tart. He's the local stud. You'd guess that just might have brought them together.'

'Shared interests? Might have made for some interesting conversations.' MacNee squinted at the mind map without enthusiasm. 'Never see what good this does, to be honest.'

'Clears out the jumble inside my head and puts it where I can see it,' Fleming said absently. 'Now, start here with Ingles. He had contact, obviously, with Davina and presumably with most of the people at the Yacht Club. Lafferty and Mrs Aitcheson didn't like him, his solicitor colleagues did.

'What we know for sure: he tried to kill Aitcheson, he didn't kill Murdoch. What we don't know: whether he killed Davina before, as he admits, he moved the body. If he did, there's a second killer out there. If he didn't, it's a fairly safe assumption that there's only one, who left Davina there for Ingles to find. Who, and why?'

'Framing him, of course – that's why. But you could be wanting him put away for good, or you could have a body to get rid of, and him an obvious suspect.'

'It'd have to be two birds with one stone. I don't buy the notion that you'd kill Davina to get revenge on Ingles. Davina wasn't a passive personality and there was a lot of anger in the way she was beaten up. She got herself killed for something she did—'

'Like blackmail.'

'Exactly. So – Ingles again. What was there she could blackmail him for? Squeaky-clean at the office, served his sentence, nothing much to lose in terms of respectability – hard to see what he would have to lose that would make it worth killing her.'

'So it's not blackmail. So she comes back, hoping to take up with him again? He loses his temper, and suddenly – bang!' MacNee smacked his fist into the palm of his other hand.

'Possible.' Fleming tapped her front teeth with her pen, considering. 'Right. Let's move on.

'Blackmail. Who is going to be vulnerable?'

'Usual suspects – married men, people with a position they don't want exposed. Normal stuff.'

'You're seeing Mrs Aitcheson this morning, aren't you? Get her blethering – cleaners always know all about their employers. Brian's given you enough to prime the pump. See if you can come back with a list.'

'From what he said, there'll be a powerful lot of names on it. Keep the uniforms tied up for the next three weeks, going round them all.'

Fleming frowned. 'OK, so we say she tried to blackmail an old flame and he flipped. Killed her, dumped the body to frame Ingles, against whom, say, he has a grudge. Then he decides to kill Murdoch too? Why?'

MacNee shrugged. 'Got a taste for it? Murdoch's been shagging his wife, say, and owes him money as well? Life's cheap, in some parts of Glasgow.'

Then he sat up. 'Here – life's cheap, right enough. Drop a

few hundreds in the right quarter, no need to soil your hands, and Bob's your favourite uncle.'

Fleming underlined Lafferty's name. 'Hold that thought. But we'll need to take it pretty cannily.

'The others we have to check out are the husband of Tansy's lovelorn lush in the Yacht Club – that can't have made him exactly happy. It would certainly give him a motive for Niall's killing; the way they all seem to have gone on in Drumbreck, it might be instructive to find out if he was in the game of Pass the Parcel with Davina too.'

'Left holding it when the music stopped and found it was ready to blow up in his face? Could be.

'Tell you who hasn't figured, though – the widow,' MacNee added. 'We all know the rule – it's the spouse as done it. And she can't just have been exactly happy with his goings-on.'

'Certainly wasn't, according to Christie. Can't fault his paperwork – his report was in the system when I came in. Says she was quite open about their bad relationship. He sounds a bit shocked that neither she nor the daughter shed a tear.'

'He's still hung up on the vandal – what's his name?'

'McLeish. Rab McLeish.' Fleming told him about the girlfriend's abortion, and MacNee winced.

'Ay, that would figure.'

'And there's a rather garbled story about a man all in black being around just before the shed was fired, which could certainly be McLeish – though Christie's inclined to doubt the witness. There's no connection that I can see with Davina, so we'd only be considering him if we accept that Greg and Jon are right about Ingles.

'And if so, there's another little problem I'd rather not have to deal with. All a bit too close to home.'

MacNee listened to the next instalment in the Stevenson saga. 'A wee thing tricky, that,' he said.

'Oh, you think? The woman is only trying already to turn my family against me – and making a good job of it, with a bit of help from my own stupidity – so can you imagine the hell that will break lose when she finds I've grassed on her husband and he's now a suspect in a murder inquiry?'

'Better get a hard hat.'

'You think you're joking! I've decided to send Jon and Tansy to the farm instead of Drumbreck – strict instructions to be tactful.'

'Make him feel better if he's to be arrested with kid gloves?'

'No. But I can tell Bill I did my best.'

MacNee cocked an eye. 'Not all sweetness and light there at the moment?'

'No,' she said again. 'And if you want me to be absolutely frank, I'm pissed off. Oh, I'll get over it, but I'm better keeping myself out of the way until I do.'

' "*Alas! Life's path may be unsmooth! Her way may lie through rough distress,*" ' MacNee began, and Fleming held up her hand.

'Hold it right there. Things are bad enough without that.' She looked at her watch. 'Time for the briefing. Come on.'

'We're packing up to go back to Glasgow today.' Adrian McConnell, coming in from checking that his own Contessa and Jason's Mirror were battened down and secure on their moorings, found his family in the kitchen at the back of the house.

The room was in a squalid state, with congealing leftover food, dirty dishes and pans cluttering every surface. Gary, strapped into his high chair, was smeared with gunk which looked like dried-on cereal and he was banging a spoon rhythmically on his tray. Kelly, oddly overdressed for this time of the morning, was eating a yoghurt, and Jason, eyes closed, was plugged into a Blackberry. Kim wasn't dressed;

wearing a slightly grubby green dressing-gown, she was heavy-eyed and very pale. She was staring into a cup of black coffee; beside it was an empty glass showing the white powdery traces of Alka-Seltzer.

Kelly looked up. 'Fine. You go. I'll come back on Sunday with Chazz.'

Behind Adrian's heavy glasses, a muscle twitched and he put up his hand to still it. 'You'll come home with your family. I'm not having you stay here with someone who's five years older, and I certainly don't trust his driving.'

'But there's a party tonight—'

'There's been a party every night. No buts, no arguments, that's it.'

Kelly jumped up. 'Oh, sure – that's it! Just take orders, like I'm your slave! No way! They'd all be, like, "Silly little kid, has to go home 'cos Daddy says!" Mum, I can stay, can't I?'

Kim looked up. 'Oh, better do as he says. What's the point, anyway? It's all ruined here, ruined.'

'You're so effing selfish!' Kelly accused her. 'Why shouldn't I get to go to the club, just because lover boy's got what was coming to him?'

'How dare you—' Roused from her lethargy, Kim raised her voice, but Adrian cut across her coldly.

'If you imagine there will be a party at the club tonight, you're wrong. Apart from everything else, the police seem to be moving in. And I think you may find we won't be the only people leaving early.'

Kim sank back. 'We might as well go. In fact, I'm not sure I can bear to come back to this place again.'

Adrian smiled wryly, but Kelly jumped up. '*What?*' she screamed. 'You want to ruin my life, don't you, just because you've made a mess of yours, and Dad's pathetic. I despise you both, you know that? I *despise* you!' She ran out, slamming the door, and a moment later the front door slammed too.

Jason opened his eyes and took out one earpiece. 'What was that about?'

'We're going home today,' Adrian said wearily.

'Oh,' Jason said, plugged himself back in and shut his eyes again.

Gary had begun to grizzle, a dreary, irritating noise.

'For God's sake, do something with that child,' Adrian snapped.

'I don't feel well. Do it yourself.'

The tic at the side of his eye was flickering again. He sat down at the table. 'Look, Kim, you'd better pull yourself together. I don't want to get caught up in all this and the sooner we're back in Glasgow the better.

'And if I were you, I'd stop all this nonsense about Niall. Everyone's having a laugh at the fool you're making of yourself.'

'You don't care about that. You want to get away because you can't face meeting people knowing that they're all laughing at *you*.'

He went white about the mouth. 'Don't – don't *dare* say that to me.' He got up, then leaned forward over the back of her chair to speak, very quietly, into her ear.

'I'm packing up to leave now. Come or don't come. I don't care. I've had enough of all this. You and Kelly have just gone too far. It can't go on like this, Kim.'

Gaping, she watched him leave. Jason, eyes closed, was still oblivious. Gary, too long ignored, started to cry in earnest.

'Oh, shut up, Gary!' she yelled suddenly. 'Shut up, or I'll slap you so hard your head will fall off.'

The child stopped on an indrawn breath, his mouth a wide 'O' of shock. Silence fell, and Kim put her head down on the table and began to cry again.

Fleming kept the briefing meeting short and to the point. The first objective, she explained, was to build a picture of Murdoch's movements on the day he was killed, concentrating particularly after seven o'clock. There would be a search of the house, and they needed to talk to his closest associates. She touched on the man's reputation, but when Wilson asked if there was a connection to Davina Watt's murder, refused to be drawn.

'The position at the moment is that Ingles has been charged with her murder, though I understand the Fiscal won't be proceeding to indictment as yet. It won't do any harm to find out who knew Watt as well, but don't let that cloud your thinking. There are other players who are in the frame for Murdoch's killing who have no link to her – like Rab McLeish, for instance, who's been charged already with vandalism to the Murdochs' property.'

That produced the only surprise of the meeting. 'Rab McLeish?' Jon Kingsley said. 'I think there was a McLeish who was a barman at the old Yacht Club – is this the same man?'

That was interesting. 'This one's a lorry driver. But we'll find out – it's not that common a name.'

'I can take that on,' MacNee volunteered. 'I'm to see Mrs Aitcheson this morning – she'll know. And I could pick off the Laffertys at the same time, and interview Adrian McConnell.'

'Good. That's it, then, everyone. Sergeant Naismith has your details. There's an incident room being set up in the Yacht Club for interviews – Wilson and Macdonald, I want you based there. One of you keep an eye on the house search and I'd like the other to focus on Murdoch's movements. And keep in mind that he could have been attacked by someone arriving in a boat. Allan, you're i/c the office end here.'

Allan looked less than happy, but said nothing. He was keeping a low profile these days.

As the officers started drifting out, Fleming stopped beside Kingsley. 'Jon, I said I'd send you to Drumbreck but I've something I want you to do instead.' She thought he looked a little put out at the idea of being removed from the centre of the action, but she paid no attention. 'I want to catch Tansy too – oh, there you are, Tansy. I'm heading back to my office. I'll explain as we go.

'I've got an awkward personal situation and I want it handled as tactfully as possible,' she said as they walked from the briefing-room on the first floor towards the stairs.

'So why pick on us?' Kingsley said, half-joking, whole earnest.

She turned to give him a frigid stare. He coloured, and mumbled, 'Sorry, ma'am.'

'Speak like that to me again and I promise you, you will be,' she said, irritated that his mood of humble penitence had disappeared quite so soon. She outlined the situation at Mains of Craigie and went on, 'You may remember he's on a charge already for attacking Murdoch.'

'The sheepdog trials.' Kerr nodded.

'That's right. So we have to take this one seriously. But I'd be grateful if you could be as discreet as possible about where the tip-off came from.' Fleming pulled a face. 'Oh, I know, they'll work it out. She will, if he doesn't. But it's just something I have to live with.'

'We'll do our best,' Kerr promised, and Kingsley asked, 'Any known connection with Davina Watt?'

'No reason why he should have.' Fleming shrugged. 'But you know what it's like in Galloway – it'll turn out she went to school with his sister or one of his wife's cousins, usual thing.

'Anyway, if you want to make me happy, find that he's got an alibi, preferably from the Moderator of the Church of Scotland, and that the dog ran away and by some wonderful instinct knew his master had moved to Mains of Craigie and came to find him, meantime having dyed his nose black because he fancied a makeover.'

'What would it be worth to find it was a conspiracy between the two of them and arrest them both?' Kerr suggested. 'That would get them out of your hair.'

'Don't tempt me,' Fleming said darkly. 'Thanks, anyway. See how you get on.'

They were standing by the staircase and Kingsley and Kerr were just setting off down it when PC Langlands appeared coming up, with papers in his hand.

'I was just bringing this for you, boss,' he called when he saw her. 'They've found the hired car. Burned out, up a track in the forest.'

Kingsley and Kerr stopped to listen. 'How badly?' Fleming asked, taking the report from him as he reached her and frowning over it.

'Totally.' Langlands leaned over to point out the paragraph. 'Fuel tank exploded, of course.'

'Won't be able to get much off it, will they?' Kerr asked, and Kingsley shook his head. 'Heat of a petrol blaze like that – wouldn't find anything with fatty traces like fingerprints or DNA. Pity, that.'

'They're taking it in for examination this morning,' Langlands added.

'We'll probably need to organize a fingertip search of the area round about at some stage, but that'll have to wait until we've tidied up at Drumbreck and can spare the manpower. I'm sure they'll have secured the site properly, but perhaps you could check that for me, Sandy. OK?'

Langlands, enthusiastic as ever, agreed and departed, with Kingsley and Kerr following him down. Fleming went on upstairs to her office.

It was a blow that there was so little likelihood of getting evidence from the car. Yet again, whoever was behind this had made sure there would be no evidence to tell tales.

Rab McLeish's connection with Davina was certainly inter-esting. He had, after all, the most obvious motive to kill Murdoch; could he, somehow, have been involved in the robbery? She remembered suddenly that the barman had normally had the safe keys in his possession and nothing could be simpler than having spares cut. Could there have been some arrangement between him and Davina? If Ingles had been wrongly accused, if Davina had come back to get money out of McLeish by threatening to expose his part in it—

But Mrs Aitcheson had caught Ingles in the act. That hare wouldn't run.

Doing all right for themselves, the Laffertys, MacNee re-flected as he stood between the fluted pillars which flanked the glossy black front door of Beach House.

He was expecting Euphemia Aitcheson, as the hired help, to open it in answer to the peal of the brass doorbell, so it was a shock to be confronted with someone who looked as if she might be able to come up with quite a number of uses for a feather duster, but cleaning surfaces was unlikely to be among them.

Gina Lafferty was, quite simply, a smasher. Tall, legs up to her armpits, dark glossy hair, eyes like an Italian film star, full lips, and below that – well, MacNee, struggling to keep his cool, decided it was wiser not to go there.

He had just produced his warrant card when a voice, from somewhere around the woman's shoulder, rasped, 'You'd better come in. Sooner you're in, sooner you're out again.'

Somehow he hadn't noticed Lafferty. His first thought was that she couldn't have kissed him yet – either that, or this wasn't a spell that could be so easily broken. Lafferty even moved like a toad, waddling squatly away without looking to see if MacNee was following him.

Gina favoured him with a smile of such high wattage that he

blinked. 'Come in, sergeant. We'll be happy to give any help we can. Such a terrible tragedy – everyone is absolutely devastated.'

He could hear the sound of hoovering from somewhere at the back of the house. As he followed Gina across the parquet floor of the hall, with its impressive staircase rising between carved pillars at the foot, the Mrs Merton question – 'And tell me, what first attracted you to millionaire Ronnie Lafferty?' – could not help but come to mind. Wonderful the things you could buy these days!

Lafferty had taken up his position in front of a white marble fireplace. Whoever built this house had been pretty keen on pillars; they featured here too, providing an unlikely setting for the present occupant. It was the sort of room that made you feel the real owners might come back at any time and throw the peasants back where they belonged.

'Get on with it, then. What do you want to know?' As Lafferty spoke, Gina went across to stand beside him.

'Perhaps it might be better to speak to you separately?' MacNee suggested.

Lafferty put his arm possessively round his wife's waist. 'We've no secrets, do we, babe?'

MacNee thought that under the expertly applied make-up she had flushed a little, but she only waited with a look of polite inquiry.

'Your movements yesterday – where were you, from seven p.m. on?'

'Quite simple – here. We were together, all the time. That do you?'

'You can confirm that, Mrs Lafferty?'

'Of course.'

She sounded quite confident when she said it; this didn't seem to be a problem area. He'd have to needle her a bit. 'And your relationship with Mr Murdoch—?'

'Perfectly civil,' Lafferty answered before she could open her mouth. 'He was my business partner. We didn't have a lot to do with the Murdochs socially.'

He needn't think he was getting away with that. 'I was asking your wife.'

'As my husband says. I never had any problem with Niall.' She didn't sound so comfortable now.

'No one said you did. In fact, just the opposite. They're saying you and he were having an affair.'

She gasped at his directness and her cheeks flared. 'I – that's—'

Oh, she definitely didn't like that, but Lafferty leaped in. 'You'd better have proof, sergeant, if I'm not to put in a complaint about you insulting my wife. And you don't, do you? All you've got is gossip from a set of poisonous old bitches.

'Take a look at my wife. They're jealous as cats. Nothing they'd like better than to cause trouble for her.'

'Maybe.' So he'd known what was going on, then: that was something MacNee had come to find out. 'And would you say the same about the violent row you were reported as having with your partner in the Yacht Club last week?'

Somehow he'd known to expect that too. 'This'll maybe come as a shock to you,' he drawled sarcastically, 'but I've been known to lose my temper. Niall and me – we've had the odd stramash over business, but it blows over.'

'What was the stramash about this time?'

'Taken an unauthorized loan out of the business. Borrowed five K to buy a sheepdog – what got into him, God only knows. Turned out to be a dud too.

'But he was going to be able to pay it back at the weekend. So if you're suggesting I bumped him off because he was owing me money, I'd have been a fool to myself if I'd done it just before he delivered, wouldn't I?'

'You believed him?'

Lafferty paused. 'Yeah. Yeah, I did, for some reason.' He sounded almost surprised; it was, MacNee reckoned, the first uncalculated response he had got.

'Where was it going to come from?'

'God knows.' Lafferty had lost interest. 'Look, five K's pocket money, as far as I'm concerned. And I've told you, we were here together all night, so whether or not I had a row with my partner isn't really relevant, is it? Unless you're suggesting my wife and I are both lying?' He stuck out his chin as if inviting a punch.

'I've heard what you said, sir. Thanks for your time.' MacNee turned to go and saw an easing of tension in their postures. 'I'd like a word with Mrs Aitcheson now. She's in cleaning, is that right?'

He saw alarm in Gina's eyes. 'Oh, I don't think—' she began, and MacNee saw Lafferty's free hand go across to grab her arm, so tightly that his fingers made indents.

'That's all right. Help yourself.'

'Thanks.' MacNee went to the door and opened it, then turned round. 'How's Paddy Riley these days? I gather he's a big chum of yours in Glasgow.'

Paddy Riley was to organized crime in Glasgow what Alex Ferguson was to Manchester United. MacNee had the satisfaction of seeing Lafferty's mouth open and shut, as if at any moment a croak might emerge. He closed the door gently without waiting for a reply.

Following the sound, he tracked Euphemia Aitcheson to a downstairs cloakroom, all gold taps and piles of fluffy towels. The bright yellow Dyson was clattering loudly on the tiled floor; it took her a moment to realize that he was there, and when she did she didn't look overjoyed to see him.

'Hello, Euphemia,' he said. 'Long time since I've seen you.'

She looked less than thrilled at the renewing of Auld Acquaintance, turning off the machine with an air of reluctance. 'What're you wanting?' she said bluntly. 'And Mrs Aitcheson'll do. I don't use my first name.'

He couldn't blame her. It must have been an additional burden in her life, along with the coarse-grained, waxy skin and flat dark eyes.

'I was having a wee chat with Brian yesterday,' he said, trying to ease into the conversation. 'Seems to be getting on all right.'

'He told me.'

His hopes of a useful, gossipy chat vanished. It was going to be awkward to ask her, flat out, to dish the dirt on her employers; he began on a different tack. 'Rab McLeish – do you remember if he was the barman at the Yacht Club at the time of the robbery, when you were injured?'

'McLeish? Aye, he was.'

'Right. But he wasn't there, the night it happened?' It crossed his mind that she could have been mistaken, in bad light and confusion, perhaps; McLeish, on paper, was a lot more likely to be violent than the solicitor described to Mac-Nee as a kind, gentle man.

'No.'

'No one else was there, just you and Keith Ingles?'

'That's right.'

She was watching him, with a sort of silent insolence that told him she was being deliberately obstructive. If that was how she wanted to play it . . .

He leaned back against the cloakroom door. 'Can you just take me through what happened that night, from when you arrived?'

Mrs Aitcheson glared at him. 'I told them a dozen times. And in the court.'

'You didn't tell me.'

She shook her head, in exaggerated disbelief at his demands. 'I went in. I heard a noise in the office and I called, "Is someone there?" and he called back, sort of anxious, "Who's that?" And I said, "Mrs Aitcheson, coming in to clean." And he said, "It's all right, Mrs Aitcheson, it's just me putting something in the safe." And I went to my cupboard and next thing I know he's coming at me with this great spike in his hands. And then he hit me. That's all.'

'And you recognized him?'

'I said. In court.' She was angry now. 'Course I recognized him. Had enough to do with him, didn't I – him and his nastiness and his, "Now, Mrs Aitchethon—"' She mimicked a posh, lisping voice savagely, then broke off. 'Anyway, got what he deserved, didn't he? Water under the bridge now.'

'OK.' She was positive, right enough, and that was a lemon which had more or less been squeezed dry. 'Brian was saying,' he went on, 'that Mrs Lafferty and Mr Murdoch were carrying on together. Did you—?'

'Brian should keep his big mouth shut,' she interrupted. 'Spreading gossip like that, without a word of truth in it.'

'He's not the only one saying that.'

'Should know better than to listen to them then, shouldn't he?'

'So you don't know anything about an affair?'

Mrs Aitcheson didn't even answer him. 'Have you finished? I've work to do.' She picked up a cloth and began vigorously polishing the gold taps.

He'd been planning to lead her on, get her talking about other scandal which might, as her job took her into the Drumbreck homes, have come her way. But the horse he was flogging was well and truly pushing up the daisies now and MacNee left with a cheery, 'Thanks for the wee blether, Euphie,' and enjoyed the sullen look she gave him.

MacNee let himself out and glanced back at the house as he left. A movement at an upper window caught his eye: Gina Lafferty had been watching him depart, but now twitched rapidly back behind a curtain.

19

'It's really pretty here, isn't it?' Tansy Kerr said, getting out of the car and looking out over Marjory Fleming's favourite view. 'Wouldn't mind living here myself – look at that blossom, and the hens pecking about!'

Kingsley, getting out of the driver's seat, grunted. 'Shame about the neighbours, as they say.' He gave a cursory glance, then turned round to survey the clutter of buildings: the old stone farmhouse, the cottage below, beside the orchard, the untidy sprawl of sheds and steadings in every possible material, from stone like the houses to polythene and red corrugated iron.

Kerr eyed him warily. He'd been in a bad mood on the way up, grumbling about being kept away from the centre of the action. 'Didn't tell MacNee to come out here to clean up the mess on her doorstep, did she?' he had said bitterly.

'What does it matter? It may have escaped your notice, Jon, but we're all in this together. We're a team. It's not a competition.'

'Oh, it may not be for *you*,' he said, his tone so patronizing that it made Kerr want to slap him. She lapsed instead into silence. She'd noticed that Big Marge always chose her confrontational moments carefully and, though it might not sit plausibly with Tansy's zany-hair-ripped-jeans style, the boss was her role model. A teeth, nails, kick-where-it-hurts row with Kingsley would have to be a pleasure deferred.

'I think we should start with Bill,' he said now, taking charge in the way that got right up her nose, considering she had longer service. 'He may have noticed comings and goings that we could check against what the Stevensons choose to tell us.'

'We'll have to find him first,' Kerr pointed out. 'He could be anywhere on the farm. So could Stevenson.'

But Bill was clearly expecting them. He emerged from one of the steadings, in heavy boots and blue boiler suit, holding a gushing hosepipe.

'I'll just turn this off and be with you,' he called.

Kerr had met Bill Fleming on a couple of occasions, including a charity ball when she had been his partner in a set of farmers for a Strip the Willow of such sustained ferocity that it made a fight after an Old Firm game look like a Sunday School picnic. She liked him; he was somehow comforting to look at, big and solid and pleasant-faced, with clear blue eyes and a ready smile.

He wasn't smiling today. He came over to shake hands with Kingsley, whom he hadn't met, and shook hands with Kerr too. He had big, hard, workman's hands, with the cracks and calloused that come from outdoor labouring.

'I suppose you're looking for Findlay.'

'Is he expecting us?' Kingsley asked.

'No. They'd heard about the murder – it was on TV last night – and I wasn't sure that you would want him given warning of your visit. But he's not far away – doing some work on a standpipe down in one of the lower fields there. I told him to take his mobile in case I needed him.'

He fished his own out of his pocket and made the call. 'He'll be about ten minutes. Do you want to wait in the house or anything?'

'Perhaps we could just check a couple of things with you,'

Kingsley said smoothly. 'The dog, first. Did you realize it was Murdoch's dog?'

Bill looked uncomfortable. 'Yes – well, yes, I suppose I did. You don't get a dog behaving like he did, totally in tune with a new master, as quickly as that. And there was that prick ear, too. But I didn't say anything. I was sorry for Fin, and I was sorry for the dog too. It was under a death sentence, you know.'

'Mmm.' Kingsley didn't sound sympathetic, and Kerr said hastily, 'But you didn't know at that time about Niall Murdoch's death?'

'No, not till Marjory came home and told me. I realized, of course, that this put a different complexion on the situation. Not that I believe for a moment that Fin would do anything like that.'

'Despite his having been previously charged with assault on Mr Murdoch?' Kingsley said coldly, and Kerr gave him an irritated glance. He seemed to be trying to put Bill's back up, a common enough technique when you were trying to bounce someone into an admission which might otherwise be withheld, but it was surely unnecessary here.

Bill didn't rise to the bait, only saying mildly, 'I suppose I would tend to put throwing a punch into a different category from murder.'

Kingsley ignored that. 'Comings and goings,' he said. 'The night before last. Did either of the Stevensons leave the farm after seven o'clock?'

'They wouldn't tell me. They would have no reason to.'

Kerr, looking at him sharply, suspected that he was, very gently, stalling. He had given an answer, but not to the question he had been asked. So much for Jon's technique!

Kingsley hadn't noticed. 'But you might have heard a car driving away – seen the car was missing? Did you see Stevenson at any stage in the evening?'

'I saw him around seven when I went out after supper to check on a delivery that had come earlier. I didn't see him after that.'

'So you couldn't say whether he was here or not? And what about a car leaving, say around ten, eleven?'

'I go to bed at ten, and after that I'm afraid I don't hear a thing. Marjory will tell you I'm a very sound sleeper.'

'How convenient for neighbourly relations,' Kingsley said unpleasantly. But, Kerr realized, he hadn't noticed that Bill had again avoided giving a straight answer. She sympathized, but he couldn't be allowed to get away with it. This was a murder inquiry.

Feeling mean, she put it to him directly. 'Bill, did you hear the Stevensons' car going out at any stage on Wednesday evening? Or notice that it had gone?'

He said heavily, 'When I went out at around nine, the hatchback wasn't there.'

'Oh, thank you, Mr Fleming. You've been *very* helpful,' Kingsley said with heavy sarcasm – as if, Kerr thought indignantly, it had been he who had prised out the information.

'That's Findlay now,' Bill said with obvious relief as Stevenson appeared up the path with a couple of collies. He stopped when he saw them and his face changed.

It was Kingsley who went forward, holding out his warrant card. 'Mr Stevenson, could we have a word?'

The dog with the prick ear came closer to his master, his eyes on the man's face, as if he sensed his unease. Stevenson squared his shoulders, as if he were going into battle.

'You'd better come down to the house,' he said.

'What's this?' Susie Stevenson, bristling, glared as Stevenson led them into the cramped room at the front of the cottage which served as both kitchen and sitting-room. 'My husband will appear in court on the date he's been given, but I don't see why we should be subjected to police harassment in the meantime.'

'May we sit down?' Kingsley said to Stevenson, as if she hadn't spoken. 'We've quite a bit to talk about, haven't we? Perhaps your wife could leave us—'

'And have my husband subjected to police brutality, without witnesses?' she shrilled, but Stevenson, looking unutterably weary, said only, 'Better do as he says, Susie. Go to Josh – see that he doesn't come wandering through.'

She looked mutinous, but when Kingsley went to the interior door and held it open, she flounced through it.

Findlay sat down on the sofa beside the little fireplace with its beige fifties tiles, and the two officers sat down opposite. The dogs had been left outside; through one of the small, deep-set windows Kerr could see the older dog with the prick ear lying down, his nose on his paws, eyes on the doorway.

'The dog outside there,' she said. 'That's Moss, isn't it?'

Findlay met her eyes for a second, then put his head in his hands. 'How did you find out?' he said, then, 'Oh, I suppose—'

'We had a tip-off,' Kerr said quickly. 'Someone gave us the information, and DI Fleming asked us to check it out.'

'Well, what would you have done?' There was hopeless anger in his voice. 'The man was going to kill him. I offered him money, but it wasn't enough. I'd tried to raise the full amount, but the bank in Kirkluce wouldn't lend, and he said it was all over. Wouldn't even talk to me any more.

'He's a brilliant dog – the best! I'd betrayed him once already, selling him to that bastard. How could I let him die?'

'Right, Mr Stevenson, suppose you talk us through it while DC Kerr here takes notes.' The emotional temperature had risen; Kingsley's cool tones brought it down again, but Kerr looked daggers at him. It wasn't up to him to order her to take notes.

'Nothing to talk through, really. I drove along to Drumbreck just as it was getting dark. There were people in the Yacht Club but otherwise there was no one around. Susie had told me where Moss was being kept so I just went to the shed and there he was. The only problem,' a flicker of a smile crossed his face, 'was the noise he made when he saw me, whining and yipping. But I shut him up, then I loosened his collar and left it attached to the chain so that it would look as if he'd slipped it, then escaped. To tell you the truth, I didn't think Murdoch would bother to go looking for him.

'Then I brought him back here – spot of black ink on his nose, and—' He shrugged his shoulders. 'That's all, really.'

'Is it? Haven't you left out one or two details?'

Stevenson looked at his interrogator. 'Well . . .' He hesitated. 'Probably, but nothing important that I can think of.'

'Nothing like torching the shed later, after you'd rescued the dog, by way of revenge? Nothing, perhaps, like being caught in the act by Murdoch and deciding to have it out with him, once and for all? You were angry, weren't you – very angry? That dog's more like a child to you than an animal, and what Murdoch was doing was murder in your eyes. Oh, maybe you didn't set out to kill him, but when you lost your temper, like that day at the sheepdog trials—'

It was a very aggressive performance, and Kingsley had raised his voice. The door to the back of the house burst open and Susie Stevenson erupted into the room.

'You're a fool, Findlay!' she cried. 'I told you I should stay. They're trying to stitch you up for murder now. They do that all the time – get you confused, so you say the wrong thing, and then when you correct it they claim you've been lying. You've seen it often enough on TV. But I heard every word. That's a false accusation, and I'm going to phone a lawyer.'

Kerr got up and came over to her. 'Mrs Stevenson, you can of course have anyone you like present. All we are doing at the moment is talking to your husband, trying to establish a background for the case. If we were going to use anything he said as evidence, we would have to caution him first.'

Sensing the woman hesitate, Kerr went on, 'Perhaps you can help us. You'll know when your husband left and when he came back with the dog. Perhaps if we knew the times involved we could work out whether he could have had time to do what my colleague suggested.' She knew the answer would be worthless – she could see Susie's eyes already narrowed in calculation of the shortest believable interval – but it had calmed her down, as Kerr had intended it should.

'Let me see,' Susie was saying. 'It must have been after seven-thirty when you left. I know because Josh had just gone to bed. And you were back by half-past eight – I looked at my watch. So you would only have had time to pick up the dog and come straight back.'

Kerr would have known it was a lie – she doubted if it was physically possible, given the narrow, awkward Drumbreck road – even if she hadn't seen Findlay open his mouth as if to speak, think the better of it and close it again.

'And then, of course, we were here together the whole of the rest of the night,' Susie finished triumphantly. 'So quite obviously, he could have had nothing to do with anything else that might have taken place.'

Kingsley had said nothing since Suzy entered the room, only observing them both with a cold, unwavering stare. Now he said, 'Did either of you know Davina Watt?'

That hit a nerve. To Kerr's astonishment, Findlay's pale, freckled skin went fiery red and Susie's mouth pleated itself into a tight, hard line.

'I – I used to,' Stevenson stammered. 'Years ago. Before we were married.'

'You, Mrs Stevenson?' Kingsley seemed only mildly interested.

'She was – around,' Susie managed.

'How well did you know her?'

Before Findlay could speak, Susie said quickly, 'Oh, she worked in the solicitors' office that Fin used for our farm, which wasn't far from Wigtown. We met her socially a few times.'

'Mrs Stevenson, meeting her socially wouldn't make your husband go bright red and you look as if you were sucking a lemon.' Kingsley sounded amused. 'We can go around asking people for gossip, or you can tell us yourselves now.'

Susie's face darkened. 'There's absolutely nothing to tell—' but Findlay took over.

'I made a fool of myself. I wasn't the first, and I don't suppose I was the last either to lose my head over Davina. Susie and I were engaged and I broke it off. It was a complete nonsense, and I realized what an idiot I had been. Susie forgave me. That's all.'

'That was my first mistake!' Susie shot at him bitterly. 'It's been one mess after another, and now this – thanks to your obsession with that stupid dog.' She turned away and stood with her back to them, arms folded, staring blindly out of the window.

'I see,' Kingsley said softly. 'Could it be that you only realized you'd made a mistake when she dumped you and moved on?'

He'd scored a hit with that one too. Findlay winced, and Kerr heard the hiss of an indrawn breath from his wife.

Kingsley pursued his advantage. 'And how did you feel when she turned up in the neighbourhood again?'

'I didn't even know,' Stevenson protested, and Susie swung round.

'Look, the woman left the place long ago. Findlay saw that she'd made a fool of him; why would it matter to either of us what she did after that?'

'All right, Mrs Stevenson. Now, Niall Murdoch – did you have any dealings with him, Mrs Stevenson?'

'We knew him slightly, as another farmer.' She met his eyes squarely. 'I haven't seen him for years.'

'Mmm.' Kingsley got up abruptly. 'I think that's as far as I want to take that angle right at the moment. Findlay Stevenson, you are under arrest. I am charging you with the theft of a valuable animal. I am now cautioning you. You do not have to say anything . . .'

Susie's outburst was spectacular; she launched herself towards the officers in a fury, but her husband caught her arm and shook it.

'Calm down, Susie. There's no point. What happens now?'

Susie flung herself free of her husband's restraint and collapsed, sobbing dramatically, into a chair. It was agreed that Findlay, with the dog, would follow them to the police HQ in Kirkluce where he would make a formal statement and the dog would be impounded.

Still smarting at the way Kingsley had treated her as his junior while he asked the important questions, Kerr got into the car and slammed the door. 'Well, that was a good way of handling the boss's request for tact! Was there any reason why you couldn't have asked him in for questioning, and charged him there?'

Kingsley was unrepentant. 'Why should someone get special treatment just because she's involved? And it broke them wide open, didn't it?'

She had to give him that; it was the truly maddening thing about Jon Kingsley – that he was good. Kerr changed her tack.

'Anyway, perhaps I could remind you not to give me orders? You're not a sergeant yet.'

He grinned. 'Act it, become it. I'd put money on Greg taking early retirement. He's pretty fed up with the job, and after his latest fiasco over Ingles . . .'

Kerr noted wryly the transferred ownership. If the fiasco had been a triumph, Allan and Kingsley would have been in it together. And she hadn't much brief for Allan, but Kingsley as sergeant would be infinitely worse.

Just to be irritating, she said, 'Don't count on it. Andy Macdonald's done his sergeant's exams already.' But she had a sinking feeling that if it came to a choice, the smart money would be on Kingsley, given his record.

Still, as they drove down the track to the main road, she added defiantly, 'Anyway, I don't care what you cracked open. It doesn't hang together. Apart from anything else, if Murdoch surprised him as he was torching the shed, how come he was in day clothes and got his head bashed in down by the boat? I still don't see that man as a killer.'

Kingsley's smile was wolfish. 'Perhaps not,' he conceded. 'But what about her?'

Donald Bailey's unannounced appearance in her office took Fleming by surprise. He must still be feeling penitent: it was normal practice for him to summon her to his, on the first floor. He must have taken the stairs too, rather than the lift, and he was breathing heavily as he came in.

He collapsed into a chair, which gave an alarming groan. 'I'm not sure about this keep-fit nonsense – not sure at all,' he grumbled. 'Seems to me that all it's likely to do is to seek out any flaws there may be in the system. But you know how it is with doctors these days – paid by results, so they're always on at you with scare stories.

'So, Marjory, how are we getting on?'

Fleming grimaced. 'The reports are coming in all the time, but nothing seems to hang together. Every time I look at it the picture seems to shift. I can't even make up my mind whether we're looking for one killer or two.'

'Don't like coincidences. Usually they aren't.'

'Tam agrees with you. And certainly, we've nothing to suggest Ingles did anything more than he admits to. They've found Davina's hired car but it's a burned-out shell so they won't get much from that.'

'Leave Ingles out of it, then. What have you got?'

'I wish I knew.' Fleming sighed. 'It's a smoke-and-mirrors job – just when you think you're on to something, you find you've been led into a blind alley. For instance, the hot suspect was a man McLeish, who's on a charge already for vandalism on the Murdochs' property. Then he turned out to have been a barman at the Yacht Club too, so would have known Davina, and I thought we were getting somewhere. But half an hour ago I had a phone call from the local sergeant who'd arrested him in the first place, and McLeish has got four mates and a bartender who can say he was drinking with them from six-fifteen onwards and by closing time he wasn't fit to walk, let alone go off for a spot of fire-raising in Drumbreck. Had to pour him into his bed, by all accounts.'

Bailey considered that. 'Hmm. Well, you know what I'm going to say, Marjory –'

She did indeed. If she had a fiver for every time he mentioned it, she could retire happy.

'– Ockham's razor. Never mind the smoke and the mirrors. What's the simple solution?'

'Someone killed Davina, then went on to kill Murdoch.'

'Go on. Features in common?'

Fleming considered that. 'The method – a bash on the head. With a stone in one case, possibly even in both, though the pathologist says it wasn't the same one. We'll know more after the autopsy, but they've got people away on holiday and as he doesn't think there'll be any surprises it won't be done till Monday. They're doing all the usual tests for fibres and so on, but whatever they find, fibres don't come with names and addresses attached.

'Anyway, I suppose you could say the weapons suggest the killer didn't go prepared, he just reacted. It's an odd combination if so – the unplanned attack, but no immediate and obvious traces left. Yet it was in Davina's case a sort of fury, given the beating-up she took.'

'So – a man, then?'

'The pathologist said a woman wasn't impossible, but quite honestly, yes, I'm assuming it's a man we're looking for.'

'There's Murdoch's wife, though, remember – you haven't mentioned her, but close to home is always the place to start.'

'I'm going out to see her later. The report on her reaction to the news is that it was cold-blooded, to say the least. And perhaps, given his alleged morals, Davina returning was a threat to their marriage or something – though from the sound of it, she'd have been happy enough to be rid of him.'

'Expensive business, divorce. Much more profitable to be a widow. It's amazing when you get right down to it, how often money is behind murder.'

'I'll keep that in mind, though I think at the moment it only opens up another hall of mirrors.'

'You keep Ockham's razor in the forefront of your mind, and you won't go far wrong.' Bailey got up. 'Well, I think you've benefited from a few pointers there, Marjory. And I'll just go and phone the ACC and assure her that we've everything in hand and expect a favourable outcome shortly.'

'One day, Don, a big black thing will come down the

chimney and carry you off, if you go on telling porkies like that.'

He smiled benevolently. 'Oh, but Marjory, I am in momentary expectation of a major breakthrough and a favourable outcome. Very shortly. That's your job, isn't it?'

Fleming viewed his retreating back with exasperation. He'd been helpful, supportive – then that final burst of pomposity, and the unnecessary tweak of the tail! Oh well, that was just Donald, and she should be used to it by now.

Still, she'd been ordered to produce a speedy result. And it was twelve o'clock already – where did the time go? She'd better get down to Drumbreck. The incident room would probably be flooded with information this morning and she ought to check out the manpower situation; she'd be interested to see what was coming in, too. She was on her feet when her mobile rang and Laura's hesitant voice greeted her.

'Marjory – is this a bad moment?'

'Not at all, Laura. I've just got rid of the Super, and I'm on my way out in a minute.'

'I hate to interrupt you at work, but I've just heard about Angus. How is he – and poor Janet? I met one of her neighbours in the High Street this morning and she was saying things were bad.'

'Oh, horrible.' Marjory sat down again. 'It's all so bleak . . .'

It was a relief to talk to her friend, even though there was little Laura could say from a professional point of view that was comforting.

'We'll just have to take it as it comes,' Marjory said at last. 'And of course I've got my hands full here.'

'How is it going? I've heard half-a-dozen rumours – it's the hot topic in the Co-op this morning.'

'I'd love to talk it through with you – might help to clear my mind, which is feeling like a junk shop where everyone has parked bits of furniture they don't want any more. But I've no idea when I'll finish tonight. I have to go off to Drumbreck now—'

'Look, you pass my door. Come in on the way back and have a cup of coffee.'

'I'll have to look in on my mother first, but I'd like that. I could get to you around six, say. I'll call you if I'm running late.'

Talking to Laura would be a good idea. Even if she did have something going with Jon Kingsley, she was reliably discreet and she had a talent for seeing clearly what Marjory, too close to the action, had missed. She just had this feeling that she was constantly being deflected in her thinking: whenever there was a lead to follow, another seemed to appear, turning her back and bouncing her off in a different direction. Smoke and mirrors, as she had said to Bailey.

The answer was, as ever, to keep going, to plough away at the routine. But in this case, where they had as yet no definite list of suspects even, relying on the process of elimination could take months and Bailey's patience was running out already. This was when you had to think, and think hard, to come up with the angle that would link it all together. She certainly hadn't managed that so far.

She had just got up to go when the 'ping' of an incoming e-mail brought her back to check it. Reports were coming in fast at the moment; she'd read them later, but if it looked urgent she'd pick it up before she went.

It was another message from DCI Chris Carter. She sat down again, and opened it.

It was short, just, 'How's it going? Has Tweedledee come up with anything? And how about the dreaded Susie? I want the next instalment. Chris.'

She reached for the mouse to click on 'Reply'. It would be therapeutic to tap into the sympathy and understanding she knew she would get from him.

Therapeutic, and dangerous. No, if she needed therapy, she had Laura. She took her hand off the mouse again. Tiffs and squabbles got resolved, and blew over, if you let them. And if there wasn't an alternative.

She'd reply to Chris tomorrow, when she wasn't feeling quite so bruised.

20

There was no one around. Drumbreck had suddenly become a ghost town, with houses blank-faced and empty-looking and hardly a car in sight. There had been several occasions, on the last stretch where the road was single-track, when Marjory Fleming had had to duck into a passing place as cars drove out, often in convoy: Dad in front in the BMW or Mercedes, Mum and the kids behind in the Chelsea tractor. When she reached the Yacht Club and got out, blinking in the bright spring sunshine, there were just two or three cars she didn't recognize as police vehicles, and out in the bay she could only see a couple of sails. There wasn't even any sign of a Press presence.

She went into the deserted Yacht Club, past the bar with its shutter down and on to the area which had been converted into an incident room, with three tables surrounded by screens for interviews and one with a couple of phones. The Force Civilian Assistant who was manning them was filing her nails and DC Wilson was sitting on the edge of one of the tables, swinging his legs and eating a sandwich as he talked to a bored-looking PC.

'Was it something you said?' Fleming asked, and Wilson grinned.

'Either that or a problem with personal freshness that no one's liked to tell me about, boss. It's been like this all morning. The exodus started about ten. Tam came in half an hour ago and said he'd walked right round the bay, ready to knock on doors, but he'd only found a couple of families still there, and they were packing up.'

'Any joy from them?'

Wilson shook his head. 'According to Tam, you'd think they'd agreed what to say. Totally shocked, terrible thing for his wife and child, but of course they'd barely known the man himself and hadn't set eyes on him for days. They were only leaving early to have the weekend to get the kids ready for school on Monday.'

'He's probably right. A chat over drinkies the night before about the party line, shouldn't wonder. Where's Tam now?'

'Across at the Murdochs' house with the team going through his effects.'

'Right.' Fleming surveyed the empty room. 'I have to admit, it's disappointing – I'd been naive enough to think that all these public-spirited people would have been queuing up to pass on any information they thought would help.'

Wilson snorted. 'Public-spirited, until the polis start asking awkward questions about them and their little chums, and then they scarper faster than a kid on a stolen moped.'

'So nothing useful come in here at all?'

'There's a couple of our lads in the marina office, looking through the books and papers,' the PC offered, and Wilson added, 'The staff were here earlier, but there was nothing doing at the marina and the sailing lessons had been cancelled, so after we'd taken their statements they shut up shop and went home. There was to have been a kids' disco this evening but that's been called off, and there was no other trade so the barman's given up and left as well.'

'Had they anything to say?'

Wilson pulled a face. 'Bit vague. The instructor girl – fit wench, Murdoch obviously knew how to pick them! She said she'd spoken to him round five when she finished a class. He was outside the boat shed holding some tackle but she didn't know what he was doing with it – taking it to a boat, probably – and she didn't think she'd seen him after that, but couldn't be sure. The barman thought he might have seen him in here around eight, but couldn't swear it wasn't the day before. The guy who's the other instructor and the one who works on the boats saw him around in the afternoon but couldn't recall when.'

'And no one noticed a boat coming in at the end there, any time after seven?'

'You wouldn't see it, unless you had a reason to go past the boat shed and round the corner to those end pontoons. The staff said it's always pretty quiet between six and eight – kids back home for their tea and adults changing for the evening. Maybe someone might have noticed something as they passed if they were coming in from sailing after seven, but all the owners who don't live nearby have gone back to Glasgow or other points north, so we'll have to track them down if we want to find out.

'We did try to get a list of yachties they'd seen around that afternoon, but that wasn't realistic – just too many comings and goings.'

Fleming was, as she had said, disappointed. She'd expected to have a problem with too much information, not too little, and she sighed. 'So – not much point in this set-up, then, is there? I'd better arrange for it to be taken out again. I'm going across to the Murdochs' to talk to her and I can find out when they think they'll be finished there – and the lads in the office as well. Mmm.' She looked round, contemplating the hole this would have made in the budget, and noticed Wilson's sandwich. 'Where did you get that?' she demanded. 'I could do with a bite of lunch.'

'They delivered a box – there.'

He indicated, and Fleming was sorting through what was on offer when Tam MacNee appeared.

'Saw your car, boss, so I thought I'd check in before I went back to HQ. Not much doing here. The McConnells have gone – at least, when I went round he had left and she was packing up the 4 × 4 by herself and swearing.'

Fleming had found a ham sandwich. 'Any luck with Mrs Aitcheson?'

'Closer than a clam.' MacNee joined her to investigate the box, coming up triumphantly with a bag of salt and vinegar crisps. Between crunches he told her that he suspected the cleaner had been given her orders by Lafferty. 'When I said I was going to speak to her, Gina got a bit antsy, but he wasn't fashed about it. Anyway, Euphie, as her friends don't call her, would only say she'd nothing to add to what she'd said in court and implied that the lovely Gina was pure as the driven snow and anything else I'd heard was just lies. If you ask me, she'll give Brian laldie for what he said to me when she gets home.'

'And what about the Laffertys themselves?'

MacNee frowned. 'Hard to get a handle on that. Stated they were together all evening, and I was inclined to believe them – as we said before, Lafferty wouldn't necessarily need to soil his hands. But he was prepared for every question I asked him. I wouldn't gasp and fall over backwards if you told me he'd plenty practice talking to the polis.

'He admitted Murdoch was owing him money. He'd borrowed from the firm to buy the sheepdog at a daft price – £5000, would you credit it? And here's me with a couple of dogs at home I'd pay you to take away. But I believed Lafferty when he said the cash wasn't an issue. Maybe the principle might be, but there seem to be a lot of folks round here who think £5000's small change.'

'All right for some,' Wilson said with some bitterness. 'If they'd like to give it to me instead, I could buy a boat and be down here every weekend. And still have change to get the wife a new handbag.'

MacNee had finished his crisps and was tipping the packet up to get the last of the crumbs when the phone rang. They all jumped; the FCA, who had rapidly stopped her manicure when the DI arrived, answered it and scribbled down a message, which she handed to Fleming.

She read it. 'That's interesting. There's a licensee in Whauphill – you know, around six or seven miles on the road to Port William – and he says he had Davina with a man in his pub last week. Saw her photo on the telly and recognized her.'

'Right.' MacNee was quick off the mark. 'I'll cover it.'

'Toss you,' Wilson offered. 'I'm fed up, sitting here.'

'No, no, laddie,' MacNee said. 'Too much excitement's bad for the young. I'm sure there's a report you could be writing. Or maybe you could borrow a nail file.'

Fleming stepped in. 'Will, you take it. Tam, you can come with me to talk to Mrs Murdoch. How's the team getting on at the house?'

'Hadn't found anything significant when I left, but they're still going through the personal things. Macdonald was hoping to get permission to check out the computer later – he understands these things. I don't think he reckons they'll be long.

'He said the daughter's been to and fro all morning, away out calling for the dog, then coming back in tears. You'll be telling her it's safe, will you?'

'Just check that one out for me, if you would,' Fleming said to the FCA. 'DC Kerr or DC Kingsley – doesn't matter which. Ask if they can confirm that Findlay Stevenson had Moss.'

Wilson was putting on the denim jacket that had been draped over the back of a chair, ready to leave.

'Have you Davina's photo?' Fleming asked. 'Just to make sure the man has it right.'

'There's one here,' the PC said. 'There's one of Murdoch too – do you want that as well?'

Wilson shrugged, but took it anyway, and left with the air of a man anxious to escape before something happens to stop him.

'Ma'am,' the FCA said, 'DC Kerr says Stevenson has admitted stealing the dog and he's been arrested and charged. And she asked me to say, "What do you reckon to Susie?" and that DC Kingsley's following it up.'

'Susie?' Fleming said blankly. 'What does she mean?'

'That was all she said.'

'You'd better call her back,' MacNee advised. Then he said, 'Hang about. I see what she's getting at.'

'Oh—' She looked aghast. 'Surely not!'

'You can't get involved, whatever. Leave it to Jon – he'll do what's needed. You're going to see Mrs Murdoch, remember.'

'Yes, of course,' Fleming said mechanically, but her mind was neither on the interview ahead nor on the likelihood of Susie Stevenson's guilt. She could only dread the domestic reaction to the sort of interrogations that lay ahead.

'Mrs Murdoch, first of all, may I say that we're very sorry for your loss. We'll do our utmost to bring the killer to justice as soon as possible.'

Jenna Murdoch nodded, but did not speak. They had tracked her down to the new flat after Fleming had checked with Macdonald for progress – none so far. Jenna had been painting; it seemed a curious thing to do at a time like this, but people had different ideas about what constituted therapy. She had led them down an uncarpeted flight of stairs into a shabby sitting-room with an unlived-in feel.

'Can I take you through the events of the past few days?' Fleming went on. 'I do appreciate this may be distressing for you, but—'

'No, carry on. You have a job to do.' She seemed quite composed.

'You last saw your husband when?'

'After breakfast he left the house. He didn't come home for lunch and then he phoned to say he wouldn't be in for supper either.'

'Did you notice what sort of mood he was in?'

'He'd been in a bad mood for the last bit – the trouble with the dog, perhaps, I don't know. But he wasn't so bad the last day or two, and that morning over breakfast he was almost cheerful. It wasn't like him, actually.'

'Why did you think that was?' MacNee asked.

'I didn't think about it really. Probably if I had I'd have assumed he'd a new girlfriend.' She looked at them challengingly as she said this, but MacNee didn't follow it up.

'Could it have been because of some money he told Ronnie Lafferty he'd be getting at the weekend?'

'Did he say that to Ronnie?' She was interested. 'I can't think where he could have been expecting to get it from. He said something about it to me too, but to tell you the truth I thought it was probably another of Niall's pipe-dreams – you know, he'd had a letter saying he'd won £100,000 and the poor fool believed it. Ronnie wasn't likely to go for that, though . . .'

'Did your husband know about Davina Watt's death?'

The woman's face became stony. 'He didn't mention it to me and I certainly didn't mention it to him.'

Fleming changed tack. 'You said Niall left the house after breakfast Wednesday morning. You didn't see him around the place after that?'

'I was here all day, working on the flat till about half-past six, when I came down to start making supper. Mirren came in shortly after Niall phoned.'

'Where had she been?'

'Oh, I wouldn't know. She's on holiday, of course – met up with some of the other kids, maybe, or off on her own bird-watching, more likely. I don't worry – it's a safe place for kids.

She knows to come back for meals, but apart from that she can do as she likes.'

'Was she upset about the situation with the dog?'

They both saw her tense up at MacNee's question. 'Oh well, she's fond of animals, of course.' She gave an unconvincing laugh. 'Naturally, she was concerned that Niall might carry out his threat to have the dog put down – though of course he wouldn't have. That was just posturing.'

'You think so?' Fleming sounded sceptical. 'Yet a lot of people seemed to believe him. Did your daughter believe it wouldn't happen?'

'Yes, of course she did.' Jenna had crossed her legs; now she crossed them again at the ankle into a tight twist.

'Not what we've been told,' MacNee said bluntly.

'What were you told, then?' She reacted defensively. 'Oh, I suppose that's the sort of thing you're not allowed to tell me! In this place you'd be very wise not to believe what you hear. They're vile, the people here—'

'You don't like Drumbreck? I can imagine it might feel very unreal, a strange sort of community.' Fleming's voice was soft now, and sympathetic.

'Unreal!' Jenna gave a harsh laugh. 'It's a fantasy – has been ever since the locals got priced out. It's their own little Happy Valley, where you buy exemption from the normal rules.'

'And you weren't tempted just to sell up and leave?'

MacNee sat back in his corner chair, withdrawing into it to keep Fleming as the focus. He had a notebook on his knee; every so often he jotted something down, then went back to studying Jenna Murdoch's face.

'Leave? Oh God, yes – from the moment I arrived and saw this white elephant. But *he*'d landed us in it – bought it, and the marina, at a sucker's price which meant we couldn't begin to get our money back until we'd – *I'd* – restored it. And before you ask,' she gave Fleming a defiant look, 'we couldn't get a mortgage, so of course there's no nice little insurance nest egg. He wouldn't have wasted money just for me to benefit.'

'Hard for you, all these years,' Fleming said blandly. 'And you never got to the point where you thought you'd just walk out? It doesn't sound as if you had a happy marriage.'

'Happy? What's that? All there was to keep me going was the promise of money later. If I walked out I'd everything to lose. And why should he—?' She broke off, biting her lip.

'You said he wasn't a faithful husband.'

'Didn't know the meaning of the word. But round here, he was hardly unique.'

'Was there anyone special, at the moment? You said you wondered about a new girlfriend?'

'I didn't even try to keep track.' She sounded infinitely weary. 'I didn't care much. He didn't either. I know he had a fling with Kim McConnell – she's just the sort.'

'But he wouldn't have been likely to leave you for her?'

She laughed again, this time with what sounded like genuine amusement. 'She's not worth it, to lose a free plumber, decorator, brickie, housekeeper – you name it. Quite hard-headed, Niall was. And I doubt if she even had exclusive rights. I noticed he's employed a very attractive new instructor – I should think she's on his schedule, if he hasn't got to her already.'

'Did she—?' Fleming began, when the mobile in the pocket of her trouser suit rang. She took it out and glanced at it, then stood up. 'Sorry, I'll have to take this. Excuse me. Tam, perhaps you could explain to Mrs Murdoch about Moss meantime?'

She went out and took the call outside in the bare, echoing hallway. It was Will Wilson.

'How about this, boss?' He sounded excited. 'The guy in the pub ID'd Davina – we'd expected that. But then he described the bloke with her – tall, dark, lick of hair over his forehead –

and I showed him Niall Murdoch's photo. That's who it was, definitely. Ten days ago – Wednesday, he thought. He remembered them coming in together a few times, some years back.

'I thought if you were talking to the widow this might be useful.'

'Oh, it will be. It will indeed. Thanks.'

Could it be that Murdoch, for some reason, had killed her, incurring revenge from one of her lovers? And why, every time a rare piece of solid evidence came in, did the case become more confusing, not less?

When Fleming went back into the room, MacNee was saying, 'So now we know that the dog's all right.'

Jenna's face had brightened. 'That's such good news. I'll need to go and find Mirren and tell her at once!' She jumped up.

'Could you spare us another minute or two, Mrs Murdoch?' Fleming spoke from the doorway.

Jenna looked at her and the light in her eyes died. Slowly she sat down again.

'Your husband was a friend of Davina Watt's, wasn't he?' Fleming sat down on an upright chair beside the armchair Jenna was sitting on, and drew it a little closer, leaning forward to look into the other woman's face.

'Oh – years ago. Yes, I suppose so. We both knew her.'

'Was she another of your husband's girlfriends?'

'Oh, probably. Like I said, I try not to know.' Her attempt to sound offhand was a miserable failure.

'And did you know that she had come back to the area? That he had seen her?'

Jenna licked her lips. 'No, I had no idea.' She looked up, straight into the searching hazel eyes, her own wide and unblinking.

'That's not true, is it?' MacNee spoke suddenly from his

place in the corner and Jenna started, as if she had forgotten he was there. 'You knew she'd come back.'

'It's easier, you know, to tell us the truth,' Fleming said conversationally. 'We'll find out anyway, one way or another. And I'm afraid in our job we have nasty suspicious minds. Lie to us, and we always think the worst.

'So what I'm asking myself at this moment is, "Why doesn't Jenna want to tell us she knew?" And there's an obvious answer, but I wouldn't want it to be true. Convince me it isn't.'

Jenna's restless hands, pleating themselves in her lap, showed her inner turmoil. At last she said, 'All right, I did know she was back. That was last week – Tuesday, Wednesday perhaps, I can't be sure. It was an accident – I picked up the phone at the same time as Niall did and I heard her asking him to meet her at the usual place. That was all.'

'And did he?'

'Probably. I don't know. He never mentioned it.'

'Do you remember what sort of mood your husband was in just before last weekend – Thursday and Friday?' Fleming asked.

'Last weekend?' Unexpectedly, Jenna gave a crack of laughter. 'Terrible! All he could think about was the stupid sheepdog trials. He was blaming the dog, because he knew he'd make a fool of himself yet again.'

'You don't think he'd anything else on his mind?'

'If he had, he didn't tell me.'

MacNee said suddenly, 'Was Davina the same as your husband's other girlfriends?' Then, as he saw her begin to frame a 'yes' added, 'I'm asking because, from all accounts, she was kinda different. And remember, you're not a very good liar.'

'Oh, all right!' she burst out. 'She was different. None of the others mattered.'

'So, if she came back, were you afraid Niall might want a

divorce before you were ready for it, financially speaking?'
Fleming was pressuring her now.

'No. No! She'd have gone off again, just like she did last
time. When she found he still hadn't any money, she'd have
been gone. And believe me, I'd have enjoyed telling her.

'Anyway, I didn't know where she was. All she said on the
phone was to meet in their "usual place" at two o'clock. I'd no
idea where that was.'

MacNee was making notes. 'You could have followed your
husband when he went to meet her.'

'No, I couldn't!' she cried wildly. 'We only have one car, for
a start. And I didn't kill my husband either, if that's the next
thing you're about to accuse me of! I was here all night. Ask
Mirren!'

'Did you not, maybe, go to bed at some stage?' MacNee
wasn't buying that one.

'Well, of course. But she'd have heard me if I went out.'

'And you'd have heard her?'

Jenna turned to answer Fleming, shock showing in her face.
'Of course I would! The stairs creak, and I'm a light sleeper.
What in God's name are you saying now?'

MacNee had withdrawn again. Fleming, her voice very
gentle, said, 'Nothing at all, Jenna, we're just exploring every
avenue. And of course, we haven't talked yet about the shed
going on fire, have we?'

'The shed? I don't know anything about the shed! It was set
on fire, I woke up, that's all.'

'And Mirren? Did she wake up, too?'

'Yes, and I told her to go back to bed.'

'And she did?' Fleming raised her eyebrows. 'What an
obedient daughter you have! You must tell me your secret.
I doubt if either of my two would have paid any attention if I'd
said they weren't to come and watch a fire.'

Jenna looked down at her fingers. 'Yes – yes, that was – well,

anyway, she did. She was tired. She'd been very emotional—'
She stopped.

'I think we'd gathered that,' Fleming said. She glanced at
MacNee. 'Anything else? No? I'm sorry we've had to press
you like this, but you will understand that it's a very serious
case.

'Is Mirren here? If we talked to her now, perhaps we
wouldn't have to trouble you both again.'

'I don't know where she is. She went out.'

'Someone can speak to her later, when she comes back.
We'll leave it there. Thank you for your co-operation.'

Jenna made no reply, didn't move as they got up to leave. As
they shut the door, she was staring at the worn carpet under
her feet, her face white and set.

Macdonald came down the stairs as they crossed the hall.
'We've just finished upstairs,' he said. 'I'm away now to check
on the computer. I'll need permission from herself to access
anything that's not to do with him, won't I? I'm not sure of the
status of the warrant.'

'I think you're right,' Fleming agreed. 'Don't take any risks. In
this case, Andy, I'd like you to be very meticulous about anything you might find in case we need to prove provenance in
court. She's in there. Get her to sign something, if she agrees.

'And maybe you could question the daughter, when she
turns up? There's something funny there – I feel it in my
bones. OK, feminine intuition – stop sniggering, you two.'

'Was I sniggering?' MacNee protested.

'Sniggering inside. Anyway, whatever you do, tell the poor
kid the dog's safe. Whatever she's done, she deserves to know
that.'

Macdonald nodded, and headed for the sitting-room while
Fleming and MacNee left the house and headed back to the
Yacht Club where they had both left their cars.

'What do you make of all that?' she said.

'There's a lot to think about. She's a bad liar, but that's not to say she couldn't have killed. She's pretty hung up on money—'

'They all are – have you noticed? Davina, Niall, Lafferty, Jenna – maybe the Super's right after all. Follow where the money leads you. Though I still wonder what this kid's been up to. Her mother ties herself in knots when you start talking about her.'

'You don't think a kid could do that, to her own father?'

'That's what they said about Oedipus,' Fleming said darkly. 'No, I don't, really – but there's something there.'

MacNee looked at her slyly. 'And what about Susie? Jon's not a fool.'

'Susie. Oh God, how am I going to cope with that? Yes, I can imagine she's probably said all the wrong things, and set everyone against her. I can believe she might want to kill Niall Murdoch because of what he did to her husband through the dog – though only just, since in my experience Susie is usually about Susie and only Susie. But I can't see her beating up another woman the way Davina was, and I can't see why she'd want to kill her anyway. And what I will say is that the further we get into this, the more I think Ingles is peripheral to the whole thing.'

'I'm with you there. I've said that from the start.'

'I'll have to find out what they think they've got on Susie – ask them to go easy unless it's—'

She broke off, seeing MacNee's expression. 'No, I can't, can I?' she said wretchedly. 'I have to back off.'

'Yup, back off. We've a few other lines to follow up on anyway. There's a connection between Murdoch and Davina now. Maybe it's him sent her the cutting, if they've kept in touch.'

Fleming seized on that. 'They'll take his prints at the

autopsy but I won't get the report till Tuesday, probably. Wait a minute. Tam, get someone at the house to lift his prints from something personal – that would save time.'

'I'll do that. And I tell you the other thing I'll do – I'll phone my pal in Glasgow – he gave me a nice wee tip for tweaking Lafferty's tail, and he'd maybe go round and have a chat with Adrian McConnell. He's the mystery man – took off before any of us had a chance to see if he minded Niall Murdoch making free with his wife.'

'Fine. I'm going to make arrangements for removing the incident room whose main use seems to have been as a café and manicure parlour. I just hope my credit with Donald's good enough to withstand the cost of that little error of judgement. Always supposing he checks, which on past form, mercifully, he doesn't.

'After that I'll head back to Kirkluce. I'll have to call in on my mother, but I'm going to have a cup of coffee with Laura around six. Want to come? She's usually got something helpful to say.'

MacNee grinned. 'Now, when have you ever known me turn down a chance to see Laura? Meet you there.'

Kingsley, with Kerr, arrived at the incident room half an hour later. 'Where can I find the marina employees?' he said abruptly to the PC in the incident room who, alone with the FCA, had again lapsed into lethargy.

'They're not here. Gone home – they've shut up shop.'

'Who authorized that?'

He didn't try to hide his irritation and the constable reacted badly. 'Didn't need authorization, did they? Expect me to arrest them, or something, in case you might happen to want to speak to them later?'

'You might have thought—' Kingsley began angrily.

'Shut up, Jon.' Kerr said sharply. She and Kingsley had

been bickering already in the car; she could accept that Kingsley had come up with this take on the case but not that it gave him the right to dictate procedure. Barging in, over-turning apple-carts as you went wasn't, in her view, construc-tive: she'd been driven to remind him of the recent results of his cock-at-a-grosset attitude to Ingles, which had left him dumped in it as well as Allan. This, she was prepared to admit, had not improved professional co-operation.

Now she said to the constable, 'Don't let him get to you. He's just a wee woolly lamb once you get under this snotty, unpleasant exterior. Let me know if you ever do – no one else has.'

The constable guffawed, the FCA smiled discreetly, and Kingsley gave her a dirty look. She went on blithely, 'You have addresses for them? Thanks.'

They waited in silence as the constable jotted them down, then held out the paper. Kingsley made to take it but Kerr got there first.

'That's brilliant. Now, Jon. I'll give you directions. And we can discuss in the car how we're to handle the questions. Discuss – that means someone says something, then the other person says something back. It doesn't mean that you an-nounce what we're going to do, and I do it. OK?'

His face black with temper, Kingsley stalked out of the club. Kerr, with a grin and a wave to the others, followed him.

'Funny the bank wouldn't lend to him,' Kerr said suddenly after they had driven for a couple of miles in silence. 'I got a loan for a holiday last year, no bother. Never even asked my earnings.'

'Extraordinary,' Kingsley drawled.

'It's not as if she hasn't a job. She works in that upmarket dress shop in the High Street.'

Kingsley didn't respond.

'Let's go and ask them why.'

He turned his head to stare at her. 'What on earth for?'

'It's an inconsistency. The boss always says you should look for anything in a story that doesn't add up.'

'"The boss says" doesn't make it right,' he said acidly. 'What does it matter? In any case, they'll only quote client confidentiality if you haven't a warrant, and I can't see you getting one for that, can you?'

'I still want to try,' she persisted. 'Let's go to the bank.'

'Let's not. Let's go and question some of the people who might have seen Susie Stevenson hanging around the place.'

'After the bank. It could be shut by the time we've done interviews.'

'Let's start with the boatman. What's his address?'

'That's for me to know and you to guess,' Kerr said provocatively.

'Stop playing idiotic games!'

'I will when we've been to the bank.'

The rest of the journey was accomplished in icy silence. When at last they drew up outside the bank, Kingsley switched off the engine and folded his arms. 'You can go. I'm not coming in to make a fool of myself.'

'Better without you.' Kerr got out and walked into the bank jauntily.

She wasn't long, and one look at her face told Kingsley she had been successful. But she didn't speak; he was forced to say, 'Well?'

'Thought you'd never ask! The loan manager was just a laddie – couldn't make up his mind if he was more chuffed at helping in a murder inquiry or feart he'd do the wrong thing.

'So I said I understood all about confidentiality, but time was important and all I really wanted was a nod or a shake of his head if I got the right answer for why they wouldn't lend. So I started with bad credit and overdrafts but then I couldn't think of any other reasons and he was starting to look desperate like someone in one of those game shows where you're allowed to mime but not say anything.

'So I said, "Look, I'm not here and you're not there. If we need something officially I'll come back with all the paperwork and we've never seen each other before." Then he just sort of burst out, "I didn't refuse, I told her they'd got it and she said she didn't want it any longer." So then I said, "Better out than in," and that was it, really.'

'OK, you were right, there was something there,' Kingsley admitted. 'She was ready to lie to the bank and to her husband. Would she be prepared to kill Murdoch to prevent Findlay from going to him direct and promising to pay him in instalments, maybe?'

'He may not have told her he was planning to steal the dog back,' Kerr pointed out. 'She'd probably have tried to stop him if he had; it was a pretty daft thing to do, with the DI right on your doorstep. She'd have been better killing the dog instead of Murdoch and putting an end to it.'

'But you've turned up something here,' Kingsley argued. 'And do we know the whole story? Is there some back connection with Murdoch, like there was with Watt? I wouldn't put it past her to have a go at anyone who got in her way, would you?'

'From what I've heard about her, no, I wouldn't. But we need to do a lot more digging. First staff address?'

'Yes please, Tansy. Thank you, Tansy. You were right, Tansy,' Kingsley said mockingly, but he was smiling for the first time that day as they drove off.

21

It was a still, sunny evening. In the walled garden at the back of her cottage, Laura Harvey was pouring lemon squash from a jug clinking with ice into a glass for Marjory. Tam MacNee was making inroads into an Export while Daisy panted at his feet, exhausted after a protracted game with a tennis ball.

Marjory had just arrived. Compared to Laura who looked cool and fresh in a sharp yellow linen shirt over jeans, she felt positively grubby in her working trouser suit. She shrugged herself out of her jacket and leaned back in the garden chair, shutting her eyes and tilting her face to the evening sun.

Laura put the glass into her hand and she sat up, drinking it gratefully. 'I've just come from Mum's. Thanks for popping in, Laura – she was so pleased to see you. Did you say anything to her about Dad? She didn't mention it, but she seemed much calmer today and I just wondered.'

Laura took her own glass and sat down. 'She's intelligent, Janet. I told her about the plaques that Alzheimer's forms in the brain, and she latched on to that. Her generation was brought up not to believe in mental illness – it was the sort of thing you just had to snap out of – and I think that somewhere at the back of her mind there was an unarticulated belief that he could do that, if she tried hard enough to help him. A physical cause – well, that's different.'

'I'd never have thought of that. Laura, would you come with us when Bill and I have to tell her that she can't cope with him at home? I'm dreading that.'

'I would, of course. But I think it'll be possible to get her to accept it gradually. As I said, she's not stupid. I enjoy my chats with her; we'll see what happens over the next bit, shall we?'

Marjory raised her glass in a toast to her friend. 'Thanks, Laura. Don't ever let them persuade you that you'd be better working from London, will you? – I need you here.'

'Maybe you could get round to solving our professional problems now too,' Tam said. 'We're in a right fankle, I can tell you that.'

Marjory groaned. 'Too many strands, all tangled together. Too many suspects.'

Laura was surprised. 'I thought you'd made an arrest, for one of the murders.'

It was Tam who groaned this time. 'Let's kid on we haven't, all right? It's what we're all doing down the nick.'

'I don't even know where to start,' Marjory said helplessly.

Laura thought for a second. 'What's the big question? The first one that springs to mind?'

'Why did Davina Watt come back?' Marjory said promptly.

'There you are! Tell me about her.'

Between them, Tam and Marjory sketched out the background, while Laura listened intently. At the end of the recital, she said, 'It seems to me that the big question you're not asking is why she went away. Look, you have this woman who disappears, changes her name, wipes out all traces of her previous life – why does someone do that?'

'Doesn't want to be found,' Marjory said, and Tam went on, 'Scared. And we know she was worried enough about Ingles to want to be told when he was getting out, wanted to be on her guard. She'd stitched him up. So when he was free, he could come looking for her – or at least go snowking around to see if he could prove what she did to him. She wanted to be long gone by the time he did that.'

'I still think she saw it as a chance for a new life too,' Marjory argued. 'Natasha Wintour – she was going to be a different person from plain Davina Watt. Natasha would get what Davina only dreamed of – only it didn't work out like that. She wanted to be a new person, but the same things happened all over again.'

'Doesn't happen. You take yourself with you, no matter where you go.'

'Right enough,' Tam approved. 'So what about the first question – what was she doing coming back here?'

Marjory was frowning. 'Something changed, didn't it? Suddenly, it was worth taking the risk. What did she want?'

'Money,' Tam said. 'Like the Super said, it'd be money.'

'It was running out, in Manchester. The man she was living with told me he'd spent his legacy, she'd tried blackmail, if we're to believe the barman, and it didn't look as if she was getting far with that. So she thought there was a better prospect here.'

'You said she was into wealthy married men. Was there someone whose interest she thought she could revive?' Laura suggested.

Tam was more cynical. 'Or someone who would pay to stop her mouth?'

'Someone,' Marjory said, 'who was horrified enough to lose control and kill her there and then. It was that sort of attack. We know that Murdoch met her – could he have had a reason to kill her?'

'From the sound of her, anyone might. But then, of course—'

They said in unison, 'Who killed him?'

'But look – I'm just thinking aloud here,' Marjory said. 'We're pretty sure she came back looking for money. He didn't have the sort of money she'd be looking for even if he was vulnerable to blackmail, which on the face of it seems unlikely. Suppose, when she met him in the pub, she told him what she was planning –

'Maybe he was her insurance policy, so she could say if she was threatened that someone knew what she was doing. Then, with her dead—'

'Or maybe before that. He might have decided to get in on the act anyway—'

'Right enough, we've seen nothing to suggest the man had scruples—'

'That fits, because he was definitely expecting he'd have money at the weekend—'

'But who from?'

Laura, watching as ideas were batted to and fro, felt the surprise of a spectator at a tennis match being asked to join in when Tam turned to her. 'So where do we go now?'

'You seemed to be getting on just fine without me,' she protested.

'Oh, we've only been covering one angle there,' Marjory said. 'There are others – the hit man employed by the Glasgow mafia, Murdoch's wife and daughter who are behaving very strangely—'

'And your friend Susie Stevenson,' Tam said slyly.

'Susie Stevenson?' Laura asked. 'Marjory's told me about the problem with her – but is she involved in this?'

'It's just Jon Kingsley flying a kite,' Marjory began, then, remembering suddenly – and with a certain unreasonable resentment – his link with Laura, added, 'Oh, he's very smart, of course, and he's picked up on something there. I haven't had a chance to talk to him yet, but Davina was so badly beaten up before she was killed that I can't imagine a woman being at the heart of it.'

Tam was less sensitive. 'Here, Laura, you and him – have you clicked?'

Laura coloured. 'No, Tam, we haven't "clicked", as you so elegantly put it. If you want a full statement about the extent of our acquaintance, I went out with him in his boat last Sunday and then he took me for a pub lunch – in Wigtown, though I'm sorry I'm afraid I can't remember the name of the pub. Then he came in for a drink after they'd arrested Keith Ingles and didn't stay because he'd to go back to work. All right, Tam?'

Tam looked abashed, and she relented. 'Actually, I wasn't much impressed then. I've told him I'm considering whether or not I want to see him again.'

Tam chortled. 'Deferred sentence to allow him to be of good behaviour, eh? That explains it.'

'Tam!' Marjory reproved him as Laura looked at him with a certain frostiness. 'It's just that Jon asked me to tell you he was being a good boy.'

'Oh, for heaven's sake!' Laura said, though she didn't sound entirely displeased.

'I must be going,' Marjory said getting up reluctantly. 'I'm going to call in to see if there's anything more at HQ, then I must get home. And so must you, Tam. Don't give him another drink, Laura. He doesn't deserve it.'

Tam rose with dignity. 'Wasn't even thinking of accepting the offer. How could I, with a wife, two dogs, three cats and six kittens expecting me back any minute?'

The women laughed, and he left. Marjory hung back. 'There's just one thing that keeps nagging at me, Laura. It's against the run of everything we've said tonight, but – children who are single-issue fanatics. Could they really kill?'

Laura was taken aback. 'Children? Yes, of course they could. If they get into manipulative hands, nothing easier. They can be more callous than adults. Think of boy soldiers in these militias.'

'Yes,' Marjory said heavily. 'I was.'

It was once again around seven o'clock when Jon Kingsley knocked on Laura's door.

'Care for a bite to eat?' he greeted her. 'I was just passing on my way home.'

There was a chop in the fridge waiting to be grilled, but suddenly that seemed rather sad. 'Why not?' she said. 'Let me get a jacket, and I'm with you. Once the sun goes in it won't be linen weather.'

As they walked to the High Street, she asked him how it was going. He made a balancing motion with his hand.

'I think I'm on to something. But I'd appreciate your input.'

Yet again, Laura had the impression that his interest in her was more professional than social. 'My consultancy fees are very high,' she said lightly, and he laughed.

'I wasn't thinking of the chippie. I booked the Vine Leaf, on the off-chance.'

The Vine Leaf was seriously expensive, which made her uncomfortable. It had been a casual invitation; of course she hadn't expected a chippie but a cheap 'n' cheerful Italian would have been more appropriate. It was as if he was trying to buy her into his team – or perhaps he just had a problem with social nuances. He wouldn't be the first man to suffer from that.

A very elegant young man welcomed them in and led them to a table with a white porcelain vase holding a single pink orchid. Laura looked around the minimalist chic of the decor and raised her eyebrows.

'My goodness, they must be paying coppers well these days,' she said dryly.

'It's "because you're worth it",' Jon said, indicating quotation marks.

Laura looked at him with revulsion. 'That's the cheesiest line I've heard in years!'

He smiled smugly. 'I thought you'd like it. It was a toss-up between that and, "This time next year, I want us to be laughing together." You may remember our first discussion about chat-up lines?'

She did, and was amused. 'You are a sod! I thought you were serious.'

'It's a talent I have. Now, let's order. Places like this take forever – confuse "taking a long time" with "doing a good job", but we can always hope.'

It came across as a bit 'city-sophisticate-slumming-it-in-the-sticks', but she was prepared to make allowances. And he did start by asking her, with apparent interest, how the new book was going; when he got round to saying, 'Would it be a bore if I asked your advice about the case?' it felt more natural, in the context of talking about each other's jobs. And anyway, she did have some curiosity to see how his take on it would differ from the one she'd heard earlier from Marjory and Tam.

'This is between ourselves, OK? I think I'm on to something. I don't know what Marjory's said to you—'

He glanced at her, but one of the first lessons she learned as a psychotherapist was to show no reaction other than calm interest. So he went on, 'There's this woman, Susie Stevenson. She and Marjory have some sort of feud that goes back to the foot-and-mouth business, but for some weird reason she and her husband are living at Mains of Craigie. Findlay, the husband, has an obsession with a collie Niall Murdoch was threatening to put down. He stole the dog back the night of Murdoch's murder, but that's not the point.

'The point is, we've discovered she's lying to us about a couple of things. The most significant is that she said she hadn't seen Murdoch for years, but two of the staff can speak to her having a blazing row with him the day before he was killed. And years ago Davina Watt almost sabotaged their engagement; it could be that she was trying to wreck their marriage, or that if Susie knew she'd returned, she thought she was. Does that work, psychologically, as motivation for murder?'

'Well, yes, of course it does.' She leaned back to allow the waiter to put down a plate of scallops in front of her. 'But surely, in police work, evidence of motivation isn't enough?'

'No, no, of course not. Motive isn't even something you have to prove, to get a guilty verdict, provided you have hard evidence. But you see, in these two cases it's hard to know how much hard evidence we're likely to get. She – or he – has been pretty clever about that.

'If we don't find something soon, we have to work towards a rock-solid theory that convinces us we know who did it. Keep the case open, wait and hope for confirmation. And you see—' He looked down, playing with the stem of his wine glass. 'I screwed up, last time. I helped my sergeant bang someone up for it who, quite honestly, I don't now think is guilty.

'Oh, I believed it at the time. You may remember how excited I was, last time I saw you – but there was someone that very evening, committing the next murder.

'So I've blotted my copybook. In the Force, you're only as good as your last conviction, and despite what I've achieved in the past, if I don't come up with the answer on this one, that's what they'll think of when they're looking to make up the next sergeant.'

He was very intense about this. Laura chose her words carefully. 'You don't think, perhaps, you're trying too hard? That without real evidence you could be in danger of picking on the wrong person again?'

'The evidence we do have seems to me to suggest Susie Stevenson. However—' He shrugged, then changed tack. 'What's Marjory thinking about this?'

'Why don't you ask her?' Laura parried.

'I don't suppose she'd tell me. She'd tell Tam, of course, and Tansy maybe. But I get left out of the loop all the time.'

The waiter came to remove their plates, and Laura had time to think about that. She could see there was a certain justice to his claim.

'As far as I know,' she said carefully, 'she's still got an open mind, looking at everything that comes in.'

Jon's face brightened. 'She'll probably go for the Stevenson angle, then. It would suit her pretty nicely, from all I can see, to have the woman carted off to jail instead of fouling her doorstep.'

'Jon, Marjory wouldn't work like that!' Laura protested. 'She'd fall over backwards to make sure she wasn't looking at it with personal bias.'

'Of course, of course.' He looked round. 'Ah, here comes your lamb and my steak. I did them an injustice about how long they'd take.'

It was a welcome interruption. Laura didn't want to go back to the subject of Marjory; she asked him instead about *Blackbird* and his yachtie enthusiasm saw them through the main course. She refused pudding, and over coffee he went back to the subject of crime. In her experience, police officers were unable to keep away from it for long.

'Psychological profiling,' he said. 'If you were asked to do a profile for these two cases – assuming it was one killer – what would you say?'

'Don't know enough about the details,' she parried. 'It's a science, not newspaper astrology.'

'Of course not. But off the top of your head?'

'I suppose – someone with an uncontrolled temper. I know Davina was beaten up, and the suggestion in the Press has been that Murdoch was bashed over the head too. Yet you tell me they've done a good job of covering their tracks, so it's someone who can think quite coolly and clearly afterwards. And someone with a lot to lose. Or,' she added, aware of having Marjory's final remarks in her mind, 'someone who doesn't see killing in quite the normal way.'

He didn't pick up on that, but he looked pleased with what she had said. 'Most of that would fit with Susie Stevenson, wouldn't it? She's calculating enough to look us straight in the face and lie; she's certainly got a temper. Her husband almost had to hold her down this morning. Thanks, Laura – you've been brilliant.'

'Hope you feel it was worth the fee,' she said as the waiter brought the bill.

'It was my pleasure. We must do this again soon.'

Marjory arrived back at the farm feeling, as her mother would have said, trauchled: not just tired, but worn down by cares.

At HQ, though Kerr had gone home, her report had been left on Fleming's desk and it hadn't made cheerful reading. Susie Stevenson was involved in this somehow, and even if Marjory still couldn't believe – especially after the talk with Laura – that these were a woman's crimes, the lies Susie had told meant this would have to be taken seriously. Tomorrow they'd be pulling her in for questioning.

She wasn't sure, either, how Bill would have taken to the morning's interviews; Tansy's report had been circumspect, but reading between the lines Marjory had picked up that Jon had been heavy-handed. Probably just because she'd asked him not to be, she thought wearily. Despite having told Laura he'd been a good boy, she'd seen precious few signs of changes in the leopard's spots.

The family were all in the kitchen eating supper when she went in. Bill came over to give her a hug and she responded, grateful that yesterday's tensions hadn't lingered.

'Had a heavy day?' he asked. 'Bad luck. Sorry – I didn't know you'd be back and there's nothing left. You know how it is when Cammie's around.'

Cammie registered a formal protest, then went on to impart the important news that he'd been selected for the district training squad. Marjory listened, with suitable exclamations, as she fetched a macaroni cheese ready-meal and put it in the microwave.

Cat, on the other hand, was finishing her supper in silence, and when Marjory asked what she'd been doing, said only, 'Hanging out with Fiona.'

'They arrested Findlay about that dog! Did you know, Mum?' Cammie went on to the second most newsworthy event of his day.

'Of course she knows,' Cat said witheringly. 'I expect she ordered it.'

'I didn't, as a matter of fact.' Marjory tried not to sound too defensive. 'The officers who came to investigate made that decision after Fin had admitted stealing it.'

'But you know what was going to happen to Moss, if he hadn't,' Cat argued. 'And they just dragged Fin off, in front of poor Susie. She told me, this afternoon.'

'That's not actually true, Cat,' Bill corrected her. 'I saw him get into his own car and drive off behind them with the dog. Susie's exaggerating, as usual.'

'You just have it in for Susie, don't you!' Cat cried. 'You're as bad as Mum. She's a nice person – and anyone would be a bit confused, with their husband being arrested.'

'I will admit, I didn't take to your Jon Kingsley myself,' Bill said. 'Aggressive young man – but Tansy's sharper, you know. She was the one who put me on the spot.'

The microwave pinged and Marjory fetched out the macaroni, peering at it unenthusiastically as she put it on to a plate and sat down at the table. 'I tell you what – let's pretend I'm off duty and talk about something else. I saw Laura today, Bill. She'd been in to see Mum, and—'

A movement outside the window caught her eye and she saw someone crossing the yard to the back door. 'Oh dear,' Marjory said with a sinking heart. 'Susie Stevenson. I don't think I'm off duty yet.'

There was a loud 'rat-tat-tat-tat'. Bill half rose. 'I'll go – try and get rid of her,' he offered, but Marjory shook her head.

'I might as well get it over with. I can't avoid her permanently. I won't close the door – you can come and help talk her down if necessary.'

The back door was next the kitchen, off the corridor leading to the mud-room; as she turned its handle, there was another furious 'rat-tat-tat'. She pulled it open.

Marjory was totally unprepared for physical attack. Without any sort of warning, Susie launched herself at her, punching and pummelling. 'Bitch! Bitch!' She was screaming. 'You did this! You did this, to spite me! You'll rot in hell!'

Marjory had the height advantage but Susie wasn't a small woman and she was stockily built. Marjory craned backwards to keep her face out of reach, and losing her balance under the onslaught, fell back against the wall. She felt nails rake her face and then a fist catch her eye. She was grappling with the woman now, trying to catch at her hands, but Susie seemed possessed.

Then Bill had reached her and had his arms round Susie, imprisoning her arms and dragging her back, away from his wife. 'Phone Findlay, Cat,' he yelled over his shoulder. 'Get him up here.'

Meg was beside him, crouched low and growling, her lip curled up to show her teeth. Cat was gabbling frantically over the phone and Cammie rushed to help his mother up.

Susie's frenzy seemed to pass; she sagged into Bill's arms, moaning, 'Bill, oh Bill! See what your wife has made me do!'

'No, I don't think so, Susie,' Bill said grimly, frogmarching her outside. 'We'll wait here till your husband comes. Marjory, are you all right?'

'Yes, yes, I think so,' Marjory said as Cat hurried over to help Cammie get her to her feet. He was pale with shock; Cat was crying.

'Oh, Mummy, your face! I'm sorry for what I said – so sorry!'

'Is it bad?' Marjory gingerly felt her smarting cheek and her hand came away bloodstained. 'Damn – that'll show. But don't worry, Cat love, it's superficial.' She fetched a wodge of kitchen towel and went over to the sink, wetting it and dabbing at her face. 'Ow!'

'You're going to have a black eye too,' Cammie said, speaking as one who knew. 'Maybe you should put something cold on it.'

'I'll get some frozen peas.' Cat, grateful to have something to do, fetched a pack from the freezer just as Findlay came running across the yard.

He looked panic-stricken, seeing his wife drooping in Bill's grasp. 'What's she done? She was in a terrible mood – I couldn't stop her coming—'

'She's made a pretty fair mess of my wife's face.' Bill did not hide his anger. 'Take a hold of her, Fin, and remove her before I hit her myself. You might be as well to take her to hospital. She must be having a breakdown – or if she isn't, she's going to be answering a charge of assault.'

Marjory came out of the kitchen, the pack of peas pressed to her swelling eye, and saw Findlay's pale face turn almost green at the sight of her. 'Oh God, Marjory, how awful! I – I don't know what to say.'

'Fin, I'd rather not take this further. You're both in enough trouble without me adding to it. Just keep her away from me, all right?'

'That's very generous of you—' he began, but Susie interrupted. 'That's not generous. She's enjoying this! Well, here's what I think of your *charity*!' She lunged out of Fin's grasp and spat at Marjory, but Bill had grabbed her again so that she didn't reach her target.

'Get – her – out. Now!' he said. 'I don't care where you go or what you do, but I want her off the farm tonight. You can't guarantee to restrain her, Fin.'

'You can't throw us out tonight,' she smirked triumphantly. 'There's Josh – you can't leave a poor little boy all on his own without his mummy or daddy.'

'Cat and Cammie will babysit till you get back, Fin. Sleep there if necessary,' Bill said, and the children, beside their mother in the doorway, nodded.

'He'll be fine. He knows us – don't worry,' Cat said reassuringly.

'You're a good, kind girl,' Susie said approvingly. 'Can't think where you get it from.' She shot a sidelong, malicious look at Marjory.

Cat flushed. 'My mother, probably. She's put up with you, hasn't she?'

'Cat—' Marjory said warningly, but Cat said, 'I know. I'm just going. Oh, Mum—'

She kissed her very gently on the uninjured cheek and she and Cammie went off down to the cottage as Fin half-dragged Susie to the car, while she protested that he wasn't to hold her arm so tightly. 'You're on their side, you bastard!' she was shouting as he forced her into the passenger seat.

It suddenly seemed very quiet. Bill shut the door.

'Dear God!' he said. 'Did you see that woman's eyes? She's flipped, or else she's on something. Are you all right?'

Marjory realized her legs were like rubber. She staggered into the kitchen and collapsed on to a chair. Meg, who had been hovering anxiously, came trotting over to push her nose into Marjory's hand.

'Yes, Meggie, yes. I'm all right, at least I think I am. I haven't looked in a mirror yet.'

'You'll need a whisky before you do.' Bill disappeared to fetch it from the sitting-room.

Marjory prodded her bruised ribs experimentally, wincing,

then touched her face again. There was a cut at the side of her mouth too, but nothing serious. She'd have some explaining to do tomorrow, though. And she'd said she wouldn't report it, but in fact, now she thought about it—

'Get that down you,' Bill said. He took her face between his hands and kissed the other corner of her injured mouth very tenderly. 'Sorry. I feel responsible for this. I read that woman all wrong – I should never have landed you with her.'

'Let's not go there. But Bill, it's all worse than you know. They think there may be evidence linking her with the murders. And I've been saying all along they weren't a woman's crimes because a woman wouldn't inflict the sort of damage there was to Davina's face.

'But she's done a pretty good job on me, hasn't she?'

22

'Crivvens! Whatever's happened to you, boss?' the desk sergeant exclaimed as DI Fleming crossed the reception area at quarter-past eight on Saturday morning.

'I haven't decided yet,' Fleming said cryptically as she headed for the stairs. Her face was very stiff and sore today; her eye was throbbing and the cut at the corner of her mouth made moving her lips uncomfortable. Two of the scratches on her face were just red lines now, but the two middle nails had bitten deeper and she had a couple of fine scabs forming which an extra layer of make-up couldn't hide.

She had only just reached her office when DC Kingsley appeared. 'I just wanted to catch you before—' Then, seeing her face, he stopped, gaping.

'Yes, Jon?' she said wearily. 'It's all right, nothing serious.'

'Glad to hear it! What happened to the other fellow?' he said flippantly, too absorbed in what he wanted to say to waste time on sympathy. He was looking pleased with himself.

'It was Susie Stevenson I wanted to talk to you about. You'll have seen my report? Well, I'd a chat with Laura Harvey last night about the case, and the psychological profile she suggested was a good fit for Susie.

'The thing is, in this case we seem to be really stuck for hard evidence. If we can work out who did it we can focus—'

'Jon, which part of the word "no" don't you understand?' Fleming hadn't the energy to spare for patience this morning. 'I've had to tell you this too many times – it's all about evidence, however dreary and tedious that may seem to be, and then we go from that to the killer, not the other way around. I don't like to rub this in, but arresting Ingles without proper evidence hasn't exactly proved to be a triumph for you, has it?'

He scowled, but she went on, 'It's still early days – we haven't had detailed analysis from the lab in either case, and they're not even going to do the autopsy on Murdoch until Monday. There's the chance of DNA evidence—'

He shrugged. 'That might clear Ingles. But could we get a warrant to check other suspects?'

That hit a nerve. 'No,' she said uncomfortably. 'I don't suppose we could. And I hear what you're saying – that this could turn out one of those nightmare open cases where we know perfectly well who did it but we can't nail them.

'That's a long way down the line, though. Thanks to the exodus from Drumbreck, asking questions is going to take longer, but there's a list of the owners of moorings and they're working through the local ones already. We'll get round the holiday homes families in time, and something may come of that. There's a lot more detailed questioning to be done before we even begin to narrow the field.'

Kingsley wasn't pleased. He'd obviously been hoping to bowl her over with his dynamic conclusions, but she wasn't about to let herself be used as a stepladder for his ambitions. She dreaded the thought of him being earmarked for promotion and in a position to do even more damage to the team she had to manage.

'Thanks, Jon.' Fleming closed the conversation firmly, and as the door shut behind him, she sighed heavily.

Kingsley was quite right that the chances of getting any warrant in connection with Susie were slim. Since the Human Rights Act, the sheriffs had become very strict about fishing expeditions. But if DNA evidence emerged, and Susie had been charged with assault, her DNA would be recorded right there in their own files.

She knew all about the anger and frustration the police felt when a man got off because the woman he had beaten up refused to report it officially so that the police could press charges, especially when there were other crimes involved. And her own situation was very close to that.

Fin had returned at midnight, having left Susie with her horrified parents. Her mother had given her sleeping pills, he said, and would take her to the doctor first thing. He himself, with Josh, was leaving next morning.

Marjory had said she wouldn't report Susie's assault. But had she any alternative?

'Here – have you an old Heilan' granny who's a spaewife?' The phone call from Tam MacNee's Glasgow contact came minutes after he arrived for work.

'Not likely, Sheuggie. If my granny'd been able to see the future she'd surely not always have backed the horse that came in last.'

'I went away round to that address you gave me last night, and here! Was there not an ambulance and a couple of cars there, and the wife going mental because her man had taken an overdose.'

'Adrian McConnell?' MacNee was astonished.

'That's him. Paracetamol – dirty stuff. We haven't heard yet if he's had his chips.'

'Was there a note?'

'Aye, there was. I'll go in later and see if I can get to fax it through.'

'Thanks, Sheuggie. I owe you one. Oh, and Lafferty – got anything on him yet?'

'He's been there and thereabouts for a few things, but we've nothing on him, as yet. I've put out a few feelers in that area to see if there's any talk about a hit man. I'll keep you in the loop. And the drinks are on you next time you're in Glasgow.'

MacNee's mind was racing as he put down the phone. What did they know about the man? Not a lot, except that he'd a wife who was a drunk who'd been carrying on with Murdoch. Would that be enough to make you want to kill yourself – or was there rather more to it than that? He'd better pass this on to the boss immediately; she might even want him to head straight on up to Glasgow today.

He was on his way out of the CID room as Kingsley came in, looking sullen. He didn't stop to ask why.

The sight of Fleming's face stopped him in his tracks.

'I know, I know!' she said. 'A parting gift from Susie Stevenson – didn't like Findlay being arrested yesterday. Still, at least she's left the farm.'

'Good riddance.'

'I know. But – am I going to report her, Tam? I sort of said I wouldn't, with them being in so much trouble already—'

'You're kidding – at least I hope you are. Apart from anything else, she's a suspect and this ties in with beating up Davina Watt.'

'I know. But I loathe the woman so I feel I have to be particularly careful that it doesn't become personal—'

'Just because you loathe her doesn't mean she's innocent,' he pointed out.

'I suppose it doesn't. And Jon's right in saying we'd be struggling to get a warrant if the labs come up with DNA evidence, whereas if she's been charged—'

'Exactly. There you are. Jon's putting his money on her now, is he?'

'He's desperate to impress the Super by getting there ahead of the rest of us, Tam. I'm trying to stop him making another big mistake, but it's not easy.'

'Why try? He can take what's coming to him.

'But wait till you hear this.' MacNee told her of the latest development. 'I'll maybe need to go to Glasgow to interview him, if he pulls through,' he finished.

'Better wait till you get the note,' she advised. 'But even if he doesn't make it, you'd probably better go and dig around the background anyway.

'Still, it doesn't mean ignoring everything else. You were going to check with Fingerprints to see if Murdoch's tally with the ones on the cutting – then we'd have at least one hard fact in this case, which would make a change. They sent it back to me once they'd finished with it – it's here somewhere.' She rummaged in one of the wire baskets on her desk and produced a plastic evidence bag. 'You might as well take it, but don't lose it – we may need it as a production in court.

'I want to have a word after the morning briefing with Andy Macdonald, see how he got on with interviewing the daughter. And I'd better report the assault. Though frankly, I won't be surprised if it turns out Susie's not fit to plead.'

There was a lot of activity at Kirkluce HQ this morning. There was overtime on offer, so that even officers who weren't on shifts had come in, but Fleming had decided to keep the briefing meeting short. She was conscious there was disappointment that they hadn't made concrete progress; most of them were well aware that the arrest of Ingles had been an error, and with no strong leads she could almost hear them thinking that the inquiry into Davina Watt's death at least was going nowhere. Even in Murdoch's case they had passed the golden period after a crime when recollection is fresh in everyone's minds – and the mass retreat of possible witnesses from Drumbreck hadn't helped there either – and from now on it would all get tougher.

She wasn't prepared to disclose the latest information about

Adrian McConnell; until they knew more about it, it could only be a distraction from the important, if humdrum, routine – the formal statements, door-stepping, the fingertip search which would take place this morning around the area of the burned-out car. But she'd also hold out the hope of forensic magic, though they'd get nothing out from the labs until after the weekend and there were tests, too, on DNA that could take a week or more to show a result.

First, though, there was the awkward business of explaining her face. She could read their expressions as they gawped at her – sympathy, in one or two cases (those were the women officers), astonishment from most, and ill-concealed amusement in the case of DS Allan, who was sitting in the centre with Kingsley beside him.

Fleming touched her face. 'Let's deal with this first and get it out of the way. I was attacked last night by one of the suspects – Susie Stevenson, whose husband Findlay works on our farm.'

She saw astonished annoyance in Kingsley's face, heard his mutter to Allan, 'Bloody woman didn't tell me that, did she?' but went on as if she hadn't.

'The details, of course, will be entered in the file once I've made a formal statement after this. But to draw conclusions would be seriously premature. Kingsley, you've broken ground on this, along with Kerr, so I want you to take it on. The problem may be that she will be unfit, so there could be a hold-up.'

'Do we have an address for her, boss?'

'It'll be in my statement on the assault.' She turned from the topic with relief, outlining the other tasks for the teams, reminding them to keep up to date with the reports. 'Greg, you've just come on duty, haven't you? Perhaps you could anchor operations here again. And now I'll hand over to Sergeant Naismith to hand out action sheets.'

As they gathered round him, Fleming singled out DC Macdonald. 'Andy, did you see Mirren Murdoch yesterday?'

'Yes. Yes I did, but I'm kind of unhappy about it.' He ran his hand over his close-cropped head. 'I was going to come and see you, boss. The kid's a weirdo. Her mother was sitting in on it, of course, and it was sort of—' He hesitated, groping for the words.

Fleming perched on the edge of a table. 'Take your time.'

'The kid just sat there, totally unfazed. It was the mother who twitched whenever I asked her anything, and it was like she was trying to protect her, but didn't really know how. Does that make sense?'

'Like she didn't know what Mirren had done, but didn't want you to find out either?' Fleming suggested.

Macdonald latched on to that. 'Yeah. But Mirren didn't stress about any of the questions – like where she was when her father was killed, just said she was in the house from suppertime on and of course Mum backed her up. Didn't know anything about the fire either till she heard her mother getting up, and then she just went back to bed, like she was told.

'Then I asked if she'd been very upset about her father's death, and that was what really spooked me. She's got these funny dark eyes, almost like they're black, and she just looked at me and said, "Well, he was going to kill Moss."

'Of course her mother got a bit frantic and started talking about how she didn't mean it, how she was in shock and stuff, but it didn't look that way to me.'

Fleming considered what he had said. 'Ingles would have to be back in the frame, if we were running with that. A child couldn't have killed Davina.'

'I'll tell you the other thing,' Macdonald went on. 'What did get a reaction out of her, was when I'd finished the interview and asked Mrs for permission to access whatever was on the computer, as part of our checks on Murdoch's effects, like we agreed, boss?'

Fleming nodded.

'And I'd swear she was just going to say yes, when Mirren went OTT. Started shouting about privacy, and her father didn't use it anyway, and we'd no right to go poking our noses into other people's business. Then of course her mother jumped in, said it was her computer and that Murdoch hadn't used it so there was no point. I tried pushing it, but in the end I got a flat refusal. And then the girl calmed down, and gave me this sort of "That's seen *you* off" look. Didn't know where to go from there, to be honest.'

MacNee glanced at Fleming. 'You were on about the kid, weren't you?'

'Yes. It just didn't feel right. OK, Andy – thanks. You did your best. Just leave it with me – I'd better go and see them myself. Where's Tansy? I know she was working with Jon on the Stevenson thing, but I don't think there'll be progress today. She'd be the best person to have along.'

'Around somewhere. I'll tell her,' Macdonald said quickly.

'I'd better go and report this now.' Fleming was not looking happy as she left.

The two men exchanged glances. 'She doesn't like the thought that it could be the kid,' MacNee said. 'But she's got problems about Susie Stevenson too.'

'Beggars can't be choosers. We'll be lucky to pin it on anyone, at this rate.'

'Where is Tansy, anyhow? Didn't see her at the briefing.'

Macdonald grinned. 'She'd a big party last night. I'm just away to ring her now. She'll be pleased.'

'Here, did your lot get Murdoch's prints yesterday?' Mac-Nee called after him, remembering the cutting he was still holding. 'She wants a comparison with this – see.' He took it out of the bag and pointed to the article about Ingles's release.

'It was in one of Davina's drawers and we're guessing it was maybe him sent it to her.'

Macdonald took it and glanced at it. 'Right. Yes, they got the same ones on his comb and toothbrush, so it's a pretty safe bet.'

'I'll away along and see if it's a match. That's where I'll be if there's a call from Glasgow.'

As the room emptied, Allan was left behind alone. It would be another day of pushing paper, of keeping all the other inquiries going, like the shoplifting gang and the wave of car crime. Better than a fingertip search, admittedly, but he felt Fleming was keeping him off the task forces deliberately, to humiliate him. He wasn't going to stand it for much longer; he'd told Jon that.

The phone ringing cut through Tansy Kerr's head like a red-hot wire. She'd taken the precaution of switching off her mobile, but this was the land-line. Groaning, she groped for it on the bedside table without opening her eyes.

Macdonald's voice was offensively chirpy. 'The boss wants you. Ten minutes ago. She's going to see the Murdochs and she wants you along.'

Tansy's tongue was thick in her mouth. 'What time is it?'

'Half nine.'

'Oh God!' She put the phone down and blinked round the bedroom of her poky rented flat. If this had been a crime scene after a burglary, they'd have been sending in victim support.

She rolled out of bed, swearing, and staggered into the inadequate shower which dribbled instead of blasting you awake, dressed in her last pair of clean jeans, a grey T-shirt she'd only worn once and picked up an acid-green hoodie she'd regretted buying from the floor of the wardrobe. She swallowed a couple of paracetamol and poured down two glasses of water, but decided she'd better get the essential fix of caffeine from the machine in the canteen. As long as Big Marge wasn't standing in reception tapping her foot.

The sunshine hit her like a blow and she fished in her bulky shoulder bag for dark glasses as she walked down the row of small terraced houses towards the High Street.

Kirkluce had not yet been hit with the curse of the super-markets, and though there were always rumours, the council had so far stood firm against them. There were still butchers and bakers and greengrocers and on a Saturday morning people who came out with their baskets for their shopping, gathering in gossiping groups and blocking the pavement as Kerr, with no very warm feelings for the charm of market town living, wove her way through them.

She reached the CID room via the coffee machine without being nobbled, at least. Kingsley was there, ready with a rude comment about her appearance as she phoned to get her orders.

'See you in the car park in five minutes,' Fleming said, and Kerr raised her eyebrows as she put the phone down.

'Sounds a bit terse this morning.'

'You'll understand when you see her. Incidentally, you left me with all the paperwork to wrap up the charge on Findlay Stevenson—'

'So?' Kerr swigged down the coffee with a grimace. 'That's what constables do, Jon, and I wrote the report.'

Bad moods were infectious. Kerr was, uncharacteristically, scowling as she went out to the car park, putting her glasses back on.

Fleming was there already, unlocking her car. She was wearing dark glasses too, and as Kerr got closer she could see there were cuts on her face. Her expression was sardonic.

'Is this a carefully contrived wet-look, or are you only just out of the shower?'

Mumbling something, Kerr got in.

'Just as well I'm driving. You look as if you could turn the crystals at twenty paces. I thought I looked bad, till I saw you. And to save you asking, I'll tell you what happened.'

Kerr listened in amazement, her hangover almost forgotten. 'Don't say Jon's going to turn out to be right again! It's not good for him.' Or for any of the rest of us, she added silently.

'This isn't proof of anything except that the woman's unstable. And right now, we need to talk to Jenna Murdoch and, more importantly, Mirren.' Fleming gave a brisk outline of the situation Macdonald had reported.

'I'd kind of like to think a kid couldn't do something like that,' Kerr said. 'But we did *Lord of the Flies* for Highers, and you begin to think he's right and they're all savages unless you force them not to be. Look at this happy-slapping stuff, and that fifteen-year-old in Stranraer who got his head kicked in by his little school chums.'

'It's fanaticism that scares me. It seems to have got to the point where, whether your religion's based on God or a football club or a belief in animal rights, it entitles you to consider anyone who doesn't bow down to your particular idol as a legitimate target for destruction.

'That's what's getting to me about this one. Mirren Murdoch's been living within a rotten marriage, and she's friendless by the sound of it too. I phoned Laura this morning, after what Andy said, and she made the point that sometimes it isn't about loving animals. It's about hating people.'

'Mum! It's the police again,' Mirren Murdoch shouted up the stairs to her mother.

Jenna, with a sick feeling in the pit of her stomach, put down the razor blade she was using to get paint spots off the window-panes. 'Take them into the sitting-room,' she yelled back, and hurried down.

It was the tall woman, the inspector – Fleming. She was wearing dark glasses this morning, looking as if she'd been in a cat-fight, and there was a younger woman with her with a green streak in custard-yellow hair and wearing a hoodie. She looked the sort that might get turned out of a shopping mall, but she was being introduced as DC Kerr. Mirren was standing in the further corner of the room, her eyes dark and watchful.

They hadn't sat down, and Jenna didn't invite them to. This time, she wasn't going to trouble to hide her irritation. 'What do you want now? The constable yesterday took statements from us both, and that's all we have to say.'

'Mrs Murdoch, I wonder if you and Mirren would be kind enough to look at the site of the fire with us? I'm not sure I understand quite what the building was or where the fire started.'

Jenna felt, rather than saw, her daughter stiffen and the knot of tension in her gut twisted again. 'I can't think what you need us for. It's surely clear enough.'

'Just one or two things, if you wouldn't mind?' The inspector moved to hold the door open and Jenna found herself being ushered through it, with the woman just behind her.

The other detective was following, with Mirren. Jenna saw her point to a small metal badge pinned to Mirren's grey cotton top.

'I'm sure I've seen that before. What is it?'

'SSPCA.' It was a grudging response.

'Oh, I went out on a call with them once. There was this awful man running a puppy farm – you wouldn't believe the cruelty—'

Jenna hung back, still looking over her shoulder, but Fleming was pointing to the shed and asking where the dog was kept and somehow she had to comply.

'Mirren must have been very relieved to hear the dog was safe after all,' Fleming said.

'Yes.' But it wasn't as simple as that, otherwise Jenna wouldn't be so worried. Mirren had known all along that the dog was all right – or at least, she'd thought she'd known. Then suddenly, she'd flipped. It was something to do with the computer; that had been clear yesterday. There was something there that she didn't want the police to find out. Jenna had tried to check last night, but it was protected with a password she didn't know and she hadn't felt strong enough to tackle Mirren about it. She wasn't sure that she wanted to know. She couldn't get out of her head Mirren's strange response to being told about her father – 'I didn't know he was dead.' It had haunted her: why should she have known?

Suddenly she realized that the pause had lengthened and the inspector was looking at her. She couldn't see the eyes behind the dark glasses but it made her feel uncomfortable.

'You're worried about Mirren, aren't you?' Fleming's voice was very gentle, very sympathetic.

To her dismay, Jenna felt tears spring to her eyes. 'Difficult time – we've been dreadfully upset, naturally—'

'She was very anxious that we shouldn't look at the computer, wasn't she? Do you know why?'

'She has a right to privacy – we all do!' Jenna blustered, but feebly.

'Children can get into a lot of trouble on the internet. It's a big problem.'

'Yes – yes. I know.'

'Have you checked what she's been accessing?'

There was a huge lump in Jenna's throat. 'She's got a password.'

Mirren and Kerr had just come out of the house. Mirren was talking animatedly and at a gesture from the detective they went to sit on the wall of the garden. Jenna made to go back to them, but Fleming was speaking again.

'I've got kids myself, Jenna. I know just how you feel about them. You'd do anything to protect them, and that's what you're trying to do at the moment. I respect that.

'But there are two things I'd say. The first is purely practical – if we need access to the computer for investigative reasons, we'll get it. It'll be slower, but we'll get it in the end.

'The second thing is that she's much more likely to need protection from the sort of people she could be meeting on the internet. She's vulnerable – from what I've seen of her, I would say very vulnerable. She doesn't have many friends, does she?'

Jenna's eyes welled over, silent tears sliding down her cheeks. 'No. But look at her now, talking to your girl there. I haven't seen her talk like that in years.'

'That's good, isn't it?'

'I – I suppose so, but it hurts. If she can't talk to her own mother, what does that say about me?'

'It says she's thirteen.'

'Oh – I don't know!' Jenna pushed away the tears with her fingers. She'd been too busy once they came here to keep up with friends herself; what she'd said about her feelings now, to this strange woman, was more than she had said to anyone for years. 'What am I going to do?'

Suddenly the gentle voice became very firm. 'You're going to give us permission to access the computer. You needn't even tell Mirren you have, if you arrange to be out of the way – take Mirren shopping or something. You do need to know what's going on, for her own safety.'

Jenna gave a shuddering sigh. 'All right. Yes, I give you permission. Though I feel I'm betraying her. But as you know,' she said emphatically, 'Mirren was in the house from just after seven o'clock. I can absolutely vouch for that.'

'We've noted your alibis,' the inspector said, which to Jenna seemed a funny way to put it, but perhaps that was just the sort of thing they had to say.

Mirren and Kerr had got down off the wall and were walking across the yard towards them. Fleming turned.

'I think that's everything. We won't take up any more of your time.'

As they left, Jenna said, 'You seemed to be having a good chat with the detective.'

'Yeah, Tansy's cool.'

'What did you talk about?'

'Oh, stuff.' Mirren walked back into the house, oblivious to her mother's hurt.

'She's in with the rougher elements of the Animal Cruelty people, as far as I can make out,' Kerr said as they walked back to the car. 'God knows what they may have prompted her to do.'

'At least I wrung out permission to access the computer. Macdonald can come down later – she's going to keep Mirren out of the way.'

The car was parked in front of the Yacht Club again. As they reached it, Kerr looked back round the sweep of the bay, with the pontoons and the pretty boats. The tide was on the turn, but the mudflats hadn't been exposed yet and under the cloudless sky the water shimmered blue. There was a swan with its wings half-raised in the sunshine and terns were fishing out towards the estuary, the strong light silvering their plumage as they folded their wings in kamikaze dives.

'You know something? I really don't like this place – gives me the creeps. Something about the atmosphere, I suppose—'

'There isn't an atmosphere,' Fleming said. 'That's what's wrong with it. A lot of people use it for acting out a sort of fantasy life – expensive hobbies and parties and drink and sex and probably the smarter drugs too – and when it looks like trouble, they leave instantly. That's not a community, that's a stage set. And just at the moment, it's a set with the flats falling down.'

As they drove off, Kerr said, 'I asked Mirren about the evening of the fire, just in the context of the dog, and she said the only time she'd gone out of the house that evening was to feed Moss, and the way she said it, I believed her. I can't see how she could have had anything to do with Niall's death.'

'Yes, it's probably true. There's just one thing. I was thinking about the pathologist's verbal report when she did her initial assessment of Niall Murdoch's body on the dock there.

'When a body's been in water it's notoriously difficult to fix a time of death. She wasn't prepared to state anything officially until she'd had time to do proper calculations based on the body temperature and the temperature of the water – presumably that'll come with the main autopsy report next week. But she did say that off the top of her head she'd be inclined to favour an earlier rather than a later time of death.

'It struck me when I was talking to Jenna. We've based the early limit on Niall phoning home at seven – but we only have her word for it, after all.'

23

Tam MacNee seldom went to Glasgow unless he had to. It was his past, and even if the series of slum flats he'd lived in, with their stinking shared cludgies on the stairs, had been torn down to make way for tower blocks where they used the lift instead, he still felt uneasily that somehow he might blunder into a time-warp and find himself back in the part of his life he had done his best to forget.

It was a smart city now, Glasgow, a City of Culture, no less, with glittering shops and galleries and posh restaurants, but underneath he could always sense the raw, raucous heart of the place, still even feel the tug of his tribal loyalty to Rangers. He'd only to hear the strains of 'Billy Boy' coming out of a pub and his mind would run on wading in Fenian blood.

Because somewhere, under the accumulated layers of respectability and police service, the old Tam was still there. He would never quite trust himself to go off into the narrow streets and alleyways which he knew like the back of his hand, to the spit-and-sawdust bars where the hard men he'd shared those streets with still drank – the ones who weren't in Barlinnie or scattered from an urn on the Rangers' pitch. He told himself he knew how they'd look now – sad and seedy, locked into a cycle of violence and ill-health – but he couldn't purge his mind altogether of that warped image, the glamour of a life lived on the edge of danger. Nothing in his life now came close to the heart-stopping thrill of escaping disaster by the skin of your teeth, because you were quicker and smarter. It was an addiction; you didn't recover, you just had to keep clear of the people pushing it.

Today, though, he would be headed for the Southern General Hospital, where Adrian McConnell had been taken after his suicide attempt in his posh house in smart Bearsden, where folk talked with a plum in their mouths and 'sex' meant what the coalman brought the coal in. He'd taken care to arrange to meet Sheuggie for a drink afterwards in a bar run by a chain nearby, where they'd taken out all the atmosphere before they brought in the red velvet benches and the fake oak tables.

Adrian McConnell's letter had been duly faxed through, along with the message that the man had recovered and was prepared to talk. MacNee had left it on Fleming's desk, along with a note to say he'd left for Glasgow.

MacNee swung the car into the inside lane of the motorway. The signs for the city centre were coming up now.

It was a pathetic missive, Fleming thought, picking it up off her desk and reading it again. Pompous, self-pitying, cold – and yet there was that hint that he would have wished to be other, if he could.

Dear Kim, I know that the first thing on your mind when you find that I am dead will be money. You can rest assured that I am not lost to all sense of duty. You and the children will be well provided-for, and you will be free to fall into bed with the next man who comes along, or else to drink yourself to death without anyone trying to stop you. The choice is yours.

Naturally, with the daily humiliations heaped upon me by you and the children, I have considered divorce. But what would be the point? I might escape from you but not from them; they would forever have a place in my life, and it

*became borne in upon me that to pursue a political career
with that sort of baggage would be to invite more public and
more excruciating humiliation.*

*I had a chance of escape a few years ago, and I have only
my own lack of courage to blame that I did not take it.
Afterwards, I told myself there would be a second chance and
this time I would let nothing stop me. The man who killed
Davina killed my dream too. That dream was hope and
without hope existence has no point.*

Adrian

How would a wife feel, getting a letter like that as her
husband's last words? And how would they deal with it, when
the death attempt failed and they had to meet each other over
the breakfast table?

Still, the confession in his letter wasn't the one she and Tam
had been hoping he'd make. Tam would question him, of
course, but this looked like yet another blind alley.

She'd have to get on up to the forest where the search was
going on, about five miles from where Davina's body had been
found. At least you could get vehicles up there and it wouldn't
mean another hike, but the whole thing was probably an
exercise in futility. She'd been hoping for evidence that this
was where the woman had been killed, but so far at least the
SOCOs hadn't come up with anything.

A quick check showed that her e-mails were unpromising –
and there was the one from Chris Carter, unanswered. She
certainly didn't have time even to think about that at the
moment.

MacNee didn't like hospitals. They smelled of despair to him,
and when he went into the ward where Adrian McConnell had
been taken he averted his eyes from the men in the other beds,
lying unnervingly limp and still or with tubes and wires

attached to them, as a nurse led him to the screened bed in the farther corner.

Adrian McConnell was sitting up, his hands folded in front of him. He looked very small and neat, wearing striped pyjamas buttoned up to the neck and dark-rimmed glasses; he was propped against pillows under a neatly turned-down sheet and white cotton blanket, like a little boy who'd been tucked in by his nanny and told not to mess up the bedclothes. His eyes were bloodshot but he was quite composed, and it was hard to imagine him as the recent survivor of a dramatic brush with death.

MacNee introduced himself. 'How are you?'

'All right, thank you.' McConnell had a small, prim mouth and a very precise way of speaking. 'I'm to be discharged very shortly.'

MacNee sat down on one of the bedside chairs. 'You'll understand we need to ask you some questions. The police have, of course, seen your note.'

'I imagined you would. But I should have thought it self-explanatory.' He spoke as if MacNee was a tiresome and unintelligent child.

'Not just entirely, sir,' MacNee said with, he felt, commendable patience. 'You seemed to suggest you had an affair with Davina Watt?'

'We had an affair, yes. Quite briefly, a bit over four years ago.'

MacNee might have been asking the man when was the last time he'd had his car serviced. 'And why did it end?'

'I covered this, I thought, quite adequately in my letter.'

'You wouldn't leave your wife and family for her, is that what you're saying?'

'I – hesitated. Yes. And then it was too late.' For the first time, he was showing signs of emotion. He was pleating his fingers as he added, with real bitterness, 'But I've paid for it since.'

'Too late? You mean she was off as usual to find some other sucker when you wouldn't play ball?' MacNee was deliberately offensive.

A spark of anger appeared in the pale eyes behind the spectacles. 'She was hurt,' he corrected him. 'She told me if I didn't love her enough to want to be with her for ever, she couldn't go on, risking more pain. "I'm ending it now," she said, and walked out. Fool that I was, I didn't go after her.

'I keep asking myself, why not? Cowardice, I suppose. She was someone entitled to big gestures, not pathetic consideration of the practicality of this or that. I wasn't man enough.'

He was talking fast now and colour began to appear in his cheeks. 'But I knew what to do if I got a second chance. I didn't think she'd ever come back to Drumbreck – after the unpleasantness with Ingles, you know – but I believed, somehow, that we'd meet. I was convinced that one day, fate would bring us together – on the tube in London, in an airport. I've run after half-a-dozen girls, thinking I recognized Davina – then they've turned, and I've had to apologize.

'You can't imagine my family life, getting worse and worse as my children become monsters of selfishness and ingratitude.' He was oozing self-pity now. 'What I had with Davina was – was unique, precious, and I threw it away. When they suggested I might run for parliament, do you know what I thought? I thought she'd know where I was and she might find it in her heart to give me a second chance.'

'You were running your life round this – this fantasy?' MacNee looked at him with incomprehension mingled with contempt.

McConnell had been animated; now it was as if all the life had drained out of him, and he sagged back against the pillows. 'It was the only time I have ever felt properly alive. I go through life wretched, half-dead – I might as well be dead, now that lawyer bastard's killed her.'

'You believe it was Keith Ingles?' It had fleetingly crossed MacNee's mind that if he'd believed Niall Murdoch had killed his fantasy lover, vengeance would have come easily to this man.

McConnell stared at him. 'Don't you?'

There wasn't an easy answer to that. 'Did you know she'd come back?'

'Not until I heard that – she was dead.' He bowed his head.

'She didn't get in touch with you? Try to tap you for money? It seems to have been the only thing she cared about.' It was intentionally brutal.

McConnell's drooping posture changed. He sat up again, rigid with indignation. 'That's a filthy thing to say! Why would she, when I would have laid all I possess at her feet?'

'Ah, but she'd have had to take you as well as the money, wouldn't she?' MacNee had taken a real scunner to this guy's delusional self-indulgence. 'Seems she was maybe doing a bit of blackmail on the side – and with you with your political career—'

McConnell pressed the bell at the side of his bed. 'I'll have the nurse escort you out. I would not have agreed to talk to you if I'd known you were going to try to sully Davina's memory.'

MacNee didn't get up. Nurses these days didn't come running when you pressed a bell. He had one last try. 'And you didn't mind Niall Murdoch having it off with your wife?'

McConnell's face twisted in an expression of disgust. 'Not in itself, no. But it was all part of what informed my decision last night.'

That was one way of describing taking an overdose. Frankly, MacNee reckoned that if he'd been Kim McConnell he'd have waited a wee while before dialling 999.

But he had to believe the man had nothing to do with either death. As he left, he asked with genuine curiosity, 'What will you do now?'

The prim little man was sitting as he had been when MacNee came in, hands folded on the smooth sheet. Behind the spectacles his eyes were blank. 'Try again. And succeed, this time. Now mind your own business, and leave me alone.'

The drive to the forest along the Queen's Way was slow today. On this sunny May morning, the tourist buses were out in force and overtaking one would only land you behind another. Or worse, a caravan.

It wasn't a hardship to have time to look at the scenery, at the vast tracts of heather-purple moorland dropping away to the south, with the pylons Fleming always thought rather magnificent striding off towards a hazy horizon, at the greens and browns and greys of moss and bracken and stone, and the dense tapestry of trees rising on the left-hand side of the road. A pair of buzzards were soaring in lazy, sweeping circles, as if they too relished the warmth of the sun on their wings.

A police car parked at the foot of a broad Forestry Road alerted her to the turn-off and an officer in a white summer shirt waved her through. There was Commission land on both sides now: new plantations of young trees still in the tubes that protected them from nibbling deer and rabbits; mature trees, growing towards a harvest in ten or even twenty years' time; great areas already untidily cleared, looking like a bone yard for trees with stumps of trunks and the whitened corpses of long-dead branches left where they fell. Firebreaks between them, with their rows of wire brooms, were a reminder that even in this climate a spell of sunny weather could have the place tinder-dry.

A makeshift sign on a stake directed her on to a smaller, rougher track and now the planted aisles of trees were crowded closer. Ahead of her Fleming could see a recovery truck, parked beside a side turning where there was a wide dead end, roughly cleared. She drove past it and stopped beside a police minibus and a white van, then walked back. There was no breeze up here; the air had a sultry feel and though the sky was still clear she thought there would be rain later.

They were just hoisting the blackened, windowless shell of the burned-out car on to the truck as she arrived. A scorched area of ground showed where it had stood; there were signs of smoke damage, too, to the nearest trees, but mercifully no more than that. Remembering how hot and dry it had been at the time, she winced.

Half-a-dozen officers in blue dungarees were working the area, two dragging and prodding at the undergrowth with long poles and four on their knees, moving backwards in parallel lines. They'd covered a lot of ground and without shade it was hot work; they were swiping constantly at the small flies attracted by the smell of their sweat. As Fleming appeared, they seized the opportunity to sit back on their heels, swigging at water bottles and wiping brows and cheeks with the backs of their hands, leaving grimy smears. The men with the poles too stopped for a breather.

'Any joy?' she asked, though not hopefully.

'Couple of drinks cans, a plastic bag, KitKat wrapper – might prove the key to the whole thing, ma'am,' one said.

'You certainly never know, constable. Nothing that might have been the weapon?'

'We-e-ell—' He gestured round about. There were stones and small rocks everywhere, the sort of thing the pathology report had suggested could have been employed. 'Plenty that could be used that way, but none we've checked seem to have been moved.'

'Hmm.' She bent down to look at a stone that looked as if it might comfortably fit the hand and lifted it experimentally. The earth below clung to it; as she forced it up, a dozen small creepy things scuttled away leaving a tiny writhing earthworm uncomfortably exposed. Taking pity on it, she dropped the stone again and stood up, dusting her hands. 'I see what you mean. Never mind – you've nearly covered it. Good work.'

Two white-overalled SOCOs were supervising the loading of the wreck and one of them came over to speak to her. She recognized the man: he'd worked on the wreck of the lifeboat last October.

'It's just the two of us here today. We got the bulk of it done yesterday,' he said.

'And—?'

He pulled a face. 'We've taken ground samples all round to check for evidence of blood, but if you ask me the car was driven here after the body had been dumped. We've gathered up bagfuls of glass fragments to take back and test for DNA – the windows, of course, would blow out with the heat – but the testing will take weeks, months, even.'

Fleming looked round ruefully. 'Bit of a waste, really, getting them up here, but the boxes had to be ticked. Still, at least it's a pretty small area and it shouldn't take much longer. It's all overtime, though.'

'That's what we all have to think about nowadays, isn't it? But we're just finished here, right, Alison?' he called to the woman who was talking to the mechanic at the truck, now ready to drive off. She nodded and gave a thumbs-up sign.

Fleming drove back down slowly behind the truck. She hadn't expected this to yield much – hoped, perhaps, but not expected. Macdonald's expedition to check out the Murdochs' computer – that was different.

When Kingsley came back into the CID room, Allan was there alone. He was reading a girlie magazine, which he swiftly slipped out of sight into a drawer. Kingsley grinned.

'Relax, it's only me. Any developments?'

'MacNee's gone haring off to Glasgow. McConnell – you know, him with the wife that puts it about?'

He nodded. 'The one Tansy interviewed. What's he done?'

'Tried to end himself but they got him in time. There's a copy of the suicide note in the file there but if you ask me it's nothing to do with us.'

'So it's just a wild goose chase?' Kingsley's satisfaction was obvious. 'I've been round asking to interview Susie Stevenson, but she's to have psychiatric assessment. And if she's not fit to plead—' He shrugged his shoulders. 'Well, we're going to have to live with it. At least we can make a coded statement that'll get the Press off our backs and keep the Chief Constable happy.'

'Oh, it's her that's done it now, is it?' Allan looked at him with dislike. 'And where does that leave Ingles? You were as convinced as me, before.'

'Look, Greg, of course I was, or I wouldn't have gone along with it when you decided to charge him. But there's other evidence now – and his house being totally clean—'

'Oh yes, you'll do whatever suits you, won't you? Anyway, what do I care? I've had enough. My notice is going in next week – and don't pretend you haven't your eye on my job.

'Still, you'd better hope Susie comes good, hadn't you? There's Andy Macdonald'll be in for it too – and he's popular with Big Marge, which is more than can be said for you. And he's away down at Drumbreck doing clever things to the Murdoch kid's computer.'

Kingsley was unmoved. 'A kid?' he sneered. 'Oh, very likely. Not. I've got a fiver says it's Stevenson. Are you on?'

It wasn't hard to bypass the kid's password; it was one of the first things DC Macdonald had been taught on the forensic technology course. And going back through her internet history, she'd been accessing some pretty strong stuff. News bulletins, with icons to click for arson, sabotage and vandalism. Graphic pictures of suffering animals which turned even Macdonald's stomach. Chatrooms, where all the talk was of violence and its justification, and hate-filled calls for vengeance. Most of this, obviously, didn't result in deaths – in this country, at least – but it wasn't hard to imagine the effect on a child with a naive, black-and-white view of life.

As he worked through, getting closer to the date of Niall Murdoch's death, the chatroom contact between Mirren and someone calling himself Cobra became more and more frequent. And eventually, there was Mirren giving him her e-mail address – exactly what they were all told not to do every time a community officer visited a school.

And now here were the e-mails, dozens of them, to and fro. His face became grimmer as he read them.

He had brought a printer with him. He installed it, printed off all relevant material, then uninstalled it again, closed down the files and made sure the computer was left in the same state as he found it. Then he gathered up the sheaf of paper and let himself out of the room.

DC Kerr was in the incident room, reading the memos on the whiteboard. The photos of Davina Watt and Niall Murdoch in life and, hugely blown-up, in death as well, dominated it and she stared at them for a long time, as if she could will the truth out of them.

Everyone was still out on their details and she had the place to herself, for the moment. She'd been meant to follow up on Susie Stevenson with Kingsley, but when she came back he'd gone already and only Greg Allan was in the CID room. She didn't fancy being alone with him; he had an unpleasant habit of making leering, suggestive comments, and though she was perfectly capable of handling him, and would have no problem with giving him a direct and painful response if he ever progressed to trying to handle her, she didn't need the aggro. She could have clocked out and gone home, since her shift had ended, but the thought of the chaos she had left this morning wasn't tempting and anyway, she wanted to hear what Macdonald might have found on Mirren's computer. She had a sort of feeling that today, at last, things were beginning to move.

There were a couple of files, bulging with reports, on one of the desks and she picked one up and sat down with it. Officers were all meant to be up-to-date with what they contained, and this was a good opportunity. Much of it she skimmed, but when she came to Sergeant Christie's accounts of his interviews with Jenna and Mirren Murdoch she began to read more carefully.

They were clear, meticulous reports. She frowned over Mirren's reaction to her father's death – such an odd thing to say! – and then, reading Kelly McConnell's statement and Mirren's response to it, frowned again. She re-read them both.

Still thinking about it, she went on through the file and stopped again when she came to the statement from James Ross. The way he sounded, she didn't exactly take to him, but she'd had a sneak in her class at school – Beryl, she was called – and in her experience their intelligence was always deadly accurate.

She needed to know what Andy had found. Could he be back yet? She glanced at her watch. If she went back to the CID room, ghastly Greg might be there on his own – but she could always go off to the canteen.

'Call that beer?' Tam MacNee's pal Sheuggie, thin-faced and swarthy, looked disparagingly at the thin liquid in the glass in front of him. 'I've tasted stronger tea in the canteen.'

'OK, I know I'm owing you. Would a nip help it down?'

'Thought you'd never ask.'

Tam fetched it and set it down, saying wistfully, 'It's jake for some. I'll have to take my beer neat.'

Sheuggie gave his evil grin. 'Shouldn't have left Glasgow, where you could walk to your work.'

'Aye, right!' But Tam could never have joined the Glasgow polis. He and Sheuggie might have been at the same school, but they'd never kept the same company. It wasn't a comfortable thought; he changed the subject, catching up on family news then slipping into shop talk.

'You'll be back at the McConnells' before long,' Tam warned. 'Carrying him out feet first, this time.'

'Hell-bent on it, is he?' Sheuggie was unperturbed. 'Pity we caught him this time, then – waste of money.'

'Waste of time too. He's not our man. But Lafferty, now – give me a wee bit of the dirt on Lafferty.'

'Ronnie? Oh, we know all about Ronnie the Puddock.'

'I know toads that'd sue for that,' Tam protested.

'Aye, likely. We know who his friends are, we know what he's doing, and he's a link with some nasty stuff. But just try pinning it on the bugger.'

'There was talk of someone lurking around the night Niall Murdoch was walloped over the head – dressed in black, something over their face. Balaclava, most like. And it just made me wonder . . .'

'It would, wouldn't it? Put out a contract, it'd cost you – oh, £200, max – that's for the de luxe version. And I can think of half-a-dozen of his toe rags who'd think it was a rare tear to do something like that. A blunt instrument, though – beneath them, I'd have thought. A blade or a gun, more like.'

MacNee sighed. 'I thought that too. Oh well, just keep stodging away with the routine, I suppose. Still, I'll away back and give him another grilling, just to get his dander up. Haven't even started checking on his movements when the girl was killed, so that should be enough to get him going. Gets riled easily, Lafferty – was daft enough to try it on with my boss, and she slapped a charge on him.'

Sheuggie set down the glass he was holding with a bang. '*What* did you say?'

'Charged him – breach of the peace. Verbal assault on a police officer, obstructing the police . . . . Open and shut case.'

'Oh, you wee dancer!'

For a terrible moment Tam thought Sheuggie in his ecstasy might rise and embrace him.

'We've been wanting his fingerprints these last five years. If we don't get a match with the ones on that Securicor heist at the very least, I'll take the wife shopping when Rangers are playing a Cup Final.'

The sun disappeared behind great livid clouds as Fleming drove back to Kirkluce. As she got out in the car park, the rain started: great, fat, heavy drops that soaked her even as she ran to the entrance.

She came in, shaking herself like a dog, and running her hand through her hair, curling now in the damp. She was on her way to the stairs when the desk sergeant called her back.

It was the motherly Sergeant Bruce who was on duty; she tutted over Fleming's injuries, then said there was someone demanding to see her.

'I tried to stall him, ma'am – told him you were out, offered to get DS Allan, but he wouldn't hear of it. It was only you he would speak to – terribly important, he said. And he was certainly in a right state – frantic, almost.'

Fleming's heart leaped. Was this, could it be the break-through they so urgently needed? But she said lightly, 'It's probably just some householder who reckons it's a waste of his valuable time to take his problems to anyone under the rank of inspector. Did he give a name?'

Bruce glanced down. 'Stevenson. Findlay Stevenson. I've put him in the waiting-room.'

She was unprepared for that; shocked, even. Either he had come to make a confession himself, or it was something significant to do with Susie – or at least, he believed it was. 'Oh,' Fleming said, then, 'Oh, right.'

She was aware that Bruce was looking after her curiously as she went to find out what the distraught man had to tell her.

24

Greg Allan was by himself in the CID room when Tam MacNee returned, tired, hot and irritable after an interminable journey which seemed to have consisted mainly of traffic jams and road works with a 40 mph limit. Allan was studying a spreadsheet, looking even more surly than usual, and only grunted in response to MacNee's greeting.

Stuff him. MacNee wasn't exactly brimming over with goodwill either. He took his jacket off, slung it on the back of a chair and sat down. He'd tried to be upbeat about a Lafferty contract killer, tried to argue with himself on the way back: a man like that, mixed up in something like this – why wouldn't it be him, rather than some middle-class woman with a hysterical temperament, or even a kid, for God's sake? But Sheuggie's words, 'a blade or a gun', kept echoing in his brain. Bashing someone over the head simply wasn't a hit man's crime. It was just that report about the sinister figure . . . but maybe it was like the Murdoch girl had said – invented to get attention.

Realistically, he'd come to two dead ends today. And there was no assurance that they were anywhere near a result elsewhere either. Marjory, he reckoned, was inclined to think it was the kid; Jon Kingsley – who, for all he disliked him, wasn't a fool – was certainly plugging Susie. Those were, he had to say, the strongest leads they had, which meant they were right back at the point where they hadn't even decided if they were looking for one killer, or Ingles + AN Other.

Maybe, as Marjory had said at the briefing – though more to keep up morale than because she believed it, was his cynical assessment – the boffins would come up with something, fingerprints or fibres or the Holy Grail of a DNA sample. But supposing they did, what they wouldn't do is tell them who it belonged to.

So back to the routine stodging, as he'd said to Sheuggie. Read the reports, tackle what's on the desk. He was on the point of picking up a printout when he noticed the plastic envelope on his desk with the outlined cutting about Ingles's release last October which they now knew Murdoch had sent Davina. MacNee took it out idly and read it.

It didn't say much. Local newspapers didn't really go in for rehashing background scandals and sensationalizing. His eyes wandered to the other items on the page: someone was getting up a petition for new public lavatories in Newton Stewart; vandalism at a children's playground – at least, one of the swings had been broken. Riveting stuff.

He turned it over. The masthead told him this was the front page – and suddenly, he froze. He looked up, staring straight ahead of him, his eyes blank. Maybe the Super had been right for once in his professional lifetime. He put the cutting away, thinking furiously.

It all started falling into place. There were obvious difficulties – but as tumbler after tumbler clicked into line, there was only one missing for the jackpot. And he thought he knew how he might be able to nudge it into place.

He jumped up, pushing his chair back so violently that it fell over.

'What's bitten you?' Allan said curiously, but was ignored.

MacNee righted it, grabbing his jacket and making for the door, without a word. He flung it open and almost cannoned into Tansy Kerr.

'Hey, watch it, MacNee! Where are you away to in such a hurry?'

'I need to speak to Euphie Aitcheson,' he said over his shoulder. 'I may be some time.'

Kerr looked at Allan, who shrugged. 'Don't ask me.'

'Do you know if Andy Macdonald's back yet?' she asked. 'I wanted to speak to him about something.'

'Haven't seen him, if he is.'

'I'll be in the canteen. Tell him, would you?' She left, and Allan directed an obscene gesture at the closed door.

He did wonder, though, what it was that had galvanized Tam like a cattle prod up the backside. He'd been looking at something from an evidence bag . . .

It took him a minute or two to find it, since it was buried under a pile of papers, but when he opened it out he couldn't see what the fuss was about. It had an outlined report about Ingles's release, and even when he turned it over, it was just the front page of an old *Galloway Globe*. He studied it for a minute, but it didn't tell him anything he didn't know already and he went gloomily back to take out his girlie magazine again.

Even after last night, she hadn't believed in Susie's guilt. Fleming paused in the corridor leading to the waiting-room, trying to collect her thoughts. Susie had, as Cat had pointed out, had a very hard time – losing the farm which was her home, having to beg her parents for a roof over their heads, finding herself eventually in a farm labourer's cottage and suffering, as she saw it, 'charity' from the woman she hated. Susie's temperament was volatile, to say the least of it, and her husband being arrested not once but twice would be enough to push anyone over the edge, into a breakdown.

But *murder*? And not just one, but two murders – murders where you had covered your tracks carefully enough to leave no traces, where you had done your best to cover your guilt by implicating someone else – she hadn't believed Susie capable of that, and it wasn't only that she had an inbuilt prejudice against any theory of Jon Kingsley's.

But then, she couldn't see Findlay in that role either. She liked him; he had always seemed to her a decent man.

Fleming took a deep breath and opened the door. Stevenson was sitting with his head in his hands, shaking. He looked up when he saw her, his face as grey-white under the freckles as the plastic carrier bag he was holding on his knees. He struggled to stand.

'No, no,' she said, hastily going to take the seat next to him. 'Sit down before you fall down. Findlay, it's bad, obviously. Tell me now. Get it over with.'

She could see him try to speak, but he was literally unable to frame the words. Instead, he held out the carrier bag. Fleming took it, looking at him questioningly, then peered inside.

There was a small, neat black handbag, a bag of quilted leather with a gold chain and linked Cs on the catch. Fleming didn't touch it. She knew what it must be.

'Davina Watt's bag.'

Stevenson found his voice. 'Y-yes. I opened it, to see – I knew Susie didn't have a bag like that. And there's her name on things inside.'

'Where was it?'

'In – in her car. I'd packed up her things at the cottage and brought them down to her parents. They'd – they'd said they'd look after Josh, so I took him in too. Bill – Bill said he was coming in to see your mother and he'd give me a lift back.

'She'd boxes and stuff, so I was unloading them and carrying them in. And then when I came to get the last box, I saw this carrier bag, stuffed in a corner. It didn't seem to have much in it, so I checked, and saw . . .'

He faltered. Wrung with pity, Fleming touched his arm. 'It's awful for you.'

'Oh God, have I done the right thing? I told Bill – he said it was all I could do, and I know that, really, but to betray her like this – it's the hardest thing I've ever had to do in my entire life.' He groaned, putting his head in his hands again.

With a heavy heart, Fleming said, 'Yes, Findlay, you did. You couldn't have done anything else.

'Now, I can't actually deal with this. I'm too personally involved. Wait here. I'll get someone to bring you a cup of tea – and I really think you should drink it – while I make the arrangements.'

With the bag in her hand, she left, and heard Findlay's racking sobs as she shut the door behind her.

'Greg said you were looking for me?' DC Andy Macdonald came into the canteen, carrying a file which he put down on one of the side tables.

Tansy Kerr was drinking coffee at a table with a couple of uniformed officers. The canteen was busy; the searchers party had returned and others were starting to drift back from their various assignments.

'Oh good!' Kerr got up. 'I've had a boring day, apart from the interview this morning. I'm off duty now but I thought I'd stick around to hear how you got on before I left.'

'Let's just say I wouldn't want a child of mine keeping the company she's got herself into on the internet.'

'Animal Liberation Front?'

'And Bite and all the rest. I've got printouts, if you're interested. Just let me get something to drink first.'

Kerr waited while he collected coffee and a Mars bar. 'I've got a theory about it, Andy. I talked to Mirren this morning and I decided two things: one, she hadn't actually killed her father and two, she was somehow in it up to her neck.'

'That would figure.'

'I hoped you'd say that. Now, there's a statement from a kid called James Ross. He saw Mirren talking to a man wearing black in the early evening. And there's another mentioning a guy the girl who lives next door saw around midnight. Dark clothes, blacked-out face – what does that suggest to you?'

'Cobra,' Macdonald said smugly.

He had her there. 'Is that an acronym?'

'Wrong "nym". It's a pseudonym, the kind used by animal liberation terrorists to glamorize thuggery.'

He went over to fetch the file. 'Look at these last e-mails. He's promised to come and rescue the dog and do a spot of fire-raising to teach Mirren's father the error of his ways. Doesn't mention any attack on him, though.'

'But that would square with her remark when they broke the news,' Kerr pointed out. 'Sergeant Christie's report claims what she said was, "I didn't know he was dead." She assumed her pal Cobra had done it – and wasn't much fazed either, by all accounts.'

'Certainly, from the tone of those websites, she wouldn't have any reason to think he wouldn't have.'

'Better tell the boss.' Kerr was excited.

'Say after contacting her in the afternoon to find out where the dog was – which he'd rescue, of course—'

'And say she told him where he would find her father—' Kerr put in.

'We could be on to something,' Macdonald said. 'Give me a high five!'

Elated, they slapped hands. 'He'll take some tracking down,' Macdonald warned.

'Hours of fun,' Kerr was agreeing when the door to the canteen opened and a woman constable came in.

'Here,' she called, 'anyone know what's happening? There's a big fuss – something's going on.'

She immediately had their attention. Kingsley, who had been talking to one of the house-to-house teams, spun round, a light in his eye.

'Breakthrough?' he said. 'What do you reckon?'

Everyone started talking at once. It was only a few minutes later that the door opened again and Fleming appeared. She was looking harassed and her black eye had gone Technicolor. The buzz of speculation died.

'Anyone seen MacNee?'

'He went out,' Tansy volunteered. 'Said he needed to talk to the Aitchesons.'

Fleming sighed impatiently. 'Damn.' She looked round. 'Macdonald – you'd better come. Kerr – no, better not. I don't want anyone who's been involved in this already.' Her eye went round the uniforms and spotted Sandy Langlands. 'You'll do. The Super's taking charge of this one himself. I'll explain as we go.'

Langlands, pink at this evidence of her confidence, followed her along with Macdonald. There was a very brief silence, and then the chatter began.

'What was that about?' Kerr said blankly.

But Kingsley was cock-a-hoop. 'You know what that means – "something we've been involved in already". Susie Stevenson – what did I say?'

'Could be Findlay Stevenson,' Kerr pointed out, but without much conviction. Bloody Kingsley, bloody right again.

'What did Tam want with the Aitchesons, do you suppose?' Kingsley wondered. 'Seems to be a bit off the pace recently, our Tam, doesn't he?' Kerr ignored that.

One of the uniforms said, 'Well, I'll wait till tomorrow to hear what's happened. They won't pay me to hang around, and anyway I've got a hot date this evening.'

There was the usual ribaldry, and a general exodus of those on overtime began.

Kerr was torn. She was curious, certainly, but she'd done a lot of hanging around already today and if she didn't get some laundry done she'd have nothing left clean. 'I'd better get home too. Are you waiting, Jon?'

'Depends. I want to have a word with Greg anyway. His shift doesn't end till seven and I'll get him to give me a bell if there's news by then.'

'You could call me too if he does.'

He said he would, and she thanked him, but without much expectation that the promise would be kept.

It was torture, this self-exclusion. Fleming had handed over formally to Donald Bailey – summoned from the nineteenth hole – and been commended for her astuteness in withdrawing.

'It could have been extremely prejudicial, you know, Marjory,' he said, repeating what she had said to him, in rather more orotund phrases. 'Any competent QC could make much of your personal animosity towards the accused.'

'They will, Donald, they will,' she warned him.

'But at least we can demonstrate that you have been utterly scrupulous in your detachment.

'It was young Kingsley who was driving this one, wasn't it? Oh, he has the faults of youth and impetuosity, but an able fellow, an able fellow.'

'Indeed. I've given you DC Macdonald for the interrogation – he's a sound man, and I've gone over questions that need asking – though of course,' she added hastily, 'you'll be directing that. And PC Langlands will be taking notes for action.'

'What's happened to Tam? I would have expected him to stand in for you, Marjory.'

'To be honest, I don't know. He was in Glasgow, checking out an attempted suicide by one of our suspects, but I haven't seen him since he got back. According to Kerr, he went out on a follow-up interview. I'll brief him if he comes back in tonight, or else tomorrow morning.'

'Fine, fine. And let's hope this is us into the home straight, eh?'

So now here Fleming was, alone in her office, seething with frustration. She could have used the time to go and see her mother, but it wouldn't be a kindness to let her see her daughter looking like something out of a documentary about violence. She phoned her instead, and found her cheerful after a visit from Bill and the children and, as always, understanding about the – in this case fictitious – demands of the job. She phoned the hospital too, for a report on her father, and found they were cautiously suggesting tomorrow as suitable for a first visit. She dreaded it, but whatever the day might bring, she ought to clear a space to go with Janet to do that. She phoned Bill too, but there wasn't much they could say beyond echoing their dismay to and fro.

Her desk had returned to its normal chaos of papers, but she couldn't find the enthusiasm to sort it out. There was a report waiting to be written on training, and reading she could do, too, on other matters, like an analysis of car crime, which looked suspiciously like a cut-and-paste job, handed in by Greg Allan, but none of it was enticing.

It would have been good to phone Laura, tell her about Susie's attack and get sympathy, but at the moment it was too difficult. Even though Laura had acted so often as an unofficial police adviser, she would feel uncomfortable mentioning the sequel, and it would be equally uncomfortable not to.

There was still, of course, that message from Chris Carter. She called up her e-mail, clicked it open and read it again. It would be better to reply tomorrow, when she might be able to say they had cracked it, she told herself, knowing she was making excuses.

* * *

'Now, let us turn to the question of timing.' Donald Bailey had taken control of the interview to this point, more or less ignoring the existence of his colleagues. 'The day Davina Watt was killed—' He clicked his fingers, and Macdonald supplied the date.

Findlay Stevenson looked bewildered. 'I – I don't know. Thursday, last week? We were staying with Susie's parents then. She'd have been working, I expect. She sometimes does mornings, sometimes afternoons until she has to collect Josh from school. You'd have to ask her.'

'Or her employer, of course.' Bailey was pleased with that thought. 'Make a note of that, constable.'

'Yes, sir.' Langlands had written it down already, under 'Action'.

'Now,' Bailey continued, 'let's take Wednesday of this week. Three days ago. You have a rather less imperfect recollection of Wednesday, I trust?'

Stevenson's mouth twisted. 'Oh yes, I remember Wednesday all right.'

'I have your statement here. Somewhere.' Bailey rooted about among the papers in front of him until Macdonald pushed the right one in front of him. 'Ah yes. You came to Drumbreck at approximately eight-fifteen p.m., reasoning, you said, that at that time there would be movement of cars and people around the place and your presence would be less conspicuous than after the arrival of the night watchman?'

Stevenson took a drink from the glass of water on the table, but his mouth still sounded dry. 'Yes, that's right.'

'You watched your chance, then simply released the dog?'
'Yes.'

'Then drove straight home, arriving back a little after nine?'
'Yes.'

Macdonald leaned forwards. 'You didn't see Niall Murdoch

at that time?' Bailey stared at him, as if he had forgotten he could speak.

'I didn't see anyone. I shouldn't think anyone saw me, either. I was doing my best to avoid being seen.'

'Finished, Macdonald?' Bailey asked acidly. 'Very well then. To resume: you came back home, where your wife was waiting for you?'

'Yes.'

'Go on, man – what happened then?'

Stevenson's eyes fell. 'We – we had a row.'

'A row? What about?'

'She didn't like me stealing the dog – said there would be more trouble. She was angry. Very angry.'

Bravely, Macdonald interrupted again. 'What form did her anger take?'

'Well – yelling and throwing things, mostly. I think she was starting to have some sort of breakdown. You probably saw what she did to poor Marjory Fleming.'

'Indeed we have,' Bailey boomed. 'A peculiarly vicious attack. And you say you were subjected to something similar?'

'She didn't attack me – just threw things.'

'And what did you do?'

'Ducked,' he said simply. 'And tried to talk her down, told her she'd wake Josh – and she did calm down, eventually. Then we went to bed.'

'Now here,' Bailey said, forming a pyramid with his fingers and leaning his chin on it, 'we come to it. Did she, your wife, leave the house at any stage during the night?'

Stevenson looked down. 'I – don't know.'

'Don't know, man? How could you not know? You can't sleep so soundly that she could get up, dress, and leave the house without you knowing?'

He seemed embarrassed. 'We – er – weren't together. She made me sleep on the spare bed in Josh's room.'

'Ah!' Bailey exclaimed in triumph. 'So you are telling us that after – what – say, ten o'clock, you could not say where your wife was or what she was doing?'

He shaded his eyes with his hand. 'No. I'm afraid I have absolutely no idea.'

'Well, I think that wraps it up! Unless there's anything else?' His look towards Macdonald defied him to suggest anything missed out.

'Not for the moment, at least.' Macdonald's was a careful response.

'Thank you, Mr Stevenson. We won't take up more of your time. And may I say you showed considerable fortitude and public spirit in coming forward with this information.'

'Thank you.' Stevenson stood up, swaying a little with fatigue and looking round as if he couldn't quite work out where the door was. Langlands hurried to hold it open, then went to intone, 'Interview terminated eighteen-eighteen,' and switch off the recordings.

'That seemed to go pretty well.' Bailey stood up with the air of one expecting applause. 'The lady certainly has some questions to answer, once the trick-cyclists let us have a go at her.'

'Yes, of course. But sir,' Macdonald framed the words with great delicacy, 'it probably struck you, just as it struck me – Stevenson has a few questions to answer himself. He's still a suspect, and of course he was there at a much more plausible time. He's basically given her an alibi until after the night watchman came on duty.'

Bailey's face registered shock, then he coughed. 'Of course, of course, as you say. This is definitely something we have to consider. A bit more digging necessary – and you see, if he were indeed responsible, who would have a better opportunity to incriminate his wife by leaving that bag in her car?'

'Yes, I spotted that too, sir,' Langlands said unwisely,

coming over holding the tapes, and oblivious to Bailey's glare, went on, 'We've only his word that he found it there, after all,' which left Bailey with nothing to add.

'An obvious point, constable. Now, I had better go and brief Inspector Fleming.'

Tam MacNee let himself out of the Aitchesons' house. He hadn't expected them to show him out with friendly waves and invitations to drop in the next time he was passing. He'd have to watch Euphie Aitcheson didn't put a knife in his back next time she caught him off his guard.

It was raining heavily and he could even hear a sullen roll of thunder from somewhere far away. He hunched his leather jacket up over his head and hurried down the path. It had taken a lot of time and effort, but he'd got what he came for in the end. It fitted, it all fitted, every last little piece of the jigsaw puzzle. All that remained to do was go back to HQ and set the wheels in motion.

But talking of wheels – he reached his car and saw with considerable annoyance that the front tyre was flat. And it had to happen in rain like this, too! He bent down to examine the problem.

He didn't hear someone come up behind him until he was almost on him. He was crouching and off-balance; he attempted to straighten up and turn to defend himself but trying to shrug off the jacket impeded him. He only managed to say, 'Kingsley, bastard—' before the jack came down on his head and he fell to the ground.

25

Marjory Fleming was running a bath. She'd declined the offer of a Bladnoch and a blether, pleading tiredness, and Bill had sent her off upstairs with sympathy and a sizeable dram, never suspecting that she could not bear to tell him about the latest developments.

The bath was running and she had just pulled on her bathrobe when she heard the phone ring, and swore. It would probably be for her, but if Bill took it, she could trust him to stall them unless it was urgent. Still, she was braced for a shout from downstairs; when it didn't come she went to test the water temperature. She was on the point of taking off her robe when she heard Bill's footsteps on the stairs, and went to open the bathroom door.

His expression was bleak. 'It's bad news. It's Tam.'

She misunderstood. Taking the phone from his hand, she said, 'Tam?' then listened with growing horror to the voice at the other end.

'Right. I'll be in shortly.' She turned off the taps and pulled the plug out. 'Did you get that?' she asked Bill.

'Not the detail. Just that they said Tam was badly injured.'

'Touch and go. Compound depressed fracture of the skull. He'd gone to see the Aitchesons for some reason. They think that when he came out he was bending down to look at a flat tyre – don't know yet whether that was part of it, but it seems likely. Someone hit him over the head, but mercifully a man came out of his house at just that moment and scared him off before he could club him to death.'

'Description?'

'The man's coming in to give a statement.' She headed for the bedroom to get dressed. 'But oh, Bill! Poor Bunty! Tam's all she has – she'll be distraught.' There were tears in her own eyes.

'You're pretty fond of Tam yourself.' Bill, standing in the doorway, held out his arms, but she shook her head.

'I can't afford to cry. I've got work to do, nailing the bastard who did this to the wall. They'd better not let me get to him first, that's all.'

The atmosphere in Kirkluce HQ was sombre. It seemed to have been otherwise a quiet night, for a Saturday: an addict found shooting up by the War Memorial, a couple of men cooling off in the cells after a fist fight and the usual flotsam of drunk and foolish teenagers drifting through. But the officers on the night shift were going about their business grim-faced, with none of the usual banter.

'Have they brought in the witness?' Fleming asked at the desk.

'In the waiting-room, ma'am.'

'Get an interview room set up. I want this recorded for the morning briefing. Are they getting on with house-to-house?'

'Three patrol cars there since eight o'clock.'

'Good. Who's around?'

'Here's the duty sheet. And DC Kingsley came in ten minutes ago. Heard it on his car radio.'

It would be out there by now, of course. That would be an added problem to handle. But it was good news about Kingsley, who was nothing if not competent. He wasn't in the CID room, but she tracked him down in the control room, listening to messages coming in. He turned as she came in.

'Nothing yet, I'm afraid. This is a terrible thing. Any more news from the hospital?'

He did, Fleming thought, look quite shaken. She'd suspected his first reaction might be that there could be a vacancy for sergeant, but of course there wasn't an officer in the Force who could hear of another's injury without thinking, 'Next time that could be me.'

'Not good. But the witness is waiting to be interviewed. Come with me, Jon.'

He hesitated. 'I thought it might help if I monitored messages—'

'More help if you think of something useful to ask him. Let's go.'

There was, disappointingly, very little that the witness could tell them. He'd come out of his house on the turning circle at the end of Duntruin Place to see a man in a dark rain jacket with the hood up standing over someone lying in the gutter. He was holding something that looked like a metal tool, and seeing the other man approach took off fast, away from him down Duntruin Place and round the corner into Duntruin Street. The witness – stout and in his late fifties – had not even tried to give chase, contenting himself with dialling 999 on his mobile.

The attacker had been, he thought, of medium height, neither particularly tall nor short, and the jacket had been either black or dark blue, but that was all he could offer.

It wasn't a lot to go on. Fleming returned to the control room with Kingsley; the phones were starting to ring now, but the best the house-to-house had come up with from Duntruin Place was someone who had seen a man in a black hooded jacket walk past a quarter of an hour before. From Duntruin Street, round the corner, came an account of a hurrying man with a hood pulled up, who had then got into a car – no description of that.

'That's almost certainly him,' Fleming said, 'but it doesn't get us any further.'

An operator turned round. 'That's a message from Car 28. They've spoken to the Aitchesons, but they didn't see anything.'

'Right. We'll need to talk to them properly,' Fleming added to Jon. 'They may be able to shed some light on what he'd been asking them. I suppose it can wait till the morning.'

'I could do that, before I come in,' Kingsley offered. 'Driving down to Wigtown isn't a problem.'

'Thanks, Jon – that would be very helpful. I'll have the briefing early tomorrow. It's my guess everyone will have heard the news by then. I'll contact the hospital again first thing.'

'What is the situation with poor old Tam?' Kingsley sounded genuinely concerned.

'I haven't by any means got a full picture, but I think they're trying to stabilize him with a view to operating tomorrow. All we can do now is pray – and pull out all the stops to get the sod who did this.'

Kingsley nodded gravely as Fleming went on, 'I'm just going to phone the Super now – I only hope I get to him before he hears a news broadcast.

'You may as well go home, Jon – but thanks for coming in.'

'Least I could do. I'll just hang on a little longer, till they've finished the house-to-house.'

'Let me know if there's anything fresh. Goodnight.'

There was more or less a full complement of officers, uniformed and plain-clothes, on duty and off, crammed into the incident room by nine o'clock next morning. As Fleming approached she could hear only low-voiced conversation, which subsided to total silence when she came in.

'First of all, Tam got through the night. He's in Dumfries – they're going to operate this morning.'

There was a buzz of relief and one or two clapped; a voice from somewhere in the middle said, quoting the old Scots motto, 'Wha daur meddle wi' Tam, eh?' and the applause grew.

'Yeah, right,' Fleming said, clearing her throat. 'So – strategy for today.

'The eye-witness's statement was videoed last night – you'll be shown the relevant part of that later. From the house-to-house interviews last night, we did get an indication of timing: the attack, we know, happened at seven-fifteen, more or less, and at seven o'clock a man matching the description walked up Duntruin Place, which is a cul-de-sac. No one saw him hanging about and he wouldn't want to be conspicuous. There's an empty house with a For Sale notice about three doors along from the Aitchesons' and it's a reasonable bet he hid in the garden there. A team will be going in to check it out – you don't need me to tell you what you're looking for.

'Apart from that, we'll be tracing Tam's footsteps, trying to work out what lead he was following. It tweaked a nerve, obviously. Someone will be checking out the Glasgow end – he was there yesterday, and we need to know what came of that. And the Aitchesons – Kingsley, did you manage to see them this morning?'

Kingsley pulled a face. 'For what it was worth. Brian Aitcheson said it was mainly about his night watchman shift when Murdoch was murdered – going over it to see if there was anything he'd remembered since he made his statement. Which he said he hadn't. That's about the size of it.'

'Hmm. Not very helpful,' Fleming was saying, when Tansy Kerr spoke up. Her eyes were red; Fleming had noticed her struggling during the bulletin about Tam.

'But he said it was Euphie Aitcheson he was going to see,' she protested. 'What did she say?'

Kingsley shot her a look of annoyance. 'Not much. Just agreed with her husband. Oh, and she complained that I'd called so early in the morning.'

But Kerr was not to be brushed aside so easily. 'He must have been there for ages! He left here in such a hurry that he almost knocked me over and that was around five o'clock. He only left the house at seven-fifteen, and it takes half an hour or so to drive to Wigtown. It wouldn't take two hours to hear that Brian Aitcheson had nothing to add to his original statement.'

Kingsley snapped, 'Well, I don't know, Tansy. Maybe they got to yarning about old times in the police force. I can only repeat what they told me.'

'That's enough!' Fleming said sharply. 'I can understand that everyone's on edge, but that doesn't help.

'We're getting numerous calls from the public, which will have to be sifted to find those that need a follow-up. There will also be intense interest from the Press and the Press Officer will handle all queries. Superintendent Bailey will be making a televised statement later.

'That's about it, unless anyone has anything – yes, Macdonald?'

Andy Macdonald rubbed his hand over his close-cropped head, a habit he had. 'I don't know if this is out of order, but if Tam was asking Aitcheson what he saw on the night of the murder, could this link in with Findlay Stevenson? We began wondering last night after he made the statement incriminating his wife whether that could just be a blind for his own activities – if Tam was on to some definite link, and Stevenson somehow got wind of it—'

Fleming's eyes narrowed. 'What time did the interview finish last night?'

'Eighteen-eighteen,' Langlands said promptly. 'I recorded the time at the end of the interview.'

'Bring him in again. We've got his temporary address?'

'Yes, ma'am,' Sergeant Naismith said. 'Small hotel in the town here. I'll arrange that.'

'Thanks, Jock. And can you set up the witness video? Have

a look at it, everyone. It's not long – he didn't have a lot to tell us, unfortunately. OK, that's it. Good luck.'

She was leaving the room when Tansy Kerr stopped her just by the door. 'Greg Allan was with Tam after he got back from Glasgow. Tam might have said something to him.'

'Where is he?' Fleming scanned the room.

'Not in yet. I think he's not on duty till eleven.'

'I see.' Fleming made her voice as neutral as she could. He must be about the only officer who wasn't here, and that included those who'd been on duty all night.

The short video clip finished. Kingsley raised his voice as people started to move. 'Just a minute!'

Fleming and Kerr turned to listen.

'Before everyone goes, I think we should have a whip-round. Just to show old Tam we're thinking about him.'

There was a murmur of agreement, which covered the sound of Kerr making a sick noise.

'A plant for while he's in hospital, do you reckon?' Kingsley was going on. 'And a large bottle of Scotch, to give him the incentive to get well enough to drink it! I'll put a box for contributions on the table here.'

Kerr and Fleming left together. Fighting back tears, Kerr said, 'He can't stand Tam. I'm not giving him a penny – I'll buy my own present for Tam. If he – if he doesn't . . .' She bit her lip.

'Don't despair. As he'd tell you himself, a dunt on the head's nothing to a Glasgow hard man.'

But as she mounted the stairs to her office, it was a quotation from Tam's beloved Burns that was ringing through her brain:

> 'An forward, tho I canna see,
> I guess, an fear!'

'Did you not hear the news about Tam this morning, Greg?' Tansy Kerr's question was pointed when Allan appeared at eleven o'clock.

He looked shifty. 'Not – not till later on,' he said, then gave himself away by adding, 'Anyway, I thought there'd be plenty people here. You don't look that busy yourself.'

'I'm checking information received to see what needs following up,' Kerr said stiffly, though in fact it was true; considering how little there was to go on, they now had saturation coverage. She was also frustrated that it was Andy Macdonald at the sharp end, while she processed useless information from members of the public who were no doubt well-intentioned, those of them who weren't several cards short of the full deck.

She'd decided unilaterally that she'd go through everything of Tam's that she could find, every notebook, every scrap of paper. Not that she was hopeful that it would yield much since Tam did a lot more thinking than writing, but at least she could tell herself she was contributing.

'Did Tam say anything to you yesterday afternoon, about a lead he had? Before he went to the Aitchesons'?' she demanded.

Allan, busying himself with trying to look busy, shrugged his shoulders. 'Not so's you'd notice. I think he deigned to say hello when he came in, but that was as far as it went.'

Kerr swallowed hard. She really couldn't afford to lash out at everyone and she was saving herself for the blistering row she was planning to have with that slimy, hypocritical reptile Kingsley. She had almost worked through the pile of messages when the door opened and a custody officer put his head round it.

'Is there an evidence bag here with a needle in it? We took it off a junkie last night. It was downstairs waiting for printing and it's disappeared. I thought one of you guys might have been detailed to follow it up.'

'Oh no. No one's been detailed to do anything, except chase their tails trying to find out who had a crack at MacNee last night,' Allan said with venom. 'Murder, mainlining, carry on, why don't you? We haven't time to worry about that sort of stuff.

'But don't let me stop you having a look around. Be my guest.'

It was only the other officer's embarrassed presence that stopped Tansy Kerr gouging his eyes out there and then.

If Findlay Stevenson had looked bad yesterday, he looked worse today. He hadn't shaved, and the checked shirt he was wearing looked as if he had slept in it. As perhaps he had, Andy Macdonald thought as he once again followed Super-intendent Bailey into the interview room, with PC Langlands bringing up the rear.

He'd come from a session with Fleming, when she had forced him to be blunt about the Super's interviewing tech-nique yesterday. She had then been equally blunt about what he had to do today.

'You've got to push Stevenson. It's vital. We could be talking about two murders and one attempted murder here. I'm haunted by the thought that if I'd been grilling him yesterday, Tam might not be in theatre as we speak.

'Maybe I flatter myself. But when you come out of there you've got to be able to tell me you know you've wrung him dry. OK?'

Though Fleming's black eye had faded to sickly yellow and the scratches on her face were less angry-looking, she was so strung-up that he could see her neck cords standing out. He'd never seen her like this before, never known her less than professional about her superiors. But everyone knew that she and Tam went back to the dawn of time, and he promised to steam-roller the man who had police promotion in his gift, feeling that not to promise would leave him in danger of grievous bodily harm.

Bailey, in his turn, cautioned him as they walked to the interview room. 'What you must keep at the forefront of your mind, Macdonald, is that this man could be a serial killer. There are two murders we are investigating, as well as this attack on MacNee. It would never do for the public to gain the impression that we are more concerned about the latter. I intend to emphasize that in my broadcast.'

'Then you'd better not let the lads hear you.' He didn't say it of course, but one of the things that kept you doing the dangerous job was that any attack on you would mean a fuss out of all proportion to the equivalent attack on Joe Public.

Bailey led off. 'Now, Mr Stevenson, we were very grateful for your co-operation yesterday.'

He paused for breath, and Macdonald cut in, 'Where were you last night, Stevenson? Because I have to tell you we weren't much impressed with what you told us yesterday.'

Stevenson looked shocked, but hardly more shocked than Bailey, whose mouth was half-open, staring at his subordinate.

Taking advantage of that, Macdonald pressed on, 'You see, we've only your word for it, haven't we, that you found the bag among your wife's belongings. And we've such nasty suspicious minds that it occurred to us that this might be quite a clever way of shifting the blame. Comment?'

Stevenson struggled for words. 'I – I – last night,' he seized on the concrete question, 'I left here and went back to the Balmoral Guest House, where I have a room.'

'Straight there?' Macdonald refused to catch Bailey's eye.

'Yes. Straight there.'

'And what did you do after that? Go out to eat?'

'I wasn't hungry.'

'So you claim you didn't leave your room after – what – seven o'clock?'

'Earlier, probably. I didn't check.' Stevenson was looking at him with dislike. 'I don't understand – what is this about?'

'Can anyone verify that for us?'

'No, of course not. I hadn't anyone in my room.'

That was good; he was getting angry, always useful. Anger meant loss of control. Oblivious now to Bailey, sulking with his arms folded, Macdonald went on, 'And what is the set-up at the Balmoral? If you leave your room, do you have to pass a reception desk with someone in attendance?'

'It's a guest house, for God's sake!' Stevenson burst out. 'Of course not! You have to ring a bell to get attention.'

'But you wouldn't ring a bell, would you, if you didn't want anyone to know you were going out?'

'Why the hell should I care?' Anger, tinged now with uncertainty. Excellent!

Macdonald switched tack. 'Do you own a dark rain jacket with a hood?'

'A *rain jacket*? I've got a green oiled jacket, but that's all.'

'Can we check your room and your car?'

'If you want – I've nothing to hide, but I would like to know what this is all about.'

'Had you any dealings with DS Tam MacNee?'

'MacNee – no.' It took a second for Stevenson to make the connection. 'Oh my God! That's the one who was attacked? You think I did it!

'I didn't. I promise you that I don't even know what the man looks like. I had no contact with him at any time. I'm simply bemused by what you're asking me.'

Macdonald gulped. In this game, the common currency was distortions, evasions, half-truths and downright lies. Your professional skill was in sifting them for the tiny nuggets of fact which might be, with a certain amount of luck, concealed within them.

Simple, straightforward truth was different. Contrary to popular belief, when it came your way – which wasn't often – it was unmistakable.

'Right,' he mumbled, as Bailey said ominously, 'Shall I take over, constable?

'Now, Stevenson, we will have to go through your movements on each of the days in question. It will help if you can think of anyone who might be in a position to corroborate any statement you make, and we will of course be instituting a very thorough investigation to see whether accepting your account is contra-indicated.'

As they went back to the Thursday of Davina Watt's death, Macdonald was left to his own bitter reflections. Thanks, boss – it could be years before he made sergeant, after this performance.

'He's not our man, Marjory.'

The wait had been interminable, and to get this news at the end of it was another blow. She'd been kept busy with progress reports – or rather, lack of progress reports – but the one useful piece of information that had come in had left her pinning her hopes on this.

'Young Macdonald gave him a bruising, but what emerged was an honest man. No alibis, but no attempt to pretend he did. No sensitivity about Davina Watt – it was patent that he felt he'd had a narrow escape, though from the sound of things it was from the frying pan into the fire. No quarrel with Murdoch either, once he'd retrieved the dog. And before you ask, Marjory – Macdonald agreed.'

Fleming had never thought him as much of a fool as others did, and she coloured at his knowing look. It was only then that it occurred to her what her demand to Macdonald that he override the boss might have done to his chances of promotion when a sergeant's job came up – which, please God, it wouldn't this very day.

'So I think we're back to considering the wife, don't you?'

'I've had bad news on that, Don. They've fingerprinted the bag, and they've found Davina's fingerprints there, and

Findlay's – as of course they would be, by his own account –
but there's no sign of Susie's. And while she's not small, I
doubt if even in a concealing jacket she'd be mistaken for a
man by several people.'

He hadn't considered that. 'No, I don't suppose she would.
I suppose, too, that the fingerprints would point to Findlay
again – no knowing when they got there . . . but as I said,
Marjory, he struck us all as a transparently honest man.

'Maybe you should rope in Kingsley again. See what he
thinks, on the basis of what we have. He's done well before.'

'He and Greg Allan were responsible for charging Keith
Ingles,' she pointed out sharply.

'True enough. But that was a young man's mistake – over-
eagerness, compounded by his sergeant's incompetence. I still
see Kingsley as a very able fellow.'

Poor Andy! Fleming agreed hollowly, then, as so often,
Bailey surprised her by saying, 'But young Macdonald, there –
good chap, too. Stood his ground, much as you do yourself,
Marjory.

'Any more word from the hospital?'

'Not since we heard they were operating. The odds are in
his favour for a full recovery.'

Bailey studied her face. 'Good odds?'

'Not – brilliant. Two-thirds, one-third.'

He got up. 'Better than the other way round. But where do
we go from here?'

The only truthful answer she could think of was, 'Your
guess is as good as mine.' She didn't think that was tactful.

'Usual lines of inquiry,' she said, which was code for the
same thing.

It was only after he had left that she remembered she had
wanted to question Greg Allan, but by that time he had gone to
lunch.

*   *   *

'Are you remembering about taking Janet to see your father this afternoon, Marjory?'

Of course she wasn't. Taken up with her worries about Tam and the hunt for his attacker, personal commitments had gone out of her mind. 'Oh Bill, I don't see how I can,' she said, not allowing herself to consider that the machine could grind on without her to turn the handle, since she was unable to bear the notion of not being on hand for any new development.

His immediate understanding shamed her. 'Of course you can't. I'll take her – Janet won't mind.'

She would, of course, but only a little. Marjory accepted the offer with gratitude and guilt, then added, 'Why don't you phone Laura, see if she'd be able to go with you? That would help.'

Bill's voice warmed. 'Of course it would. Actually, she'd probably be much more use than either of us in supporting Janet.'

'Of course she would,' Fleming agreed heartily. Her emotions, as she put down the phone, were so confused that she was glad when Allan's knock on the door prevented her from having to examine them.

'Greg, come in. I just wanted to ask you about Tam, yesterday afternoon,' she greeted him. 'Tansy said you were in the CID room when he came back from Glasgow.'

'I told her.' Allan looked positively resentful at having been summoned. She really was going to have to do something about the man, once the immediate crisis was over. 'He said hello and that was it. Then later he left without saying anything, except to tell Tansy where he was going. Just about knocked her over in his hurry. He'd knocked over his chair already.'

'Really? What was that about?'

'No idea.'

His bored tone annoyed her. 'Allan, I shouldn't have to ask

you for maximum co-operation. I don't feel you're trying. What was he doing that might have prompted him to leave so hurriedly?'

'How should I know?'

This wasn't merely verging on insolence. She got to her feet. 'Stand up, sergeant. Stand to attention.'

Startled, he did as he was told.

It was a technique she had used before, though never on him. She had the height advantage; she moved round the desk to stand in uncomfortably close proximity. He shifted uneasily.

'I said, attention!'

His hands stiffened by his side. He wasn't a brave man; she had scared him.

'Let's start again. You're going to tell me every tiny detail you can remember of what happened after MacNee came in.'

Allan licked his lips. 'He came in, sat down – no, took his coat off and put it on the back of his chair. Then sat down. Looked at some papers. I was working too, of course,' there was a whine in his voice, 'so I wasn't watching him, particularly. But then I saw him looking at that cutting with Ingles's release in it. It was after that he went out.'

She remembered the cutting. Was this the key they had been looking for? 'Where is it?'

'On one of the tables. I took it out to have a look at it but it didn't mean anything to me. I just left it there.'

'Go down and get it. At the double.'

He needed no second invitation to leave, but before he reached the door, she added, 'And sergeant, behave like that again and you're on a charge for insubordination.'

The news from the hospital was good, as far as it went. Tam was out of theatre, in the recovery room, and the policeman on guard duty had been told to expect him to return to a private room, rather than to intensive care. The trouble was, it wouldn't be for some time that they would know whether or not there was brain damage, or even whether he would escape the danger of infection, ever-present in hospitals today and to which he would, as Bunty told Marjory in an emotional phone call, be particularly vulnerable.

The news about the cutting Tam had been reading was not, however, good. Allan, looking frightened, had come back to report that he couldn't find it, though the evidence bag was still there. Another, more exhaustive search failed to find it either. Allan confessed that he had left it lying on the desk; if it had found its way to the floor, a cleaner might easily have thrown it away.

There was no note of the date. Fleming had questioned Allan, now all eagerness to oblige, about the other contents, but all he could remember was that it had something about the loss of the Knockhaven lifeboat, which didn't narrow it down much: its shocking, deliberate wrecking and what followed had dominated the local Press for weeks on end.

Fleming sent him to find out the precise date of Ingles's release from prison, and the *Galloway Globe* had been alerted to look out back copies for the month of October.

They would track it down before long, but what haunted her was the thought that she, like Allan, might look at it and find, like him, that it meant nothing to her.

The afternoon briefing was, indeed, brief. Fleming talked up the news about Tam and the gloom lifted a little. There was also another encouraging development: officers searching the grounds of the empty house had found clear footprints in the damp soil of a flower-bed, behind a bush where anyone standing would be out of sight but still could keep an eye on the road outside.

But there was little more that could be done that day and

some of the off-duty officers had already drifted away. Kerr, too, was missing, but Kingsley had collected a gratifying amount; he was planning to drive with the gifts to Dumfries, and promised to pump the nurses for any further information.

Allan had produced the date of Ingles's release and, waiting impatiently for the fax from the *Galloway Globe*, Fleming had listened patiently to Bailey rehearsing his statement for TV. It was a comprehensive list of the usual clichés – 'despicable attack', 'several promising lines of inquiry', 'wonderful public support' – while saying absolutely nothing. 'Perfect,' she told him, and he went away happy.

At last the fax was brought to her office. Fleming seized it and ran her eyes first over the second page with the outlined article, then turned it over.

26

Jon Kingsley's hands were shaking as he got into his car, which disturbed him. He made a fetish of total self-control and his talent for thinking on his feet amounted to genius, but this had been – challenging.

Just one more big problem – the biggest, perhaps. But hey! Four times already it had looked like certain disaster. He'd faced it down. He'd come through. He was cool with this, of course he was. And his hands weren't shaking, not when he gripped the wheel.

Yet these last nightmare weeks! Like battling the mythical hydra – cut off one head, two grew in its place. The flashbacks too: mockery in Davina's face as she turned to him in the parked car, then horror as his eyes flared and he lashed out at the little bitch; her helpless screams as he punished her. Then silence, until the thud of the stone on her head. Well, blackmail, for God's sake, when she'd handed Jon the safe keys and planted the cheques in Ingles's house herself to frame the man! But he'd no leverage; she'd another life, could vanish into it, he couldn't. It had felt good, afterwards, and it had felt good again to line up Keith Ingles as fall guy, one more time.

So near, so near! Calculating bastard! A normal man, finding the woman he loved dead – he'd have touched her, wept, held her close, called the police. It would all have worked. His hands curled tight round the steering wheel in remembered frustration. Oh yes, he'd screwed up there; Ingles was an ex-con now, not a respectable lawyer. And even the clincher, her handbag to be 'discovered' under a floorboard on a later visit – that had been thwarted by Fleming banning him and Greg Allan from the site.

Don't think about what hadn't worked. Needed his mind clear and calm. Needed to think how brilliant he'd been. But somehow, it all kept playing in his mind like a disjointed film.

Murdoch's call coming in, right there in the police station, telling him he hadn't finished. The man standing there on the pontoon, out of sight of the rest of the marina, not a boat in view, bending to check the holdall for the cash. Then his arms going up in shock, as the blow from the weighted sock – so simple, so clever! – caught him. The muffled splash as he went into the water; a tinier splash as the weight sank. And Jon's own jaunty walk back – who would remember just another yachtie in a navy hooded sweatshirt, strolling past?

Then the alibi, his masterstroke – that had worked. Oh yes! That was serious class!

And Laura, lovely Laura – how useful she'd been! Gullible, of course. He'd basked in her sympathy for the pressure he'd to take from his father. That was the father who'd abandoned the family when Jon was three. Perhaps, when he'd finished this off, he could take her more seriously. She was attractive, clever, had money; what more could he want? Only that she could get him ahead in the job – the job he loved, with the power it put into his hands – and she could do that too.

That was something he could think about, to take his mind off what lay ahead. Another meal at the Vine Leaf, perhaps – the food had been better than he expected. And she'd get used to sailing, get her sea legs in time . . .

Fleming saw what Tam had seen; of course she did. The photograph on the front page, of Kingsley and Kerr leaving the Knockhaven town hall after the funeral tea, captioned 'Detectives pay their respects to lifeboat victims'. DC

Jonathan Kingsley was quoted in the article too, making some anodyne comment about the tragedy.

So Davina had known that her old acquaintance, Jonathan, was back in the area, in the police force. So? Blackmail? But they'd established that Ingles had definitely done the robbery – was there some scandal in Kingsley's past that might cause trouble for him now he was a policeman? It was hard to imagine what it could be, these days, when nothing in the sexual line was taboo and the police force was positively going out of its way to recruit gays and transsexuals.

They'd need to question Jon about this, but she had a growing fear that it was another red herring. After all, now she thought about it, on the night Murdoch was killed, Laura had mentioned him being there having a drink, and she knew that he and Allan had worked till late, getting the reports and the admin on Ingles finished.

So what was it that Tam knew and she didn't, which had sent him off hotfoot to talk to the Aitchesons for hours?

The hour of maximum danger lay ahead. Kingsley shuddered – but he mustn't shudder. He must remain ice-cool, as he always did. He needed luck, but Lady Luck was his best girl at the moment. Planting the handbag in the cottage at the Flemings' farm would have been seriously risky, but there he was, refused permission to question Susie, and hey, look – it's the boot of her car, standing open! And then Macdonald this morning, with his suggestion of Findlay as the attacker – how lucky was that?

And the luck of finding the cutting, too, lying in full view on MacNee's desk. He'd known at once MacNee was on to him, and knew, too, why he'd gone to the Aitchesons'.

Jon had to be unsuspected. Somewhere he'd have made the contact that left a trace, and if the trace was there, forensic tests would find it. If only that interfering fool hadn't appeared before he could finish off the little sod!

He would, though, given luck, and after that, he'd be safe. *Luck, be a lady!* Who would remark on the pinprick of a syringe on someone who had probably had a dozen injections? And who would be surprised at cardiac arrest, in the circumstances?

And if MacNee got AIDS from the needle, it would hardly matter, would it? The sick joke pleased him; he started to laugh, then scared himself by finding it hard to stop.

She'd checked. Kingsley and Allan hadn't left till just after midnight on that Wednesday night. Fleming was still puzzling when her desk phone rang. 'It's DC Kerr. I have Mr Aitcheson here with me, ma'am. Is it all right if I bring him up?'

'Yes, of course.' She put down the phone, frowning. Kerr had been unhappy this morning about what the Aitchesons had said about Tam's long visit, but it was perfectly possible he'd gone to check something first. And Kerr's judgement could well be skewed, given how upset she was about Tam.

When Kerr came in behind Brian Aitcheson, there were spots of high colour in her cheeks and her eyes were very bright. She began without formality. 'This is something you have to hear urgently. Tell her, Mr Aitcheson.'

The big man looked hangdog. 'Tam came yesterday to persuade Mrs A to agree that she'd maybe kind of, well, exaggerated her evidence to the court. She didn't want to admit it and I got sort of mad with him myself, for he just sat there and argued, or just sat there, really. She gave in, in the end.'

Fleming was mystified. 'But why should she – er, exaggerate? What do you mean?'

'She was feart that swine Ingles would get off. He'd made her life hell, with his lies and insinuations about her, and she knew it was him, she'd heard his voice! So why shouldn't she say she saw him, just to make sure no clever-clever lawyer could make something of it?'

'So she just heard him, she didn't see him. Why did Tam think that was so important?'

Aitcheson shook his head. 'Sorry. No idea.'

'And did you tell DC Kingsley this, when he spoke to you this morning?'

Kerr could bear it no longer. 'He never went there at all. He lied to us. You see, if Mrs Aitcheson just heard a voice—'

'*What?*' Fleming heard what she was saying but it didn't make sense. It wasn't possible – Kingsley? Her eyes fell to the photograph in front of her, to the bright-faced young man, and suddenly she saw it all, with deadly clarity. Keith Ingles's voice, Niall Murdoch's phone call . . . 'Oh God! He's a brilliant mimic, isn't he? I haven't heard him, but rumour has it that he does a brilliant Big Marge.'

It was all there. What was hard to accept was that throughout, as he tried to manoeuvre one suspect after another into the position where the police believed that they had found their murderer even if proof was lacking, she had considered him guilty only of overweening ambition.

'So the night Murdoch was killed, when he had a complete alibi from the time of Murdoch's phone call home—'

She stopped. 'Oh God! He's on his way to the hospital in Dumfries right now, taking the present to Tam.' Seeing Kerr's face, she added, 'Don't worry, Tansy – there's someone on duty, and anyway, Kingsley wouldn't be dumb enough to try anything on, but I'd better alert them, even so.' She was dialling as she spoke, and broke off to say, 'Get me the number of the officer guarding Tam MacNee. Urgently.'

'Och, he'll be fine if you ask me,' said the cheerful constable outside MacNee's private room. 'Tam's a hard nut to crack, and like they say, it's only his head.'

Kingsley didn't know him, but marked him down immediately as a bit of a clown, and his confidence grew. 'You're
not wrong there, mate!' he said chattily, setting down a pink
azalea, which was in a fancy wrapper, and a large bottle of
Scotch, which wasn't, on the table beside the constable's chair.

'What state's he in at the moment?'

'Still unconscious. But according to one of the nurses – right
wee cracker, she is – that's maybe just still the anaesthetic. He
came through it fine, according to her.'

'That's great news. I tell you, back in Kirkluce it's been like
working in a funeral home today, all tiptoeing around speaking
in hushed voices.

'OK if I go in and put these by his bedside so he can see
them when he opens his eyes? We thought seeing the Scotch
would give him a real incentive. I won't disturb him.'

'I doubt if you could, right now. On you go – his wife's with
him, but that's all right.'

Kingsley recoiled. 'His wife?'

'Oh aye, but she's a real nice buddy. She'll not mind. She'll
be pleased the lads think so much of him.'

'Oh – oh, I couldn't intrude. I'll just wait for a bit, till she's
gone.' He could feel sweat appearing on his upper lip.

The fool was oblivious to his reluctance. 'Och, away you go!
Don't be daft – she'll be glad of a wee chat, just sitting there
and him not able to say a word to her. And she could be here
for hours yet.'

'Even so, she may want her privacy. I tell you what, I'll go
away and see if I can find a cup of coffee. Come back in a while
when she'll have gone home.'

'Suit yourself. But it seems kind of daft, when he won't
know you're there anyway. I could take it in for you later, if
you want.'

Was that a note of suspicion in the man's voice? Desperately, Kingsley said, 'The thing is, later he'd maybe have

come round, could say a word or two so I could tell the lads. I'll stick around for a bit anyway.'

He suddenly became aware that the man was looking over his shoulder. 'Well, pal, something tells me that maybe you won't, after all.'

Kingsley couldn't move. He'd blotted out the voice of uncertainty that had been screaming at him in the car, and there was nothing he could do. He stood stock-still as four uniformed police officers reached his side, and one said, 'Jonathan Kingsley, I am detaining you on suspicion of attempted murder. You do not have to say anything, but anything you say will be taken down and may be used in evidence against you.

'And take off your shoes. We'll be needing them, and all the others you've got at home, for comparison.'

She had never seen anything like the Press onslaught. Fleming collapsed behind her desk, feeling battered after running the gauntlet at the entrance to the Kirkluce HQ; the thumping on the roof and windows of the car, the machine-gun rattle of the cameras and the blinding flashlights as they were held against the windscreen. And it wasn't just her car, it was everyone's, from the Super down. They felt in a state of siege and intimidated women officers were arriving in tears after being mobbed and shouted at.

'Can't you do something?' she had demanded of the Press Officer, a professionally calm and charming woman.

'*You* bloody do something!' she snarled. 'Arrest the whole damn lot of them – I don't care! I've bent over backwards to be helpful till I feel like a sock that's been turned inside out, but it hasn't made a blind bit of difference. I'd say they were reptiles if I weren't afraid of being sued for defamation by pit vipers.'

That had, at least, made Fleming smile, but it didn't last long. She had a meeting with Donald Bailey ahead, and she

must calm herself first, since he would need no encouragement to go nuclear, with predictable results.

Checking her voice-mail and e-mail wasn't exactly soothing,
but among the e-mails was a name she recognized. She still
hadn't replied to Chris Carter's last message: this one was
labelled, 'Sorry.'

It was quite long. It said just what needed to be said, about
Tam and about the Jon Kingsley catastrophe. He showed the
perfect understanding that was balm to the soul.

Marjory and Bill had talked long into the night last night,
but for all his sympathy he kept reassuring her with, 'But you
and Tam got him in the end, remember. He was a policeman –
OK, not good, but he's not the first rotten apple and I don't
suppose he'll be the last. These things happen.'

She couldn't deny that, but nor could she find the words
fully to explain her own feelings. It wasn't just the terrible
burden of guilt at having failed to see what was under her nose;
it was that every time something like this happened, trust – the
trust of the public, the vital trust among colleagues – was
broken. Repairing it, like restoring fine china, would put it
together again, even quite impressively, but evidence of the
damage would still be there. She felt as if the shame was her
shame, from belonging to the body Jon Kingsley had been part
of as well.

There was always a glass wall between police and public:
she and Chris Carter were on one side of it and Bill was on the
other. And whatever the demands of the day, Chris's message
needed an immediate, and grateful, reply. But he had ended,
half-joking, 'I'm sure I could organize a fact-finding mission to
study the investigation methods of the Galloway Force.'

He'd left it open for her to treat it as she wished, and the
temptation was there – 'Why not? And then a return visit to
study yours?' But playing with fire meant not just getting
burned yourself; it started conflagrations that destroyed homes.

Ignoring the constantly ringing phone, she set herself to write a considered reply. There were many deletions, but in the end she felt it was the best she could do: not hurtful, but final. It ended, 'I can't think Manchester would have much to learn from us, sadly. Good luck in the future, and thanks for all your help. Marjory.'

She re-read it, hesitated, then pressed 'Send'. It was done now.

'It's intolerable, Marjory, absolutely intolerable!' Superintendent Bailey's face was an alarming shade of puce. 'We must apply to the Sheriff Court for an injunction, the High Court if need be. An exclusion zone for five hundred yards around the station.'

'Let's think it through, Don. What sort of headlines would we get after that? Police arrogance – public right to know . . .'

He glared at her as if Press persecution could be laid to her charge. 'So what do you suggest?'

'You have to accept that it's a big story. A huge story. Two murders, one attempted murder – mercifully they haven't made the connection with the attack on Mrs Aitcheson, though that will come. Throw in a bent copper, with one of his victims being another policeman, fighting for his life – if I sat down and thought for a fortnight, I don't think I could come up with a bigger one, unless you could add a connection to Princess Diana's accident in Paris.'

'Yes, yes,' he said testily, 'I know all that. And don't go on to tell me they have a valuable job to do in the public interest. What I want to know is, how to stop them doing it?'

Fleming tried not to, but she began to smile. Bailey was affronted for a moment, then realized what he had said and smiled reluctantly. They began to laugh, disproportionate laughter which might be an effect of stress, but they both felt the better for it.

Dabbing his eyes with a blue silk handkerchief, Bailey said at last, 'That's all well and good, Marjory, but we still have the problem.'

'I know we do. But I wonder if we should involve the Chief Constable – oh, I know, he's been on to you already,' as Bailey, with a pained expression, made to speak, 'but he could perhaps contact the editors, or the proprietors if necessary. Explain that we're anxious to work with the Press, we rely on them, blah, blah, blah – I'm sure he can write the script – but they are currently impeding the police in the ordinary execution of their duties. Civilian staff, who man emergency calls, are afraid to come in, and this is something we would have to explain to the public. He could even hint that we might put out one of our younger and prettier policewomen to cry on camera. I have one in mind – nice wee lass, probationer, who's been in tears this morning already.'

Bailey looked at her with respect. 'You may be wasted in the Force, Marjory. Have you ever thought of politics?'

'Never. I'm a rotten liar.'

'Glad to hear it. Not like some.' He sighed. 'What's the state of play?'

Sighing seemed to be contagious. 'His attack on Tam – no problem. The footprints in the garden matched the shoes he was wearing and they found the jack with –' she gulped '– blood and tissue on it in his car.

'Davina's murder: I was going to brief you on that. The labs have fibres from her clothes, and now they have his for comparison, it's likely they'll get a match, though there's always the danger that he may have destroyed the ones he was wearing. But they're comparing the grit on the soles of her shoes with the grit on his, and that may well produce results.

'We still don't know where he killed her, though I'd guess it was in her car, so there's nothing to hope for there. And we don't know how she contacted him either – possibly even by a letter sent here, since she's unlikely to have had another address and his number doesn't appear in the list from her mobile, which they've checked through now. Murdoch's does, though, which confirms what we knew already.'

'She was a bit foolhardy, surely, agreeing to meet Kingsley face to face?'

'I think she was probably foolhardy by nature. She'd tried it on with the men in the bar in Manchester and even if she wasn't successful, she got away with it. And I'd guess she told Niall Murdoch what she was doing as a safeguard, but Kingsley's attack was so sudden she hadn't the chance to use it.'

'And where are we on Murdoch?'

'Ah. We may never get him on that one. There's no evidence of contact between the two, though Murdoch made two or three calls to the station here, but with the vandalism problems that was hardly surprising and there's no record of who he asked to speak to. We can no doubt prove from phone records that Kingsley made the call to Jenna Murdoch but the rest is guesswork. This may just be one of those cases where we know who did it and stop looking, but haven't evidence that will stand up in court. Ironic, really – that's exactly the outcome he had been working towards, only with someone else as the prime suspect.'

Bailey shook his head. 'A sad business!'

'As far as the attack on Mrs Aitcheson goes, Ingles's lawyer will appeal his conviction and have it set aside as unsafe, no doubt, but Ingles will have to be charged with perverting the course of justice in any case. The only evidence against Kingsley is likely to come from tracing the money he used to buy his boat, but that'll be hard to prove, after all this time. And he's not about to confess.'

'He's said nothing?'

'Nothing at all – sat throughout the six hours' questioning in total silence. We kept him there the full time,

working in relays. Perhaps we shouldn't have allowed
Tansy Kerr to give him his character quite so forcibly,
but it was therapeutic for her and the tape's never going to
be evidence. A death stare can't be shown in court to prove
murderous intent.'

'And what about you, Marjory – what did you say?'

Her eyes fell. 'I didn't say anything, except what was
professionally necessary. I didn't trust myself. Once I started,
I don't know where I would have stopped.'

He nodded gravely, 'Understandable. But you'd wonder
how he ever thought he'd get away with it.'

'According to Laura Harvey, supreme self-confidence is a
psychopathic characteristic. Poor Laura – she's taking it badly
that she didn't pick up on it.'

'If my recollection of lectures in criminal psychology – dim,
I grant you – serves me, they can be clever at covering up too.
If it's any consolation, tell her she wasn't the only one who was
fooled. I had Kingsley pencilled in for promotion when the
next sergeant's job came up.

'And speaking of sergeants – any word on Tam today?'

'Stable is the official verdict, but Bunty's worried. They
found there had been a haemorrhage putting pressure on the
brain and though they've relieved it and he's been able to
speak to her, we won't know for a while yet what the damage
is. I'm going along to see him this afternoon.'

It wasn't easy to talk about it. Fleming got up. 'I'd better get
back to my office. Working through the voice-mail alone looks
like taking all day, and there's a report to be written.'

'Oh, incidentally, before you go, also on the subject of
sergeants,' Bailey rummaged among his papers to find a form,
'Allan's requested to leave the Force as soon as it can be
arranged.'

'Good riddance!' Fleming said with feeling. 'It's been positively unpleasant of late with Allan and Kingsley trying to set

up their own little private mafia. The CID room will be a much happier place without the two of them.'

Bailey gave her a sardonic look. 'A CID room that's all sweetness and light? Dear me, Marjory – I hadn't realized you were quite so naive.'

Laura was waiting for Marjory to pick her up to go and see Tam. She was in her pleasant garden, with the sun shining and Daisy cheerfully rootling around among the bushes, but she wasn't happy.

She was depressed first of all at being so credulous. She, of all people, should be able to recognize manipulation when she saw it, yet she'd accepted Jon's account of his pushy father as a textbook case – which was probably where he'd got the idea. She'd suspected he was using her, certainly, but on the couple of occasions when he'd kissed her she'd found herself responding with enthusiasm. Sexual attraction notoriously blunted your perceptions.

Was she just another desperate woman, with a ticking biological clock, flattered by the attentions of a man five years younger? Thirty was looming; thirty, with a failed marriage behind you and no steady relationship since, was an added reason for depression. How she envied Marjory with her Bill, settled in a partnership that was steady as a rock!

Happy as she was with her writing and broadcasting, much as she loved this place, was it enough? She had real friends here and what she thought of as a 'real' life, connected with her neighbours and the community as she could never be in London. But eligible men didn't exactly happen along very often.

There were agencies, of course; she'd had friends who'd used them, with great success. But perhaps she just needed a change . . .

Then Daisy barked, she heard Marjory's knock on the door

and she hurried to answer it. At least it was good news about Tam. She picked up a bag with grapes she had bought and opened the door.

'Do you think he'll thank me for grapes, or would he rather a deep-fried Mars bar?' she said gaily, then stopped when she saw Marjory's face. 'What's happened?'

'Another bleed in the brain. They're going to have to operate again.'

'Oh no!'

Marjory followed her in; the dog ran round their feet, puzzled at getting no response to her welcome. They sat down outside and for a moment neither said anything.

Then, 'How's Bunty?' Laura asked.

'As you would expect. She's got a couple of sisters there, propping her up.'

'That's good.'

There was another silence. Then Laura said, with an attempt at cheerfulness, 'Oh, come on, Marjory – you know Tam! He won't give up. And here I was feeling low, and expecting the visit to cheer me up.'

'I have to say I'm pretty low myself. Laura, I went to see Dad today.'

It was, Laura knew, the first time she had gone. 'And—?' she said gently.

Marjory's eyes filled with tears. 'Laura, it was terrible! And that place – I'm sure they do their best, but it smells of urine. And the noises the patients make . . . But it was Dad that was worst of all.' She was really crying now, struggling to find a tissue in her bag. 'We never had an easy relationship, but you know, I was so proud of him. So tall and impressive in his uniform when I was young, my hero, really, and even after he retired he never looked anything but immaculate. This after-noon he wasn't properly shaved, and he was wearing a dressing-gown he'd dribbled on. And he didn't know us –

he started yelling at us whenever we arrived, started lashing out. They had to come and give him an injection.'

'Was Janet with you?'

'That was the shaming thing. She was much better than I was. She comforted me – said it wasn't Dad, that he'd gone. She's accepted he'll need looking after, and she's started looking for the best place. Was that your idea?'

'I thought she'd be better off with something constructive to do. And I asked around to find out which were good – there's a new doctor at the Health Centre who was very helpful, and I gave her a list.'

'Is that the one Mum was talking about? Mid-thirties, "a braw young man", she said.' Marjory gave her friend a side-long look. 'And single.'

'Oh, for goodness' sake, Marjory!'

'I didn't say it. Mum did,' Marjory said, eyes wide and innocent. 'She said we should maybe have a dinner party for him, make him feel welcome in the neighbourhood.'

Laura protested, but it lightened their mood. After Marjorie had left, promising news of Tam whenever there was any, she went back out into the garden, smiling. With friends like Marjory, who needed agencies?

She still wasn't quite convinced. She was recording a programme in London in a couple of weeks' time; perhaps she'd extend her visit to a month, see how she felt about a faster pace of life.

Instead of heading for home, Marjory took the Kirkcowan road, heading towards Wigtown and Drumbreck. It felt necessary, somehow, to put things to rest.

It had all been about money from the start – those who had too much, and those who envied that and greedily took it. Drumbreck had created itself as a fantasy, a self-indulgent play-world where the rules didn't apply and life was a game with no consequences. Would this make any difference?

She didn't think so. Money meant that unless you got caught in the fallout, you could remove yourself until everything was clean and nice and ready for you to start your game again. Next weekend, or maybe the one after, they'd be back, a little shaken by all that had happened, circumspect for a while, perhaps, but slowly and surely they would revert to the way of life that suited them, decadent and unhealthily exciting.

Marjory parked her car once more outside the Yacht Club where there were a few other cars parked. The club itself looked deserted and the marina was closed, but there was some activity by the boats and there were a few other people strolling in the evening sunshine.

She set off along the road that skirted the bay. The tide was half-way out; oozy, khaki mudflats were exposed, but there was still deep water round the pontoons. As she watched, a motor launch backed out from its mooring, then roared off towards the estuary, its prow well clear of the water.

There were windows open in the Murdochs' house – perhaps in the flat where paint was drying. She wondered what Jenna would do – sell up and clear out, or stay and run the marina, probably more effectively, now she had a free hand? Marjory didn't envy her struggling through the teen years with that strange, introverted child. And she wondered, too, about poor Moss, in police kennels somewhere. He belonged to Jenna now, of course, but he'd never be happy as a pet. Still, look on the bright side: Mirren, who was so much more sensitive to animal feelings than to human ones, might suggest reuniting him with his master.

There was no sign of life in any of the other houses. She walked on past the McConnells' cottage, as far as the Laffertys' grander abode. It would be interesting to see what happened there. A request for his fingerprints and DNA had come in already from Tam's pal in Glasgow – oh, Tam, Tam! She bit her lip, and stopped to look over towards the marina and the Yacht Club.

The Laffertys' might be the smartest house, but it wasn't at the more salubrious end of the bay when the tide was out. From the exposed mud, warmed by the sun, came a smell of decay, and there was rotting vegetation where small flies were hopping in a moving carpet.

With a shudder, Marjory turned and walked back. She had almost reached the end of the road when one of the strolling couples came towards her.

'Lovely evening,' she said.

'Lovely place,' the woman said, indicating with a gesture the pretty houses and the soft hills and the brightly painted boats. A pair of swans had appeared, as if they were working on commission.

Marjory smiled and nodded, and went back to her car. She was finished here; she must put it out of her mind. Home now – home, which had become her sanctuary once again. Home to Bill and the kids. And if she thought of a clever, arrogant, lonely man it was only for a moment. She had better pick up bread and milk on the way. They were always running out.

Read on . . .

Discover the next book in the DI Marjory Fleming Series

LAMB TO THE SLAUGHTER

A sunny evening, a tranquil garden – and an old man
brutally gunned down on his doorstep.

In the market town of Kirkluce, a proposed superstore
development has divided the population in a bitter war.
The low-level aggression of bored youth has turned
sinister, a bloodied sheep carcass is abandoned in the
streets and teenage bikers, terrorising a woman to
breaking point, are impossible to control.

Then a second victim is killed in what seems a random
shooting. DI Fleming will not accept that the crimes are
motiveless, but she struggles to make sense of the two
murders, when nothing makes sense any more and no
one will believe anything. Not even the truth.

Out now in paperback and ebook.

HODDER

THRILLINGLY GOOD BOOKS
FROM CRIMINALLY
GOOD WRITERS

CRIME FILES BRINGS YOU THE LATEST RELEASES FROM
TOP CRIME AND THRILLER AUTHORS.

SIGN UP ONLINE FOR OUR MONTHLY NEWSLETTER AND BE THE FIRST
TO KNOW ABOUT OUR COMPETITIONS, NEW BOOKS AND MORE.